There was a vi... light and then, ... above their hea... building slowly ... inexorably to a roaring, deafening crash as if the cave was collapsing on top of them.

Selena cried out, her voice lost in the uproar, and stumbled forward, her hands reaching out to Alexis, who caught her and held her until the last terrifying echoes of the thunder died away and all she could hear was the tumultuous thud of her own heartbeat.

And beneath her cheek his—like the relentless rhythm of a drum.

His hand moved down, impelling her silently to look up at him. To read his intention in the sudden flare of his gaze as he bent and his mouth found hers, gently, sensuously, coaxing her lips to part for him.

She leaned into the heat and strength of his body, welcoming his kiss, responding with bewildered ardour as it deepened and a shiver of pleasure feathered enticingly across her skin.

When, at last, he took his lips slowly from hers she made a small, lost sound in her throat that never became an actual word—even if she'd been able to think of one.

She registered that the crackle of the lightning had become less frequent and the answering thunder had become a sullen mumble in the distance.

'The storm is over.'

There was an odd silence, then he said quietly, 'On the contrary, Selena *mou*, I think it is just beginning.'

Secret Heirs of Billionaires

There are some things money can't buy...

Living life at lightning pace, these magnates are no strangers to stakes at their highest. It seems they've got it all... That is until they find out that there's an unplanned item to add to their list of accomplishments!

Achieved:

1. Successful business empire

2. Beautiful women in their bed

3. *An heir to bear their name...?*

Though every billionaire needs to leave his legacy in safe hands, discovering a secret heir shakes up his carefully orchestrated plan in more ways than one!

Uncover their secrets in:

Unwrapping the Castelli Secret by Caitlin Crews

Brunetti's Secret Son by Maya Blake

The Secret to Marrying Marchesi by Amanda Cinelli

Demetriou Demands His Child by Kate Hewitt

The Desert King's Secret Heir by Annie West

The Sheikh's Secret Son by Maggie Cox

Look out for more stories in the
Secret Heirs of Billionaires series, coming soon!

THE INNOCENT'S SHAMEFUL SECRET

BY
SARA CRAVEN

First Published in Great Britain 2017
By Mills & Boon, an imprint of HarperCollins*Publishers*
1 London Bridge Street, London, SE1 9GF

© 2017 Sara Craven

ISBN: 978-0-263-92520-3

Our policy is to use papers that are natural, renewable and recyclable
products and made from wood grown in sustainable forests. The logging
and manufacturing processes conform to the legal environmental
regulations of the country of origin.

Printed and bound in Spain
by CPI, Barcelona

Former journalist **Sara Craven** published her first novel, *Garden of Dreams*, for Mills & Boon in 1975. Apart from writing—naturally!—her passions include reading, bridge, Italian cities, Greek islands, the French language and countryside, and her rescue Jack Russell cross Button. She has appeared on several TV quiz shows, and in 1997 became the champion of UK TV show *Mastermind*. She lives near her family in Warwickshire—Shakespeare country.

Books by Sara Craven

Mills & Boon Modern Romance

Inherited by Her Enemy
Seduction Never Lies
Count Valieri's Prisoner
The Price of Retribution
The End of Her Innocence
Wife in the Shadows
His Untamed Innocent
The Innocent's Surrender
Ruthless Awakening
The Santangeli Marriage
One Night with His Virgin Mistress
The Virgin's Wedding Night
Innocent on Her Wedding Night
The Forced Bride
Bride of Desire

Seven Sexy Sins

The Innocent's Sinful Craving

Men Without Mercy

The Highest Stakes of All

Visit the Author Profile page
at millsandboon.co.uk for more titles.

CHAPTER ONE

SELENA SAW THE letter as soon as she opened the front door, the blue airmail envelope unmissable against the brown matting.

She halted abruptly, recognising the Greek stamp, her stomach lurching as a sudden image blazed into her mind of tall bleached columns rearing into an azure sky, with a pool of grass hidden among the fallen stones at their feet. And the soft murmur of a man's voice in the sunlight, and the brush of hands, lips and warm, naked skin against her own.

She gasped, the plastic carrier bag she was holding slipping from her numb fingers, sending the lemons it contained bouncing and rolling down the narrow hall to the foot of the stairs.

Before she realised almost in the same instant that the untidy scrawl on the envelope could only be Millie's. No one else's. And alarm was replaced by growing anger.

Nearly a year of silence, she thought, her throat muscles tightening. And now—what? Another diatribe of recrimination and accusation with the pen scoring the paper just as her sister's furious voice had scraped across her flinching senses in that last disastrous telephone conversation?

'It's all your fault,' Millie had accused tearfully. 'You were supposed to help—to put things right. Instead you've behaved like a brainless idiot and ruined everything for both of us. I'll never forgive you, never, and I don't want to see you or speak to you again.'

And the phone had gone down with a crash that sounded as if it was in the next room rather than hundreds of miles away in a *taverna* on a remote Greek island.

Leaving her with the knowledge that there was little she could have said in her own defence even if Millie had been prepared to listen. That she had indeed behaved like a fool and worse than a fool.

But she'd suffered for what she'd done in ways that Millie could not even imagine, or was determined to ignore.

Because since that phone call, there'd been nothing. Until now…

She was sorely tempted to leave the letter lying there. To step over it and walk into her living room and begin the new life that had filled her thoughts on the bus journey home.

Except it wouldn't just go away. It wouldn't disintegrate or vanish on a breeze. And, in spite of everything, curiosity would be bound to get the better of her in the end.

She bent stiffly and picked up the envelope, walking through the living room, and tossing it on to the worktop in her small galley kitchen, before filling the kettle and setting it to boil.

She'd originally planned to make a jug of fresh lemonade, clinking with ice, and enjoy it in the warmth of her tiny courtyard. A quiet celebration of this unexpected fresh start.

Now what she needed instead was a caffeine rush, she thought bleakly, taking the jar of coffee and a beaker from the cupboard.

While the kettle was coming to the boil, she went back to the hall, collected the lemons, and put them in the fruit basket.

Idiotic, she told herself, to panic like that. Needless, too. Had she really thought, even for a moment…?

No, she told herself harshly, her hands clenching into fists. You do not—*not*—go there. Not again. Not ever.

She made her coffee strong and carried it outside, settling herself on the elderly wooden bench in the shadiest corner, making herself recap the previous events of the morning and try to recapture something of its optimism.

She had been alone in the classroom, taking down the wall display for Mrs Forbes and putting it in a folder while she considered rather anxiously how she should occupy the unpaid six week summer break ahead of her, when her reverie was interrupted by the arrival of Mrs Smithson, the head teacher.

She said briskly, without preamble, 'Lena, we heard last week that Megan Greig has decided not to return after her maternity leave. Her job as teaching assistant has therefore become a permanent instead of a temporary post, and the staff and governors agree with me that it should be offered to you.' She gave Selena a brief, friendly smile. 'You've worked very hard and become a real member of the team at Barstock Grange. We all want this to continue, especially Mrs Forbes, and hope you do, too.'

'Well—yes.' Selena was aware she must sound dazed, having expected to be once more jobless and probably homeless by Christmas. 'That—that's terrific.'

This time, Mrs Smithson's smile was broader and tinged with relief. 'Then we're all pleased. You'll be sent official confirmation in the next week or so. And—see you next term.'

Selena's state of euphoria had lasted throughout her journey home and the short walk to her tiny terrace property. Until, that was, she'd opened the door...

She didn't need to be subjected to another rant, she thought wearily, or, indeed, to the other possibility—a request to borrow money.

If so, she's going to be disappointed, she told herself, because I'm skint.

Besides, I need to concentrate on my own priorities, like looking for somewhere else to live where children and animals are allowed.

She and Millie had always wanted a pet, she remembered, but Aunt Nora would never agree, clearly believing that two orphaned nieces were sufficient responsibility.

And, considering what had happened, perhaps she'd been right.

Over the years, it had become clear to Selena that

Miss Conway had offered her late sister's children a home more from a sense of duty than any warmer feeling, family visits having been few and far between. But, as she got older, she'd realised that her aunt's decision owed an equal amount to self-interest.

Her valued role as a pillar of local society in Haylesford might have taken a serious knock if word had got out that she'd allowed her nieces to be put into care. A lot of people might have felt that charity should begin at home.

Having experienced it, Selena wasn't so sure. Eleven years old, shocked and wretched with the loss of her parents, killed in a collision with a hit and run driver, it hadn't seemed to matter where she and Millie went, or what happened to them, as long as they were together.

Although they were as different as chalk and cheese, physically as well as temperamentally.

Millie, two years her junior, was a golden girl, small, curvaceous and pretty, her hair a deep, rich blonde which curled slightly. Selena was tall and on the skinny side of slender. Her eyes were grey to Millie's blue, and her skin much paler than her sister's peaches and cream complexion.

But the big difference was her hair, almost at the silver end of the spectrum, and totally straight, spilling halfway down her back, even when confined to the thick braid insisted upon by Aunt Nora.

Hair like moonlight...

Oh, God, she thought, as memory stabbed at her suddenly, viciously. Not dead as she'd believed and hoped, but brutally alive.

She sat rigidly, her nails digging into the palms of her hands as she tried to force that particular memory back into the oblivion it deserved.

No one would ever say it to her again. She'd made sure of that long ago, leaving the long silky strands on the floor at the hairdressing salon in Haylesford in exchange for a *gamine* crop with feathery tendrils framing her face and giving emphasis to her high cheekbones.

Yet another difference between us, she thought, as she made herself think about Millie again.

She looks like Mum, and I take after Dad's side of the family, she reflected, swallowing past the lump in her throat. He always claimed he had Viking ancestry and that's where our colouring came from. On the other hand, he tended to wing his way through life like Millie, while my mother was the steady, sober member of the partnership. As I believed I was.

But whatever the reason for Aunt Nora's reluctance to take them on, it couldn't be a dislike of children because she ran a private junior school for girls and a very successful one, catering for those needing extra help to pass the examinations for their very expensive senior schools, or, as it was known, a crammer.

Not that she and Millie were ever enrolled at Meade House School, even though they were both under thirteen. Instead, they were both placed very firmly in the state system.

Her long-term plans for them, however, she'd kept to herself, Selena thought drily.

She drank some more coffee, wondering why she was re-treading these well-worn paths all over again. Especially when she'd told herself the best way to survive was to shut the door on the past. Think only of the future.

Or was this simply deliberate prevarication? Delaying the moment when she'd have to deal with Millie's letter, still in the kitchen, silently demanding her unwilling attention.

Time to get it over with, she decided as she finished her coffee and went indoors.

The single piece of paper inside the envelope looked as if it had been ripped from a small notebook.

'Lena' Millie had written. 'We have to talk. It's an emergency, so please, please call me.' She'd added the telephone number, including the code, and signed off 'M'.

Short, but not too sweet, thought Selena. And it's almost certainly about money because Rhymnos is bound to be having its share of economic problems.

Or has her life on a small Greek island already palled and could this cry for help involve a one-way ticket back to Britain?

But to do what—and to live where? Well, hardly here, that was for sure, sharing a cramped bedroom with a three-quarter-sized bed, not to mention a shower room not much bigger than a cupboard.

And apart from some undistinguished GCSEs, Millie had no qualifications for any career except bar work or waitressing. And she'd probably had her fill of both by now.

Surely she can't imagine there's a remote possibility that Aunt Nora's been in touch and all is forgiven?

If so, dream on, Millie, she thought. She's out of our lives for good and all.

And why didn't you ring me if it's all so urgent? Especially as I sent you my number along with the address.

She realised she'd crumpled the letter in her hand, and smoothed it out again on the work surface.

The phone number Millie had given clearly demonstrated that she was still living with Kostas at his *taverna*, named Amelia in her honour. But maybe that was only temporary.

And although it was tempting to take the coward's way out and pretend the letter had never come, Millie was, in spite of everything, her sister and wanted her help.

She said aloud, 'I can't let her down.'

Steeling herself, she picked up the phone. It was answered on the second ring. A man's voice.

She kept her voice cool and steady. 'Kostas? It's Selena.'

'Ah, sister, you have called.' Across the miles, she could hear the relief in his tone. 'How good to hear you. But I knew it would be so. I told my Amelia that she must not disturb herself with worry.'

'Things have obviously been—difficult for you all,' she said. *And that's putting it mildly.*

'*Po, po, po.* Now we look for better times.'

'Yes,' she said. 'Of course.' She paused. 'Is Millie around? Can I speak to her?'

'At this moment, no, sister. The doctor has ordered she must rest, and she is sleeping.'

'The doctor,' Selena repeated, frowning. 'You mean she's ill? What's wrong with her? Is it serious?'

'I cannot say. It is a woman's thing, and she feels

scared and very much alone.' He hesitated. 'My mother is here, of course, but—it is not easy, you understand.'

I bet, thought Selena, remembering Anna Papoulis in her unrelieved widow's mourning, her headscarf framing her sharp face with its narrow-lipped, bitter mouth set in resentment of her son's foreign bride.

However, it seemed as if the marriage was surviving, which was some relief.

'It is you that she wants. Again and again she says it, and she weeps.' His tone became eager. 'If you would come here—be with her for a while—she would soon be better. I know it. And there is a room for you here with us. I prepared it in hope.'

She was shocked into silence. And disbelief.

Rhymnos, she thought. He actually thinks I can go back to Rhymnos? After everything that happened? He must be crazy.

'No,' she said at last, her voice harsh. 'That's impossible. You know it is. I—I'm needed here.'

'But things are different now,' he persisted. 'You have nothing to fear, sister. People have gone,' he added, his voice heavy with meaning. 'The island has changed. You will be safe here. Safe with us.'

I thought I was safe before. Believed Millie was the one in danger. Yet I was the one to be betrayed and I still have the scars.

He went on quickly, 'And my Amelia wants so badly to see you—to be with you. I cannot bear for her to be disappointed.'

No, she thought. That's how it all began. Because Millie mustn't be disappointed. Because two of her classmates were having a holiday in Greece, for the first time without their parents, and asked her to go with them. And she cried when Aunt Nora said, 'At seventeen? Absolutely not.'

Tears on their own probably wouldn't have worked, but reinforcements arrived in the shape of Mrs Raymond, mother of Daisy, whose idea the trip had been, and, in her way, as formidable as Aunt Nora.

'I think one has to allow them some independence at their age,' she'd pronounced majestically. 'Demonstrate that we trust them. After all, they'll all be off to university next year.'

Daisy and Fiona, perhaps, Selena had thought drily. Millie—only if she started doing some work.

'And Rhymnos is only small and quiet, not crowded with nightclubs, which means fewer opportunities for mischief,' Mrs Raymond had added. 'The hotel, too, is family run and has a good reputation. The girls are so keen for Millie to go with them, and she's bound to be disappointed if she's left behind. Besides, there's safety in numbers, you know.'

It all sounded too good to be true, Selena had thought with sudden unease, hoping that Aunt Nora would stick to her guns.

But, albeit reluctantly, she'd eventually agreed, leaving Selena to shrug and decide it was none of her business.

Which only proved how wrong it was possible to be.

Because, suddenly and incredibly, it had become her business, turning her entire life upside down.

Kostas was speaking again. 'If it is a matter of cost, I

shall happily pay the airfare to Mykonos, and the ferry transfer. I ask only that you come to us—for Amelia's sake. She hopes so much to see you.'

She said crisply, 'That was hardly the impression she gave when we last spoke.'

He sighed. 'But in all families, sister, things are said in anger and then regretted. And I am relying on your compassion for a sick girl.'

Selena bit her lip. Put like that, she thought, she could hardly refuse. And yet she was aware again of that odd sense of unease. Although, he'd said things had changed...

But I haven't changed, she thought. I know that now. And perhaps I never will until I have the courage to face my demons and put them finally to rest. And maybe that time has come.

She took a deep, painful breath. 'Very well, Kostas, I'll come as soon as I can get a flight—which I will pay for myself, thanks all the same. I'll be in touch when I have the details.' She added, 'And wish Millie well for me.'

She occupied the rest of her day with some heavy duty housework, trying to ignore the small voice in her head telling her that she'd clearly learned nothing from her past mistakes and was, once again, behaving like an idiot.

Because she knew how doubtful it was that Millie would make the same concessions for her, if their positions were reversed.

But she could probably live with herself, she thought

drily. Whereas I couldn't—especially if this illness of hers turns out to be something really serious.

And, in that case, what kind of medical attention could Millie expect in so small a place?

If she needs to come back to England with me, I'll deal with it, even if it means finding an even bigger place.

She decided to have an early night, in view of all she had to do the following day, hoping, too, that sleep would silence that little warning voice—at least for a while.

As she undressed, she embarked on a mental list of what she'd need to take with her to Rhymnos, remembering that the high summer temperature could soar to forty degrees plus.

Reaching for her nightdress, she glimpsed herself in the wall mirror and paused, wondering if the events of the past year had altered her in any significant way. But, apart from her severely shorn hair, her critical gaze could see no real change. Her breasts were still high and rounded, her waist small, her stomach flat and her hips gently curved.

I look, she told herself ironically, almost untouched. And found her laugh turning into a sob.

She spent a wretched, restless night and was sorely tempted, when her radio alarm went into action, simply to silence it, pull the covers over her head and stay where she was.

The coward's way out, she thought wryly as she swung her feet to the floor and headed to the shower.

Her first visit was to the letting agency, to register her new requirements, followed by a wander round a cheap and cheerful fashion store which still had a few pairs of cotton cut-off pants, tee shirts and even a one-piece swimsuit available in her size and within her limited budget.

Working on the premise that she wasn't sure how long her stay would last or if she'd be returning alone, she booked a single flight at the travel agency, and bought some euros, knowing she would have to use them carefully because she could afford no more.

But her most difficult task was still ahead of her, she reminded herself as she emerged into the street, subjecting her, no doubt, to more disapproval and more pressure. Except this time, she'd have a positive response to make. An actual workable plan for the future.

She heard her name called and turning saw Janet Forbes coming towards her smiling.

'I'm glad I've seen you,' she said. 'I was planning to get in touch anyway and have a chat, over an iced coffee maybe, or are you too busy?'

'No, that would be great.'

They went to a cafe with a veranda overlooking the river, its banks busy with families sunbathing, eating ice cream and feeding the ducks.

'I wanted to say how delighted I am that we'll be working together again next year,' Mrs Forbes began as they sipped their coffees under the shade of the awning.

'Megan was a nice girl and very conscientious, but I always felt that she was simply filling in time. Whereas you…'

She paused. 'I wondered if you'd ever considered getting a BEd and becoming a teacher yourself, because I'd say you were a natural.' She added swiftly, 'Not that I want to lose you, of course. Please don't think that.'

Selena was all set to declare herself perfectly happy with her lot. Instead, to her own astonishment, she heard herself say, 'I did start training but got no further than the second year.' She forced a smile. 'Family problems.'

'Well, that's a great shame.' Mrs Forbes gave her a thoughtful look. 'You could always go back to it, you know. It's never too late to start again.'

That, Selena thought, is what I keep telling myself. Maybe it's time I believed it.

'One day, perhaps,' she said. 'I mean, I'd love to, but right now I have—other priorities.'

'Well, do bear it in mind for the future.' Mrs Forbes got to her feet, collecting her bags. 'I hate to see talent wasted.' She patted Selena on the shoulder. 'Maybe when your family problems are behind you.'

Except, thought Selena, watching her go, you don't know the half of them. And I can never tell you, or anyone else, what happened two years ago.

Or that I'm still struggling with the aftermath.

CHAPTER TWO

SHE SUPPOSED SHE ought to move. Go back to the store and buy some of the clothes she'd seen. The absolute minimum would do and was all she could afford anyway.

But being accustomed to living on not much could stand her in good stead if her life changed in the way she hoped.

Not 'if', she told herself, but 'when'.

And in celebration, she recklessly ordered another iced coffee.

How strange, she thought, when she'd been watching Janet Forbes so closely, admiring her classroom technique, her patience and ability to engage the children, and keep them interested and focussed, that, all the time, Mrs Forbes had been watching her. Deciding to encourage her into teaching.

Not blackmail her into it.

She'd been sixteen, quietly delighted with her GCSE results when Aunt Nora had dropped her bombshell. Informed her that all her university expenses would be paid as long as she, and eventually Millie, too, agreed to teach at Meade House after graduation.

Otherwise, Selena could forget the Sixth Form and college, leave her comprehensive school and find a job.

'I had to settle your late parents' debts as well as bearing the costs of your upbringing,' her aunt had stated coldly. 'I expect to be repaid, Selena. And Amelia, of course, will have to do the same.'

She paused, allowing that to sink in. 'And kindly stop looking as if your death sentence had just been pronounced. At Meade House, you and your sister will be guaranteed a continuing home, careers and security. A little gratitude would not come amiss.'

How am I supposed to look, Selena had wondered, when every plan—every dream I had of getting away from Haylesford and being my own person—has been virtually knocked on the head?

For a moment, she'd been prepared to say *To hell with it* and take the risk, but she knew that she could not make choices that would also affect the future of fourteen-year-old Millie. That was neither right nor fair.

And once her agreement had been obtained, however unwilling, there had been a perceptible easing of Aunt Nora's strict regime, leading eventually, inevitably to Millie being permitted her Greek holiday with her friends.

Selena had found a vacation job in a cafe, one which turned out to be short-lived because one showery July day her aunt slipped and fell in her garden and ended up in hospital with a broken leg.

Aunt Nora, ensconced in a comfortable private room, received her sourly. 'They won't allow me to go home until I've mastered using these crutches.' She gestured disdainfully to where they stood, propped against the wall. 'But even with them, I'm going to require help, and Amelia, of course, is leaving for Greece in ten days' time.'

Lucky Millie, Selena thought grimly.

As she'd suspected 'patient' was hardly the word to describe her aunt, who kept her on the run from first thing in the morning until last thing at night, with the help of the little handbell she kept beside her at all times.

In addition, Millie had fussed endlessly over her packing, claiming exclusive access to the washing machine and ironing board, and providing Aunt Nora with another excuse to grumble.

It was almost a relief when Mrs Raymond arrived with Daisy and Fiona to drive them all to the airport.

One less problem to handle, Selena thought, as she closed the front door.

'Dr Bishop says I shall need physiotherapy when the plaster is eventually removed,' her aunt announced the following week. 'He has given me a list of reliable practitioners who pay private visits.'

'Isn't it available on the National Health Service?' asked Selena.

'Not to the extent that I shall require,' Aunt Nora said coldly. 'Dr Bishop says it was such a serious fracture that I shall probably have to learn to walk all over again.'

Selena thought drily that Dr Bishop, rightly nicknamed Old Smoothie by Millie, excelled at telling her aunt exactly what she wanted to hear, and hoped the physio would have more sense.

And, talking of Millie, apart from an initial text announcing that Rhymnos was great, they'd heard nothing from her.

Still, she decided, philosophically, the parents of Daisy and Fiona were probably in the same boat, and, anyway, wasn't no news supposed to be good news?

She'd been into town the afternoon the girls were due back, taking a list of her aunt's requests to the public library. She expected Millie to have arrived when she got back, yet there was no clutter of luggage in the hall.

The flight must have been delayed, she thought, then heard her aunt calling her, her voice high and angry, and found her sitting upright, two bright spots of colour in her cheeks emphasising her unusual pallor.

She checked, the terrible memory of her parents' accident striking at her, making her feel sick to her stomach with fright. 'Has—has something happened?'

'Oh, yes.' Her aunt's voice shook with fury. 'Your sister, it seems, has involved herself with some local yob on that island and decided to stay there—to set up house with him. Apparently she'd gone from her hotel room this morning with all her things. The other girls had to leave without her.

'Well, I won't have it. I will not allow her to disgrace me, to make me ridiculous in front of the whole town— a child of her age. However there's nothing I can do about it, so you'll have to go over there and bring her back.' She added ominously, 'Before too much harm is done.'

Selena sank down on the nearest chair. Typical, she thought bitterly, that her aunt should see the situation in terms of personal disgrace rather than the danger to Millie and the potential ruin of her future.

She said, 'Who is the man? Do Daisy and Fiona know?'

'It seems he's the barman at the Hotel Olympia where they were staying. His name is Kostas.' Aunt Nora pronounced the name with acute distaste then held out a piece of paper that had been crumpled in her hand. 'She left this note.' She shuddered. 'Mrs Raymond could hardly look me in the eye. I blame her entirely for allowing this trip in the first place and then badgering me to let Amelia be part of it.

'But that, of course, won't stop her telling the entire town what's happened. She's probably already started.'

Selena read the note frowningly. Millie said simply that she was not coming back to England because she loved Kostas and was staying with him.

So, not much room for negotiation there, she thought.

'As you can see, there's no time to lose.' Aunt Nora was regaining some of her old briskness. 'So, you go there, you find her and you bring her back. That's all there is to be said.'

She added decisively, 'I will not have my plans for the future of the school wrecked by some childish infatuation. Men like this barman should be locked up.'

Selena tried to reason with her, pointing out that Millie was not a child and it might be better to let her realise her mistake and return of her own accord.

And how, she asked, would her aunt manage without her, only to discover that Aunt Nora had already booked a live-in carer.

'Terribly expensive,' she'd said sourly. 'I hope Amelia realises the inconvenience she's causing.'

But nothing Selena said made the slightest difference, which was why, only two days later she found herself on board the ferry from Mykonos with the harbour at Rhymnos already in sight.

She was in no mood to appreciate the attractive scene it presented, with its tangle of *caiques* and motor cruisers, and beyond them the row of *tavernas* and shops fronting the waterside.

And above them, on the hillside and not nearly as impressive as its name, picked out in large blue letters on the white walls, stood the Hotel Olympia.

Enemy in sight, thought Selena grimly as she picked up the big canvas satchel that served as her luggage and slung it over her shoulder.

As she came ashore she was assailed by a chorus of whistles and other bids to attract her attention by the young men mending fishing nets or waiting on tables at the *tavernas*.

No wonder Millie, released from the kind of purdah existing at Meade House Cottage, had been such easy game for an unscrupulous local, she thought.

Daisy and Fiona, with obvious reluctance, had volunteered a few details—his full name, Kostas Papoulis, young, good-looking, full of himself, and—with a shrug—sexy.

Besides, Daisy had added with faint malice, she hadn't thought that he was that interested in Millie. Just—playing around.

Selena wanted to slap her. Hard.

On the other hand, if this had also occurred to Millie by now, it might make her own task much easier.

The short walk up to the hotel was blisteringly hot, and she began to think longingly of iced water.

From the road, a path led up through borders bright with flowers to a terrace running the length of the frontage, and a pair of glass doors.

The foyer was light and airy, with a marble floor and a polished reception desk, currently unattended.

But Selena headed straight for the door labelled 'Bar', immediately opposite, and, drawing a deep breath, she walked in.

Once again, it seemed entirely deserted. Where was everyone? she wondered, as she looked about her. It was as if the entire establishment had been abducted by aliens.

Which the aliens could have done with her good wishes, she thought, just as long as they hadn't taken Millie.

But as she hesitated, she heard above the hiss and bubble of the coffee machine on the end of the counter, an unmistakable chink of bottles coming from behind a curtained doorway at the rear of the bar itself.

She walked to the counter, sliding her bag from her shoulder to the floor, and coughed loudly. When there was no immediate response, she followed it up with an imperative, 'Hello.'

The curtain was swept back, and a man appeared, clipboard in hand, his frowning gaze scanning her impatiently.

Selena found she was staring back, hoping she didn't

look as shocked as she felt because he bore little resemblance to the arrogant young stud described by Daisy, or any of the grinning lads she'd encountered at the harbour.

For one thing he was clearly older, probably in his late twenties, tall, swarthy, and in need of both a haircut and a shave, with a lean muscular body clad in jeans and a faded red polo shirt that emphasised the easy strength of his chest and shoulders.

Not conventionally handsome, she thought, aware her throat had suddenly tightened, his dark eyes brilliant, the nose and chin strongly marked, the mouth cool and sculpted with a firmness that suggested he was very much in charge of himself and his surroundings. Someone with—presence. And more.

She thought, *Oh, God, Millie, you stupid, stupid girl. He's miles out of your league. What have you done?*

He broke the silence, his voice deep and resonant as he addressed her in what was apparently German.

She said, 'I don't understand,' and saw his scrutiny sharpen and become more searching.

If you're thinking I could be trouble, you've got it in one, she informed him silently.

His English was excellent, with only a faint trace of an accent. 'I apologise for my mistake, *thespinis*. I was misled by your hair.' His gaze rested on the gleaming pale blonde mass tumbling over her shoulders, and for a startling moment, it was as if he'd touched it. Run his fingers through the length of it.

'But I was telling you that the bar is closed at this time of day, unless, of course, you wish for coffee.'

She lifted her chin. 'No thank you. I've only come for my sister.'

'Then I am afraid you must look elsewhere.' He glanced pointedly past her at the unoccupied array of glass-topped tables and small easy chairs, set in comfortable groups. 'Most of our guests are by the pool at the back of the hotel, or on the beach. Is she a resident?'

'You tell me. After all you're the only one likely to know her exact whereabouts.' She glanced at her watch.

'So shall we stop playing games? Just take me to her and she'll be off your hands and on the way back to Mykonos and the airport on the next ferry.'

'An excellent plan.' His voice was crisper. 'But there is a problem. I do not know either your sister's identity or where she may be found. Except it is plainly not here.'

Selena gasped. 'You mean she's already left? She's on her way home?' She glared at him. 'I suppose I should be grateful to you, but I'm finding it difficult.'

'It is also unnecessary. I was not aware of her presence here, or her departure. I suggest you conduct your enquiries elsewhere,' he added with cold finality and turned as if to go back to the store room.

'And I suggest you answer my questions,' she flung after him, aware that she was trembling inside, and not simply with temper at being so summarily dismissed. 'Otherwise I shall go to the police and tell them you've taken advantage of a vulnerable seventeen-year-old. That you've kept her here to have sex with her, forcing her friends to return to the UK without her, and causing endless worry to her family.'

She added contemptuously, 'I thought the Greeks were supposed to respect foreign travellers.'

'We do,' he said. 'Although your female compatriots do not always make it easy.' The contempt was echoed and the frown was back in force. 'She was staying here, your sister and her friends? Their names?'

'Raymond, Marsden and—and Blake.' She heard her voice quiver slightly and snatched at her self-command.

'Ah, yes.' He nodded. 'I remember some of the staff speaking of them.' His tone suggested the comments were not to their credit.

Well, he was the last person with any right to pass judgement.

'Whatever their opinions, nothing justifies your behaviour, Mr Papoulis.' She was about to say 'And I insist you bring Millie here immediately,' when she was stopped in her tracks by the realisation that he'd started to laugh.

'I'm glad you're amused,' she said scornfully. 'However, the police may not share your sense of humour.'

'They may,' he said, still grinning. 'When they hear I have been mistaken for my own barman. And they would undoubtedly tell you that, when you burst in, all guns blazing, *thespinis*, you should make sure they are aimed at the right target.'

He put down the clipboard and held out his hand. 'Allow me to introduce myself. I am Alexis Constantinou and I own this hotel. Kostas is merely employed here, when he can take the trouble to work,' he added sardonically. 'But at least I know the reason for his absence this time, and that he cannot use the excuse that he is ill.'

Numb with embarrassment, and bitterly aware of the mockery in his dark eyes, Selena allowed her fingers to be gripped briefly in his.

'So Kostas has sweet-talked your young sister into his bed,' he went on musingly. 'Strange. He usually confines his attentions to rather older women—the single, the divorced, so...' He paused, his gaze once more drifting down her hair. 'So—she must have made quite an impression.'

Her skin warming, she said tautly, 'I don't find that particularly reassuring.'

'Nor would I,' he said unexpectedly, 'if she was my sister.'

He turned to the shelf of bottles behind him. 'I think you need a drink, *thespinis*, and so do I.' He poured something amber into two glasses and gave her one. 'Five-star Metaxa,' he said. 'A universal remedy. Especially for shock.'

She said tautly, 'You don't seem particularly shocked over your employee's behaviour.'

'No,' he agreed. 'However, it is an irritation.'

He came round the bar and took the drinks to a table, motioning her to join him. She obeyed reluctantly, bringing her satchel with her.

Alexis Constantinou eyed it with faint amusement. 'You travel light, Kyria Blake.'

'It's going to be a brief visit, Mr Constantinou. I intend to find my sister and persuade her to leave this—

this cut-price Casanova she's involved with and come home.'

His amusement deepened. 'You have quite a turn of phrase, *thespinis*.'

'Thank you.' She added tautly, 'And if I may say so, perhaps you ought to exercise more vigilance over your staff's out-of-hours activities.'

'I make sure they do their job,' he said. 'I do not claim to be anyone's moral guardian. And perhaps your sister and her friends are the ones in need of guidance.'

'How dare you,' she flared. 'Millie is totally inexperienced. He's taken advantage of her innocence.'

'You paint a moving picture,' he said, clearly remaining unmoved. 'Now let us drink.' He raised his glass, touching it to the one she was holding, '*Yamas*. That means—to our health.'

She didn't like the way the toast seemed to unite them, but took a cautious sip, suppressing a gasp as it trailed fire down her throat.

'What is that?' she asked when she could speak.

'Brandy. To give you strength for your search. And— to calm you.'

She bit her lip. 'I'm perfectly calm, thank you.' And wished it was true. Because she was suddenly all too aware of him watching her. Glanced away and found herself instead looking at the hand clasping his glass. At the long fingers and well-kept nails, and the way his thumb was playing with the glass's stem.

Even with the width of the table between them, he seemed too close for comfort.

She went on hurriedly, 'If you'll just give me Mr

Papoulis's address, I'll go and let you get back to—whatever you were doing.'

'Stock-taking,' he said. 'As for Kostas's address,' he added with a shrug, 'I doubt if that will help. Like the rest of the staff, when he is working, he has a room here, but this, I am told, he has not used for several days.'

The implication in his words was obvious, Selena thought, swallowing.

'And when he's not working?' she demanded.

'He lives with his widowed mother,' he said. 'But she is very pious, so I doubt you will find your Millie there, either.'

She said half to herself, 'Then what am I going to do?'

'I am sure that is not a request for my advice,' he drawled. 'But I shall offer it just the same. Go home, *thespinis*, and wait for your sister to come to her senses.'

She took another gulp of brandy. 'And if he's keeping her here against her will?'

'Once again you are allowing your taste for the dramatic to run away with you,' Alexis Constantinou said softly. 'Kostas, believe me, has no need to use force.'

'You take all this so lightly.' Her voice shook. 'When I'm worried sick, and I—I can't leave without her.'

She paused. 'I shall have to go to the police.'

'I would prefer that not to happen.'

Her voice rose indignantly. 'You're actually protecting him?'

'No,' he said, with faint grimness. 'I am protecting the reputation of my hotel. And for that, I am prepared to help you. Give me a day, maybe two, to make enquiries.

To find where he is and if your sister is indeed with him. But that is all. After that, it is up to you. Do you agree?'

Selena stared down at the table. Almost in spite of herself, she could feel the warmth of the brandy quelling her inner trembling. A sense of something like hope growing in its place. Which was, of course, quite ridiculous under the circumstances.

She said, 'How do I know I can trust you?'

'Because stock-taking bores me,' he said. 'I want my barman back. His absence is inconvenient.'

She glared at him. She said mutinously, 'In that case—I suppose we have a deal.' She reached for her satchel and got to her feet. 'Thank you for the drink, and I hope your plan succeeds.'

'Wait,' he said. 'I need to know where to contact you.' He eyed her narrowly. 'You have made a reservation, found a place to stay, of course.'

She hesitated. Fatally. 'Not yet, but I'm sure I'll find somewhere.'

'I do not doubt it.' His tone was cynical. 'With that hair and those eyes, *pedhi mou*, you will be overwhelmed with offers in the first moment. In fact, your sister, wherever she may be, is probably much safer.'

She was shaken by that altogether too intimate reference to her appearance. She said coldly, 'I'm a university student, Mr Constantinou. I can look after myself. I can make my own arrangements—and my own enquiries.'

'The English, I think, have a saying,' he drawled. '"Famous last words." Perhaps you know it.'

'Nevertheless…'

'Nevertheless, *thespinis*, you will not go into the

town asking for a room to rent. I shall not permit it. Besides, how can you enquire about anything when you do not speak Greek?'

He rose to his feet. 'The Olympia is fully booked, but I have a small flat on the top floor for my personal use. You may stay there.'

'We have another quaint old saying in my country.' She faced him, lifting her chin. '"Out of the frying pan into the fire." Maybe you've heard that, too.'

He said silkily, 'And you, *pedhi mou*, should not jump to conclusions. I shall stay at my house, the Villa Helios, on the other side of the island. A safe enough distance, wouldn't you say?'

There were a lot of things she would like to have said, but she only managed a reluctant, 'Thank you.'

Alexis Constantinou nodded. 'Now I will speak to my housekeeper about your accommodation. And you perhaps should finish your brandy.'

As he walked to the door, Selena said, 'Why have you changed your mind suddenly? I—I don't understand.'

'You think I should not concern myself over the well-being of an innocent and inexperienced girl?'

'A moment ago you were implying that Millie's problems are all of her own making.'

'I still do,' he said. 'But the innocent I speak of is not your sister, *thespinis*, but yourself.'

And he walked out of the bar, leaving Selena staring after him.

CHAPTER THREE

'EXCUSE ME, DO you want to order anything else? Only there are people waiting for tables.'

The aggrieved tone of the waitress jolted Selena back to the present.

'I've finished, thank you.' She tried a smile. 'I'm sorry, I was miles away.'

Worlds away. An ocean of pain away, she thought as the girl gathered up the used crockery and walked away with a faint sniff.

Back in the honeyed trap that she'd thought was kindness. Caught by a man who was neither innocent nor inexperienced.

And now she had to go back to where it all happened. To Rhymnos—the place where she'd ruined her life and broken her heart.

At the same time, it was her chance to prove to herself that she had survived. Even mended.

As she left, she passed the young couple waiting for her table, and saw that the man was wearing a baby sling across his chest, cradling an infant obviously in its first weeks of life, its over-large cotton sun hat slipping down over a red, crumpled, sleeping face.

Saw, too, the way the young father looked down proudly at his child, then exchanged smiles with the pretty girl beside him in shared delight.

Selena felt a sudden twist of agony inside her, as if a hand had reached into her and wrenched at her heart, then she turned slowly and walked away, to tackle her final and most important problem.

The interview had proved just as difficult as she'd anticipated, she thought unhappily as she walked home.

'You're going on holiday?' Mrs Talbot had radiated disapproval. 'Do you think that's appropriate?'

'Unavoidable, I'm afraid,' Selena had returned quietly. 'And it's hardly a holiday. My sister is ill.'

'All the same, you'll be missing scheduled visits, which is very disappointing—for everyone.'

She was almost tempted to cancel, but, in the end, she simply sent Kostas a text with the time of her flight.

She made herself a cheese salad before she emptied and cleaned the fridge. Then she stuffed the contents of her linen basket into a large carrier bag, and set off to the nearby launderette.

She'd taken a book to read, but she found it difficult to lose herself in the story when other thoughts, other memories persisted in intervening. In pushing aside all other considerations.

Forcing her to go back to that first day on Rhymnos and that fateful encounter at the Hotel Olympia.

Left alone in the bar, she'd taken one more sip of brandy, then pushed the glass away. She'd already made one idiotic mistake, she reminded herself, and there was no need to muddle her thinking any further.

Because she had to decide very quickly whether to remain here and accept the help Alexis Constantinou had offered, or grab her bag and run.

In principle, her mission had seemed simple enough. Come to the hotel, confront this Kostas, who might be having second thoughts himself by now, and convince Millie that a holiday romance was not a commitment for life, and it was time to go home.

It had never occurred to her, or presumably Aunt Nora, that the pair might disappear.

And where would she go, anyway? If the Olympia was full, it might not be easy to find a respectable alternative—although Alexis Constantinou's offer of his private flat hardly qualified as that, either, in spite of his assurances.

And relying solely on a Greek phrasebook wasn't going to be much help in tracking down the runaways.

I should have done more homework in advance, she thought bitterly. If I'd been allowed to, of course.

However, she was here now, and her main concern was finding Millie, for which, galling as it might be, she probably needed the help of Alexis Constantinou.

It doesn't matter, she told herself, gritting her teeth. After all, the sooner you trace Millie, the quicker you can leave.

Suddenly restless, she rose and wandered over to the glass doors, which ran the length of one side of the bar, and walked out on to the balcony beyond with its flight of marble steps leading down to another area of garden, bright with flowers and shrubs and surrounded by hibiscus hedges. And beyond that, hazy with heat, the infinite blue of the Aegean.

Apart from a faint sound of splashing from the pool area, it was very quiet.

If I was here for a different reason, just one guest among many, I'd probably not want to leave, either, she realised with a swift pang.

She remained where she was, letting the peace soak into her, until a sound from the bar behind her made her turn hurriedly in time to see a tall, thin man with a heavy black moustache place a tray with a pot of coffee and a plate of pastries on her table.

'For you, *thespinis*,' he announced. 'Kyrios Alexis, he say it is long before dinner.'

'Oh,' Selena said disconcerted. 'Thank you.' Then remembering one of the words she'd learned on the plane, she added, *'Efharisto.'*

He inclined his head. *'Parakalo,'* he returned politely. 'I am Stelios and I manage the hotel for Kyrios Alexis. Anything you wish for, please ask me.'

Presumably that did not include a missing sister, Selena thought as he vanished.

The coffee was a strong filter brew, and the food turned out to be delicious little cheese tarts, still warm from the oven. Selena ate every scrap.

She had just drained her final cup when she was joined by a middle-aged woman wearing a neat black dress and an air of unmistakable authority.

She pointed to herself. 'Androula, *thespinis*. Housekeeper. Your room waits for you.'

She picked up the satchel and waited for Selena to accompany her.

A lift at the side of the foyer whisked them to the third floor. Androula led the way along the corridor to a pair of double doors at the end, which she unlocked, then stood aside allowing Selena to precede her into a spacious sitting room, with comfortable sofas and chairs upholstered in deep blue linen grouped round a massive square coffee table, its surface tiled in cream and gold.

As she looked round her, two girls emerged from another room, one carrying an expensive leather suitcase, the other a linen laundry bag.

As they passed Selena, they smiled shyly, but their eyes were alive with curiosity.

They must be wondering why they've been asked to clear the decks, she thought drily. However, it seemed that their boss was a man of his word after all and she only wished she could feel more at ease with the situation.

The bedroom was uncompromisingly masculine, almost disturbingly so, with shutters at the windows instead of drapes, dark fitted furniture, and what seemed to Selena to be an ultra-wide bed, made up with immaculate white linen, and a brown and gold coverlet in a Greek key pattern folded at its foot.

A door in the corner led into a bathroom almost as big as the bedroom, with a large walk-in shower as well as a tub, and twin basins in the long mirrored vanity unit, indicating, perhaps, that the owner did not always lack for company.

As if, she reminded herself swiftly, it was any business of hers.

Nevertheless it seemed she would be maintained pretty much in the lap of luxury during her brief stay, although she would have to make it clear to Mr Constantinou at their next encounter that she'd come prepared to pay for her board and lodging.

At least Aunt Nora has allowed for that, she thought. So I won't be obliged to be in his debt more than I can help.

She turned to Androula. 'Thank you.' She made an awkward gesture. 'It's lovely.'

The housekeeper inclined her head politely. 'You rest now,' she said. 'I will send someone to bring you to dinner at eight o clock.'

And on that, she departed, closing the outer door behind her. And, Selena realised in horror, locking it, too.

She was just about to rush over and beat on the panels, shouting 'Come back,' when she saw, just in time, another key lying in the centre of the coffee table, and realised her host was probably not the floor's sole occupant. And allowed herself a faint groan of relief that she hadn't made an utter fool of herself twice in one hour.

She's right, she thought. Maybe I do need to rest. Also—get a grip.

She retrieved her forlorn cotton robe from her bag and went to the bathroom, where she took a long, satisfying soak in the tub, then stretched out in the middle of that vast bed and gratefully closed her eyes. She was asleep within minutes.

It was already after seven when she awoke, and for

a while she lay watching with languid pleasure how the evening sunlight slatted through the shutters across the marble tiles.

Yes, she had to get ready, but it wouldn't take long. There weren't any anxious choices to make over how to dress for dinner. There was her denim skirt with a white top, or her denim skirt and the other white top.

Travelling light has its advantages, Mr Constantinou, she addressed him silently as she wriggled off the bed.

It was the prettier of the two maids she'd seen earlier who came to collect her and escort her to the restaurant on the ground floor, and her sideways glance, although polite, conveyed she was not greatly impressed by either the denim skirt or the other white top, or by the fact that Selena, on some inexplicable impulse, had plaited her hair into the severe braid preferred by Aunt Nora.

But then, thought Selena, I'm here on business, not out to impress—anyone.

The dining room was a large, airy room, most of its tables already occupied, and Selena attracted little attention as a waiter conducted her to a secluded corner partly screened from the rest of the room by a trellis supporting foliage plants growing in terracotta pots.

As she sat down, Selena realised it was the first time she'd ever eaten alone in a hotel. What a sheltered life you've led, Miss Blake, she mocked herself.

It had only just dawned on her that the table was set for two when Alexis Constantinou appeared, sauntering across the dining room, exchanging smiling greetings with the other diners as he approached, and clearly heading straight for her corner.

Oh, please no, she begged under her breath as her tense fingers crumpled the linen napkin she was spreading on her lap.

'Kalispera,' he said as he took the chair opposite. 'That means good evening.'

'Yes,' she said shortly. 'I picked up a few words on the flight. That was one of them.'

No one would have mistaken him for a barman now, even someone with an Olympic gold for leaping to conclusions, she conceded ruefully.

He'd shaved, for one thing, and the elegant, pale grey suit he was wearing was offset by a charcoal shirt, carrying the unmistakable sheen of silk, and open at the neck, revealing several inches of bronzed, hair-darkened skin, which it would be safer to ignore.

No, not handsome, she thought in sudden bewilderment, but stunningly, mind-blowingly attractive in a way she'd never encountered before. Or never been aware of, at any rate.

By contrast, she must look like something the cat dragged in.

'Excellent.' He smiled at her. 'Perhaps during our acquaintance, we will be able to extend your repertoire.'

'I doubt if there'll be time.' She adjusted a perfectly placed fork, crossly aware that her skin was warming. She added hurriedly, 'I'm hoping that you have some news for me.'

'I have certainly made enquiries among the staff,' he returned. 'But so far, without result.'

'Perhaps they're shielding him.'

'I never thought he was that popular,' he said drily. He paused. 'It seems, this time, he took the trouble to be discreet.'

This time, Selena repeated under her breath and winced.

He saw and said more gently, 'Forgive me. I meant it might indicate that this time he could be genuinely in love.'

'In two weeks?' Her objection was instant and vehement. 'That's ridiculous. No one could possibly fall truly in love that quickly.'

'You don't think so?'

'Of course not. People have to—to like each other first. Be friends. Enjoy each other's company. Have shared interests, and learn respect for each other's opinions.' My God, she thought. I sound like my great-grandmother.

His brows lifted. 'That is how it was for you?' His tone was politely interested.

And what was she supposed to say to that? To admit she could count the number of her dates, all strictly casual, on the fingers of one hand?

It might be best, safer, she thought uneasily, to make him think she was involved. 'Yes,' she said defiantly. 'As a matter of fact.'

'And that is how it sounds, *pedhi mou*.' His dark eyes glinted at her. 'Matter of fact.'

A change of subject seemed well overdue. She said, 'What do you keep calling me?' She tried to pronounce the words as he had.

'It means—my little one.'

She lifted her chin. 'Then please don't say it again. It's—demeaning. I am not a child.'

'Po, po, po,' he said softly. 'Then why tie back your beautiful hair like a little girl at school?'

'Because it's cool,' she said. 'And neat.'

'Ah,' he said. 'That is how you see yourself, perhaps?'

'I'm too busy to give it much thought,' she retorted. 'Besides, all that's important to me right now is my sister's well-being.' She paused. 'How do we go about finding her?'

'Quietly,' he said. 'Another reason not to go to the police. People talk and news travels fast. It is better your sister does not know you are here to collect her, so she and Kostas do not run away to another island, or even to the mainland and add to your difficulties.'

He beckoned and a waiter arrived at the table with an ice bucket, a gold-foiled bottle and two flutes.

'Champagne?' Selena asked incredulously. *Another first.* 'What is there to celebrate?'

'As yet, nothing.' He shrugged. 'So let us toast a beginning. The launch, if you wish, of our quest and its ultimate success.'

She could hardly refuse, even though she felt out of her depth, caught in some swift, disturbing current that she ought to resist.

The wine was cool, crisp and tingling against her dry throat, as other waiters began to bring plates and a dish containing some kind of green vegetable like small fat cigars.

'*Dolmades,*' her companion told her as they were served. 'Vine leaves stuffed with lamb, rice and herbs.'

Warily, she sampled a bit, then, surprised and delighted, another larger mouthful, savouring the various flavours, and saw him smiling at her.

'Good?'

She nodded. 'Wonderful.'

As was the grilled swordfish with sauté potatoes and salad which followed. And, of course, the champagne, its bubbles seeming to dance along her senses.

The dessert was just right, too—a bowl of fruit to share—peaches, and marvellously sweet figs that he told her had come that day from the garden at the family villa.

'You must have a lot of trees,' she commented, glancing at the now-crowded dining room.

'They are not for everyone. I had them brought specially to welcome you to Greece.'

She flushed. '*Efharisto*, Mr Constantinou.'

'*Parakalo,*' he returned. 'And must we be so formal? As I have told you, my name is Alexis.'

'I think formality is best,' she said. 'Under the circumstances.'

'Even though you will be spending tonight in my bed?' His question was soft and her flush deepened hectically as she struggled for composure.

She said jerkily, 'Please stop saying things like that. In Britain, it could be considered harassment.'

'But now you are in Greece,' he said with a shrug. 'And I have only spoken the truth, unless you plan to sleep on a sofa or the floor.' He paused. 'Tell me something. Why did you not come on holiday with your sister?'

'I had a vacation job. Besides, she was coming with her friends.'

'And your parents permitted this?'

She bit her lip. 'My parents were killed in a car accident. Our aunt acts as our guardian and though she wasn't keen on the holiday at first, she was persuaded by one of the mothers that they'd be fine on such a small island.'

'Yet human nature is the same everywhere. And you had to give up your job to come here?'

'I'd already done so. My aunt tripped in the garden and broke her leg and needed me at home.'

'So how does she manage without you now?' He was frowning.

'She's paying someone,' Selena said shortly. 'Now may I ask you something?'

'If you wish.'

'How is it you speak such good English?'

'My mother was born in America. Although she came to Greece to give birth to me, their only child, she and my father lived mainly in New York, and continued to do so after their divorce when my time was divided between them.'

'That must have been—difficult.'

'Divorce is always hard for children,' he said quietly. 'It is better to deal with mistakes in marriage before they are born.'

She was silent for a moment. Then: 'I suppose in that way we were lucky,' she said slowly. 'My mother and father adored each other and we felt surrounded by happiness. When they were—taken like that, it was dreadful for us, but I've thought since that it was good for them to be together. That if just one had died, the other who was left would never have recovered. They'd have been just part of a person.'

She stopped abruptly, shocked by what she'd said, what she'd let him see—this disturbing stranger that she wasn't even sure she could trust.

She remembered trying to say something similar to Aunt Nora when she was younger, and what the cold reply had been.

'I'm sorry,' she added quickly, trying to force a smile. 'I know that sounds—ridiculously morbid.'

'No,' he said. 'It does not.' He paused. 'Has she been kind to you, this aunt?'

'Yes. Of course.' She straightened her shoulders, silencing inner voices, drawing down mental blinds. 'It can't have been easy for her to be saddled with two pre-adolescents, but she's coped wonderfully.'

He inclined his head politely. 'So wonderfully that your sister cannot wait to escape, whatever the means.'

'My sister,' she said, 'as you've admitted, has been seduced by a serial womaniser, and is probably, and quite naturally, scared of the repercussions.' She added, 'We live in a small town and there's bound to be unpleasant gossip, so I'm here for damage limitation, not to burden you with our family history.'

'It is not a burden.' He signalled to a waiter. 'I suggest that after coffee, you go up to the flat and get some

sleep. You have had a long and worrying day, and tomorrow the search truly begins.'

'Thank you,' she said. 'But I think I'll sleep better
without coffee.' She rose, and he, too, got to his feet.
'Goodnight, Mr Constantinou.'

'*Kalinichta*, Kyria Blake.' His smile was tinged with
irony. 'Until tomorrow, then. Sleep well.'

He didn't add 'in my bed' this time but he might as
well have done, Selena thought mutinously as she made
her way across the dining room.

And knew, if she looked back, as she had no intention
of doing, she would find him watching her go.

Her laundry finished, Selena removed it from the
tumble dryer and folded it with care, aware that her
hands were shaking.

I should have left the next morning, she told herself
for the thousandth time. Got up early and slipped away,
leaving a note at the desk, thanking him and saying I'd
decided to pursue my own enquiries.

Instead, there she'd been, back in the restaurant,
breakfasting on fresh orange juice, warm rolls with
honey, and a pot of strong filter coffee, staring through
the windows at the sunlight dancing on the water. And
forbidding herself to look round every time the faint
squeak of the double doors announced a new arrival.

But when her meal was over without any sign of
Alexis Constantinou, she was at a loss what to do next.

Perhaps he'd had second thoughts about helping her,
she told herself. After all, he had a hotel to run. So she
would simply revert to Plan A: go to the police and risk
the gossip mill alerting Millie and her boyfriend.

But as she walked out into the foyer, he was waiting for her by the reception desk, casual in cream chinos and a black shirt, sleeves rolled to the elbows, and unbuttoned almost to the waist this time, she saw, her throat tightening.

'*Kalimera.*' His dark glance appraised her own white cut-offs and navy tunic top, then rested briefly on her hair, once more deliberately plaited into a long braid and hanging down her slender back. But he made no comment. 'Did you sleep well?'

'Yes,' she said, adding awkwardly, 'Thank you.'

'And you have eaten, so we can go.' Briskly, he ushered her out of the hotel and through the garden to a Jeep, waiting at the gate.

She hung back. 'Go where?'

'To find Adoni Mandaki, a local fisherman who is also a friend of Kostas.' He handed her into the Jeep, then swung himself into the driver's seat and started the engine. 'I heard in a bar last night that his boat is missing, but he himself has been seen in the town, drinking and playing *tavli* as if its absence did not disturb him, and he has no living to earn.'

'A boat.' Selena bit her lip. 'Do you think Kostas and Millie have left Rhymnos?'

'That is what I hope he will tell us,' he said as they drove down the hill towards the harbour.

She said slowly, 'So, after you sent me to bed, you came down here asking questions about my sister. It didn't occur to you that I might want to be there to hear the answers? And maybe ask some questions of my own?'

He shot her a swift glance. 'It occurred,' he said. 'But I dismissed it.'

'Ignoring the fact that I had a right to be there.'

'To do what? To shout at everyone in English until they told you what you wanted to hear?' His mouth twisted. 'Believe me, it would not have worked. And I decided you needed a night's rest.'

She stiffened. 'Then maybe you'd consult me in future before making any more arbitrary decisions.'

'I will try to remember. In return, perhaps you will now agree to call me Alexis. And tell me your name also.'

'Why is that necessary?'

He shrugged a shoulder. 'Because it suggests that we are on—friendly terms.'

Selena stiffened. 'I think it might imply rather more than that,' she said icily.

'So, people will see me spending a day in the sun with a pretty tourist,' he countered. 'What of it? Once we have found your sister, you will persuade her to leave with you and go, and that will be the end of it.'

He paused. 'Surely that is worth the temporary inconvenience of my company?'

She said reluctantly, 'You make me sound very ungrateful.'

'No,' he said. 'I think you are frightened, and you have reason. It is no easy thing you have been asked to do—to come all this way to a strange country and alone, when you cannot speak the language and do not know where to look.'

He sighed abruptly. 'I see this and I should have

more patience. And perhaps you could try to trust me. Believe that I wish to help you.'

'Yes,' she said. 'Thank you—Alexis.' She hesitated. 'And my name is Selena.'

'Selena,' he repeated, his brows lifting. 'In our language Selene—the goddess of the moon.'

'But people usually call me Lena,' she added hastily.

'Sacrilege,' he said softly. 'For a girl with hair the colour of moonlight.'

She felt an inner jolt as if she'd missed a step downwards. Knew, too, that she was blushing. 'And Millie's really Amelia,' she went on, aware that she was babbling. 'Perhaps she's named after a goddess, too.'

'Alas, no,' he said. 'But maybe to Kostas, she is Aphrodite herself. We shall soon find out.'

'I hope so.' And she meant it.

Because, as she'd suddenly realised, however scared she might be for Millie, she, too, was in danger, with an equally urgent need to get away.

CHAPTER FOUR

YET NOW HERE she was—once more flying to Millie's rescue, she thought wryly, as, back at the house, she began her packing. But this time the situation was very different, because she would be spared the agonising possibility of encountering Alexis again.

As Kostas had confirmed, he had indeed gone for ever, as she'd been told in that horrifying interview all those months ago.

And now, surely, she could begin to look to a future with hope, not regret.

God, what a fool I was, she thought bitterly, extracting a folder of photographs from a drawer, and tucking one of them into her bag. 'Trust me,' he said, and I was naïve enough to believe him.

And telling herself that, at the time, she'd had little choice was no excuse.

Because, even as they drove along the quayside that first morning in search of Adoni, she could have said she'd changed her mind and requested him to take her to the police station instead.

But she didn't because she was already starting to flounder in a maelstrom of unaccustomed emotions.

At the same time, the bustle at the harbour held its own fascination, too. The air still held the aroma of last night's charcoal grills. The *caiques* were unloading their first catches amid shouting and laughter. Owners of souvenir and clothing shops were unrolling awnings and bringing out their display stands, and at the *tavernas*, cloths were being anchored to the tables with plastic clips, tiled floors hosed down and tubs of geraniums watered.

As the Jeep went past, people called smiling greetings to Alexis, who waved in acknowledgement.

Like a royal progress, Selena thought with faint amusement.

'Do you always get this kind of reception?' she asked.

He shrugged. 'Only when I have been away for a while. Many of those who live here regard the world outside Rhymnos as a dangerous place and are glad to see I have returned safely, and that all is as it should be again.' He shot her a swift glance. 'You find that strange?'

'I find everything about this situation strange,' she returned tautly.

'Yet you will soon accustom yourself, I promise.'

But I don't want to become used to this place—this way of life, she thought, her throat tightening. I can't afford that.

They reached a dilapidated warehouse, hardly more than a shack, its doors standing open. Deftly, Alexis slotted the Jeep between two trucks on the other side of the road, and switched off the engine.

'Adoni sleeps here sometimes when he is not on his boat,' he said. 'Wait here while I see if he is sober enough to talk.'

'I want to come with you,' Selena protested.

'But I wish you to stay where you are,' he said softly.
'I have my reasons.'

Which of course take precedence, she thought resentfully watching his tall figure stride across the road and
disappear into the dark interior of the building.

Unless she was there, how could she be sure he'd ask
the right questions?

On the other hand, she had no real wish to encounter a Greek fisherman with a hangover.

There was a haze over the sea and the heat was building steadily. It was going to be a scorching day, she
thought, pulling off her broad-brimmed cotton sunhat
and using it languidly to fan herself.

Her thin tunic was already clinging to her damp
skin, and she was just hoping that Alexis's interrogation would not take too long or she might melt, when he
emerged from the shack accompanied by another man,
stout, bearded and clad only in a pair of sagging shorts.

Some Adonis, she thought critically.

However, he appeared to be doing all the talking, and
was smiling at the same time, which might be a good
sign, while Alexis stood, head bent, listening.

As she watched, she suddenly realised that she, too,
was under scrutiny. That Adoni had spotted her and
was staring openly, his smile broadening into a grin as
he made some comment to Alexis.

Then they both laughed, clapped each other on the
shoulder, and Alexis walked back to the Jeep.

As he swung himself into the driving seat, he turned

to her, shrugging and spreading his hands almost ruefully.

'Look disappointed, Selene *mou*,' he whispered urgently. 'Pout a little.'

'Disappointed?' she echoed, staring at him appalled.

Had Adoni refused to help—pleaded ignorance? Had
they come so soon to a dead end?

As her thoughts rampaged, Alexis reached out a
hand and clasped the nape of her neck, his fingers
lightly stroking the silky skin under the pale blonde
braid.

Taken totally by surprise, she felt her pulses leap and
the quivering ache of an unfamiliar tremor along her
senses. In sudden panic, she tried to push him away,
but she was too late. He was already drawing her towards him, pulling her against him, imprisoning her
hands between their bodies, holding her helpless, while
his mouth took her parted, outraged lips in a long and
very thorough kiss.

A kiss for which nothing in her life so far could possibly have prepared her.

She was conquered, consumed by the pressure of his
mouth moving on her, enjoying her, by his clean breath
sighing into hers and the heated intimate glide of his
tongue against her own.

Half drugged by the heat of the sun, its golden
clamour against her closed eyelids and the warm, male
scent of his skin, she found herself prey to feelings—
to needs she had not known existed until that moment.

She thought dazedly: I have to make him stop.

And then: I never want him to stop.

Because something—some sensation was uncurling deep inside her, sending out little tendrils of pleasure that were beginning to bloom and grow and which, instinct warned her, could easily overwhelm her.

And then suddenly, with a shock as brutal as a slap across the face, she was free, and Alexis was sitting back at a decorous distance watching her, his expression unfathomable.

He said coolly, 'I hope I have not caused permanent damage to your hat, *agapi mou.*'

Numbly, she looked down at it, crushed in her hand, and suddenly her predominant emotion was shame that she'd allowed him to—maul her in full view of anyone who cared to look. And although he had certainly not been brutal, her mouth felt hot. Swollen.

'You.' Her voice almost choked as her hands clenched into belated fists. 'How *dare* you…'

'Be calm.' He held her wrists, fending her off with the utmost ease. There was a note of laughter in his voice. 'As I thought I made clear, I want Adoni to see you disappointed, Selene *mou*, not dangerous.'

'You *wanted* him to watch that—that disgusting performance?'

'I wanted him to watch you being consoled for the loss of our romantic trip together in the seclusion of his boat.'

'But—the boat is supposed to be missing.'

'Why, yes,' he said. 'As he explained when I suggested hiring it for the day. I was too late, he told me. A friend had already borrowed it—for his honeymoon.'

'Honeymoon,' Selena repeated dazedly. 'You mean that Kostas and Millie are married?'

He sighed. 'No, I merely changed the words he really used in order to spare your blushes.'

'Oh,' Selena said and began to smooth the creases out of her hat, her fingers all thumbs. She swallowed. 'And you let him think that you—that I…'

'Wished to share the same delight,' he supplied courteously as she stumbled to a halt.

'Did he actually say it was Kostas who'd borrowed his boat?' She jumped to safer ground.

'No,' he said. 'Because he knows that Kostas should be working at the hotel not off somewhere enjoying his new lover, and assumes that his absence has not been reported to me. A real beauty, he told me. Such golden hair, such eyes. A hot little English honey.'

'Oh.' Selena bent her head, covering her face with her hands. 'Oh, God.'

He said, 'If you are going to weep, Selene *mou*, can you wait until we have more privacy? I do not want the whole of Rhymnos to think I ill-treat you.'

She straightened defiantly, glaring at him. 'I have no intention of crying. I'm too angry. How do you think it makes me feel—hearing that Millie's been discussed—leered over like that—when she doesn't deserve it?' She took a breath. 'Because whatever Daisy and Fiona may have done, she wouldn't have been involved. I know it.'

He was silent for a moment, then he said quite gently, 'You are at university, *ne*? And in the vacations, you work.'

'Most students do.' She was defensive.

'So you have not always been there to see, perhaps, that she has changed. That maybe she is no longer the little sister—the child of the family. That she has grown up—spread her wings.'

Selena gasped. 'What are you saying?' she demanded. 'That she chased Kostas—not the other way round? That she's the one to blame for all this?'

He sighed. 'No, Selene *mou*. That is not what I mean. Just that the situation may not be as clear-cut as you believe.' He started the engine. 'But first we must find them, and do so quickly. Adoni tells me there is going to be a storm.'

And as she glanced up incredulously at the cloudless sky, he added drily, 'And where the weather is concerned, at least, he is never wrong.'

Almost as soon as the harbour was left behind, the road became little more than a rutted track, with the sea on one side and a scatter of small single storey houses on the other, their gardens neatly tended, with chickens pecking in the dust and the occasional goat tethered on the verge.

And behind them, stretching away towards the grey and amethyst rocks crowning the hills in the centre of the island, the ancient twisted trunks of olive trees, their leaves shimmering like silver in the sunlight.

'Don't the locals complain about this surface?' Selena asked, grabbing the side of the Jeep after one particularly severe jolt.

'Not that I have heard. Besides their transport is accustomed to it,' he added, indicating two donkeys peacefully browsing in the shade of a tree.

She said in a hollow voice, 'Oh, I see.'

'I think you are beginning to.' There was faint amusement in his voice, and she flushed.

'I can't help it if things seem strange. I haven't been abroad before.'

'And even now it is business, not pleasure, that brings you—and alone.' He paused pointedly. 'To me, that is strange.'

'But hardly my choice,' she returned coolly. And let him make what he would of that.

'So,' she went on, 'where are we going?'

'To look for Adoni's boat. Where else?'

'But it could be anywhere.'

'I think not. It is hardly a luxury yacht,' he added drily. 'Nor is it equipped for a long voyage. So it is probable they have moored where they can have access to a beach and some form of shelter, and on Rhymnos such places are few.'

He shot her a swift sideways glance. 'Try to relax, Selene *mou*. We will find them, and soon, I promise you.'

She nodded. She said in a stifled voice, 'I keep thinking this is all a bad dream and that, in a minute, I'm going to wake up back in Haylesford with Millie asleep in the next room.'

'Truly? Is this place where you live so dear to you?'

No, she thought. And it never will be. But right now it represents a kind of security.

She said quickly, 'Of course. It's my home.' And paused. 'You must feel the same about Rhymnos.'

There was an odd silence, then he said almost harshly, 'Yes, I do.'

She looked at him, startled at his tone, then by the sudden starkness she saw in his face and the grim set of his mouth.

Was shocked to find herself wanting to put her hand on his arm. To say, *Tell me what's wrong. What's troubling you...?*

And thought that she must be going crazy, because, in reality, that was the last thing in the world that she needed to do.

Keep your distance, she warned herself urgently. Be polite now, grateful when you get Millie back, and leave it at that.

She turned slightly, staring at the sea, noticing that it had become smoother, like a sheet of glass, and that a ridge of pale cloud seemed to be building on the horizon.

It looked as if Adoni's prediction about the weather was coming true after all, she thought uneasily, transferring her attention to the olive groves clustering on the other side of the track.

She said, trying to sound like an interested tourist, 'People must use a lot of olive oil.'

'They use what they need,' he said. 'Most of it now goes for export.'

'From a tiny place like this?' She was astounded.

'Yes,' he said. 'Until quite recently, each household gathered and pressed its own olives and stored the oil. But it was felt they deserved a wider market, so the islanders were persuaded to join a co-operative and now their olives are collected and processed at a new, modern plant on the other side of the island and sold worldwide under the Rhymnos label.'

Selena's eyes widened. 'I think it's on sale in the supermarket near the university. Do the bottles have a picture of three stone columns?'

He smiled faintly. 'The pillars of Apollo, all, sadly, that remains of his ancient temple.' He paused. 'I shall be happy to show it to you.'

'I'm afraid there won't be time,' she said quickly. 'Millie and I have to return to the UK on the first available flight.'

'Of course,' he said. 'In the pleasure of your company, Selene *mou*, I had almost forgotten.'

She reverted hastily to the safer topic of olive oil. 'Was it you who persuaded the islanders to join this co-operative, by any chance?'

'I was not alone,' he said. 'Our priest, Father Stephanos, supported the scheme, and most of the headmen of the villages, who knew fishing and tourism would not make Rhymnos self-sufficient. And fortunately, I had contacts in the States in advertising, as well as marketing and distribution, which I could offer as an incentive.'

His smile was rueful. 'But it was not easy. The idea of a co-operative held little appeal at first. Now they can take pride in its success.'

And they're grateful, too, Selena thought. It explains the royal progress earlier. And maybe it means that I can trust him, that it's good to have him on my side, even if his main concern is the good name of his hotel rather than Millie.

The journey proceeded in silence, Alexis driving steadily, scanning the sea as they went. It now looked like burnished steel, she saw uneasily, and the sky had almost disappeared behind a grey veil, through which the sun's disc burned with a sullen orange.

At the same time, she realised that the Jeep was slowing. Alexis pulled over on to the rough grass at the side of the track and parked in the shade of yet another olive tree.

She craned her neck to look past it. 'Have you seen the boat?'

He looked at her, frowning slightly. 'No, but this is the only other place where they could have come ashore, and there is a good, dry cave. If they are using it, they may intend to return. There may be signs of this, so I am going down to check.'

Selena scrambled out. 'I'll come with you.'

His frown deepened. 'You would do better to stay here,' he advised brusquely. 'The path is difficult.'

'Do you think I care?' She confronted him, chin lifted. 'If there's anything in that cave, I—I want to see it.'

There was a brief, taut pause, then he said quietly, 'Whatever horrors you are imagining, *agapi mou*, put them out of your head. The most I expect to see is water—the remains of food—perhaps a blanket.'

'It makes no difference. I want to look for myself.'

When she saw how steep the route to the beach really was, she began to regret her intransigence, and when Alexis paused at the edge of the cliff and silently extended his hand, she took it without demur.

Their descent was slow and wary, and she found it was better to concentrate on the loose stones threatening to roll away under her feet than to look down at the beach.

When they finally reached the foot of the cliff, she realised she'd been holding her breath and, as she released it with a gasp, wondered if that was due to the gradient or more to the firm clasp of his fingers round hers.

Releasing herself, she said quickly, 'I don't see any cave.'

He pointed to a huge boulder. 'The entrance is behind there.'

He strode off across the beach, and she followed more awkwardly, her feet sinking in the coarse, gritty sand. An apprehensive look upwards told her that the overcast of cloud had now blotted out the sun completely.

It had become very still, as if the world around them was waiting. Gathering itself. That she and Alexis were all that moved in a silent landscape, and she suddenly remembered the saying, 'The calm before the storm.'

As she reached the rock, she paused as she saw the narrow entrance it was guarding and the darkness beyond.

She'd never experienced even mild claustrophobia, but there had to be a first time for everything, and in spite of the oppressive heat, she felt a quick shiver run down her spine.

At the same moment, she glimpsed a jagged flash over the sea, followed by a sullen rumble of thunder and the first few heavy drops of rain, sharp and cold against her skin.

Alexis was gesturing at her impatiently from the opening to the cave. 'Come quickly,' he called. 'Run.'

As she reached him, he took her by the shoulders,

turned her sideways and thrust her through the gap, following immediately behind her as outside the rain was gathering to a deluge.

It was dim in the cave, but, as her eyes adjusted, she realised that after the cramped entrance had been negotiated, it opened out quite astonishingly, its roof well over six feet high at the front, allowing Alexis to stand upright, but tapering down to less than four feet at the rear. However, it was also completely empty.

Her voice shook with disappointment. 'They haven't been here.'

Another jagged flash tore at the sky outside, bathing the cave for an instant in a strange green light.

Alexis said something under his breath and bent to the sandy floor. When he straightened, a short length of heavy silver links was dangling from his fingers.

He said, 'Someone has—and not so long ago, or this would have been hidden by the sand.' He looked at her. 'You know this?'

Selena stared at the broken chain, her throat tightening. She said huskily, 'It's the bracelet I bought Millie for Christmas,' flinching as another crack of thunder echoed around them.

As it died away, he said, 'Then you had better take it,' and dropped it into her hand.

She pushed it into her pants pocket. 'So she was here—with him. Oh, where are they? What has he done with her?'

There was another violent flash of eerie green light and then, almost at once and right above their heads, an ominous rumble building slowly and inexorably to a roaring, deafening crash as if the entire cliff was collapsing on top of them.

Selena cried out, her voice lost in the uproar, and stumbled forward, her hands reaching out to Alexis, who caught her and held her, wrapped closely in his arms, his hand stroking her hair, until the last terrifying echoes of the thunder died away, and all she could hear was the tumultuous thud of her own heartbeat.

And, beneath her cheek, his—like the relentless rhythm of a drum.

He lifted his head and stood for a long moment, unmoving, giving her the odd sensation that the entire world had suddenly shrunk to the circle of his arms and that, once again, it was waiting in breathless anticipation.

That she herself was poised—on the edge of some momentous discovery, her whole being suffused by a warm and unfamiliar languor.

His hand moved down, brushing a few damp strands of hair from her temples, then tracing her cheek and the delicate line of her jaw with his fingertips. Impelling her silently to look up at him. To read his intention in the sudden flare of his gaze as he bent and his mouth found hers, gently, sensuously coaxing her lips to part for him.

She leaned into the heat and strength of his body, this time welcoming his kiss, responding with bewildered ardour as it deepened, and a shiver of pleasure feathered enticingly across her skin.

His hands slid down her body to clasp her hips and pull her even closer, making her frankly aware of his arousal, and, to her shocked astonishment, of the heated, melting ache of her own needs. Unguessed-at, perhaps, unbidden—certainly, but frighteningly potent just the same, turning her suddenly into a stranger to herself.

When, at last, he took his lips slowly from hers, she made a small, lost sound in her throat that never became an actual word, even if she'd been able to think of one.

She lifted her shaking hands and pushed aside the edges of his shirt, her fingers tracing the uncompromising line of his shoulders before they drifted down to discover his muscular torso and the way it clenched under her untutored touch.

His hands were moving, too, swift and deft as he unfastened the buttons that closed her tunic and slipped it down, baring her to the waist. He cupped her rounded breasts in his palms, his fingertips teasing her nipples into hard and aching peaks, then drew her against him, grazing them with his hair-roughened chest until she could have cried out with the delight that pierced her to the core of her womanhood, that made her burn and melt.

As if the body she had fed and clothed but never been remotely tempted to share with anyone had taken on a life and purpose of its own, fierce and unrecognisable.

That showed her, at last, the mystery of desire.

But not, she realised dazedly, its answer.

Because the hands that held her, although still gentle, were putting her away from him. Distancing her.

Isolated on the other side of the space between them, she saw those same caressing hands ball into fists and become hidden in the pockets of his chinos. Watched the muscles move in his throat as he swallowed.

He said quietly and harshly, 'This—should not have happened. Forgive me.'

For an instant, she was transfixed, knowing there was nothing to forgive. That wherever he had led, she would have gladly followed. That he must have known that.

Yet he had still turned away.

Pride came to her rescue, and the self-containment that the past nine years had taught her. She turned her back, pulling her top back into place, fumbling with the buttons.

She said over her shoulder, 'I should apologise, too. I—I'm not usually afraid of thunder, but I thought the roof was going to collapse and I—panicked.'

In the part of her mind still functioning on the rim of reality, she registered that the crackle of the lightning had become less frequent and the answering thunder had become a sullen mumble in the distance.

She added, with a kind of ludicrous brightness, 'But at least the storm is over.'

There was an odd silence, then he said quietly, 'On the contrary, Selene *mou*, I think it is just beginning.' He paused again. 'Now let us resume our search.'

And he led the way out of the cave and back to the Jeep.

CHAPTER FIVE

BEHAVE AS IF it didn't happen, she told herself repeatedly as she scrambled back up the cliff, this time without assistance. Or as if it was just a random incident to be shrugged away and forgotten.

Back on level ground, she paused, shading her eyes against the emergence of a watery sun and staring out to sea as if she could conjure up Adoni's boat by sheer force of will. Then, her breathing under control, she followed Alexis over to the Jeep.

When she arrived, she found that he'd produced a towel from somewhere and was using it to wipe away the rain that had gathered on the front seats.

'So, where do we go from here?' She gestured towards the Aegean, keeping her tone brisk. 'If they're just sailing around, how can we possibly trace them?'

'By helicopter, perhaps.' He screwed up the damp towel and tossed it in the back of the Jeep.

'Helicopter,' she repeated and managed a short laugh. 'Now why didn't I think of that? And I suppose you have one available?'

'Of course.' His glance was sardonic. 'Or I would not have suggested it. It is at my house.'

She absorbed that with a gulp. 'You didn't think of using that first?'

'Yes,' he said. 'But I decided, wrongly it seems, that tracking them this way would be a simple matter.'

'Maybe you don't know Kostas as well as you thought.'

'I will not,' he said softly, 'make the obvious remark about your sister, Selene *mou*.'

Her search for a crushing retort was halted as she realised he was stripping off his shirt.

'What—what are you doing?'

'Making sure you are comfortable for the rest of our trip.' He folded the shirt into a neat pad and put it on the still-damp passenger seat. 'Shall we go?'

He was about to start the engine when there was a loud trill from the mobile phone in the well between the seats.

He answered it brusquely, then listened for a moment, his expression, she saw, changing from impatience to incredulity. Then he barked off a response and switched off the phone, sitting in silence for a moment, staring through the windshield.

She said, 'Has something happened?'

'Why, yes, *agapi mou*.' He started the Jeep. 'It seems that we shall not need the helicopter after all. Adoni's boat is back in the harbour and Kostas and your sister are now at my house, together with his mother, who shares your views about their relationship and has been saying so very loudly.' His lip curled. 'My staff have had a dramatic morning.'

She bit her lip. 'I—I'm sorry.'

She could only hope that all this signalled the parting of the ways and that Millie would be glad to put Rhymnos and its mistakes behind her and go quietly back to England.

And she won't be the only one, she reminded herself without pleasure.

He said, 'I thought you would be jubilant.'

She looked down at her hands, clenched together in her lap. 'I'm just trying to figure out what to say to them both.'

'You have only to talk to your sister,' he said, adding with a touch of grimness, 'I shall deal with Kostas. And his mother.'

'Oh,' she said. 'Well—thank you.' She paused. 'Millie—and Kostas. Do they still seem to be speaking to each other?'

'Speaking, holding hands and refusing to be parted, also loudly. Not, I think, what you wanted to hear.' He glanced at her frowningly. 'You were hoping she would simply leave without an argument?'

'Well, naturally.'

'You are an optimist, Selene *mou*.' He paused. 'So— let us speak of your aunt. Clearly, she has money. How much do you think she would be willing to pay for your sister's return?'

'You mean—Kostas might be bought?'

'Who knows?' His tone was cynical. 'But, in the end, money tends to speak louder than words of love.'

Selena bit her lip. She said quietly, 'I doubt she'd even consider it.'

'And, in that event, what awaits your sister in England?'

'School. Some important exam results. College interviews.' She saw his mouth twist and added hastily, 'Oh, and her eighteenth birthday in a few weeks' time.'

'A few weeks,' he repeated softly. '*Po, po, po.* Then you do not have much time,' he added and put his foot down hard on the accelerator.

She was braced for another bone-shaking trip, but almost at once found they were joining a broad, level road, apparently of recent construction and cutting across the middle of the island. It was a bleak landscape consisting mainly of wide stretches of stone and scrub and dominated by the huddle of rugged hills at the centre and hardly, she thought, justifying an access like this.

Until she saw they were approaching a collection of single storey buildings, composed of concrete blocks and corrugated iron, enclosed by a high wire fence, with a large sign at the entrance displaying three golden pillars.

'Oh,' she said. 'Is that where the olive oil is produced?'

'*Ne.*' He slanted a smile at her. 'Not beautiful, I agree. But efficient.'

'Is that why it's here—in the middle of nowhere?'

He tutted reprovingly. 'Rhymnos,' he said, 'is too small to have a nowhere. Everything is close to somewhere. In this case—where a dream became an idea and the idea moved to reality.'

'I'm not very good at riddles.'

He shrugged a shoulder. 'If you were staying, I could explain.'

She kept her voice light. 'As it is, I shall just have to live with my curiosity.'

'And so,' he said softly, 'shall I.'

A comment she deemed it wiser not to pursue.

The road stretched out in front of them, winding its way round the bottom of the hills, the barren landscape giving way to more olive groves, but interspersed now with well-kept orchards growing lemons, peaches and figs.

And beyond them, at last, standing alone in its spacious grounds was the Villa Helios, a sprawl of white stone, topped with faded green roof tiles and set against the coruscating blue of the sea.

Now *that*, thought Selena, catching her breath, that *is* beautiful. She was aware of Alexis shooting her a sideways glance and smiling as he interpreted her reaction.

He drove round to the rear of the villa and parked in a yard where chickens scattered, clucking indignantly at the intrusion.

Selena followed him to an open doorway, bracing herself as they walked down a passage lined with store and laundry rooms to another door leading straight into a large kitchen, seemingly crowded with people.

For a moment there was silence, then, just as Selena had registered that Millie was not one of the crowd, this was hideously broken by a series of piercing shrieks from a thin woman clad in funereal black from her headscarf to her shoes, who was seated at the massive central table.

Selena took an involuntary step backwards, stumbling a little, and felt herself caught and steadied by Alexis's hands on her shoulders. Immediately the screeches increased in volume and a middle-aged woman in a neat grey dress came forward spreading her hands in a kind of helpless embarrassment, murmuring in Greek. She was plump, her dark hair streaked with grey and drawn into a bun on top of her head. Her round face suggested that her expression was usually merry and that her black eyes would twinkle, given the opportunity. Only they weren't twinkling now.

Alexis said something quiet and savage, half under his breath, then crooked an imperative finger to summon a young girl in a maid's uniform.

'Go with Penelope to your sister, Selene,' he directed. 'I will join you when I have spoken to Kostas.'

Selena found herself guided out of another door and down a short passage into an impressive entrance hall and across to a pair of double doors. As the girl reached to open them, Selena halted her. 'Do you speak English…er… Penelope?'

'*Ne, thespinis.* When I was a child, I lived in America.'

'Then can you tell me why that woman started screaming when we arrived?'

Penelope's pretty face was lit by a swift smile. 'Madame Papoulis is very devout—very modest, *thespinis*. She was offended that Kyrios Alexis was not wearing a shirt.'

Selena's eyes widened. 'But she's been married,' she exclaimed. 'Surely she can't be that shocked.'

Penelope shrugged. 'There are many kinds of marriage, *thespinis*. Maybe we should pity her husband, *ne*?'

And on that, she ushered Selena into the room beyond.

'What are you doing here?' was Millie's defensive greeting as the door closed behind Selena.

Her face mutinous and unsmiling, she was perched on the edge of a sofa, clad in tiny white shorts and a skimpy black bikini bra, her finger and toe nails lacquered gold.

'And hello to you, too,' Selena returned equably. 'I came to see if you were all right.'

Millie hunched a shoulder, putting the bra top in peril. 'Of course I am. Didn't Daisy and Fiona pass on my message?'

'Such as it was.' *Don't lose your temper. Just walk to a chair and sit down.* 'Didn't it occur to you that Aunt Nora would be worried sick?'

'Worried, no,' Millie returned calmly. 'Mad as fire, yes. However, I've now written to her, explaining everything, and asking her to send my birth certificate and some other stuff. Will you make sure she does it?'

'Your birth certificate?' Selena stared at her. 'Why?'

'Because I'll need it to get married as soon as I'm eighteen. Greek law.'

'Married?'

Oh, God, thought Selena. *I sound like an echo. And that's why Alexis said there was no time to be lost.*

She took a deep breath. 'Millie, for heaven's sake, think what you're doing. You're throwing away your future...'

'On the contrary, my future is going to be with the man I love.'

'Someone you hardly know.'

'I knew within the first hour. So did he,' Millie said defiantly. 'You may be content to slave away for our beloved aunt for the rest of your life, but I want something different. Something better. And I'm taking it.'

And if she means it, thought Selena, with a sudden, joyous lift of the heart, then I'm also off the hook.

She said slowly, 'I had my reasons for doing what Aunt Nora wanted, but now they no longer apply. So, let's get back to you. Do you really imagine you can both live on what Kostas earns from seasonal bar work?'

'I can work, too. Besides, he won't always be just a barman,' Millie said defiantly. 'He has ambition. He's going to have his own *taverna.*'

'But until then, where will you live?'

'Well—at the hotel.' For the first time there was a note of uncertainty in her sister's voice. 'Of course, Kostas will have to clear it with his boss, but that shouldn't be a problem. And I can be—a chambermaid or something,' she added with a vague gesture.

Bold talk from someone normally incapable of making her own bed, Selena thought cynically.

She said, 'I wouldn't count on it, Mills. If there are any staff vacancies, they'll almost certainly be offered to local people.'

She paused. 'Anyway, you're so young to be making this kind of decision. You need to see more of life— meet other men—before you settle down.'

'Oh, for heaven's sake, Lena.' Her sister sighed. 'I'm

not a virgin, and I've been on the pill since I was sixteen, so I probably know more about "life", as you put it, than you do.

'I came out here to have a good time with a couple of mates and I certainly didn't expect to fall in love. Nor did Kostas, let me tell you. But it happened, and whatever you think, it ain't going to change.

'And I'm relying on you to get Aunt Nora on side,' she added. 'After all, you'll be the blue-eyed girl from now on. Make her see I'm entitled to live my own life.'

At the same time curing world hunger I suppose, Selena thought despairingly.

As she tried to marshal her arguments for another attempt, there was a rap at the door and Alexis walked in, once again fully clad, and trailed by a young man, who, in spite of his sulky expression, still managed to be spectacularly good looking with the build of a Hollywood action hero.

Selena could see the attraction, but was far from reassured.

'Kostas. Darling.' Millie jumped up and hurled herself at him. 'Is everything fixed?'

'*Ochi.* No, *kougla mou.*' He sighed. 'Kyrios Alexis says that you should return to England with your sister.'

'But I've already made it clear to her that I'm not leaving Rhymnos.' She turned wide eyes and a pretty smile on Alexis who appeared curiously unmoved.

'Surely you can understand we want to be together and find a little corner for me, while we wait to be married. I promise that I'll be no trouble.'

Alexis spoke bleakly. 'Forgive me, *thespinis*, but you

have already caused more trouble than you can imagine. The staff accommodation at the hotel is for single occupation only and I make no exceptions. Also your presence may continue to distract Kostas from his work.' He paused. 'You wish him to keep his job, do you not?'

'Yes, of course.' The blue eyes began to swim with tears. 'Why are you being so cruel?'

'Perhaps in order to be kind.' His dark face was harsh. 'Marriage is a serious business and this has not started well. You both need time to think—to reflect. Mistakes once made are not easy to put right.'

'But this is not a mistake.' Kostas turned on him. 'My Amelia is the only woman I shall ever want.' He struck his chest with a clenched fist. 'I cannot live without her.'

Alexis's mouth tightened. 'Very dramatic,' he said coldly. 'Perhaps you should seek work with the National Theatre.' He jerked his head towards the door. 'There is food waiting for you in the dining room. Go and eat while I talk with Kyria Blake.' He paused. 'And you, *thespinis*, should dress in something more discreet before you are seen by your fiancé's mother.'

They went reluctantly, Millie, having apparently abandoned the idea of weeping, sending him a fulminating glance instead.

'So,' Alexis said when they were alone. 'As I feared, you are having problems, Selene *mou*. What will you do now?'

'I don't know.' Selena bit her lip. 'I can hardly force her to the aircraft, kicking and screaming. I suppose I should really talk to my aunt.'

He pointed to a side table. 'The telephone is at your disposal. You know the code?'

'Yes,' she said. 'Thank you.'

'Then I will leave you to make your call.' At the door, he turned. 'I wish you luck, *agapi mou.*'

She was sitting on the sofa Millie had vacated, gazing unseeingly into space, when he came to look for her some ten minutes later.

'The conversation did not go well.' He was stating a fact, not asking a question, as he scanned her pale face.

'No. She was—furious.' She tried and failed to smile. 'With me even more than Millie, I think.'

Fool of a girl—completely useless—can't have been trying.

The words stung at her.

She said, 'I've been told I have to make Millie see sense, however long it takes.' She swallowed. 'And I'm forbidden to go back without her.'

'Po, po, po.' He sat down beside her, not touching.

'She has little understanding of love, this aunt.'

'You think it's really that?' she asked wistfully. 'That they genuinely love each other?'

'Who knows?' He shrugged. 'Only time can tell. When I spoke earlier to Kostas, he claimed to care for your sister very deeply. Perhaps it is the first time in his life that he has felt this for a woman.'

Selena sighed. 'All the same, I have to try again to change her mind.'

'But not at once, perhaps,' he said musingly. 'Let them think that you have accepted the situation, and that you are only staying on to give your aunt's anger time to cool.'

He added, 'Who knows? If they are no longer persecuted lovers, their romance may lose some of its excitement, especially if passion is exchanged for convention.'

He paused. 'Tell me—can your sister cook? Clean a house? Look after hens—even milk a goat?'

She stared at him. 'Millie? Of course not.'

'Then for Kostas's sake, she must learn,' he said briskly. 'I will have your belongings brought from the hotel, Selene *mou*. You and your sister will stay here as my guests. My housekeeper will act as chaperone when Kostas comes to visit your sister. Eleni has a fierce reputation,' he added drily. 'So he will attempt no further liberties.'

He paused. 'And your sister will spend time each day with my staff, learning to cook and clean.'

She drew an incredulous breath. 'Millie will never agree to all this.'

'I think she will, *agapi mou*, when it is explained to her that this is the path that leads to her wedding.'

He added softly, 'I shall also suggest that Father Stephanos gives her instruction in the Greek Orthodox faith, which may soften the attitude of Kostas's mother to the marriage.'

Ridiculously, she found herself bristling. 'Why should she object?'

'Because she will already have picked out a suitable bride for her only son,' he said calmly. 'Does this not happen in England, too?'

'Not where I live. But do whatever you must to stop

her screaming again,' she said reluctantly. 'Although I really don't see the point of encouraging them to get married.'

'This is not encouragement,' he said with a touch of grimness. 'More a demonstration to your sister of what she may expect as the wife of a working man on Rhymnos. Who can say what her reaction to this new regime will be.'

She said slowly, 'You think she'll hate it and want to leave.'

'We can hope. You have a better idea?'

'No,' she admitted reluctantly. 'But once again, you're being put to a great deal of trouble.'

'It's no problem. And while your sister is occupied, you, Selene *mou*, will learn to relax. To be free to swim, and to sunbathe. To drink wine and, I hope, enjoy all that Rhymnos has to offer.'

He got to his feet and walked to the door. 'After all, where else do you have to go?'

And left her staring after him.

With hindsight, she realised how easy it had been. How stupidly, terrifyingly easy to tell herself that she was only agreeing to this for Millie's sake.

That it might only be a week or so before her sister decided she'd had enough of Greek home economics and would prefer to go back to Haylesford.

The time would soon pass, she told herself and when, mission accomplished, she arrived back with Millie, their aunt might, for once, be forced to eat her words.

At least she had to try it and see if it worked.

Upon which, the door re-opened abruptly and the plump woman in grey entered.

She said without preamble, 'I am Eleni Validis, *thespinis*. If you will come with me, I shall show you your room.'

As Selena scrambled to her feet, the housekeeper crossed the room, opened the wide glass doors that almost filled one wall and slid back the shutters beyond, revealing a spacious courtyard with a large swimming pool at its centre.

Skirting the pool in Eleni's brisk wake, Selena felt the heat like a blow.

More shutters, another pair of glass doors and she found herself in a capacious bedroom, with cream walls, matching floor tiles, and filmy cream and gold drapes at the windows. Confronting her was the widest bed she'd ever seen, its snowy linen set off by the midnight blue coverlet folded across its foot.

Facing it, and flanked by an array of louvred wardrobes in pale wood, was an archway leading to a bathroom tiled in glowing mother of pearl.

In the centre of the ceiling, a large fan murmured softly as it turned.

She swallowed and turned to Eleni. 'It's—beautiful. Thank you.' She smiled. 'I mean—*efharisto*.'

But there was no responding smile, just a brief inclination of the head. 'Lunch will be served in an hour, *thespinis*. Yorgos will come to take you to the dining room.' And, on that, she crossed to the door opposite and disappeared into a white-walled passage.

So much for Greek hospitality, thought Selena, feeling a little bleak. But maybe they're accustomed to a better class of visitor and infinitely less aggravation.

Having explored her new domain, she would have dearly loved to cool down in the walk-in shower, or even soak in the deep tub, but was deterred by her lack of clean clothes to change into.

But she soon found an hour was a long time to be alone with one's thoughts—especially when they were as potentially disturbing as hers were becoming.

It was almost a relief when the passage door was flung open and Millie marched in, scowling.

'Kostas has gone,' she announced tragically.

'Gone?' Selena repeated on a note of hope.

'His brute of a boss has taken him back to the hotel.'

'Oh,' said Selena, sighing inwardly as hope died. 'Well, that is where he works.'

'And about as far from this place as it's possible to get,' Millie flung back. 'But if they're hoping to keep us apart, it won't work. Kostas intends to borrow his cousin's motor bike.'

She glanced around, her frown deepening. 'Easy to see who's going to be the skivvy round here. This room is twice the size of mine.'

'If it matters so much, we could swap.'

'What—and disobey the orders of the great god Constantinou?' Millie asked derisively. 'You must be joking. He practically owns the island and everyone in it. They all jump to his bidding.'

'Including you,' Selena said drily, noting the demure blue chambray dress Millie was now wearing. 'Isn't that your school uniform?'

Millie grimaced. 'I wore it to the airport to avoid grief from Aunt Nora. And I thought it might do me some good with Kostas's mother. Fat chance. As soon as she saw me, the old bag started beating her chest with her clenched fists and screaming. You've never heard anything like it.'

That's what you think, Selena informed her silently.

'Kostas brought us here hoping his boss would speak to her for us,' Millie continued angrily. 'Tell her he approved of the marriage. We had no idea she'd got here first.'

Selena said quietly, 'She was probably worried about his disappearance. And maybe the skivvying, as you call it, will be worthwhile if Mrs Papoulis thinks you're trying to learn to be a good Greek wife.'

'I wouldn't bet on it.' Millie paused. 'And why are you still here? Why didn't Mr Constantinou take you back, as well, to pick up your stuff and catch the ferry?'

The million dollar question, thought Selena.

She said carefully, 'Because I'm also trying to avoid grief from Aunt Nora. She's angry because you won't come home with me.'

'Too bad,' said Millie. 'Besides, Rhymnos is my home and I'm not leaving, now or ever, so you're in for a long wait, babes. Enjoy.'

And in a whirl of blue chambray she was gone, leaving Selena standing rigid in the middle of a beautiful room that had suddenly become a trap of her own making.

Or his, she thought. And shivered.

CHAPTER SIX

LUNCH PROVED TO be a simple affair of grilled chicken with a Greek salad, accompanied by a light and crisp white wine and followed by fresh fruit.

To her surprise, Selena found sheer hunger overcoming her stomach's nervous churning and ate every bite.

'Not exactly a banquet,' Millie commented sourly as they drank the thick, sweet Greek coffee. 'Any more than this place is a mansion,' she added, giving the cool blue-washed dining room a derisive glance. 'And there isn't even an infinity pool. You wouldn't think the Constantinou family were billionaires.'

Selena put down her cup, suddenly breathless as if she'd been kicked in the ribs.

She thought, That's nonsense. He owns a hotel, that's all. Although even that might represent untold riches on such a small island.

And yet…

As if she'd returned to a half-finished puzzle, pieces began to fall into place.

Even if billionaires didn't usually do their own stock-taking, they could find the money to fund roads and olive oil processing plants, and successfully launch a new product in an already thriving market.

Besides, there'd been that casual reference to contacts in the States and, of course, the helicopter as if that mode of transport was the norm.

Not to mention the effortless way he'd taken charge. His assumption that she would follow his advice, allow him to solve her problem and, finally, accept his hospitality.

A powerful man, she realised dazedly. Accustomed to doing exactly what he wanted. To using his power and being obeyed. To—using people.

In all sorts of ways…

Stop right there, she adjured herself fiercely.

Somehow she managed to keep her tone casual. 'Perhaps they don't like to flaunt their money in the current economic climate. That is—if it's true.'

'Of course it is,' said Millie. 'Kostas says they have homes in Athens and New York as well as this house. Eleni was born in New York, which is why she speaks such good English. She used to be Madame Constantinou's maid and she met Yorgos while the family were here on holiday. He didn't want to leave the island after they were married, so he became the major-domo here with Eleni as housekeeper. All nice and cosy. Although they have more to do since Alexis returned.'

She added more quietly, 'Kostas says he quarrelled with his father over his plans for Rhymnos. Or so everyone thinks.'

Selena's brows lifted. 'Kostas appears to be a mine of information,' she said drily.

Millie shrugged. 'I told you. The Constantinou family is a big deal on Rhymnos. However, I'm still getting married and I'll need my birth certificate. So don't forget.'

'I'll do my best,' Selena said drily. 'And I've remembered something else.' She delved into her pocket and produced the silver bracelet. 'I came across this on my travels.'

'I wondered where it had got to,' said Millie. She gave Selena a winning smile. 'The clasp's a bit dodgy so maybe you could get that fixed, too, and send it with the other stuff.'

She finished her coffee and stood up. 'Now, I'm going to change out of this foul dress and catch some rays by the pool.' As she turned to the door, it opened and Eleni came in with a tray and an apron which she handed to Millie.

Her voice was pleasant but firm. 'You will clear the table, if you please, *thespinis*, then bring the tray to the kitchen. Hara, our cook, will show you where everything is kept, and afterwards you will help her to begin preparations for the evening meal.'

Millie gasped. 'But we've just eaten,' she objected. 'And it's sweltering.'

'Even so, you will find that a tired and hungry man will require to be fed.' Eleni was inexorable. 'You must accustom yourself, Kyria Amelia.'

Selena braced herself for the hissy fit of the century. Instead Millie's shoulders slumped and she muttered a grudging acquiescence and began to pile the remaining china and cutlery on to the tray.

Selena cleared her throat. 'Can I do anything to help?'

'That would not be appropriate, *thespinis*.' The older woman spoke with chilly politeness. 'Not for a guest of Kyrios Alexis.' She beckoned to Millie. 'Come, little one.'

Well, that's me told, Selena thought without pleasure.

She hesitated for a moment, debating whether or not to go back to her room but decided it would be better not to treat it as her sole option, or it might soon seem like a prison cell.

Instead, she slid open the door to the courtyard, and emerged cautiously, feeling once again as if she was walking into a wall of heat.

During lunch, cushioned loungers and parasols had been arranged temptingly round the perimeter of the pool.

Selena dragged the nearest one into a patch of shade, adjusted its parasol to cover her completely, and lay down, aware within minutes that her pants and tunic were sticking to her sweat-dampened body.

She sent the pool a longing look, knowing at the same time it would make no difference when her bag arrived from the hotel, because her swimsuit was still in England.

I packed for a flying visit, she thought, not for sunbathing and swimming.

Just one of many reasons not to hang around but to go home and brave Aunt Nora's wrath.

The prime one being her need to avoid any further involvement with Alexis Constantinou.

Not that there's been much, she tried to tell herself.
And certainly nothing serious. Especially on his part.

On the contrary, he'd merely been—amusing himself
by playing with the senses of someone he'd instantly
recognised as being totally inexperienced. Something
of a novelty, no doubt, in the world he moved in.

Even something of a novelty in her own world, come
to that.

But, for whatever reason—a belated sense of de-
cency, or, more probably, a suspicion that her innocence might prove sexually unrewarding—he had not
allowed those moments in the cave to proceed to their
obvious conclusion.

Well, why would he, when he could probably have
his pick from most of the women in the world?

And she should be grateful that he'd thought twice
and go while the going was good.

Except there was still a chance—in fact, a distinct
possibility—that Millie might start to have doubts, now
that romance had truly collided with reality. Her expression in the dining room just now had indicated as much.

And if so, Selena told herself resolutely, I should stay
to help tip the balance, maybe. I just hope she doesn't
take too long to come to her senses.

While she ignored the sneaking suspicion she might
just have taken leave of her own.

But as the days passed, Selena was forced to the conclusion that both her hopes and her fears were equally
groundless.

To her surprise, Millie's sulks over the new regime
had been relatively short-lived. She had accepted that

she would only see Kostas on his afternoon off, and that part of their time together would be spent with Father Stephanos, so that she could learn about the Greek Orthodox religion.

Even more amazingly, she'd developed a penchant for cooking under the good-natured direction of Hara the cook, a large well-built lady who looked like a walking advertisement for her own skills.

In fact, the moussaka Millie had produced for lunch with something of a flourish the previous week had been delicious.

The plan, Selena thought grimly, was clearly not working. While her co-conspirator in all this seemed to have vanished off the radar.

Because, in nearly three weeks, Alexis Constantinou had not paid a single visit to the Villa Helios. Not a sight. Not a sound. Not even a message.

Not that she wanted him there, she hastened to assure herself, but although it had been a novelty at first to relax by the pool in the bikini airily proffered by Millie—'It belongs to Fiona. I must have packed it by mistake. Something else for you to take back when you go'—she was beginning to find it lonely, which was odd for someone so used to her own company, she thought wryly.

Also, even if she'd been interested in acquiring a tan, it was difficult to relax when each day increased her conviction that she was not truly welcome at the villa.

Eleni and Yorgos remained coolly polite and unswervingly formal while Penelope, whenever Selena tried to engage her in conversation, clearly could not wait to scuttle away.

She'd spent some of her time exploring her immediate surroundings, becoming familiar with the villa's layout around the central courtyard, while beyond the gardens at the rear and towards the broad headland, she'd found the landing area for the helicopter and the massive shed where it was kept.

But most of the time, she occupied herself with the small cache of British and American thrillers she'd found in a cupboard in the *saloni* and which, according to Eleni, had been left there by 'my lady, Madame Constantinou'. The information, accompanied by a heavy sigh, reminded Selena that Alexis had mentioned his parents were divorced.

Selena sighed, too, as she closed the current Elmore Leonard and prepared to go inside and change. Kostas was due soon, possibly accompanied by Father Stephanos, and Eleni had hinted heavily on the first occasion that it would be unbecoming to be seen in a bikini during these visits.

So, it was back to a cotton top and her button-through denim skirt, of which she was already heartily sick even though it was returned to her, like the rest of her meagre wardrobe, beautifully laundered after each wearing.

However, she just had enough time for another swim, she decided, walking to the pool and poising herself for her dive. This was the real luxury of the Villa Helios, she thought. Not the king-size bed, or the power shower, but this secluded expanse of turquoise water, the total opposite of the crowded public baths in Haylesford where it was almost impossible to swim even a few metres uninterrupted, and she would miss it when she left.

In fact, it was all that she would miss, she added with a touch of defiance, and dived in.

She powered one swift, invigorating length, relishing the coolness of the water against her warm skin then, as she turned, she took a deep breath and submerged completely, enjoying once more the sensation of being enclosed in a silent world ruled by the glow of the sun.

Only to become suddenly aware that a shadow had fallen across the brightness ahead of her, shifting with the ripples on the water as she got nearer.

Gasping, Selena surfaced, grabbing at the tiled rim with one hand and pushing her wet hair back from her face with the other as she looked up. And found Alexis, waiting silently. Looking down.

Something—an amalgam of joy and fear—lurched inside her. Joy at seeing him again at last. Fear of revealing too much of the thoughts and dreams that had haunted her waking and sleeping since he'd walked away from her at the hotel.

The unguessed at longings, potent and unforgettable, that he'd awoken in a few short moments. And as quickly regretted. That, she knew, was what she should remember, just as much as she needed to hide the rest.

He said, 'Did I startle you, Selene *mou*?'

She hunched a shoulder. Tried for nonchalance. 'A little. I didn't know you were expected.'

'I was not.' He added softly, 'And I did not expect to disturb a water nymph.'

'Oh' seemed the only, if inadequate, answer to that. She felt silly, there in the water, gaping up at him like a goldfish in a bowl, but as she went to haul herself out of the pool, he reached down, his hands firm under her armpits, and lifted her bodily, and all too easily, on to the tiles.

In the next instant, he'd unslung the towel—her towel—draped across his shoulder, and wrapped it round her, tucking in the edge above her breasts to secure it.

The contact with her skin was infinitesimal, but it ran like wildfire through every pore—every nerve-ending.

'I think,' he said quietly, his dark gaze holding hers endlessly, almost mesmerisingly, 'that we need to talk.'

'Yes—perhaps so. I—I'll just go and get dressed...'

'And I will wait here.' His hands descended on her tense shoulders, directing her towards her room.

She showered, then rough-dried her hair, dropping the brush twice, her fingers all thumbs, knowing—and resenting that she was unnerved by Alexis's sudden re-appearance.

We'll talk and he'll go, she told herself. That's all there is to it, so calm down.

She opened the wardrobe and reached for the shelf where her clean underwear was deposited each day. But although her lace-trimmed briefs were there in a neat pile, there was no sign of her bra. Oh, hell, she muttered under her breath. It must have been taken to Millie's room again.

And she didn't have time to hunt through that particular chaos.

She picked a white vest top in ribbed cotton, which, she decided, was sufficiently concealing, then buttoned on her denim skirt, and went out into the courtyard to join him.

She said flatly, 'Obviously, we need to discuss Millie and what to do next, because Plan A has failed and we don't have a Plan B.'

She paused. 'Did you know that a couple of days ago, she actually made a feta cheese? *A feta cheese.* For Kostas to take to his mother.' She sighed. 'You have to admit she's been clever.'

'Determined, certainly.' His tone was dry. 'But Anna Papoulis is equally so, and her mind is fixed on a substantial dowry for her handsome boy.' He paused.

'Perhaps if your aunt will give her nothing, she might be persuaded to come here and say so. It could lead to the result she desires.'

He added brusquely, 'Her leg must have healed by now.'

Selena hesitated. 'It's out of plaster, but apparently she's having serious physiotherapy every day. And her mind is made up. Millie goes home. No compromise.'

His brows lifted. 'So, you have spoken to her?'

'Only briefly. She's either having treatment or she's out.' Selena shrugged. 'Her friends are gathering round, taking her for little trips in their cars to provide her with a change of scene.'

'She would not regard Rhymnos as a change of scene?' Alexis asked ironically.

'No,' Selena said baldly. 'As a climb-down.'

She looked down at the ground. 'You really think

that Millie having no money could be a deal-breaker
and Kostas's mother will force him to give her up?'

'She will try,' he said drily. 'But perhaps she will
discover that love is not so easily dismissed from the
heart and the mind.'

'Then you believe Kostas really does care about Millie?'

Alexis shrugged. 'He shows every sign of it. In my
bar now, he sells only drinks, not his—company.'

Selena flushed. 'Well, that's a good choice,' she returned awkwardly.

'He is fortunate he can make it.' There was an odd
harshness in his voice, and she looked up at him, startled.

His smile was reassuring. 'But on this lovely day, I,
too, have choices and I choose to show you Rhymnos—
if you will come with me.' He added wryly, 'Your aunt
should not be the only one to have a change of scene.'

She knew she should not do this. That she should invent an excuse—any excuse. But she could hardly claim
to be busy when he'd found her in the pool.

And maybe she could risk one day in his company
before she finally admitted defeat and went home. Or
what passed for home anyway, she thought wryly, imagining the atmosphere that her failure would engender.

Although she didn't have to stay in Haylesford, she
reminded herself. Millie's future was no longer a consideration, and she could get on with her own life.

If she could find another job before the next term
began, she could even begin to establish her future independence right away.

He said, 'Well, say something, Selena *mou*.' His tone was faintly mocking as if he was expecting her to refuse his offer. 'Just tell me if you wish to be left in peace.'

Peace. The word stung at her brain, sending her into renewed turmoil.

What peace is there in never seeing you again? she wanted to cry. When I know that, in spite of myself, you've been there in my head every day and every night since I arrived on this island.

Do I really need to deprive myself of a final hour or two in his company—knowing how precious their memory will be? Or to let him know I'm scared to be alone with him?

She met his quizzical gaze with sudden recklessness, her mouth relaxing into a smile. 'I should like to see more of Rhymnos—before I leave.' Adding, *'Efharisto.'*

'Parakalo,' he returned and smiled back at her. 'So—shall we go?'

And that, she thought, was how, swiftly and easily, she'd made the choice which had changed her life for ever.

CHAPTER SEVEN

It HADN'T SEEMED like that at the time, of course.

He was just being a good host, she'd told herself, but that hadn't stopped her wanting to dance at his side as they made their way out of the courtyard. And not even glimpsing Eleni frowning at the *saloni* window could spoil her mood.

So where could they be going? she wondered as he started the Jeep. After all, there couldn't be much of the island that hadn't been already covered during their search for Millie and Kostas.

Unless he was planning to take her back to the cave…

Even the thought of it was enough to send her body tingling into dangerous warmth, shocking her with the force of her own yearning.

To hide her confusion, she hurried into speech. 'This is very good of you.'

'Not at all.' He paused. 'I thought you might like to discover a little more about our most important industry.'

Geography and economics…

Disappointment was almost choking her but she kept

her tone bright. 'Am I going to see round Rhymnos Oil? How marvellous.'

'Not now,' he said. 'Not today.' He turned the Jeep to the right, following the rough road along the coast, between the sea and yet more olive groves, all new territory for her. 'Instead, we shall go back to where it all began.'

With some history thrown in...

Her mouth was beginning to ache with the effort of smiling, but she persevered. He was being kind and she needed to be grateful. Which was all he would expect from her in return.

But already, she was far too conscious of his presence beside her. Much too aware of his dark sculpted profile and the movement of his lean, strong hands on the wheel of the Jeep, evoking memories of his touch it was far safer to forget.

She forced herself to turn her head and concentrate on the sea, the faint breeze barely troubling its azure smoothness today as it stretched out to the horizon and beyond. A distance that, very soon, she would be covering on her journey back to England.

The prospect of her return and its inevitable confrontation with Aunt Nora was not one she relished.

She would be thankful when term recommenced and she could lose herself in the demands of her course work, she thought, feeling her eyes sting and telling herself it was just the dazzle of the sun on the water.

'What troubles you, Selene *mou*?'

His question jolted her. She hadn't realised she was being observed in her turn and she looked back at him, flushing a little. 'Oh, the usual back-to-reality blues, I guess.'

'Rhymnos has not seemed real to you?'

No, she thought, as longing tightened her throat. Because of you, it's turned into a wild, impossible dream. And I don't want to wake...

By some superhuman effort, she shrugged. Kept her tone casual. 'Well, hardly—under the circumstances. If I'd come here on my own account, it might have been different.'

'Ah,' he said softly. 'Then do you think you will come back?'

If you asked me, I'd stay...

And where had that come from? she asked herself wretchedly, nailing on another smile and thanking heaven she hadn't spoken aloud. 'Oh, one day, perhaps, in the distant future when I'm no longer a struggling student but qualified and working. Who knows?'

'Who, indeed, *agapi mou*.' There was an odd note in his voice. 'So we must make the most of what time we have left.'

Sudden anger flared inside her. She wanted to turn on him. To demand, 'If you think that—if you *really* think that, then why have you stayed away all this time? Why have you left me alone to wonder—and suffer through these empty days? And what's this afternoon all about? Crumbs from the rich man's table?'

But she bit back the words, because these were dangerous questions which, in all honesty, she had no right to ask. And, probably, would receive answers she didn't want to hear.

Leave it there, she adjured herself. Accept what there is. Hope for nothing more.

She realised that Alexis was turning the Jeep inland up a well-worn track through the shade of yet another massive olive grove, their route flanked by trees with trunks so gnarled and twisted they looked a thousand years old. And perhaps they were long past their 'best by' date because for the life of her, even by craning her neck, she could see no sign of any fruit.

Eventually, she broke the silence. 'Are these your trees? I suppose you must be thinking of replacing them.'

He shot her a swift, amused glance. 'Yes, they are mine and, on the contrary, Selene *mou*, I am expecting them to bring me a wonderful harvest in November.'

'Truly?' She gave the overhanging branches another dubious look.

'The olives are still tiny,' he said. 'But they are there.'

She was half expecting him to stop the Jeep and show her, but he drove on, accelerating up the slight slope which, eventually, rose more steeply as it took them out of the shelter of the grove towards the grassy upland beyond.

Where he stopped, parking the Jeep under another massive tree, its leaves shimmering in the sunlight.

He reached into the back of the Jeep and extracted a rucksack. He said, 'From here we walk, Selene *mou*.'

'Oh.' She swallowed, glancing at the rock-crowned hills ahead of them. 'I'm not really dressed for mountaineering.'

He slanted a smile at her. 'You need not fear. It is not far and we go round, not up.'

The tussocky grass, studded with wildflowers, was springy under her feet, and Alexis reached for her hand and steadied her as they walked, skirting the steeper slopes as they headed round the curve of the hill.

And there cradled in its folds as if set down there by some giant hand were three tall pillars of creamy stone rearing towards the sky from their flat rocky platform, all of it encircled by grass, green as an emerald.

Instantly, prosaically familiar from bottles on a supermarket shelf and yet, in their proper setting, startling and somehow alien, part of an entirely different world, ancient and mysterious.

Alexis said softly, 'The pillars of Apollo, *agapi mou*. All that still remains of his temple. My own private sanctuary since I was a young boy. Where I have always come to think about what I truly wanted from my life. And the place where Rhymnos Oil became for me more than just a dream.'

She took a deep breath. 'It's—beautiful.' She hesitated. 'But it can't always have been private. Not with holidaymakers swarming all over it.'

He shook his head. 'They come to Rhymnos for the beaches and *tavernas*. There's nothing here to tempt them. It is not Delphi. There's no cave for an oracle or glorious statuary waiting to be uncovered like buried treasure. It is just another small ruin.'

She said quietly, her heartbeat quickening, 'But special to you.'

'Yes. For so many reasons.' He paused, looking at her, his gaze broodingly intense as it held hers. 'Shall we go down?'

The slope of the ground was gentle but Selena felt as if she was standing on the edge of an abyss. That one false move and she would fall quietly—endlessly into oblivion.

You don't need to be here, whispered the voice in her head. You already know what you're doing with your life. You can't risk any second thoughts—especially when they're foolish and impossible.

But you can always step back. Take your hand from his. Make an excuse. Tell him you're leaving early tomorrow and you need to pack. Tell him something. Anything that will get you back to safety.

Only to hear herself say haltingly, 'Yes, that would be good.'

Silence folded round them as they walked down to the temple. Not the hush she'd sensed on that other day before the storm, but something deeper and even more intimate than the clasp of his fingers round hers. And infinitely more dangerous.

At the foot of the slope, the ground levelled out, its cover of grass even as a carpet, soft and springy underfoot.

Alexis released her hand and she moved forward, climbing up the two steps which led to the rocky floor of the shrine, and looking across to the tumble of fallen masonry below the columns, which, she supposed, must once have been an altar.

How many thousands of years ago, she wondered, had people built this place and come there with their offerings?

A breeze like a sigh moved between the columns,

bringing with it a delicate almost spicy scent. Oregano, she thought wonderingly as she breathed it, mint and thyme. Did they grow wild here?

She turned to ask Alexis and saw that he'd taken a rug from his rucksack and spread it in the shade of two large rectangular stones and was now reclining, very much at his ease, drinking from a bottle of water.

He produced another, uncapped it and held it out to her. 'Are you thirsty after our walk?'

It made no sense to deny it. She walked back slowly and took the bottle from him, taking care to sit on the furthest edge of the rug.

How quiet it was, she thought, letting the water trickle blissfully down her throat. And—how remote. Too remote and too quiet.

And she needed to leave, she told herself with sudden unease, while she still could.

Find some excuse to cut the afternoon short and go back to the house. But what could she say? That her sister would be worried, when he must know as well as she did that Millie never gave her a second thought?

But she could at least break this dangerous silence.

She rushed into speech. 'Why Apollo? I thought Zeus was the most important Greek god.'

He smiled. 'On Rhymnos, it was always Apollo. Eleni's mother, who was my nurse when I was a baby, was born here, too, and she filled my head with all the old legends. How he was Apollo the Healer, the god of music and poetry as well as prophecy. How as Phoebus Apollo he drove the chariot of the sun across the sky each day.'

'Wow.' This was better. This was casual conversation, she thought as she smiled back. 'A god of many talents. And I thought all he did was chase girls.'

'He found time for that, too,' Alexis agreed solemnly. 'Or he would have had no sons.'

'And that was important—even for a god?'

'I think—for anyone,' he said, after a pause. 'Besides one of his sons, Asclepius, became the father of medicine and another, Aristaeus, taught the Greeks agriculture. How to keep bees, to look after livestock, to grow olives, and even make cheese.' He added lightly, 'So we should be thankful.'

She matched his tone. 'While I know who's really responsible for Millie's sudden expertise in the kitchen.'

'Efharisto,' he said. 'I thought you would blame me.'

'Hardly.' She sighed. 'She seems determined to prove herself, but I still feel it's far too soon for her to commit herself like this.'

'Ah,' he said softly. 'So you do not believe that sometimes all that it takes is a look—a word—in order to be lost for ever?'

Selena swallowed. 'No, I don't,' she said defiantly.

Adding silently, *I can't—I won't believe it. I need it to be impossible. Need it so very badly...*

'Tell me something, Selene *mou.*' His tone was almost idle. 'How many times have you telephoned to England since you came to my house?'

She gave him a wary look. 'I suppose—about six. And I intend to pay for my calls before I leave,' she added defensively.

'That will not be necessary.' His tone permitted no

argument. 'But all these calls, I think, have been to your aunt's house. None of them to your man.'

Damnation, she thought, biting her lip. Why had she ever thought it was a good idea to invent him?

She said stiffly, 'I think that's my business.'

'Even so, how will he regard so long a silence?'

She lifted her chin. 'He'll understand.'

'Understand?' Alexis repeated incredulously. 'In his shoes, I would have been here before a week had passed, searching the island for you.'

'I told you—he's busy.'

'So busy that he can forget the smoothness of your skin, the scent of your hair, the sweetness of your mouth?'

She gasped, feeling a rush of hot colour suffuse her face.

'You—you have no right to say such things,' she accused breathlessly.

'I have every right.' He spoke with quiet intensity as he took the bottle from her hand, replacing its cap and setting it to one side. 'Because I, may God help me, have forgotten nothing. And I never can.'

Her mind was suddenly in freefall. He did not seem to have moved, yet the space between them had somehow dwindled to nothing.

And, equally somehow, he'd recaptured her hand, brushing its palm gently with his lips, his teeth grazing the soft mound at the base of her thumb, sending little tremors shimmering through her nerve endings.

She closed her eyes, shutting out the image of his dark head bent so near her own.

She thought, *Oh, God, I have to stop this. Now...*

But the heavy beat of the sun against her eyelids was already echoing in the thud of her pulses, as if telling her over and over again 'too late—too late.'

And then he was raising her hand, placing it on his shoulder and she could quite easily have snatched it back, but instead found her fingers tracing bone and muscle, then curling into the warmth of his skin beneath the crisp cotton shirt as his arms went round her drawing her to him.

His hands slipped under her top, and as he stroked her bare back, following the path of her spine up to the delicate wings of her shoulder blades, she found her body involuntarily arching towards him, her lips parting in a tiny gasp of remembered delight at his touch.

In the next instant, his mouth sought and took hers, probing its inner sweetness, teasing her with the glide of his tongue against hers, while his hands slid deftly round her body, cupping her untrammelled breasts, strumming her hardening nipples with his thumbs until they burned and ached with a pleasure that was almost pain.

She moaned softly into his mouth, melting into his kiss, sharing its ardour, answering its demand and basking in its moisture as her tongue tangled with his in enthralled exploration. Her body was straining against his as if seeking to be absorbed into its heat—its strength. Her reeling mind, dismissing the shyness and reticence that until then had been her safeguard, was telling her that this was what she'd been born for.

This hour. This place. This man.

When at last he raised his head, his dark eyes looked blurred, almost dazed. He said unsteadily, his voice hoarse with yearning, 'Do you know how lovely you are, Selene *mou*? How badly I need to look at you—to know how beautiful you truly are.'

She stared back at him, her eyes widening as she realised what he was asking. And, for a moment, she was assailed by doubt, wondering how she would endure it if the next time their eyes met, she saw disappointment.

'*Se thelo poli, agapi mou.*' His words were a whispered caress, turning any remaining fear to hunger. 'I want you so very much, my darling. Let me know that you want me, too.'

Selena sat up slowly. She put her hand against his face, running her fingers along his cheekbone then down to the strong line of his jaw, savouring the faint roughness of his skin.

Taking a deep breath, she pulled her vest top over her head and tossed it aside, then lay back on the rug, smiling up at him.

She saw a muscle move in his taut throat, then he bent to her, taking one rounded breast and then the other in his lips and suckling them gently, his tongue flicking the tumescent nipples with sensuous precision.

And she heard herself cry out huskily in a voice she hardly recognised. A voice that expressed a longing as deep and as urgent as his own.

'Yes,' he said. 'Yes, *matia mou*. I promise.'

He began to unbutton her skirt, beginning at its hem, then moving slowly, even carefully, up to the waist band, before peeling the edges apart, as if unveiling some infinitely precious work of art, leaving her with only a last few inches of lace-trimmed fabric to cover her.

Letting her see the glow in his gaze, and the tenderness and pleasure that curved his firm mouth as he studied her.

As he started to touch her again.

His fingers were almost miraculously gentle, feathering across her shoulders and stroking the soft underside of her arms before returning to her breasts, his lips following the path of his hands over every curve and hollow. Moving downwards with tantalising languor, smoothing the flatness of her stomach, and toying with the inner whorls of her navel. Outlining the graceful jut of her hip bones, then sliding a hand under the rim of her briefs and easing them off, stripping her deftly and completely.

She heard him draw a deep sighing breath as he looked down at her, his hands gliding the length of her body from throat to instep, and then back to her slender thighs, stroking them, coaxing them apart as if he knew that the soft trembling of her flesh was prompted as much by shyness as excitement.

'Trust me, *agapi mou*.' The whispered words were raw. 'Let me learn to please you a little.'

His hand moved, exploring the delicate folds of her womanhood to find the tiny aching mound they concealed and caress it slowly with his fingertips.

His touch still gentle, but also wickedly sure. Banishing any lingering doubts and leading her instead to acceptance. And, unhurriedly, to the sensual tumult of physical arousal.

The time for resistance, if it had ever been a possibility, was long gone.

Selena lay, eyes half-closed in surrender, every thought, every nerve ending concentrated almost painfully on her body's astonished response to every new, delicious sensation.

Hearing the tiny moan she was unable to control as his subtle, all too knowing fingers pushed lightly into the silken, soaking heat of her, pausing, waiting, perhaps for some sign of discomfort, before penetrating her more deeply. Offering her a sweetly piercing foretaste of her future initiation.

She moved restlessly against the thrust of his fingers, instinct telling her that she wanted the future to become the present. That she needed to feel his skin naked against hers. To know the stark male hardness of him sheathed inside her and possess him in turn. And found herself reaching for him, fumbling with the fastening at the waistband of his chinos.

'Ah, no, *matia mou*.' His voice ragged, Alexis captured her wrists, placing her hands at her sides. Holding them there. 'This is for you, my sweet one. Only for you.'

And bent to her again. Only, this time, using his mouth, his tongue brushing like gossamer against her burning tumescent urgency. Circling it, flickering on it fiercely—exquisitely.

Making her writhe and quiver in helpless almost shocked abandonment at this ultimate intimacy, and, at the same time, becoming aware of some strange knot of tension tightening deeply, inexorably inside her, taking her to the very edge of endurance.

Her voice pleading, breaking, she cried out something that might have been his name, then the knot snapped and she was free, flung wildly into a tumbling, throbbing chaos where the sharp, sweet, clenching spasms of pleasure were hardly distinguishable from pain.

Held there, then slowly released, the tremors dying away leaving her body and its senses calmed and at peace as she floated back to the reality of Alexis's arms holding her close and his voice murmuring softly, tenderly in his own language. Plus the additional discovery that she was looking at him through a blur of tears.

Shaken by all kinds of embarrassment, Selena sat up, scrubbing at her eyes like a child while she tried desperately to think how to react, silently cursing the lack of sophistication that might have carried her through this awkwardness. And eventually decided only the truth would do.

She swallowed. 'I—I don't know what to say.'

He said quietly, almost ruefully, 'I think I, too, am a little lost for words, Selene *mou*.'

She bit her lip. 'However, I think I should get dressed—unless you...' She stumbled a little. 'Unless, of course, you want...'

He reached for her clothes and handed them to her.

'As I told you, *agapi mou*. This was for you alone.' He smiled at her, adding softly, 'I can wait.'

He got to his feet and walked away towards the tem-

ple, waiting, his back turned, while Selena huddled on
her garments. For which, she realised, she was grateful. Absurdly so in view of what he had just seen and
done. But now, in the aftermath, she felt distinctly self-
conscious. And uncertain. Also uncomfortable as her
clothing seemed to rasp against her still sensitised skin.

At last, she said, 'I'm ready.' And when he remained
where he was, staring silently ahead of him, she repeated the words more loudly.

He turned back instantly, smiling again but this time
with an obvious effort. 'My apologies, Selene *mou*.

'Once again, I was thinking.'

Thinking, she wondered, or regretting?

And this question continued to occupy her own
thoughts all the way back to the villa.

CHAPTER EIGHT

She must, Selena thought, have taken leave of her senses. Although it might be fairer to say she'd been robbed of them. Or seduced out of them.

Except, her common sense told her it had not been a conventional seduction by any means. In fact, she wasn't really sure how to describe it—or justify the long, sweet shiver that ran through her as she remembered.

But what should she make of the subsequent silent journey back to the villa?

Thankfully, she was alone. Millie, absorbed in Kostas, probably hadn't noticed her absence, so she had time to recover her equilibrium and come to terms with what had happened.

Because, very soon, she would have to face Alexis again at dinner, without blushing, stammering or falling over her feet.

And it seemed important that when they met, she should not be wearing the clothes he had so recently removed with such lingering skill.

Do not, she adjured herself, pressing her hands to her burning cheeks, even go there. Stay sane.

A change of clothing didn't offer much choice. The blue tunic also held memories best forgotten. So she decided on her Capri pants and the nondescript white shirt, bought in her final school year.

Also, she needed to do something with her hair. Leaving it loose would only remind her of his fingers twining it as he kissed her, and plaiting seemed too obvious, so she simply scooped it back, securing it at the nape of her neck with an elastic band.

But her precautions, if that's what they were, proved unnecessary because Alexis was not at dinner, having returned to the hotel, according to Millie, taking Kostas with him.

Selena ate her meal on autopilot, her mind veering between blankness and bewilderment.

It seemed, after all, that he'd just—walked away. That he'd just been playing some unkind game with her senses. Amusing himself by breaking down the inhibitions of this little English virgin who'd come blundering into his life.

And who would waste no time about blundering right out again, she told herself, her throat tightening.

'For God's sake, Lena,' Millie said impatiently. 'Are you deaf or in a trance? I've asked you twice when you're going back to England because I really need my birth certificate.'

'Would tomorrow suit you?'

'Well—fine.' Millie gave her a surprised look. 'I really hope Aunt Nora doesn't give you a hard time,' she offered awkwardly.

Selena shrugged. 'I expect by now she's accepted the situation. Shall I send the paperwork here?'

'No, to Kostas at the hotel.' Millie paused. 'I'm leaving, too, going to stay with his Aunt Evanthia, who lives just outside town.'

Selena's brows rose. 'His mother's sister?' she enquired dubiously.

'His father's. Chalk and cheese, apparently.' Millie gave a slight giggle. 'It'll be more convenient, and besides, I guess we've both overstayed our welcome here, don't you?'

In my case, from the moment I got here, thought Selena. She said quietly, 'Probably.'

She was packing her bag when Eleni came in with a small pile of clean laundry.

Selena looked across the bed at her. 'I'm returning home tomorrow, Kyria Validis. Will your husband be able to drive me to the ferry?'

She saw a flash of surprise in Eleni's eyes and what she'd have sworn was relief but the housekeeper's voice held only its usual unemotional civility.

'Of course, *thespinis*. You wish to take the morning boat, perhaps? Shall I tell Yorgos ten a.m.?'

'That would be perfect,' Selena returned equally levelly.

At the door Eleni hesitated as if she was about to say something else, then turned and left in silence.

Selena sighed and added the clean clothes to her bag, switching her thoughts determinedly to her travel plans. She wasn't sure how soon she could get a flight from Mykonos, but there was enough credit on the cash card

Aunt Nora had grudgingly supplied to tide her over for a night or two.

But any uncertainty would be worth it if it rescued her from the present situation.

If, she thought, it saves me from myself. From this stranger I never knew existed, but who's living in my head. In my body…

But then she'd never been seriously attracted to anyone before. She'd always been too busy—or too shy.

Until now…

She bit down hard on her lip, tormented by the memory of how swiftly and eagerly she'd surrendered.

As if her life had been spent waiting for this moment. This man.

Delusional, she thought. Pathetic.

And how long would it take to get over this ridiculous weakness? To forget Alexis with the same ease that he had demonstrated over her—leaving without a word?

When term starts, it will be easier, she told herself. Until then I'll get a job—waiting on tables, stacking shelves—anything to keep me occupied.

And soon these weeks in Greece will seem like a bad dream.

If she'd thought an early night would relax her, she soon discovered she was wrong. At last, around midnight, she finally fell into a restless doze, only to find herself suddenly sitting bolt upright, staring into the darkness, her heart hammering.

The room felt airless and oppressive, so maybe this was why she couldn't sleep properly, yet it seemed churlish to complain of the heat when before long she'd be faced with an English winter.

However, it might be worth risking a stray mosquito by pushing back the shutters in search of a night breeze from the pool.

Her nightdress clinging to her, she slid off the crumpled bed, pushing back her hair from her damp forehead and relishing the coolness of the floor against her bare feet.

The shutters glided noiselessly open and she stepped through into the courtyard, and halted abruptly, aware that she wasn't alone. That someone who'd been stretched out on one of the loungers in front of her was rising to his feet.

And not just someone, she realised incredulously as Alexis said softly, 'So there you are.'

She found her voice. 'What are you doing here?'

'Waiting,' he said. 'Again. For you.'

'You went back to the hotel.'

'I had some business to complete.' He was watching her, barefoot like herself and tightening the belt of his towelling robe. 'It is done, so I returned.'

'Yes—but...' She hesitated nervously.

'But?' he queried.

Selena spread her hands almost helplessly. 'You said you were waiting but you couldn't possibly know that I'd still be awake, let alone that I'd come out here.'

He shrugged. 'I was unable to sleep. I thought you might have the same difficulty.' He took a step towards her. 'And for the same reason.'

'I—I don't know what you mean.'

He clicked his tongue reprovingly. 'That is unworthy of you, *agapi mou*. Also untrue.'

'I—I'm just concerned about the journey,' she improvised swiftly, almost desperately. 'You see, I'm leaving tomorrow. Going home.'

He walked to her. He said huskily, 'Then it is as well we have the rest of the night.' And lifting her into his arms, he carried her down the courtyard to a room at the end where a shaded lamp burned dimly beside the bed.

His room, Selena thought dazedly. His bed. Also waiting...

And she needed to say something—do something to stop this here and now before the afternoon's mistake turned into the night's disaster.

Instead, she found herself turning her face into his shoulder, her resolution faltering as she breathed the scent of his skin, her body curving ever more closely to the warmth and strength of his own.

Just this once, she begged whatever gods were listening. Let me have this one memory and then I'll go far away. Back to my old life, but able to deal with it in a better way.

And she slid her arm round his neck, pulling him down to her waiting lips. His kiss was tender but beneath the gentleness, she already sensed a new dark urgency—a force as yet unleashed, and found herself suddenly hesitant.

Alexis lifted his head, looking down into her widening eyes. 'You must not be afraid, *matia mou*,' he murmured as he put her down on the bed. 'Not of me.

Never of me. How can I hurt my own soul?' He smiled at her, stroking the curve of her face then walked over to fasten the shutters and draw the filmy curtains, closing them in together before taking off his robe.

Beneath it, he was naked. And, although she had no grounds for comparison, magnificently so, she realised, any initial shyness or apprehension dissolving, and her gaze absorbed, even hungry as he came back to the bed. And to her.

'Don't look at me like that, *agapi mou*.' There was laughter in his voice as he stretched out beside her. 'You will embarrass me.'

'How do I look?' she whispered, smiling as he drew her into his arms.

'Like a little cat,' he said softly. 'With a saucer of cream.'

And he began to kiss her again, his mouth caressing hers, then skimming her forehead, her eyes, her cheekbones and slowly back to her parted, eager lips.

He slid the straps of her nightgown from her shoulders and eased it down her body until she was completely free from its thin folds.

He said softly, 'I have dreamed of you like this, *agapi mou*, naked in my bed, your hair like moonlight on my pillow. And now my dream has come true.'

He tossed her nightgown to the floor and began to stroke her breasts, her nipples rising and hardening under the skilful play of his fingers, drawing a sigh of pleasure from her, which turned to a husky moan as his lips took each dusky peak in turn and suckled them slowly and sweetly.

'Exquisite,' he whispered against her skin. 'Like perfect roses, Selene *mou*.'

Then once again, his mouth found hers, capturing its soft contours, his tongue moving like silk against her own, and Selena wound her arms round his neck, playing with the thick hair that grew at its nape, surrendering to the implicit promise of his kiss.

His hands slid down her back, tracing the pliant length of her spine and moulding the slight curves of her buttocks, as he gathered her closer, so that the proud strength of his penis pressed against her belly, and she felt the hot rush of moisture between her thighs that signalled her body's readiness to welcome him.

She moved beneath him, her body seething, restless, her hands exploring him in turn, closing round him, cupping him with unashamed greed.

'Please.' She hardly recognised her own voice. 'Oh—please.'

'Soon,' he whispered hoarsely. 'Have patience, my sweet one. First, let me protect you.'

He lifted himself away, reaching into a drawer in the night table, extracting and tearing open a small packet.

Safe sex, she thought from some still rational corner of her brain. That was what he meant, of course. But there could be no such thing. Even from her limited and incomplete experience she knew that. Because sex was wild—exciting—dangerous—taking your mind and your body by storm. Never *safe*…

Then he came back to her, and she stopped thinking as his hand reclaimed her, his fingertips parting the delicate petals of her womanhood to find the liquid heat they sheltered.

She arched towards him, gasping as, once again, he stroked her swollen crest, awakening it to aching delicious torment. Urging her towards release, then holding back, making her wait, prolonging her anticipation of the exquisite moment.

Her mouth searched for his, kissing him feverishly, almost desperately, sobbing soundlessly, her teeth grazing his bottom lip.

He said her name softly and fiercely. Then his hand moved with intense precision and took her at last over the edge, her body convulsing harshly as she was lifted to the peak of rapture.

She cried out, brokenly, blind-eyed with joy, and, in the same moment, was aware of him raising himself, moving across her, his arms braced on either side of her, before entering her still throbbing body with one powerful, fluid thrust.

For an instant, he paused, his gaze intent, even questioning, as if searching hers for a hint of reluctance or discomfort. Then, gently, unhurriedly, he began to push more deeply into her, making her want more.

So much more. Making her realise it was all there— waiting for her.

Telling her to reach for him. To grasp his shoulders. To lift her legs so that they locked round his lean hips. To move with him—against him—in this unique rhythm. To feel herself closing round the strong heated hardness of him, her muscles holding him. Taking all of him in this driving compulsion to be one with him.

At once, the pace of their joining quickened.

Intensified. She was caught, carried along by the fierce current of their mutual desire, every atom of her being concentrated on the sensations that seemed to be once more gathering inside her, drawing her, incredibly—inexorably—on a renewed ascent to pleasure.

No, she thought dazedly. Impossible so soon…

Yet, at that moment, it was there. She was seized and flung out, gasping, trembling and crying out wordlessly into the stormy tumult of climax, and, at its height, she heard Alexis groan harshly and felt his body shudder into hers in his own fierce release.

They lay still entwined together as their ragged breathing steadied and a kind of peace returned. At last, Alexis withdrew from her gently and went to the bathroom.

When he came back to the bed, he pulled her into his arms, cushioning her head on his chest, pushing her sweat-dampened hair back from her forehead.

'So, my heart's angel,' he whispered. 'Have you nothing to say?'

She gave a lingering sigh. 'It was—unbelievable.'

'I am sorry you think so.' There was laughter in his voice. 'I shall try to be more convincing next time.'

She giggled softly. 'And when will that be, Kyrios Alexis?'

'When I have recovered a little,' he returned, kissing the top of her head. 'It was only the gods who were made all-potent and untiring when they made love, *agapi mou*. Sadly, they denied mortal men the same gifts, and gave them only to women.'

She snuggled closer. 'How very unkind of them.'

'I have always believed so. But I thought, while we waited, you might like to learn a little Greek.'

'Why not?' She traced a pattern among his chest hair with her forefinger. 'What do you want me to say?'

'Let us begin with—*s'agapo*.'

'*S'agapo,*' she repeated obediently. 'What does that mean?'

'It means,' he said softly, 'that you have told me you love me.'

She gave an indignant gasp. 'Oh—but that's…'

He silenced her with a kiss. 'Is it untrue? Do you still claim that love cannot happen so quickly or so completely?'

She was silent for a moment, then she said huskily, 'Yesterday, I'd have said yes. Now—I just don't know any more. And it's not just about—this. It's when you take my hand and I—I feel suddenly—safe. As if…' She hesitated.

'As if you have come home?' Alexis supplied gently.

'Because that is how it is for me, *matia mou*.'

'Then why did you—vanish like that? Leave me out in the cold again?' She stopped abruptly. 'Oh, God, that sounds awful—so *needy*.'

'But I also have needs, Selene *mou*. And a question for you to ask me. *M'agapas?* Do you love me?'

She said quickly, painfully, 'Alexis—you don't have to…'

Only to be halted by another kiss.

'Ask me,' he whispered.

She lifted a hand. Touched his cheek. '*M'agapas*, Alexis *mou*?'

He took her hand. Held it. He said quietly, 'Yes, my beautiful one. I think almost from that first moment. And I shall love you for the rest of my life.'

He paused. 'But, I will confess I did not bargain for it. Maybe I felt there was no place for it in my life, and that is why I distanced myself.'

His mouth twisted. 'Only to discover that there was not an hour in every day that I did not think of you. When I did not long to be with you, to see that little jerk of the chin you give when you are about to cut me down to size.

'Or when I did not remember how you felt in my arms and the sweetness of your mouth.

'But when I came back, you told me you were leaving.' He drew a deep breath. 'That must not be, *agapi mou*. Not now. We cannot return to the cold when we belong together.'

Selena bit her lip. 'But I must go back. Millie needs her birth certificate and...'

'There is time for that. Time that we need together.' He spoke firmly. 'Stay with me here, *matia mou*, until I am free to travel to England with you.'

She stared at him. 'But my aunt...'

'I shall face her with you,' he said. 'When that time comes.'

Her little laugh was breathless. 'You must really love me.'

'Believe it.' He sounded almost fierce. 'Believe it always.'

He framed her face in his hands, brought her mouth to his, the kiss deep, lingering and warmly sensuous, leaving her sighing with pleasure.

She ran her fingers over his chest, stroking the flat male nipples, tracing the strength of his ribcage, enjoying the quickening of his heartbeat at her touch.

Emboldened, she let her hand drift down across his abdomen to rest on his hip and then slip further, feeling him stir and harden as her fingers clasped him. Caressed him.

Alexis sank back against the pillows, eyes half-closed and a faint smile playing about his mouth.

He said very softly, 'What are you doing, Selene *mou*?'

'Being a little cat,' she whispered back. 'Waiting for my next saucer of cream.'

She woke to the dazzle of sunlight and Millie's voice saying, 'Wake up, Lena, for heaven's sake. You've got a ferry to catch.'

Selena shot bolt upright, gasping, to the realisation that she was not only back in her own room, but once more chastely clad in her nightdress.

As if, in fact, the previous night had never happened.

But the slight aches she was experiencing, plus the feeling of languid well-being suffusing her told a different story.

Alexis, she thought, must have carried her back here and put her to bed like a little girl. And she suppressed a giggle.

Millie handed her a cup of coffee. 'It's all been kicking off here,' she said. 'Eleni and her beloved Kyrios

Alexis, the one who can do no wrong, having the mother and father of all rows.'

Selena's hand jerked, nearly spilling the coffee. 'Do you know what it was about?' She tried to sound casual.

Millie shrugged. 'How could I? I don't speak Greek. But I expect I can find out from Kostas,' she added. 'He knows everything that goes on.'

She paused. 'Don't forget about my bracelet, and you'd better return Fiona's bikini to her, if she still wants it.

'And please do your best to mend fences for me with Aunt Nora. Get her to come to the wedding. Apparently on Rhymnos, they know how to throw quite a party.'

She left Selena feeling dazed and uneasy. And when, bathed, dressed and bag in hand, she found Yorgos waiting to drive her to the ferry, her bewilderment increased.

Had she dreamed the night before? Had it all been just an extreme exercise in wish-fulfilment? Had she simply imagined that Alexis had told her that he loved her—not once, but so many times in that long and rapturous night? Had asked her to stay?

Because if it had been real, then where was he? And knew she could not ask.

'My wife is unwell,' Yorgos said awkwardly as he placed her bag in the car. 'But she wishes you a safe and pleasant journey, *thespinis*.'

Selena stared ahead of her, bleakly certain she'd been the subject of the earlier row. She swallowed.

'Please—thank her for...' She could hardly say *for making me welcome* or even *comfortable*, but managed, 'For looking after me.'

It was a silent journey, Selena battling with her increasingly unhappy thoughts and Yorgos clearly wrapped in his own worries.

When they arrived at the quayside, the ferry was just entering the harbour.

As Selena left the car, she reached for her bag but found that Yorgos had already retrieved it and was clutching it to him, with an air of mulish determination.

Her heart sank. She was clearly going to be put aboard the ferry, and he was going to wait until it had departed. It was like being deported, she thought, burning with embarrassment.

She summoned a smile from somewhere and held out her hand. 'I can manage, Yorgos. You don't need to stay.'

She was braced for an argument, but he said nothing, just stared past her, his expression turning to one of dismay.

Selena glanced round and saw Alexis standing a few feet away, hands on hips, his sunglasses pushed to the top of his head.

Their eyes met. As his smile reached out to her, she felt the bleak emptiness melt inside her.

'Kyria Blake is my responsibility, Yorgos.' His voice was quiet. 'You may return to the house.'

Yorgos muttered something, his shoulders slumped as he put down the bag, then got back in the car and drove away.

There was a silence, then Alexis said, 'So, *agapi mou*. Did you really think I would let you slip away, out of my life?'

She looked at him gravely. 'I wasn't sure. Millie told me that Eleni was upset earlier. I—I don't want to cause you more problems.'

He shrugged. 'There was a difference of opinion. At times, Eleni forgets I am no longer in the nursery. But it need not trouble you.'

He paused. 'Unless you really wish to go?'

Mutely, she shook her head. And let him take her hand in his and lead her away.

CHAPTER NINE

HER HAND IN HIS, making her feel cherished. Safe and wanted, then and throughout the days and nights which followed.

But—above and beyond all—loved in a way she'd almost forgotten could exist, their mutual passion tempered with tenderness and consideration, her body free of its inhibitions flowering, opening to him at his touch.

And she was spoiled, too. Alexis had insisted on taking her on a shopping trip to Mykonos, and while Selena had refused to consider any of the more extreme fashions in the designer boutiques, she now had several bikinis with matching wraps, gorgeous silk shirts in jewel colours to wear with slim-fitting white pants and pretty dresses that floated like clouds for their evenings together.

Things he'd whispered that he would enjoy taking off and her smile told him she would enjoy that, too.

Most days they drove out together, lunching off freshly caught fish at small seaside *tavernas*, often returning to the Pillars of Apollo to make love in the drowsy heat of the afternoon. They often dined out in the evenings, too, at places where there was traditional Greek music and dancing in which Selena, in spite of her initial protests, was made to join.

'You must learn, *matia mou*,' Alexis told her. 'So you can dance at your sister's wedding.'

However, none of their rovings around the island, including a tour round the ultra-modern, ultra-efficient olive oil factory, took them back to the villa, confirming for Selena that she had indeed been concerned in Alexis's 'difference of opinion' with Eleni, which troubled her. Instead, his apartment at the hotel had become their own private domain, and if the staff there also disapproved of her presence, they hid it well, Stelios leading them in treating her with smiling courtesy.

Except for Kostas who seemed to be going out of his way to avoid her.

She'd sought him out once to suggest that Millie might join her occasionally beside the pool or on the stretch of sandy beach below the hotel gardens, only to receive a point blank refusal.

'You are the pillow friend of Kyrios Constantinou, and that has caused more problems with my mother,' he told her sullenly. 'It is better that my Amelia stays away.'

She was tempted to remind him he was hardly in a position to adopt the moral high ground, but decided it would be more politic to keep quiet, telling herself that things would sort themselves out. Although she wasn't sure how.

The only time she was separated from Alexis was on

his trips to Athens when he would generally be away for at least twenty-four hours.

Selena missed him desperately during these brief absences, finding it difficult to sleep without his arms around her, and asked at one point if she could accompany him, but he'd refused. 'Athens is a sad place now, *agapi mou* and not always safe,' he told her gently and she'd reluctantly accepted his explanation.

However, when he warned her that his next trip would take much longer, lasting a week or more, she decided, instead of moping, to go back to Haylesford, not just for Millie's sake, but her own.

To break the news to Aunt Nora that she was putting her career plans on indefinite hold and returning to Rhymnos, and weathering the storm that would inevitably follow.

But Alexis seemed restive about the scheme. 'Wait a little, *matia mou*, until I can go with you,' he urged.

But Selena, under pressure from Millie, anxious about the date of her wedding, remained adamant.

'I can handle Aunt Nora,' she told him with more confidence than she actually felt. 'And I'll be back before you are.'

'You promise it?' he asked, his voice oddly sombre.

'Cross my heart,' she said. 'Besides, I have to go because Stelios did magic to get me on a flight and I can't let him down.'

His smile was thin. 'I must remember to thank him.'

'You do that,' she said and kissed him.

Yet the night preceding his departure, there was a fierce almost desperate edge to his lovemaking, which took her to new heights of pleasure but left her afterwards feeling forlorn to the point of sadness, even before they'd said goodbye.

And her mood wasn't lifted by the grey skies and rain that greeted her in England. By the time she reached her aunt's house from the station, she was chilled and damp.

And there was no one at home. She went into the kitchen and switched on the kettle, then went up to her room. The bed was freshly made up, indicating that her phone message had been received and she was expected, so presumably her aunt's absence was only temporary.

She ate a hasty meal of scrambled eggs on toast and drank two cups of coffee, then walked into town, first to the jewellers where Millie's bracelet was mended while she waited, then to the travel agency to book a return flight to Mykonos for the following day.

She was on her way back to the house when a girl's voice said, 'Hi, Selena,' and she turned to see Daisy and Fiona.

Just what I need, she thought, responding with a polite, 'Hello.'

'So, where's Millie?' Daisy looked around as if expecting her to pop out from behind a lamppost and shout *Boo*.

'On Rhymnos,' Selena said evenly. 'Preparing for her wedding.'

'Wedding?' Fiona echoed. 'How amazing. We thought she'd have had enough of the Greek stud scenario by now, didn't we, Dais?'

'Well—there you go,' Selena said briskly, trying to edge past them.

'So, in all this time, you didn't manage to talk her out of it,' said Daisy, and giggled. 'Or did you stay because you'd been talked into something yourself?'

Selena, to her annoyance, felt her colour rise but she managed a shrug. 'I think a career is a better choice. She doesn't.' She added, 'I'll tell her I saw you.'

'And make sure she invites us to the wedding,' Fiona called after her.

When pigs grow wings, Selena thought as she walked away. I'm not even sure I'll be invited myself, judging by the way Kostas spoke the other day.

'Pillow friend,' he'd called her, which sounded marginally better than 'mistress' or 'tart', but it meant the same and, knowing it had exposed her to the contempt of Anna Papoulis, stung like a thorn in her flesh.

And was painful in another way. Because it was so very far from 'wife'.

There, she thought, unhappily. I've said it at last. Faced the fact that in all this time, Alexis has never mentioned marriage. Never suggested that my staying with him should become permanent...

Or not in the way I've secretly hoped.

Perhaps he was just waiting until Millie and Kostas had their wedding. Or maybe not.

For a moment, she felt troubled, then pulled herself together as she remembered the warm, moonlit nights and his hands and mouth caressing her—arousing her. But above all, his voice whispering, *'S'agapo.'*

I love you...

And wasn't that what mattered? All that really mattered?

She sighed. If she said it enough times, she might even start to believe it.

Back at the house, she retrieved the 'Personal' file from the bottom drawer of her aunt's desk, extracting Millie's birth certificate and medical insurance documents and, after a moment's thought, her own, although, as she reminded herself firmly, it was unwise to make assumptions.

Now there were other practical matters to be considered, such as the contents of her wardrobe. She knew from Alexis that winters on Rhymnos could and probably would be cold, wet and stormy, so jeans and sweaters and her fleece would be useful. The rest could be bagged up for charity and she'd make a start on that now.

Because I can't wait to be out of here, she thought, hurling a blameless navy skirt into the reject sack. And back with the man I love, adding determinedly, on whatever terms.

She was just tying up the last sack when she heard a car arrive, then drive away and the rattle of a key in the front door.

Back from another little trip, she thought as she braced herself and went downstairs.

Aunt Nora was in the hall, removing her light waterproof jacket.

'So you're finally here,' she commented acidly. 'And Amelia with you, I trust.'

'Well, no, she isn't.' Selena forced a smile. 'You're looking well, Aunt Nora. I hope your leg has quite recovered.'

'It's still painful. I have to use a walking stick much of the time. So, where is your sister?'

Selena abandoned any further attempt at evasion. 'She's on Rhymnos,' she said. 'Planning her wedding. And she hopes you'll be one of her guests.'

There was an ominous silence. Then: 'So she intends to continue with this madness.' Aunt Nora drew a deep breath. 'Why did you allow this to happen, Selena—against my express wishes?'

'Because I couldn't prevent it.' Selena lifted her chin. 'And now I don't even want to. They love each other.' She paused. 'And there's something else you have to know. I've also met someone and tomorrow I'm going back to Rhymnos to be with him.'

Her aunt's voice shook with anger. 'You dare to say this to me—that you're throwing away your university place—the career I've offered—everything I've done for you? My God, your ingratitude is beyond belief.'

Selena said gently, 'I have tried to feel grateful, but somehow it never quite works. You want me to become a teacher, not for the good of the community, but to provide you with cheap labour at your expensive school. And I'd have done it, for Millie's sake. But she's decided her own future, setting me free to do the same.' She smiled. 'And I'm doing it. So if I do decide to teach, it will be on my terms.'

'Bold words,' said Miss Conway. 'Which you may well regret, my dear, when the summer's over and your boyfriend gets tired of you and throws you out. Or simply goes back to his wife.'

She paused. 'But you're right. Millie is a lost cause,

and I want nothing more to do with her or her Greek peasant. You, however, could still be of service to me, and when you discover you've made a terrible mistake, I might be prepared to give you another chance.'

Selena said woodenly, 'I'll bear it in mind.' But inwardly, she was still smarting over the wife comment.

Not that she believed her, of course. Yet there'd been times when she'd found Alexis watching her, his expression guarded. Other times when he'd seemed about to say something—but remained silent.

But when she'd queried this, his answer was invariably, 'I was thinking how very beautiful you are, *agapi mou*.'

Which was lovely to hear, but somehow left her still wondering…

Trust Aunt Nora to score a direct hit on my insecurity, she thought bitterly. And thank heaven she won't have many more opportunities.

It was cloudy but still hot when she reached Rhymnos. She'd left a message the previous day to let the hotel know she was returning, but no one had been there to meet her from the ferry, and she found herself transferring her heavy suitcase from hand to hand as she trudged up the hill.

There was no one at the desk when she walked in, so she headed straight for the lift, retrieving her key from her bag as she pressed the button.

Opening the door to the suite, she was immediately halted by the unexpected smell of cigar smoke, and as she paused, putting down her case, a large, powerfully built man in a crumpled cream linen suit, his dark hair streaked with grey, strolled out of the bedroom, a cheroot smouldering between be-ringed fingers.

At the same time, she realised there was another man, younger, thinner and wearing glasses, seated on one of the sofas with a briefcase beside him.

For an absurd moment, Selena thought she'd come to the wrong floor—the wrong room—and braced herself to back out apologising.

But then the man with the cigar spoke, his Greek accent spiked with transatlantic overtones. 'So you will be Miss Blake.'

Dark eyes under heavy grizzled brows swept her in a frank assessment that made her burn with embarrassment and indignation.

He turned to the other man. 'I can see the attraction, Manoli. That golden beauty and innocence combination would tempt a saint.' He sighed. 'And as we both know too well, my friend, my son is no saint.'

She found a voice. 'I'm sorry, but I don't understand.' She looked round almost wildly. 'Who are you—and where is Alexis?'

'My name is Petros Constantinou, and this is my family lawyer, Manoli Kerolas. As for Alexis…' He shrugged broad shoulders. 'He is in New York where he belongs and where he will remain from now on.' He gestured with the cigar. 'Now take a seat, young lady, while we discuss terms.'

'I prefer to stand.' Selena lifted her chin defiantly, aware that her heart was pounding and she felt deathly cold. 'And there is nothing to discuss.'

He sighed. 'As a favour to all of us, don't make this harder than it needs to be. Just accept that the party's over and get on with the rest of your life. Because you won't be seeing Alexis again, here or anywhere else. It's finished, *pethi mou*. Over.'

The words thudded into her like stones, and she forced herself not to flinch.

'I don't believe it,' she said. 'I'll never believe it until he tells me so himself.'

'That's not going to happen.' His tone was bluntly dismissive. 'My son's good at beginning things, but, as you've just found out, bad about ending them. He prefers that done for him. It's one of his weaknesses, I guess, like his attraction to willing blondes and his sentimental attachment to this island.

'But the olive oil project can run itself now, so he can devote himself to his neglected business and family duties in New York.'

He smiled. 'No doubt, marriage and fatherhood will at last encourage him to focus on what is important in his life, rather than trivial diversions, however attractive.'

'Marriage? Fatherhood?' Selena's throat was dry. 'What are you talking about?'

'Ah,' he said. 'You didn't know Alexis was about to be married?' He gave her a derisive look. 'But why would you spoil a beautiful romance by asking awkward questions?'

She said hoarsely, 'He wouldn't do this. He couldn't. He loves me.'

'I'm sure he told you so.' His voice was almost be-

nign. 'Like most men, he would say anything to keep
a pretty girl in his bed. But he is promised to a girl he
has known since childhood, and the marriage will be
celebrated almost immediately.'

He paused. 'In fact as soon as I have dealt with such
extraneous matters as yourself, Miss Blake.' He beckoned to the lawyer. 'Now, in order to save my future
daughter-in-law undeserved heartache, we need you
to sign this.'

'What is it?' Her hands were clenched in the pockets of her jeans, her nails digging into her palms. Using
one pain to fight another. Keeping it at bay until she
could be alone.

His voice was hard. 'A legal undertaking that you
will not contact my son again under any circumstances
or disclose your past encounters with him here to any
part of the media. In return for your agreement, I will
arrange for two hundred and fifty thousand pounds ster-
ling to be deposited in your bank account.'

He paused. 'Call it compensation for your disappointment, although I am sure you will have no difficulty in finding a new protector to replace Alexis.'

Selena said thickly, 'How—how bloody dare you! I
won't sign a damned thing and you can keep your filthy
money. But you don't have to worry.' She swallowed
past the tightness in her throat. 'Do you really imagine
I want to *think* about your son ever again, let alone *see*
him or *talk* about him? If so, you must be mad.'

She indicated the door. 'Now perhaps you'll go.'

'This is Constantinou property, *thespinis*.' The lawyer spoke. 'It is for you to leave. Although you may first

collect any clothing or gifts you received from Kyrios Alexis during your time together.'

She bent and retrieved her case. 'No.' Her voice shook. 'You can keep them, too.'

She added, 'I want nothing from any of you—not now—not ever.'

And managed, somehow, without stumbling or yielding to the pain and grief waiting to swamp her, to turn and walk away.

As she emerged from the lift, her legs shaking under her, she saw Kostas standing in the doorway of the bar and managed to remember the errand that had sent her back to England.

She took the envelope containing the documents and the bracelet from her bag and handed it to him, somehow keeping her voice even. 'For Millie.'

His glance slid away. He said hurriedly, 'I am sorry for this trouble that has come to you,' and went back into the bar.

After that, it all became ridiculously simple. The ferry was still loading at the quayside, and when she reached the airport on Mykonos there was an empty seat on a late afternoon flight.

It was almost as if the Fates, too, were conspiring to be rid of her.

She bought a ticket for Haylesford because she could think of nothing else to do.

Knowing there was nothing she could say in her own defence that could possibly justify this sordid, hideous little episode.

That she'd gone willingly and, above all, unquestioningly into the arms of a man about to marry his child-hood sweetheart, who had used her and now, cynically ditched her, without even the courage to face her him-self with the truth.

Just because he'd told her he loved her and she had wanted so desperately to believe him…

Not an excuse, she realised, that would cut any ice with her aunt, even if she could bring herself to use it. And she could just imagine the grim triumph that would greet it.

As the train pulled into Stilbury, the stop before Hay-lesford, obeying an imperative she barely understood, she grabbed her case and got out.

She walked into the town, found a cheap hotel and took a room for the night. The next day, she emptied her bank account for the advance rent on a tiny bedsit, and took a job as a waitress in a busy gastropub, full-time and with long hours but her own tips.

Not great, she thought, but work. Because work was the answer. The magic formula that would let her forget Greece and everything that had happened there.

And perhaps, at that desperate moment, she even believed it might be possible.

CHAPTER TEN

YET HERE SHE WAS, on board the ferry once again as it approached Rhymnos, the heat of the rail burning through her clothes as she leaned against it, her hands clenched in tense fists at her sides.

Up to the moment when she'd boarded the plane, she'd told herself that she didn't have to do this. That there was still time to change her mind. But the chance of a rapprochement with Millie had decided her.

Kostas said things had changed, she thought, and he was right. The harbour had been enlarged, and smart motor yachts now outnumbered the fishing boats.

She made herself look past them at the white building on the hill, hoping against hope that this might have been transformed, altered beyond recognition, or, preferably, demolished, its associations buried with it.

Knowing, at the same time, that she couldn't be that lucky. That there wasn't even the palliative of a board announcing 'Under New Ownership'.

Kostas was waiting when she disembarked and insisted on carrying her bag. 'I am thankful to see you, sister. My Amelia will be so happy.'

His *taverna* was at the far end of the harbour, clean and colourful with its tubs of geraniums and red and white awning. Obviously busy, too, with all the outside tables taken.

Heaven alone knew how he'd raised the money to acquire it, she thought in bewilderment, but the gamble seemed to have paid off.

They went through the bar into the kitchen where Anna Papoulis was lifting a large dish of moussaka from one of the ovens, her normally sour expression deepening when she saw Selena, while totally ignoring her polite, *'Kalimera.'*

No change there, then, Selena thought wryly, following Kostas through a curtained doorway and up a flight of wooden stairs to the first floor.

Her room, situated at the end of a narrow passage and overlooking a rear yard with bins and crates, was small and little more than basic, with a low bed, covered by a thin red blanket, a narrow cupboard for her belongings and a rag rug on the hastily swept floor.

Ah well, she thought, I'm not planning a long stay. Only to remember, with a sudden pang of alarm, that was what she'd said the first time she came to Rhymnos, and how disastrously that had turned out.

But that was then, she reminded herself. This was now, and she was a different person.

Kostas deposited her bag on the bed and gave her an anxious look. 'You will come to my poor Amelia?'

'That's what I'm here for.' She kept her voice upbeat and even managed a reassuring smile.

But the smile slipped a bit when she followed Kostas

along the passage to the main bedroom and found his poor Amelia in a pretty blue dressing gown reclining in the middle of a very large bed, with a dish containing a half-eaten bunch of grapes beside her and clearly as far from death's door as anyone wearing mascara and lip gloss could possibly be.

'Oh.' She put down the magazine she'd been reading.

'So here you are. I'd begun to think you'd changed your mind.' Her eyes widened. 'What the hell have you done to your hair?'

'Cut it,' said Selena. 'Hello, Mills.'

She walked across and sat on the edge of the bed. 'I thought you were ill.'

Millie grimaced. 'I am. I've never felt so dreadful in my entire life. I can't stop being sick, but I get no sympathy from the old bat downstairs. She seems to think I should still be waiting on tables. It would serve her right if I threw up over the customers.'

She added, 'That's one of the reasons I wanted you here, because I thought you'd understand.' And paused. 'Or perhaps you were one of the lucky ones and didn't get sick.'

The room was hot, but Selena felt icy cold. *One of the lucky ones...*

She tried to speak steadily. 'Millie, are you telling me you're pregnant?'

'Yes, of course. Naturally, Kostas is turning cartwheels, but then he doesn't have to suffer like this.' She took another grape. 'Fruit is all I can eat. It's a nightmare.'

No, thought Selena, her throat closing. I'm the one

having the nightmare. After everything that's happened, how can she be doing this to me?

She got to her feet. 'I believe morning sickness usually ends after the first trimester, unless you're very unlucky. In any event, it's hardly an emergency.' She walked towards the door. 'I hope all goes well for you.'

'Where are you going?'

'Back to the UK. Where else?' Selena's tone was crisp.

'But you've only just got here,' Millie protested. 'Besides, it isn't just the baby, Lena.' She was kneeling on the bed, her voice faltering and sounding very young. 'We have big, big problems and we need your help.'

Of course they did, thought Selena, unease crawling across her skin like the scrape of a nail on glass.

Every instinct was screaming, was telling her to go, yet she found herself hesitating. She said, 'I presume it's about money. Yet the *taverna* seems to be doing well.'

'It is. Which makes everything so much worse.'

'What does?'

Millie's face was flushed, her eyes tearful. 'To know we've been cheated. And that we may lose it all—our home—our living—everything.'

And she threw herself, sobbing, against her pillows.

Selena came back to the bed. 'Don't, Millie,' she said gently. 'You need to keep calm—for the baby's sake,' she added, stumbling a little over the words. 'Now, tell me how you've been cheated.'

Her sister gulped. 'The *taverna* didn't belong to the guy who made the deal with Kostas, and now the real owner wants it back.'

Selena stared at her in genuine shock. 'Surely your lawyer should have picked up on any query over the title?'

Millie looked away. 'It was all handled privately. We didn't have a lawyer.'

'Well, you need one now,' Selena said briskly, wondering if Kostas was certifiable.

Millie still wasn't looking at her. She said in a low voice, 'We hoped you'd help us.'

'But that's ridiculous.' Selena spread her hands in exasperation. 'I'm going to be a teacher. I haven't a clue about Greek or any other kind of law.'

'But if you talked to the owner, you might persuade him to change his mind.'

'Why on earth should he listen to me?'

And, as if from a far distance, she heard Millie say, 'Because it's Alexis Constantinou. He's back, staying at the hotel and he wants to see you.'

'You lied to me. Both of you. How could you do that?'

She faced the pair of them, her body rigid, her mind still reeling under the shock of it. The agony of another betrayal…

Millie looked at her beseechingly. 'If we'd told you the truth, you wouldn't have come. And we're desperate. We have nowhere else to turn.'

'Then nothing's changed.' Selena's tone bit. 'I won't see him.' And then ruined it by asking, 'Is he alone?'

Kostas looked at the floor. 'Here—yes. Elsewhere? Who knows?'

Who indeed? Pain struck at her again, harsh and

deep, telling her all her attempts at putting the past behind her had been totally in vain. As if she was still the naïve, gullible idiot who'd believed everything he'd told her.

Who'd even dared to dream…

Until, of course, his father had ripped off her rose-tinted spectacles and revealed Alexis for what he truly was…

She said slowly, 'Are you sure it's him and not his father asking for me?'

'What has his father to do with it?' asked Millie. Kostas, however, remained silent.

He looks almost guilty, thought Selena, although being an idiot was hardly a criminal offence or even a mortal sin.

But, having arranged to have her cut so brutally from his life, why was Alexis now trying to force her into another confrontation?

This threat to ruin Kostas and Millie was placing her in an impossible predicament.

If she refused to see Alexis, he would win. In fact, the offer of negotiation had to be a deliberate ploy on his part. He knew exactly what her reaction would be, and he could assign the blame to her if Kostas and Millie became homeless.

But she would not allow that to happen, she told herself with icy purpose. She could not let him think she was too scared—too broken to face him. If all she had was pride to carry her through, then she would make it enough.

She said quietly, 'Don't cry any more, Mills. It's bad

for the baby. And—yes—I'll talk to him if that's what
it takes, but I promise nothing. I'm quite sure he has
his own agenda.'

She looked back at Kostas who was still avoiding her
gaze. 'Has he mentioned a time and place?'

He cleared his throat. '*Ochi*. Not yet.'

Instinct told Selena that there was obviously more
to this than met the eye, but at the moment she had
enough to cope with.

'Right.' She moved to the door. 'Now I think I'll have
a shower and relax for a while. OK?'

And on their subdued murmur of assent, she left
them to it.

The shower was refreshing, but there was no question of relaxation afterwards.

She still could hardly believe what was happening,
or why. Was unable to credit how Alexis could have the
gall to treat her like this—to add insult to the terrible
injury he'd already inflicted.

Proof if proof were needed that he'd never cared for
her, she thought, fighting the wave of pain and grief that
threatened once more to overwhelm her.

That all the warmth and tenderness he'd shown her
had simply been a ploy to entice her, pliant and, above
all, unquestioning, into his bed, and keep her to provide him with sexual entertainment until his real world
claimed him back, and he could simply walk away.

He must have known how she felt. Had it amused
him to make her admit she'd surrendered her heart as
well as her body?

Had this ruthless pursuit of his own pleasure always

been there, under the charm and allure, only she'd been too besotted to see it?

And perhaps Eleni's forbidding attitude had been an attempt to warn her away before too much harm was done?

She must have asked herself these questions a thousand, thousand times, until she'd finally decided it was time she stopped looking for answers and—moved on. Or as much as she could under the circumstances. She'd thought she was succeeding.

Yet here she was, once again in torment. Knowing that her wounds were still raw.

Among the many things, she realised, her throat tightening, that she needed to keep hidden when, eventually, she had to face him again. Most of all, the precious photograph now propped against the bottle of water on the rickety bedside table.

She picked it up and studied it, her heart clenching in tenderness in response to the small, laughing face with the lively dark eyes.

'Not long now, darling,' she said softly. 'And we'll be together always—and that's a promise.' She kissed the photograph and put it back on the table.

She would not wait, cowering, to be summoned, she decided. Tomorrow, she would take matters into her own hands and go to Alexis. Let him know he had a fight on his hands.

Pleading tiredness after her flight, she went to bed early, intending to plan some kind of strategy.

But it was hard to concentrate as she lay naked under the single sheet, listening to the sounds of *bouzouki* wafting up from the *taverna*, and remembering, in spite of herself, the long evenings of eating, drinking and music under the stars.

How she'd clapped her hands to the rhythm as she watched Alexis dance with the other men, more grace-ful, more virile than any of his companions, before she and the rest of the girls were summoned to form a long line with the men, laughing and breathless as they dipped, swayed and spun between the tables in sim-ple, uncomplicated happiness.

How, later, in his arms, her body had moved to a very different rhythm. Been urged to a pleasure so deep it was almost pain.

And became aware, with shame that her body was stirring at the memory, her nipples hardening against the linen that covered them.

She turned over, pressing her face into the hard pil-low.

'Damn him.' Her whisper ached in the darkness. 'Damn him to hell.'

'So,' Selena said briskly. 'What I need from you is paperwork—something to prove that you bought the *taverna* in good faith, and that you might be due some compensation.'

'We don't want compensation,' said Millie. 'Just to keep the Amelia. Besides, I don't think there is any paperwork. Kostas says it was a private arrangement.'

'He told me the same thing.' Selena gave her sister a level look. 'Mills, I really need to know what you and Kostas aren't telling me.'

'There's nothing, honestly.' Millie was clearly bewildered. She got to her feet. 'I'm going shopping before it gets too hot. We want some more cucumbers.'

Selena stopped her. 'I'll get them on my way back. You stay in the shade and rest.'

'You are sure about this?' Millie subsided into her chair again. 'Wouldn't it be better to wait until he sends for you?'

'Not from where I'm standing.' Selena smiled at her. 'Stop worrying.'

She set off along the waterfront and up the hill to the hotel, just as she'd done that first time all those months ago.

Stelios was at reception when she walked in. He looked up and smiled. 'Kyria Blake.'

She made herself smile back at him, easily and confidently. '*Kalimera*, Stelios. Is the boss around? I really need to speak to him. But if he's busy I can come back later.'

But will I? Or, if I wait, will I lose whatever reserve of courage brought me here and run...? Except I can't do that. I have to go through with it now, whatever happens.

'No, no, he will see you now.' Stelios reached for the internal telephone. 'He has been expecting you.'

Yes, she thought. Of course. What else did I think? But now the fight begins.

She stood beside him in the lift, carefully unclenching her hands, and making herself breathe slowly and evenly. Reminding herself why she was there. Rehearsing in her head what she had to say.

Reminding herself that she was here to confront her demons and conquer them at last.

'Kyrios Alexis is having breakfast,' Stelios informed her as he unlocked the door to the apartment and ushered her inside.

She nodded. *'Efharisto.'*

'Parakalo,' he returned and backed out, closing the door behind him.

She crossed the empty sitting room and went into the bedroom, deliberately averting her eyes from the unmade bed.

The long windows stood open and Alexis, barefoot and barelegged in a white towelling robe which emphasised the deep bronze of his skin, was sitting at the table on the balcony, drinking coffee, the remains of his meal—fruit, fresh bread and cherry jam—pushed to one side.

She walked slowly forward and he looked round, staring at her, his eyes narrowing.

His face seemed thinner, she thought, its features more deeply accentuated. And, above all, tired.

'Kalimera.' He indicated the chair on the other side of the table. 'Would you like coffee?'

She sat. 'There's only one cup.'

'How can that matter,' he said softly, 'when we have already shared so much?'

Clearly, he was not going to make this easy for her.

She met the mockery in his eyes. 'But not,' she said, 'for some time.'

'Yet you are here now. Allow me to express my pleasure.'

Selena lifted her chin. 'To negotiate,' she said crisply. 'Nothing else.'

'Nothing? I fear you must think again.'

And suddenly, every word she had planned to say, every careful argument she'd devised, went out of her head.

Instead she heard herself asking the question she'd promised herself would remain taboo. 'Why didn't you tell me you were going to be married?'

He said levelly, 'Because I hoped it would not be necessary.'

While she was still reeling from this, he added, 'Why have you cut off your hair?'

Hair like moonlight...

She pulled herself together. 'Convenience.'

'No,' he said with sudden harshness. 'Sacrilege.'

She had a sudden memory of the hairdresser saying anxiously, 'Are you quite sure?' How, she'd nodded silently, then sat looking down at her hands, clenched in her lap, as the shining silver-blonde lengths fell to the floor.

She took a deep breath. 'Perhaps we should turn to the problem of the Taverna Amelia.'

'The difficulties of your sister and her worthless husband can wait. I used them only as an excuse to bring you here.' His smile chilled her. 'We have the matter of a personal debt to discuss—you and I.'

'What debt?' Selena shook her head. 'I—I don't understand.'

'You owe me a child, Selene *mou*,' he said softly. 'Or did you think I would not find out?'

She stared back at him, hardly able to breathe, her whole body rigid with shock.

How could he know? she asked herself desperately. How had he found out that she'd been pregnant? Or what had become of the baby since?

At the same time realising that it was not tension she had seen in his face but anger. And directed, unbelievably, at her.

'I—I don't know what you mean.' She could barely recognise her own voice.

'Do not lie to me, *matia mou*—my eyes—my beautiful, shining, innocent eyes.' His voice was harsh, his face inimical. 'Eyes that made me believe that it might be possible at last to love—to trust. What a fool I was.'

He paused. 'Tell me—was it my son or my daughter— the child you gave away so carelessly to strangers?'

Oh, God, how could he do this? Describe in such terms the hardest decision she'd ever taken in her life?

'Alexis,' she said desperately. 'Alexis—you must listen to me…'

'I am listening. Waiting for an answer to my question. Boy or girl?'

'A boy.' She bent her head, her throat tightening uncontrollably. Terrified in case she broke down in front of him—this bitter stranger.

When he was born, they had to sedate me because I was hysterical—unable to stop crying—calling out for you… While afterwards I was alone, having to concentrate on simply staying alive—keeping body and soul together somehow, when really I wanted to die myself.

She looked at him, afraid of what he might see. She said dully, 'If that's what you wanted to know, may I go now, please?'

'You will leave when I permit you to go. Not before.'

She glanced up, startled, at that and felt his smile scrape across her senses.

He added, 'You see, Selena *mou*, I require you to remain here with me until you have given me another child, to replace the one you were so quick to abandon. And, in that way, paid your debt to me in full. Do I make myself clear?'

CHAPTER ELEVEN

THE DISTANCE BETWEEN them seemed to have widened—become impassable. Terrifying.

She said hoarsely, 'You don't—you can't mean it. Alexis—the past is gone and we can't change it—any of it. We have to look to the future—get on with the lives we've chosen.' She added with difficulty, 'With the—the people we've chosen.'

'You refer to your man in England?' His gaze rested sardonically on her bare hands. 'If he is still in your life, he seems in no hurry to marry you.'

And now was not the time to admit there was no such person nor ever had been, she thought.

She lifted her chin. 'No,' she said clearly. 'I was speaking of your wife.'

'I have no wife,' he said.

'Oh.' She paused. 'You're divorced?' *Why was she even asking?*

'No,' he said. 'There was no divorce, because there was never a marriage. I broke off the engagement.'

She said huskily, 'I—I don't understand.'

He shrugged. 'I do not require your understanding,

Selena *mou*, only your cooperation as I think I have made clear.'

She rose. 'And I came here solely to discuss the legal problem over the ownership of Taverna Amelia and try to reach a settlement.'

'Sit down,' he said. 'And listen to me.' He waited until she unwillingly resumed her seat. 'There is no problem. Kostas knows the *taverna* and the land it stands on belongs to me. And I want it back.'

She fought her dismay. Tried to sound confident. 'Then, at some point, he's been misled. And at least he deserves the purchase price repaid.'

His glance was derisive. 'You are the one who has been misled, Selena *mou*, because he paid nothing. And now you are here to induce me to be merciful, and with-draw eviction proceedings against him and his preg-nant wife.' He paused, adding sardonically, 'You are a fertile family, it seems.'

Best to ignore that, she thought, biting savagely into her lip. 'But Kostas worked for you. You encouraged him to marry Millie. Why have you turned against him?'

'Once again, you are mistaken. It was Kostas who turned against me.'

Selena stifled a groan. I knew it, she thought. Knew there was something very wrong.

She said carefully, 'But why should he do that?'

'He imagined that marrying your sister would give him some kind of privileged standing with me.' His shrug was cynical. 'I had to show him he was wrong. He decided to take his revenge.' His mouth tightened. 'A great mistake.'

She bit her lip. 'Am I allowed to know what he did?'

He shrugged. 'Why not—as it also concerns you.'

'Me?'

'Of course,' he said. 'What other weapon did he have? He had somehow learned of my engagement and that my father was pressing me to honour the arrangement and marry the girl.'

'Your childhood sweetheart,' she said.

'Never.' His tone was scornful. 'But what is one more lie among so many? I had indeed met her once or twice as a child. Her father, Ari Sofiakis, was a business colleague of my father's in the early days of the Constantinou Corporation.

'Katerina was her father's princess, spoiled, whining and detestable and the intervening years had not improved her. Her interests in life were fashion magazines, chocolates and cosmetic surgery. I doubt we had a thought in common.'

'Then why did you agree to marry her?'

'I did not. It was put to me as a done deal and I refused absolutely. At first my father argued that this would deeply offend the Sofiakis family, and I retorted he should have obtained my consent before proceeding.

'And then he told me the truth. That, years before, he had made corrupt payments to civic officials in order to secure lucrative contracts for our companies. That Ari Sofiakis knew of this and my marriage to Katerina was now the price of his silence.

'By this time, you see, he had realised that other potential bridegrooms for his precious child were being deterred by the stories of her extravagance and temper tantrums and he was becoming desperate to find her a rich husband.

'Unless I complied, he, my own father, would end up in court and almost certainly go to jail, which would be a catastrophe for Constantinou International and, by association for me, his only son.'

She said shakily, 'But that's blackmail on both sides.'

'Of course.' He shrugged. 'I was presented with two intolerable choices, and I chose reluctantly to protect my father, and agreed to an engagement.

'But the wedding, I made clear, must wait. I had already committed myself to trying to protect Rhymnos from the worst effects of the economic crisis and nothing would change that.

'But I told the Sofiakis family that if Katerina would agree to a small, hasty wedding, she was welcome to accompany me to the island and share whatever privations that might involve.'

He added casually, 'It was a safe offer. Katerina, I knew, would never willingly travel further from Manhattan than the Hamptons or Cape Cod and after both she and her mother had indulged in a series of increasingly hysterical scenes, the marriage was safely postponed.

'Before my departure, I hired a team of investigators to take a close look at Ari Sofiakis. I wasn't hopeful. He had a reputation for utter probity in his business life and was known as a religious man and a major donor to charity.

'At the same time, I had my lawyers and accountants working in the background to make me totally independent from Constantinou International.' His voice was expressionless. 'I had learned my lesson.'

She said, 'And your investigators found something?'

'Yes,' he said. 'When I had almost given up hope. In his charity work. One small, insignificant organisation, run by an order of nuns, helping potential immigrants to adapt to life in the US, and supported regularly and generously by Mr Sofiakis and a number of his friends and other prominent members of the community.' He paused. 'Which did not include my father.

'The team found this—odd. When they looked deeper, they found the nuns long gone and their house sold. While the immigrants, most of them illegal, but all female and beautiful, were high-class and expensive call-girls with Ari a faithful and long-standing client.

'They telephoned me in Athens with the news and I flew straight to New York to confront him, not knowing my father, under pressure from his family, had also been busy. Mr Sofiakis agreed to end the engagement but then had to invent some reason to placate his wife and daughter. I almost felt sorry for him.'

His mouth hardened. 'Until my father told me that my relationship with you was over, too, and I should turn my attention to finding myself another bride from our community.'

'When I said I would marry you or no one, he advised me not to waste my time. That you were a greedy tramp who had let yourself be bought off for a quarter of a million pounds.

'His lawyer even produced a document you had signed, promising to give me up, and congratulated

me on my "lucky escape".' He pronounced the words
with distaste.

She said numbly, 'And you believed them?'

'Not my father, perhaps,' he said. 'But I had no reason then to doubt Manoli. I had been at college with his
younger brother, and looked on his family as friends.'

'Whereas I was just a pillow friend,' she said scornfully. 'One of many, no doubt.'

'If you expect me to apologise for my past, Selene
mou, you will be disappointed.'

Their glances met—clashed—and she was the first
to look away.

'How did you discover the truth—about the money?'

'Months later, when my father unwisely fired Manoli.
By then I had separated myself from Constantinou International, and offered him a job. He broke down and
confessed you had rejected the pay off, and that my father had signed the document in your name, gambling
rightly on my not recognising your signature and being
too shocked to question its validity.

'I told him the job offer stood and booked an immediate flight to England, to find you.' He paused. 'In the
town where your aunt has a school.'

Her head went back. She said hoarsely, 'You saw
Aunt Nora?'

'Yes,' he said. 'And heard her, too. How you had refused her help, her offers of support. How your hatred
of me had caused you to reject our baby at birth.

'Some might say I owe Kostas thanks for putting an
end to my illusions about you,' he added bitterly. 'But
somehow I cannot be grateful.'

Her head swam. She felt herself gulping in air, struggling not to fall to pieces after this new blow. Because she needed to concentrate her energies on finding a way out of this nightmare.

Not unscathed—she would carry his anger, his accusations with her like a scar—but hopefully with her self-respect still intact.

'Yet you still used him to bring me here.' Her voice was brittle.

'If you'd known I had sent for you, would you have agreed?' He watched her look away and nodded. 'I thought not.'

But was that the truth? How many times had she imagined standing before him—asking the questions that haunted her?

I can never tell him that, she thought achingly, because I dare not let him see that the answers to those questions still matter to me.

That, God help me, he still matters—in spite of everything...

She said, 'So, I have to tell Kostas that he's lost his home and his living.'

'I think, Selena *mou*, that he already knows.' He shrugged again. 'His time on Rhymnos is done.'

He paused, watching her, his eyes lingering on her mouth. 'And now shall we turn to our more personal negotiations?'

'There is nothing to discuss.' She looked back defiantly. 'I have no intention of—co-operating as you put it. The idea disgusts me—as it should you.'

'Such indignation,' he returned softly. 'Yet I am only

being practical. I am a single man who needs an heir. I require you to provide one for me. If I had known you had already done so, I would have induced you to hand him over to me, instead of hastily abandoning him to strangers.'

She said thickly, 'I—did not—abandon him. Before he was born, I was living in one room, able only to work part-time and receiving benefits.' She swallowed. 'It took me longer than it should have to—recover—afterwards, and that's when he was taken to—to live with another family.'

'You did not think to contact me—his father?'

'No, because I thought—I'd been told—that by then you'd be married. I—I didn't want to intrude on your new life.'

'How noble.' He studied her through half-closed eyes. 'And how much you must have regretted refusing my father's money.'

'Never,' she said. 'Not for one moment.'

'You were content to simply—let your baby go?'

Content? If hearts could break twice, mine would have done so.

She kept her voice steady. 'The decision was made for me.'

'How convenient,' he drawled. 'Then let me tell you what I have decided. That you shall become, in effect, a surrogate mother. After the birth, I shall legally adopt the child, son or daughter, leaving you to walk away unencumbered once again. Although I shall naturally pay for your services.'

She stared at him, shaking with disbelief—and with

her own mounting anger as it mingled with the renewed pain at his treatment of her.

'How generous.' Her voice vibrated with scorn. 'But I do hope you're not offering another paltry two hundred and fifty thousand as your father did. My starting price would be at least double that amount.'

There was a long, taut silence. Apart from the sudden clench of a muscle in his jaw, he was motionless, his dark eyes studying her as if he had never seen her before.

'So,' he said eventually. 'You have actually managed to surprise me, Selene *mou*. But at least we now know where we stand. And I will pay whatever you ask, although I advise you not to allow your greed to run away with you. Do we have a deal?'

She drew a quick, harsh breath. 'No,' she said raggedly. 'We do not and we never will, you—you unutterable bastard. How could you even think so?' A sob she could not control rose in her throat, as she pushed back her chair and stood up. 'I think you're utterly vile and despicable—and I only wish to God that I'd never met you.'

He, too, got to his feet, taking a step towards her, bringing him too close for comfort—or safety. Making her dizzily aware of the warm, familiar scent of his skin.

Reviving memories that were poignant as well as dangerous.

'Truly?' His voice was harsh. 'I wish I could feel the same—but, even now, I cannot.'

If he came any closer she would be lost and she knew it.

Stay calm, she whispered silently. And walk away.

But when she reached the outer door he was beside her, his hand on her arm.

She recoiled. She said between her teeth, 'Do—not—touch me.'

'Forgive me, but there is something I must know.' There was a strange, almost anguished note in his voice. 'My son—what is his name?'

The empty passage ahead of her became a sudden blur, but she forced back the tears.

She said huskily, 'Alexander.' And fled.

'You,' she said. 'You dared to ask for my help, when you knew what you'd done? When you'd ruined my life?'

They were alone in the bar. Millie was resting upstairs and Madame Papoulis, muttering, had gone to buy the forgotten cucumbers.

Kostas's face was wretched. 'I was angry, sister, because I asked Kyrios Alexis to lend me money to buy my business and he refused me. He said that if I wished to marry, I should work and save for my wife, not borrow what I might not be able to repay.'

He hit his chest with a clenched fist. 'In that moment, he made me feel less than a man, and I wished to make him sorry.

'At his house, I had heard Eleni and Yorgos talking when they did not know I was there, speaking of the marriage in America arranged for him by his father. How there would be great trouble if Kyrios Petros found out that Kyrios Alexis had a pillow friend who had taken his eyes and his heart.'

She winced. 'So you told him.'

'*Ne*. And he promised I would be rewarded. I only wanted the money Kyrios Alexis had refused, but he offered me this *taverna*, which was not his to give. He cheated me.'

She said icily, 'I hope you don't expect sympathy.'

'I expect nothing. My life is finished.' He looked up pleadingly. 'Please, sister, do not tell my Amelia that I am to blame for our loss. I cannot bear for her to know.'

'I think she'd prefer honesty,' she said crisply.

'And it might be best if I caught the afternoon ferry.' *In case Alexis comes looking for me.*

Just the thought made her throat tighten in a mixture of panic and desolation.

'But if you leave like this, your sister will wonder.' He gave her another beseeching look. 'For her sake, stay a little longer.'

'Until tomorrow,' she said stonily. 'Then I'm gone.'

'I am thankful.' He sighed. 'I hoped you would persuade Kyrios Alexis to forgive me, so that my Amelia and I can keep our dream.'

And what about my dream—my hopes—my loss? she wanted to scream at him. *And the price I paid—that I'm still paying? That I only get to see my little boy once a week, and at the occasional weekend. That now his foster parents are talking about adoption, and I shall have to fight to keep him.*

She took a deep breath. 'I think you'll just have to buckle down and—start again—somewhere else.' She got up from the table. 'I'll see if Millie's asleep.'

Not just asleep, but dead to the world, she thought as

she peeped round the door. She went to her own room, and sat on the edge of the bed, staring into space.

Her meeting with Alexis had left her sick and shaking inwardly. Would it have been easier to endure, she wondered, if they'd met on neutral territory, instead of somewhere still charged with memories?

Their bedroom, she thought achingly, its balcony overlooking the lawns and the sea beyond, rippling to the edge of the beach in its own quiet, endless rhythm, and where, at night, she would watch the moon carving her silver path across the water.

The room, too, where one warm, golden afternoon their baby had been conceived…

She remembered waking from a delicious dream and reaching for him to find the space beside her unoccupied. She slid naked from the bed and went to find him.

He was in the bathroom, his dark hair still damp from the shower, standing at a basin, a towel draped round his hips, deftly removing the last traces of lather from his chin with his razor.

He saw her in the mirror and smiled, the glint in his eyes showing his appreciation for the provocative picture she made, framed in the doorway.

Selena walked across and slid her arms round his waist, pressing her face against the warm skin of his bare back, breathing the scent of his soap, and marking the length of his supple spine with small, soft kisses.

She unfastened his towel and let it fall to the floor, her hands sweeping slowly down over the taut male buttocks to the muscular length of his thighs.

She heard him gasp softly then the rattle of the razor slipping from his fingers into the basin. His body tensing under her caress, he leaned forward, his head bent and his hands gripping the edge of the tiled surround.

Her lips moved downward, tantalising him with every kiss, her teeth grazing him gently as she slid a hand between his legs, cupping him, teasing him with her fingertips, then reaching for his rigid, straining shaft and stroking it until he groaned aloud.

He turned, lifting her as if she was featherweight, then lowering her on to his loins and filling her with one smooth thrust.

Selena clung to him, arms round his neck, her legs wrapped round his hips. Their mouths were locked together, their tongues tangling, in a silence broken only by the rasp of their breathing and the sound of flesh against flesh as she rode him, demanding, challenging in her glorious abandonment, her muscles gripping him, urging him on, taking him deeper and deeper still.

The harsh, exquisite ascent to pleasure was already building inside her, surging towards its peak, then overwhelming her, convulsing her in such an agony of delight that she cried out into his mouth.

And in the next instant felt him explode, his climax white-hot within her.

Afterwards, they found their way, somehow, to the bed and lay for a while, exchanging quiet kisses.

Eventually, Alexis lifted himself on to an elbow and looked down at her, stroking a strand of hair back from her sweat-dampened face.

He said slowly, half to himself, 'I did not intend that.'

It was unexpected and she gave him a questioning, almost anxious glance. 'Are you sorry?'

'No,' he said, and kissed her again. 'No, my beautiful one, my angel, I could never be that.' His smile was faintly rueful. 'But I meant to be wise for us both.'

And only some weeks later, when she first began to feel sick in the mornings, did she realise, as he must have done at the time, that it was the only time they'd had unprotected sex.

Which had left her to face, totally alone, the most terrifying, heart-wrenching moments of her life…

CHAPTER TWELVE

'GO BACK AND talk to him again, Lena, please. Say whatever you have to, but make him listen.' Millie looked dreadful, her face pale, her eyes swollen. 'After all, he was crazy about you once. Everyone knew it.'

Selena bit her lip. She had agreed with Kostas to tell her sister that she'd tried to reason with Alexis, but that he'd remained totally intransigent.

Her worry that Alexis might come to the Amelia to repeat his offer in person had proved unfounded, but that was the only positive in the day so far.

She said briskly, 'What's past is gone, Mills, and we have to accept that. And downstairs there is a full house wanting dinner. So, do something about your face then come down and charm the customers before your mother-in-law has a total fit.'

'What's the point?' Millie asked despairingly. 'When we're about to lose everything anyway.'

Selena stood up. She said evenly, 'Because you're facing a fresh start and for that you'll need every penny you can make, including tips.' Adding, 'As I once did.'

* * *

When she got downstairs next morning, she found Kostas, looking heavy-eyed, sweeping the *taverna* floor.

He saw the bag she was carrying and frowned. 'You are truly leaving?'

'I did say so.'

'But the manager at the hotel brought this for you.' He went to the bar and produced an envelope. 'I hoped it might be from Kyrios Alexis saying he had thought again.'

'I think the age of miracles is past.' She took the envelope and went outside to read it, aware Kostas was watching anxiously from the doorway.

The note was brief. 'The deal I offered is no longer on the table and you have nothing further to fear from me. I wish you well.' And his initial.

'Does he want to see you again?' asked Kostas.

'No,' she said. 'He's—just saying goodbye.'

She read it again, her heart thumping, asking herself what could have prompted this total *volte face*.

Well—practical considerations, probably. One day, he would meet someone he wanted to marry, and an adopted child born from a supposed surrogate mother in another country would require too much explanation.

Or had he simply decided to take 'no' for an answer?

She thought—*It's over. I'm free.*

So, why wasn't she jumping for joy?

Worse still, why did she feel suddenly so lost—so scared?

Because I have a tough time ahead, she told herself. I have to find an affordable two-bedroom flat where

children are allowed, then let the authorities know I'm
in steady full-time employment, and that Alexander no
longer needs fostering and should be living with me.

After all, I've already missed out on too much of
his babyhood...

And paused, biting her lip. Because, it occurred to
her with all the force of a blow, she was not the only one.

I can't do this, she thought. Whatever Alexis thinks
of me, I can't walk away and leave him with—nothing.

She folded the note and put it in her shoulder bag.
She said, 'Can I leave my other things here, Kostas?
There's something I need to do before I go.'

Stelios was standing on the terrace in front of the
hotel, talking to an elderly couple. As they departed, he
turned to her, his smile fading, his tone formal. 'Kyria
Blake. How may I help you?'

She said, 'I need to see him. Will you tell him it's
important—please?'

'He is not here, *thespinis*. Last night, he went back
to his house, and later today he leaves for Athens.' He
added flatly, 'I do not know when he will return to
Rhymnos.'

'His house?' she echoed, reckoning up the cash she
had with her. 'Then can you get me a taxi?'

He looked at her in astonishment. 'There is only one
on the island, *thespinis*. It belongs to Takis, and today
he attends his uncle's funeral.'

She said, 'I see. Well, it doesn't matter,' and turned
away defeatedly.

'Kyria Blake.' His voice was gentler. 'I think, maybe,
it could matter very much. If you allow, I will drive you.'

'I can't ask you to do that.'

'You do not ask,' he said. 'I offer. Come.'

As they approached Villa Helios, Selena could see that the helicopter was out of the hangar and waiting on its pad.

She said, half to herself, 'It's too late.'

'No, no.' His tone was reassuring. 'See—Panayotis is still working on it, making checks. There is time.'

Eleni answered the door, red-eyed. 'Kyrios Alexis is not here,' she said in answer to Stelios's urgent question. 'He has gone to a meeting. I do not know when he will return.'

Selena stepped forward. 'Eleni—you're upset. What's happened? It's not—Penelope?'

'My daughter is in New York, with my lady, Madame Constantinou. When the house is closed up, we with Hara will be joining her there.'

'Closing the house? But I thought he was born here.'

'It is true, *thespinis*, and his mother will be deeply, deeply grieved that he should decide such a thing. She loves this house and hoped her grandchildren would be born here.' Eleni sighed. 'So many times she has said so.'

'Then why is he doing this?'

'Because he says his life is now in America. That there is nothing for him here.' She gave Selena a sorrowful look. 'He is a changed man, Kyria Blake.'

'Yes,' Selena said quietly. 'It would seem so.'

Stelios said, 'Shall I drive you back to the town, *thespinis*?'

'I suppose that would be best.' She turned back to

Eleni. 'Do you have any idea where Kyrios Alexis is having this meeting?'

'None, Kyria Blake. He took the Jeep and went.'

Her thoughts were whirling as she accompanied Stelios back to the car, trying to make sense of what she'd just heard. The house—closing. Alexis leaving Rhymnos for ever.

And at the same time, she found herself re-thinking everything that had happened between them.

Knowing that she needed to be totally honest with herself.

Admit she'd hoped that his coldness and contempt would be a kind of salvation for her, releasing her at last from the anguish of loving him. From the utter futility of hoping that—somehow—somewhere—there might still be a future for them both. Forcing her to accept that it was indeed—over.

Yet aware that here she was again, trapped in a maze of bewilderment, knowing there were now other questions that needed answers.

Realising that, without them, she would have no peace. Would be left wondering in some bleak wilderness.

She said under her breath, 'I have to find out. I have to…'

And suddenly she realised where Alexis would have gone.

Stelios was frankly unwilling to set her down at the track through the olive groves. 'Kyria Blake, this is a lonely place. Visit Apollo's temple if you wish, but I shall wait for you here.'

'There's no need,' she said as she got out of the car. 'I'm sure I shan't find it lonely at all.'

Difficult, she thought. Perhaps, in the end, impossible. But, for a while at least, not lonely.

'I shall still wait, *thespinis*,' he called after her.

'For half an hour, in case you are wrong.'

But, just as she'd known it would be, the Jeep was there, parked in the usual place.

She ran for most of the way and she was breathless when she finally reached the ridge and looked down into the precinct.

He was leaning against one of the pillars, a dark figure in the sunlight, his shoulders slumped as he stared towards the sea.

Motionless and solitary beyond belief, Selena thought, her heart twisting as she started down the slope.

Not there this time to make plans for the future, but to accept the defeats of the past.

And so lost in his thoughts that he was unaware of her approach until she said his name when he turned sharply, almost defensively.

'If you have come to say goodbye, it is not necessary. I thought my note made that clear.' His voice was harsh.

'It was perfectly clear,' Selena returned. 'But I decided I needed to clarify a few issues, too. Because I don't want us to part like this when there are still things that need to be said.'

'You wish me to apologise for the deal I proposed to you? Very well. The suggestion was shameful. Is that what you wish to hear?'

'No. Although I hated what you said, it was—almost understandable—considering what you were told.' She shook her head. 'I didn't know my aunt hated me so much.'

'You are saying she lied?'

'Yes,' she said. 'I am. I never contacted her when I returned to England. I suppose it was cowardice, but I couldn't bear to hear what I knew she'd say. And I'd always intended to leave what passed for home anyway.

'I moved to a larger town a few miles away where no one knew me. But one night, a few months later, an acquaintance of hers from Haylesford had dinner at the restaurant where I was working and told Aunt Nora that she'd seen me, that I looked well and appeared to have put on weight.

'So—she came to check. She sat at a table in the corner and watched me all evening. When I left, she was waiting outside—and she went on the attack.

'Oh, not physically,' she added quickly as Alexis took a step forward, his face darkening. 'Shouting—calling me names—saying that Millie and I were both disgusting little whores and worse. Totally out of control, using words I'd no idea she knew. Screaming that I'd disgraced her—damaged her good name for ever. That she would never be able to hold her head up in Haylesford again.' She tried to smile. 'She even mentioned nurturing vipers in her bosom.'

'I think the vipers would be most at risk,' he said. 'Go on.'

'There were some people passing and a man came over and asked me if I was all right or if I wanted the police to be called, and after that she calmed down a little. Began talking very reasonably and rationally about my pregnancy being still in the early stages, and how it could easily be terminated. That she would pay to have it done privately at some clinic in London and afterwards I could go back to university, complete my training and teach at her school, just as planned.'

She shuddered. 'In a way, the shouting was better.' She paused. 'When I told her I wouldn't consider abortion, and was going to have my baby, she became very quiet—very cold. Said I had twenty four hours to come to my senses, or she would make me sorry.

'That all contact between us would end. That I, and my bastard, could starve in the gutter for all she cared. And that she would change her will so that neither Millie nor I would ever see a penny of her money.' Again she attempted a smile. 'The ultimate threat.'

He said, 'But ignored.'

'Yes.' She sighed. 'Millie was furious when she found out and stopped speaking to me. She obviously thought I should have agreed to an abortion. But, now she's pregnant herself, she probably understands.'

'But I do not,' he said. 'If you had a choice, why wait until the child is born to be rid of him?'

She swallowed. 'It—it wasn't like that. After the birth, I—I was in a bad way. I had some kind of breakdown and the doctors and social workers felt I was in no fit state to look after myself, let alone a baby.

'And—and they were probably right. So I agreed to have him fostered until I could get on my feet again, find decent work and provide him with a proper home.

'But although I never saw or heard from Aunt Nora again, she must have been keeping tabs on me and discovered all this.'

She gave him a steady look. 'So when you arrived on her doorstep, she saw the perfect way to make me sorry. And did so.'

There was a silence, then: 'My God,' he said quietly. 'We are neither of us fortunate in our relations, Selene *mou*.' He paused. 'They are good people who are looking after Alexander?'

'The Talbots,' she said. 'Yes, good—and kind. Sticklers over visitation arrangements with me, but loving to him.' She paused. 'Maybe too much so because it will be hard for them when I take him back.'

She added, stumbling a little, 'But not as hard as it's been for me being without him all this time. Not able to watch him grow. Learn about things. Missing his first smile, first tooth, first step.'

She reached into her bag. 'Having to depend on things like this.' She handed him the photograph. 'I want you to have it. That's one of the reasons I'm here.'

He looked down at the photograph. He was very still but Selena saw a muscle move in his throat.

At last, he said quietly, 'You plan to take him back— to be with you.'

'I always did,' she said. 'I just had to prove, among other things, that I could find steady employment, which I now have and a decent place to live. I'm working on that.'

She hesitated, her heartbeat quickening. 'And when it happens, I'll have a deal to offer you. Access to your son. The right to visit him, and have him visit you wherever you happen to be living. To share in decisions about his education, well-being and future. To be his father.'

There was a long silence, then he turned away. He said, 'You are generous, but my answer must be—no.'

She was shaken to the core. 'You—don't want to see him—be with him? I—I don't understand.'

'When we first met, I told you how it was when my parents parted. How I was pulled between them, spending time with one, then the other. I remember seeing my mother cry when the car came for me and I had to say goodbye. Later, I realised she always feared that one day my father would decide to keep me. Demand sole custody.

'I swore then I would never do this to my child, or to his mother.'

'But—Alexis—you're not your father. I know I could trust you…'

'How do you know?' He swung back to face her, almost savagely. 'When I have kept the truth from you, believed insane lies about you, and offered you a bargain which was an obscene insult. Holy Mother, I hardly know myself any more.'

Her voice shook. 'I thought maybe we could put that behind us. Start again—for Alexander.'

'Tell me something.' He walked over to her, put his hands on her shoulders. Looked down on her, his gaze searching, intent. 'Why did you refuse to consider a termination of your pregnancy?'

'I—I don't know. It just seemed the wrong thing to do.' She tried to pull away. 'Let go of me, please.'

'No,' he said. 'That is an evasion. I insist the truth, or there is no hope for us.'

She said with sudden bitterness, 'Oh, you want your pound of flesh, don't you, Kyrios Constantinou? Then here's the truth—for better or worse and to hell with you!'

She swallowed, aware that slow tears were trickling down her face. 'Because all I could think of was that this baby—this tiny thing growing inside me was part of you. All I had left of you. And I could not bear to let that go.

'And when he was born, I wanted to die of unhappiness knowing that you would never know him—' her voice cracked '—or even hold him.'

Alexis's arms were round her, drawing her close. 'Don't cry,' he whispered into her hair. 'My beloved, my precious girl. I have you now, and I shall never let you go again.'

'But you're leaving,' she sobbed into his shoulder. 'Closing the house and going to America.'

'Because I could not bear to stay here without you. There wasn't one place without some memory of you to torment me.' He paused. 'I tried so hard to stop loving you, *agapi mou*. I told myself that I could take you— use you, then dismiss you without emotion. Make you suffer as I had done.

'Yet when you walked on to our balcony yesterday, I knew how impossible that was. That it would be like tearing the living heart out of my body. But I could only think how much I must have made you hate me.

'Today I came here only to say goodbye for the last

time. Instead, once again I began to think, and I realised that the name you had chosen for our son might mean you still cared a little. That I should not give up hope.'

'And I couldn't understand why you'd changed your mind—decided to let me go,' she said. 'And I needed to know. So I made the photograph my excuse to come and find you.'

'And, of course, you knew where I would be.'

'Yes, I knew.' She remembered something. 'Oh, God, Stelios is down on the road, waiting for me.'

'No,' he said. 'He will have gone by now, probably to the house to tell them I will be staying—after we return from England with our son.

'So will you break the rules, *matia mou*, and live with me until Father Stephanos can marry us?'

'Oh, I think so.' Her eyes were still misty, but her dawning smile was radiant. '*S'agapo*, Kyrios Alexis. *M'agapas?*'

'For as long as we both live, Kyria Selene.' He bent his head and began to kiss her slowly, even gently at first, the first touch of his mouth on hers a promise of future joy as they sank down to the grass, breathless and laughing, in each other's arms.

EPILOGUE

IT HAD BEEN a wonderful party, thought Selena, gazing dreamily through the window of the *saloni* into the gathering darkness.

There'd been tables in the gardens, groaning with food and drink, music, dancing, and what seemed to be the entire population of Rhymnos there to celebrate not just the first anniversary of her wedding to Alexis, but to drink to her health and happiness as she awaited the imminent birth of their second child.

There were exceptions, of course. Anna Papoulis had been one absentee and Kostas had been there only to deliver Millie and baby Dimitri to the festivities and collect them when it was over.

Although Alexis had allowed them to keep the tavern and stay, Kostas clearly still felt awkward around his powerful brother-in-law.

Millie, however, had no regrets about her mother-in-law's absence.

'Miserable old witch,' she'd muttered. 'Honestly, Lena, she's a nightmare. Every time I put Dimitri down for a nap, or if he makes the slightest sound, she's there, picking him out of his cot, so now he expects it and screams blue murder if he doesn't get instant attention.'

She'd looked across the courtyard to where Maria Constantinou, Alexis's mother, was sitting quietly with Xander on her silk-clad lap, the pair of them engrossed in the story she was reading to him. 'Really, you don't know how lucky you are.'

'On the contrary,' Selena said gently. 'I really, really do.'

She'd been a bag of nerves when Alexis first took her to America and the big rambling house on Long Island to meet his mother, only to find there'd been no need to worry as Madame Constantinou had come running to meet her, folding her into a scented embrace, and smiling through happy tears.

'At last,' she said. 'At last Alexis brings me a daughter to love.'

From the first, she'd been wonderful with Xander, unfazed by his small serious face and silent bewilderment at finding himself among strangers in such very different surroundings, coaxing him gently out of his shell and even persuading him to call her Ya-ya.

By the time they left Long Island, he had also come to accept that the tall young man who carried him on his shoulders, taught him with endless patience to swim and played ball with him as long as there were hours of daylight was 'Papa'.

And that 'Mama' was no longer the sad, quiet girl who had come each week to visit him in that other house which was already becoming a distant memory, but someone who sang and laughed and cuddled him as well as devising with Papa some wonderfully noisy games at bathtime.

Also that a visit to the kitchen at the house in America and here on Rhymnos was invariably rewarded with beaming smiles, petting and some freshly baked and delicious treat.

It had not taken long for him to see that he was on to a good thing, Selena reflected tenderly, and she was thankful for it. Thankful, too, that the Talbots' angry predictions that he would be traumatised if he left their care had been counterbalanced by the love that had surrounded him since the first day, turning his acceptance of his new life into a minor miracle.

She put a hand to her throat, gently fingering the exquisite diamond pendant that Alexis had fastened there only hours ago.

'A small memento, my dearest love, of a wonderful year,' he'd whispered, his lips caressing the nape of her neck. 'And of a perfect day.'

Their sole disagreement had been when Selena had suggested that if their new baby was a boy, they should follow custom and give him his grandfather's name Petros, which Alexis had firmly vetoed.

'He would see it as a sign of weakness,' he declared.

'But, darling, he's still your father,' Selena protested. 'No matter what he's done, you can't want this estrangement to last for ever. Besides,' she added, 'if we make the first move, then we occupy the moral high ground.'

'I doubt he knows such a thing exists,' he returned, his mouth twisting. 'And the baby will be a girl. My heart tells me so.'

A daughter who would be called Maria, a decision already mutually and joyfully arrived at, which had caused Madame Constantinou to weep with happiness.

And maybe it was still early days to talk of reconciliation between Alexis and his father, and she should wait and allow time to do its healing.

'So here you are, *agapi mou*.'

She jumped a little as her husband's voice reached her.

Alexis came to stand behind her, his arms sliding round her, his hands resting gently on the mound of her belly. 'I thought Nicos advised you to rest.'

'I wanted to unwind a little. Perhaps wait for the moon to rise.'

'We'll watch for it together. And then you must obey your doctor's orders.'

She said, keeping her voice casual, 'Is Nicos still here?'

'Yes, in the dining room drinking coffee with Mama. He said to tell you he asked Xander if he would prefer a sister or a brother, and our son replied he was hoping for a donkey.'

She giggled. 'He's talked about nothing else since the Stephanides foal was born.'

'Perhaps I should ask Takis if he would sell it. We can tell Xander it is a gift from the baby.' He paused. 'How is our little one?'

'Remarkably peaceful for a change. And seems to have changed position.' She relaxed against him. 'But my back has started to ache, so perhaps I've spent too much time on my feet. A massage later would be much appreciated.'

'It will be my pleasure.' He kissed the top of her head and they stood in silence for a while, simply content to be together, until Selena moved, sharply and uncomfortably.

'What is it?' Alexis was alerted instantly.

'My back. It's not just an ache any more.' She drew a deep breath. 'I think maybe I should go and lie down while you tell Nicos I seem to be having contractions. Quite quick ones. And warn Mama and Eleni, too.'

He said hoarsely, 'Ah, dear God,' and lifted her gently into his arms, carrying her swiftly and safely to their bedroom.

'This should not be happening here like this,' he said as he placed her on the bed, and helped her out of her pleated silk dress. 'I should have insisted that we stayed in America, where you would have the best of care.'

'As I shall get from Nicos.' She reached up and stroked his cheek lovingly. 'Because I want this baby born here, as you were, with everyone I love around me. It—it's important to me,' she added, her voice shaking a little.

'Ah, *matia mou*,' he said softly and bent and kissed her.

Left alone, Selena felt absurdly calm.

A perfect day, Alexis had called it, and this would be its unexpectedly perfect ending.

The contractions were getting stronger, and she made herself relax and breathe through them, each one bringing her a step closer to the moment when she would hold their new child in her arms.

A baby conceived one magical afternoon as the early autumn sun turned the temple columns to fire.

Our little Maria, she thought, or—maybe—it might be Petros, after all. I'll just have to trust Apollo the Healer. And she smiled.

* * * * *

If you enjoyed
THE INNOCENT'S SHAMEFUL SECRET,
why not explore these other
SECRET HEIRS OF BILLIONAIRES *stories?*

THE SHEIKH'S SECRET SON
by Maggie Cox
THE DESERT KING'S SECRET HEIR
by Annie West
DEMETRIOU DEMANDS HIS CHILD
by Kate Hewitt
THE SECRET TO MARRYING MARCHESI
by Amanda Cinelli
BRUNETTI'S SECRET SON
by Maya Blake

Available now!

'I'm going to leave, Scott, and I suggest you don't try to stop me.'

He straightened, his broad shoulders squaring as he faced Sarah with narrowed eyes. 'Are you planning on leaving me for good?'

'I don't know yet. We'll have to wait and see.'

'What does that mean, exactly?'

'It means I need some time away from you, Scott. Time to think and to work out what I should do.'

'I don't want you to leave,' he growled. 'Look, I'm sorry for what I did. Sorry I jumped to conclusions.'

'No,' Sarah said, resisting the temptation to accept his apologies and stay. 'Scott, we don't even *know* each other. I can see that now. We got married way too quickly. All we have between us is lust. And that's not enough for me. I need to have a husband who truly loves me and trusts me unconditionally.'

'You expect too much.'

'Perhaps. But I refuse to settle for less.'

Marrying a Tycoon

Australia's most eligible tycoons
meet their match at the altar!

Magnate Scott McAllister believes he has the perfect
compliant wife—until she defies him! Suddenly he
discovers the passionate nature she hides…
and is determined to awaken it!

The Magnate's Tempestuous Marriage

Available now!

Tycoon Byron Maddox doesn't do commitment, but
shy PA Cleo intrigues him instantly! He wants her in
his bed—but will he want her to wear his ring?

Look out for Byron and Cleo's story, coming soon!

You won't want to miss this dramatic, passionate duet
from Miranda Lee!

THE MAGNATE'S TEMPESTUOUS MARRIAGE

BY
MIRANDA LEE

First Published in Great Britain 2017
By Mills & Boon, an imprint of HarperCollins*Publishers*
1 London Bridge Street, London, SE1 9GF

© 2017 Miranda Lee

ISBN: 978-0-263-92520-3

Printed and bound in Spain
by CPI, Barcelona

Born and raised in the Australian bush, **Miranda Lee** was boarding-school-educated, and briefly pursued a career in classical music before moving to Sydney and embracing the world of computers. Happily married, with three daughters, she began writing when family commitments kept her at home. She likes to create stories that are believable, modern, fast-paced and sexy. Her interests include meaty sagas, doing word puzzles, gambling and going to the movies.

Books by Miranda Lee

Mills & Boon Modern Romance

Taken Over by the Billionaire
A Man Without Mercy
Master of Her Virtue
Contract with Consequences
The Man Every Woman Wants
Not a Marrying Man
A Night, A Secret…A Child

Rich, Ruthless and Renowned

The Italian's Ruthless Seduction
The Billionaire's Ruthless Affair
The Playboy's Ruthless Pursuit

Three Rich Husbands

The Billionaire's Bride of Vengeance
The Billionaire's Bride of Convenience
The Billionaire's Bride of Innocence

Visit the Author Profile page
at millsandboon.co.uk for more titles.

PROLOGUE

SARAH SAT AT her desk, twiddling her thumbs, bored to tears. Thank God it was Friday. Only a couple of hours to go and the working week would have ended, as would her tedious stint in Contracts and Mergers. Sarah hadn't become a lawyer to spend her days filling out forms and asking people to sign on the dotted line. Anyone could do that. It didn't take four years of study, doing a law degree.

When she'd been offered a job at the prestigious legal firm of Goldstein & Evans, Sarah had imagined herself becoming the champion of the underdog, righting wrongs and representing innocent people in court. Instead, in the seven weeks since she'd joined the firm in January, she hadn't even come close to setting foot in a court. She'd spent one week in Conveyancing, two in Trustees and Wills and then two in the family law section, which had not been to her liking at all. Still, at least it had been more interesting than what she'd been doing this last fortnight.

Sarah was infinitely grateful that next week she would be moving on to the criminal and civil defence team, which was more her cup of tea. They had a pro bono section where some of the lawyers—usually the new ones, she gathered—were assigned to people who needed but could not afford legal representation. Sarah was looking forward to that.

Meanwhile, she rolled her eyes as they returned to her laptop where she'd been filling in time, doing some research on a client who was coming in to sign a sales contract at three o'clock. For a diamond mine, no less! His name was Scott McAllister and he was supposedly some hotshot mining magnate whom Bob— her current mentor—said she should have known. Apparently he'd been on the TV a lot lately, because of a nickel refinery that was going bust, whose threatened closing down would cost a lot of jobs. Sarah wasn't a great watcher of news programmes so she didn't have a clue who he was.

The Internet, however, had a reasonable amount of information on Scott McAllister. One of Australia's youngest mining magnates, he had his finger in a lot of mining pies, having interests in iron ore, gold and coal as well as nickel and aluminium. And now diamonds, she added to the list. Apparently, he'd got his start after his prospector father had died over a decade earlier, the son soon discovering that two of his parent's seemingly worthless purchases of land held hidden treasures. One had some decent-sized deposits of iron ore underneath which had originally looked like useless rock. The other was chock-full of brown coal.

Bingo! Good old Dad. Luck, it seemed to Sarah, had played a big part in this McAllister's success. Not according to Bob, however, who insisted their client was a very astute man, who had a history of buying rocks of his own and turning them into diamonds, for want of a better word.

'Several reports stated that the diamond mine he's buying today is all mined out,' Bob had told her earlier today. 'But a man like McAllister wouldn't be buying it if that were the case. Clearly, he knows something that the present owners don't know.'

He'd sounded full of admiration for the man. Sarah wasn't quick to admire any man. But she'd looked him up just the same out of sheer curiosity.

Clicking onto a different site, she encountered a photograph of him that didn't tell her much other than he was very tall and very well built. It had been snapped at a work site where all the men, including the owner, were wearing yellow safety vests and yellow hard hats. The caption underneath disclosed it was a recent photo, taken at the nickel refinery last month during a strike. It was impossible to see what McAllister really looked like as he was also wearing sunglasses. Amazing how much the eyes told you about a man's looks. What she could see of his face was large and tough-looking, with suntanned skin, a strong nose and a squared jaw that could have been carved out of granite. A frown on his high forehead gave him a thoughtful look, but the set of his mouth was hard and uncompromising. He was reputedly only thirty-five, but he looked older. Not married, she'd also read, and decided that wasn't surprising. He didn't look like the type of man many women would take to, despite his wealth.

Bob's phone started to ring. Muttering a swear word under his breath, he swept it up to his ear. Thirty seconds later he swore even harder.

'Sorry,' he apologised to her. 'But McAllister has arrived early and the other parties aren't here yet. Neither have I finished reading through this damned complicated contract. Look, could you do me a favour and go down and welcome him? Take him up to the boardroom on the next floor and get him a coffee, or a drink or whatever he might like. You're good at that sort of thing.'

Sarah had no doubt she was. She'd been doing nothing much but getting coffee for Bob and his cohort since she started in this section. Might as well have been a waitress as well as a clerk. But her mother had taught her good manners, and excellent social skills. So she just smiled and said it would be her pleasure.

He beamed back at her. 'You are such a good girl,' he said.

Sarah might have taken offence if Bob had been any less than the sixty-three years he was. She was twenty-five years old. Twenty-six this year. Hardly a girl!

Rising, she smoothed down her skirt and pushed her hair back from her face before making her way from the office and along the hallway to Reception, glad in a way to have something to do. And to be honest, she was quite curious about the man she was about to meet, curious to see what he looked like without those sunglasses.

She spied him straight away, sitting all alone on one of the black leather two-seaters that dotted the large reception area. Dressed in a dark grey business suit, a white shirt and a rather dreary navy tie, he was leaning back with his arms outstretched along the back of the couch, his right foot hooked up over his left knee. His shoes, she noted, were clean but far from new. Fashion, she realised, was not one of this man's long suits. Maybe mining magnates didn't care about such things.

Disappointingly, his eyes were closed, but she could see the rest of him more clearly. His hair was dark brown and cut very short on top, and even shorter at the sides; a very macho look, which suited him. His nose was bigger than she'd originally thought, but his face could handle it. His mouth was wide and his top lip on the thin, slightly cruel side. His bottom lip was fuller, though not full enough to soften his hard face.

Even before he opened his eyes, Sarah knew Scott McAllister wasn't a traditionally handsome man but there was something about him that she found perversely appealing. Odd, since she'd never been attracted to big macho-looking males, always finding them physically intimidating. She much preferred lean, elegantly handsome men who had more brains than brawn.

She stopped a metre short of his feet and cleared her throat. 'Mr McAllister?' she said, a sudden burst of nerves making her voice higher than she would have liked. Her drama teacher at school had once called her voice lilting. She found it a touch girlish, not a voice designed to make a great impact in court. But she was working on it.

His eyelids rose, and she finally saw them. His eyes...

An icy grey, with surprisingly long lashes. Not hard. But definitely on the cold side. Yet strangely hot at the same time. Hot and hungry. They took her in with one long sweeping glance, *all* of her, making her breath catch and her cheeks colour. Not a fierce blush but a blush all the same. How humiliating!

'That's me,' he drawled as he unfolded himself and stood up, towering over her own five feet eight. And she had heels on as well! Not high heels admittedly, but still...

Her neck craned as she gazed up at him, her mouth having gone annoyingly dry. Suppressing a groan, she surreptitiously licked her perversely dry lips and adopted what she hoped was still a sophisticated persona.

'The present owners of the mine aren't here yet,' she said with one of those coolly composed smiles she could summon on autocue. 'So Mr Katon sent me down to look after you till they arrive.'

He didn't return her smile. Just stared at her, his eyes like molten steel.

A returning heat started up deep inside her, melting her core and making her want to do and say the most outrageous things. The control she had to exert over herself was enormous.

'If you'll follow me, sir,' she suggested, still coolly polite on the surface.

'Sweetheart,' he said, a small smile now lurking at the corners of that cruel yet sexy mouth. 'I'd follow you into hell.'

Sarah's mouth dropped open, the realisation hitting her with a certainty that was as strong as it was seductive that she felt exactly the same way about him.

CHAPTER ONE

Sydney, fifteen months later...

SCOTT STOOD AT the window behind his desk, staring blindly out at the view. Not that there was much of a view. The office block that housed the head office of McAllister Mines stood in the southern end of Sydney's CBD, not down at the more picturesque harbour end of town. There was no soothing water to look at. No sparkling Opera House. No beautiful parks or gardens. Just traffic-clogged streets and rather boring buildings.

Not that anything would soothe Scott that Monday morning. Never in his life had he felt such emotional upheaval. He'd been distressed when his father had died. But death, Scott decided, was easier to cope with than betrayal. He still could hardly believe that Sarah would do this to him. They'd only been married a year, yesterday their first wedding anniversary. And whilst Scott harboured a degree of distrust in the female sex, Sarah had been different from the women responsible for his cynicism. *Very* different. That she would cheat on him seemed...incredible.

The text—with photos attached—had arrived on

his business phone last Friday afternoon, shortly after he'd finished meeting with a Singapore billionaire who was staying on the Gold Coast, and whom Scott hoped would help solve his current cash-flow problems. Fortunately, he'd been alone at the time, as his first reaction had been utter shock. Followed by total disbelief. Gradually, however, he was forced to accept the evidence before his eyes. The incriminating photos, after all, had been crystal-clear, all of them stamped with the time and the date when they'd been taken. At lunchtime that very day.

And then there had been the accompanying message.

Thought you might like to know what your wife is getting up to when you go away.

It had been signed, 'A friend'.

Hardly, Scott thought bitterly. More likely a business enemy of his, or a jealous female colleague of Sarah's. His wife was the sort of girl who would inspire jealousy in other women. *And* in her husband. Not that that meant Sarah was innocent. His father used to say that if something looked like a duck, waddled like a duck and quacked like a duck, then the odds were pretty high that it was a duck. It didn't take Scott long to accept that his wife was having an affair with the superbly dressed, very handsome bastard who featured in those damning photos.

Scott would never have thought himself capable of the kind of black jealousy—and almost uncontrollable fury—that had seen him abandon his PA, Cleo, on the Gold Coast to finish his business negotiations for him, making the excuse that Sarah had been taken ill, then flying straight home to confront his adulterous spouse.

But he hadn't confronted her straight away, had he?

A measure of guilt—or was it shame?—curled in his stomach at what he had done.

He'd meant to have it out with her immediately, still harbouring some vain hope that there might be a logical explanation to this nightmare. But when he'd strode into their apartment that evening, she'd literally thrown herself at him, seemingly overjoyed by his cutting his business trip short to be with her. Her kisses had been wildly passionate, more so than usual. Whilst their sex life up till now had been more than satisfactory, Sarah was not an aggressive partner. She always left it up to him to make the first move; to take the lead in bed matters. Not that night, however. She'd been quite bold with her actions, touching him intimately as she'd kissed him.

Guilt, he decided now in retrospect.

Perversely, after she'd fallen asleep that night, exhausted from their sexual marathon, *he'd* been the one who'd felt guilty. Crazy, really. Why should he feel guilty? *She* was the guilty one. *She* was the adulterer, not him.

She'd blatantly lied to him about what she'd done that day—telling him she'd been shopping at lunchtime for a fabulous anniversary present for him. But he knew exactly what she'd been doing at lunchtime that Friday.

He'd left her then and gone to his study where he'd acted like the Neanderthal he felt like, drinking himself into oblivion before passing out on the sofa.

Which was where she'd found him the next morning.

And where their final ugly confrontation had begun...

It hadn't been pretty, Scott still stunned by the accusations Sarah had thrown at him. And the names. In the end, she'd walked out on him. And she hadn't come back.

By Sunday night Scott was forced to accept that Sarah might never come back.

Something that should have pleased him no end, but, perversely, it hadn't. As much as he wasn't the type of man who would countenance having a wife he couldn't trust, Scott couldn't get past the niggling doubt that maybe he'd been wrong to jump to the conclusion he had. Maybe he'd made a terrible mistake.

A knock on his office door startled him out of his troubling thoughts. 'Yes?' he bit out as he turned away from the window.

Cleo came in somewhat tentatively, the look she gave him speaking volumes. There was worry in her dark eyes and concern on her face. Scott had given her a potted version of the truth when he'd arrived this morning, knowing that it would be impossible to keep lying to Cleo. She wasn't just his PA. After three years of working closely together she'd become his friend as well. She'd been more shocked than he was, if that were possible, declaring her disbelief openly.

'Sarah would never be unfaithful to you, Scott. That girl loves you to death!'

Yes, well, he'd always thought so too. But obviously, he was wrong. Cleo, as well.

Scott would have shown her the photos, if he still had them. But he'd given the phone in question to his head of security last Saturday afternoon to have the damned things investigated.

Showing Harvey the photos of his wife with another man had been mortifying to say the least, but he simply had to make sure the photos were genuine and discover who had sent them. Plus he wanted to find out everything he could about the man involved. Lord knew what he would do once he found out his identity.

The man in the photos was facially handsome but he wasn't as tall or as well built as Scott, his frame on the lean side. Elegant, though. And a snazzy dresser. Scott hated him with a passion.

'Harvey just rang to say he was on his way up,' Cleo said, interrupting his jealous train of thought. 'Do you want me to get you both some coffee?'

Scott had been waiting for Harvey to report back to him all morning, but now that the moment was here he wished he'd never started on this course of action. He should have made Sarah stay and talk to him; should have insisted on her explaining those photos. Though what explanation could there possibly be? She hadn't denied their veracity. Her outrage that morning had been directed at him, and what he'd done the night before. Okay, so he should have shown her the photos as soon as he arrived home but he hadn't. Naturally, he'd still been too angry with her the following morning to apologise for what she called his caveman mentality. Her attempts to put the blame on him had almost worked, too. After she'd stormed out of the apartment, he'd begun to think that maybe she was innocent.

Till he'd looked at the photos again.

Scott's teeth clenched down hard in his jaw after which he glanced up at his patient PA. 'No coffee right now, thank you, Cleo,' he told her, doing his best to sound normal and not like a man about to face a firing squad. 'Oh, and, Cleo...thanks for standing in for me last Friday. I don't know what I would do without you.'

Cleo shrugged. 'Afraid I didn't do you much good. The investor made it obvious that he didn't like dealing with a female, especially one who's under thirty. Still, if you want my opinion, you're better off without his money. I didn't like the look of him at all. He had shifty eyes.'

Scott smiled a wry smile. Cleo had the habit of judging people by their eyes. And strangely, she was usually right. She'd prevented him making errors in judgment several times. And she had liked Sarah, had thought her the loveliest, nicest girl. He supposed no one could always be right.

'I'll scratch him off as a potential partner, then,' he said.

'That would be my advice. Still, you'll need to find someone else quick smart, Scott, or you'll have to shut down the nickel refinery. Maybe the mine as well. You can't keep running both at a loss indefinitely.'

'Yes, I know that,' he bit out. 'Look, do some research and see who might be open to investment. Someone from Australia maybe. Ah, Harvey's here. Come in, Harvey.'

Cleo left them to it, Harvey's poker face revealing absolutely nothing as he walked in. Harvey was in his mid-fifties, a big burly man and totally bald, with a craggily handsome face, an uncompromising mouth and cold blue eyes. He'd spent twenty years on the police force and another ten as a private detective before he'd become Scott's head of security. His bouncer-like appearance made him an excellent bodyguard, a job he'd done for Scott on occasion. Being a successful mining magnate did have its hazards, especially when a mine had to be closed, even temporarily. Despite his blue-collar appearance—Harvey was wearing jeans and a black leather bomber jacket—Harvey was also an IT expert, an invaluable security tool in this day and age.

Scott shut his office door then waved Harvey to one of the two armchairs in front of his desk.

'So what have you found out?' he asked straight away, hiding his escalating tension behind a brusque tone.

Harvey's eyes carried the closest thing to compassion that Scott had ever seen in them.

His heart sank, his stomach swirling with sudden nausea. Slumping into his office chair, he scooped in a deep breath then let it out slowly. 'From the look on your face, I presume you haven't any good news to tell me.'

'No.'

A man of few words, was Harvey.

Scott gathered himself in readiness for the worst. 'Okay, shoot,' he said.

Harvey leant forward and placed Scott's phone on the desktop before settling back into the chair.

'First things first,' he said matter-of-factly. 'The phone used to send you those photos was a throwaway. Couldn't be traced.'

'I suspected that,' Scott said. 'Were they real, though? The photos?'

'Yes. They weren't doctored in any way.'

Scott swallowed the bile that rose in his throat. 'What about the dates and times they were taken?'

'Also real. I was able to confirm everything by checking the hotel's security vision. They have cameras set up everywhere.'

'And what hotel was it?'

'The Regency.'

Scott's gut tightened. The Regency was a five-star hotel that was a stone's throw from the building where Sarah worked. 'What else have you found out?' he asked, resigned to more bad news.

'I spoke to a member of the bar staff who was working last Friday at lunchtime. He remembered Sarah.'

Of course he did, Scott thought grimly. Any man who wasn't blind would remember Sarah. She was a stunning-looking girl with long creamy blonde hair, big blue eyes and a mouth that would tempt Saint Peter himself. Add to that a slender but shapely figure that was always housed in softly feminine clothes and you had a package that drew every man's eye— and kept it.

Scott had never forgotten the first moment he'd laid eyes on her. It had been just on fifteen months ago. He'd been in the process of buying a clapped-out diamond mine he'd had a hunch about and had arrived early for an appointment at Goldstein & Evans, a Sydney legal firm he always used for signing business contracts. Sarah had been sent to greet him, acting more like an accomplished hostess rather than the newly graduated lawyer that he'd soon found out that she was. Scott had fallen madly in love at first sight. She'd confessed to him one week later on their third dinner date that she'd been similarly smitten with him.

And he'd believed her. Three months later she'd become his wife. One year later, it looked as if she was about to become his ex-wife.

Scott cleared his throat. 'What else did the barman say?'

'He said they looked pretty cosy together. Sat off in a very private corner. Didn't drink much. Just talked. Then after about fifteen minutes, they upped and left.'

'Right,' Scott bit out. They both knew exactly where they'd gone. The photos had told the story. First, the man had gone to Reception and booked a room. Then they'd ridden up in the lift and gone into the room, not emerging till forty-five minutes later.

'On the plus side, the barman did say he'd never seen her in there before,' Harvey added.

Terrific. But there were other hotels in Sydney's CBD. Heaps of them.

'The guy looked familiar, though,' Harvey went on. 'Been there with some other woman on a few occasions. A brunette.'

'Did you find out who he was?'

'Yup. His name is Philip Leighton. Mid-thirties. A lawyer.'

'And he works for Goldstein & Evans.'

'Spot on. In the family law section. He specialises in divorces. Society divorces mainly. People with money. His own family is wealthy. His father's a senator. Word is Mr Leighton has his eye on going into politics himself. He's not married and doesn't have a permanent partner. Quite the ladies' man, according to a work colleague of his I spoke to this morning. "A silver-tongued charmer" was the way this chap described him.'

Scott tried to blank his mind out to where that silver tongue might have been, but it was impossible, a black cloud of jealousy descending to darken his mood further. He hated being taken for a fool. And Sarah had taken him for a fool. Her outrage last Saturday morning had all been a sham to deflect attention away from her own guilt. The plain truth was Sarah had allowed herself to be seduced by that smooth-looking bastard.

Maybe if you hadn't been going away on business so much lately, it wouldn't have happened...

God, now *he* was making excuses for her!

Scott sat up straighter in his chair before sending his head of security what he hoped was a composed look. 'Is there anything else you have to tell me about my wife's relationship with this Leighton fellow?'

'Only that she didn't go to him after she left you on Saturday. He owns a house on the North Shore, and there's no sign of her—or her car—at his address.'

Was he relieved at this news? He didn't feel relieved. His gut churned some more.

'She's probably gone to stay at Cory's,' Scott muttered. 'He's her best friend. Sarah met him at university.'

Scott didn't elaborate, mostly because he didn't know all that much about the circumstances behind his wife's close friendship with the young architect. It came to him suddenly that he didn't know all that much about his wife's past all round. She'd told him during their whirlwind courtship that her mother was dead and she was estranged from her father and her only sibling, an older brother. There'd been a bitter divorce when she was a teenager, with the brother siding with the father, despite the bastard being unfaithful to his wife. He'd never questioned her further about her past. He'd also never grilled Sarah over her friendship with Cory, mainly because he wasn't worried about Cory. He rather liked the fellow. And Cory liked him back.

He probably doesn't like me now, Scott thought. *Not after Sarah told him what I did last Friday night.* And she would have. She told Cory everything. They were like two teenagers sometimes, laughing and chatting to each other on the phone for hours. Scott would have liked to be a fly on the wall at Cory's place right at this moment. Though possibly he wouldn't find out anything. It was Monday, after all, and both of them would be at work.

Suddenly, Scott wanted Harvey gone so that he could make some enquiries of his own. He stood up and strode around his desk where he stretched out his hand.

'Thank you, Harvey. You have gone over and above. I am most grateful.' At least he now knew where he stood. Though he still didn't know everything. And it was eating away at him. Did Sarah love this man? Had she ever loved *him*? Scott could have sworn she did. But then, he could have sworn she would never have cheated on him.

And she had.

'My pleasure, boss,' Harvey replied, rising to take

Scott's hand. 'Sorry I wasn't able to bring you better news.'

'Like our one-time Prime Minister said, Harvey, life isn't meant to be easy.' Or love. Because he still loved his unfaithful wife. Lord knew why!

As soon as Harvey was out of earshot, Scott took out his personal phone and brought up the number for Sarah's workplace. When he found out she wasn't at work, having called in sick, he wasn't sure what to think. Sarah never took days off, going into work through thick and thin. She loved her job, especially since being stationed permanently in the firm's pro bono section, which helped people without the funds to pay for a lawyer. She'd worked on a variety of cases so far, including one of unfair dismissal plus several sexual discrimination cases, most of which she'd won. It certainly wasn't like her to take a day off work without good cause.

Scott frowned. Clearly, Sarah was still upset. But with him, or herself? Maybe she'd only been unfaithful the once. Maybe she regretted it as soon as she'd done it. Maybe that was what her behaviour last Friday night was all about, her trying to make it up to him for what she'd done.

Suddenly another truly appalling thought occurred to Scott. Maybe she'd run off with this Leighton fellow, taken off interstate or even overseas.

Scott's heart did a savage somersault, then stopped entirely. 'Is Mr Leighton in this morning?' he somehow managed to ask the receptionist, his voice gravelly.

'Yes, he is, sir. Do you wish to speak to him?'

Relief had Scott quickly pulling himself together.

'Not right now,' he said firmly. But he would. Soon. First, he needed to speak to Sarah. Depending on what she revealed, *then* he would be speaking to Leighton. Though he doubted it would be a civil conversation. Scott could feel his temper rising just thinking of that sleazebag who thought nothing of seducing another man's wife. There was no doubt in his mind that Leighton would have been the one to make the first move. Sarah simply wasn't the un-faithful type.

Or was she?

It was becoming clear to Scott that maybe he didn't know his wife at all!

Shaking his head, he brought up Sarah's number, expecting that it would be turned off as it had been all weekend. It wasn't, but it *was* engaged. Who was she talking to? Cory? Or her sleazebag lover? On top of that, where was she? Still at Cory's place, probably.

Scott didn't hesitate, knowing that he couldn't sit there in his office, stewing over things. It was time to face Sarah again, and to insist on knowing where he stood. Grabbing his suit jacket from the coat stand in the corner, he dragged it on then hurried out to where Cleo was sitting behind her desk, frowning at her computer screen.

'Have to go out, Cleo. Things to do. Cancel any appointments I have this afternoon and take the day off. You deserve it.'

Cleo glanced up and sighed. 'You're not going to do anything foolish, are you, Scott?'

'Not today. I did that just over a year ago.' When he'd married a girl he didn't really know, a girl who was an enigma in this day and age.

Because Sarah had been a virgin when he'd met her.

As he hurried down to the basement car park Scott began to wonder with some of his old, well-earned cynicism towards the opposite sex if she'd had a secret agenda in keeping her virginity so long. Now that he thought about it through less rose-coloured glasses, how she'd got through high school then university untouched, along with two years backpacking around the world, was beyond credibility. Unless she'd always wanted to marry money, and had seen her virginity as the perfect weapon to ensnare the right rich sucker. Namely him.

Scott had come across quite a few gold-digging females since he'd made it big in the mining world, but none of them had been virgins. Not even close.

He hadn't questioned Sarah's inexperience at the time; had accepted her explanation that she'd been wary of the opposite sex for a long time because of her cheating father. He'd also eagerly swallowed the added seductive reason that till he came along, she'd never met a man who'd made her really *want* to have sex with him.

Not that she'd used the word, *sex*, at the time. She'd said make love with. Naturally. Nothing crude about Sarah. She was the epitome of femininity, her large liquid blue eyes windows to a soul that seemed as pure as it was incapable of deception.

More fool him. They said love was blind. *Well, they were right*, he thought angrily as he jumped into his Mercedes and gunned the engine. But he wasn't blind now. And he wanted answers. Lots of them!

CHAPTER TWO

'Are you sure you don't need me to drive you over there, sweetie?' Cory said. 'You might need help to carry things. I can easily take the afternoon off work. We have flexible hours here.'

'Thanks for the offer, Cory, but I would rather do this by myself.'

'And you're quite sure Brutus won't be there?'

Sarah winced at the new nickname Cory had given Scott. Not that it wasn't appropriate. The man was a brute to do what he had last Friday night, all under the guise of passion. Her stomach curled at all that she had allowed, and enjoyed. That was the worst part. How much she had enjoyed Scott's ravishing of her entire body. Her face flamed at the memories of the humiliating noises she'd made, the way she'd pleaded with him not to stop.

When she'd found out the next morning that he'd acted out of jealousy and revenge, her shock had quickly changed to fury.

'You don't honestly think he wouldn't have gone to work, do you?' she said bitterly. 'Trust me when I say only an atomic bomb landing on him would keep Scott away from his precious office on a Monday morning.'

'From what you told me, last Saturday morning was a little like an atomic bomb going off.'

Sarah was not a girl who lost her temper easily. But when she did…

'I can't tell you how mad I was!'

'You don't have to, sweetie. I saw for myself when you arrived at my place. You were spitting chips. Till you started crying, that is. For a while there over the weekend, I thought I might need a life jacket.'

'Please don't try to make me laugh, Cory. That man has broken my heart. What he did was unforgivable.'

'Why? Because he acted like a lot of men might have acted? When I found out Felix was cheating on me I was hotter for him than ever.'

'But you didn't love Felix and I *wasn't* cheating on Scott!'

'But it looked like you were…'

Sarah groaned. 'I know. I know.'

'I think you should call Scott and explain why you were at that hotel with your lawyer friend. After all, from what you told me those photos were pretty damning.'

'And then what? Scott says sorry and we just go on to live happily ever after? I don't think so, Cory.'

'Ah, I forgot. You're a Scorpio. They never forgive or forget. By the way, has it crossed your mind to wonder who might have sent those photos in the first place?'

Sarah sighed. 'I've thought of little else all morning.'

'Someone you work with perhaps?'

'No one comes to mind.'

'It has to be someone who hates you. Or hates Scott, more likely.'

'It could be the same person who told Phil those rumours about Scott and Cleo,' Sarah speculated.

'You're absolutely right,' Cory said excitedly. 'I told you from the first that it had to be some kind of set-up. Otherwise how could he or she have been at the right place at the right time to take incriminating photos of you and Phil at that hotel? That's far too coincidental. I think it has to be someone you work with, Sarah, someone who saw you leave together that lunchtime and followed you.'

'But who?'

'Search me, sweetie. But I do know that if you let this destroy your marriage, then that person has won.'

'It's Scott who's destroyed our marriage,' Sarah bit out. 'The bottom line is he didn't truly love me, or trust me. He jumped to conclusions and didn't give me the chance to explain. He didn't care how I would feel because he doesn't really care about me. I can see now that I was only ever a trophy wife to him. Arm candy to be trotted out at social functions, with the added bonus of sex whenever he felt like it. When he's home, that is. Which has become less frequent during the last six months. I actually thought he'd cut his business trip short last Friday so that he could be with me on our anniversary weekend. What a fool I was in more ways than one.'

'Wow. You're still very angry with him, aren't you?'

'You can say that again. Look, I must go. The cleaners would have left by now and I want to be out of the apartment before Brutus gets home.'

'You're calling him Brutus now,' Cory pointed out drily.

'Yes, well, if the cap fits he should wear it.'

'You do realise that hate is the other side of love.'

'Oh, yes. I certainly do. Have to go, Cory. I'll see you tonight.'

'I'll bring home Chinese,' he offered. 'And some nice wine.'

'That would be lovely. Thank you.'

Tears pricked at Sarah's eyes as she hung up. Cory was a dear friend. And so kind. Whatever would she have done without him this last weekend? Sarah didn't have a lot of friends, her few girlfriends from high school having drifted away after she left school and went to university. The same thing happened after her poor mother died at the end of her first year of university. Unable to study—or grieve properly— Sarah had taken off to go backpacking around the world. By the time she returned to Sydney University two years later, her earlier student friends had also moved on. Her own fault, Sarah accepted, having not kept in touch via social media, depression dogging her footsteps for such a long time, especially during the first twelve months of her backpacking getaway. Europe remained a blur, nothing of the incredible sights she'd seen touching her soul or brightening her life. She'd gone from city to city in a fog.

It wasn't till she'd reached Asia that the fog had finally lifted. Maybe it was the truly warm, gentle people she'd met there. The children had been especially adorable and the twelve months she'd spent travelling through India and Thailand and Vietnam had banished her depression, plus her bitterness, showing her that maybe it was still possible for her to overcome her wariness where men were concerned and find love. Maybe even get married and have children. Though that had seemed a stretch at the time.

Still, by the time she'd come home to Sydney and resumed her studies, she'd been way more open to at least try to give the opposite sex a chance. Though she'd still had no intention of leaping into bed with anyone in a hurry. It had been an enormous stroke of luck that during her first semester back at Sydney University she had met Cory.

Sarah smiled wryly as she looked back on that time in her life when she'd imagined Cory might just be 'the one' to banish her wariness of the opposite sex—and sex—for good. Not only was he fun to be with, he was quite gorgeous to look at. Very sexy with his blond hair, bedroom blue eyes and a buffed body. Whilst she hadn't been mad for him—she hadn't known what it was to be mad for a man back then—she had found him attractive. He'd seemed attracted to her as well. The 'life of the party' type, Cory had insisted she join the university book club and movie club with him and soon they'd been going out together. It wasn't till she'd finally decided to take the big step and sleep with him that Cory had been forced to come out and tell her he was gay. Apparently, up till then he'd tried to deny it, even to himself, afraid that his parents would reject him.

But they hadn't. After that, she and Cory had remained close friends, with Cory dating like-minded men and Sarah eventually becoming resigned to going to her grave still a virgin. Because no way had she been going to go to bed with a man she didn't truly love and trust; trust being the most important part. In her mind she'd pictured a straight version of Cory. Someone sexy and intelligent and kind.

Unfortunately, she'd never seemed to meet such a man, not even when she'd left university and secured a plum job at a large legal firm that had wall-to-wall men walking around their corridors, men who had showed they found her *very* attractive. But none of them had done anything for her, not even Phil, who was super handsome and super intelligent and really very nice. Too old, however, at thirty-five. Despite her lack of success so far, Sarah had kept dreaming that one day she would meet Mr Perfect, fall madly in love, get married and have at least two perfect children.

Scott McAllister's entry into her life had blown apart all Sarah's misconceptions over the kind of man she imagined falling madly in love with. For starters he looked even older than Phil, yet it turned out he was the same age. He *wasn't* traditionally handsome. Neither was he university educated. In fact he'd never even gone to high school, spending his teenage years travelling the outback with his prospector father. Despite that he was obviously intelligent, a self-made mining magnate with perhaps more money than manners; the strong silent type who didn't waste words, or time. Superbly fit, with the body of a champion boxer, Scott McAllister was a macho man in every way, bull-dozing his way into her life with very little subtlety.

She'd never forgotten the moment they'd first met, Scott's normally icy grey eyes glittering with a raw animal lust as they'd travelled over her from top to toe. Her body had flamed in instant response. And from that moment, she'd been his. It had been just a matter of time. He'd asked her out to dinner within five minutes of meeting her. And she'd been unable to say anything but yes, her body consumed with desires which had been as corrupting as they'd been compelling. How she'd lasted three dinner dates before succumbing to Scott's constant requests to go home with him afterwards was a miracle.

Of course, he'd been stunned over her being a virgin. But not displeased. In fact, he'd seemed quite taken by the idea, confessing that he'd never been with a virgin before.

Soon, she hadn't been able to get enough of his big, strong body and his passionate but still considerate lovemaking. She'd adored how safe she always felt in his arms. How truly loved. Feeling truly loved was just as important to Sarah as the physical pleasure she experienced in bed with Scott.

Or so she'd believed, till last Friday night...

'Don't think about that night any more, Sarah,' she lectured herself aloud. 'You'll go mad if you do.'

Shaking herself violently, Sarah went in search of her handbag and car keys. Ten minutes later she was heading across the harbour bridge, making a list in her head of what she had to collect from the apartment. Work clothes, of course. She couldn't call in sick every day. Neither could she go in there wearing the jeans she'd worn all weekend, or one of Cory's track suits, which was what she was wearing today. She needed toiletries too, of course. And the rest of her make-up. After her argument with Scott last Saturday morning she'd bolted out of the apartment with nothing much. Her going-out clothes could wait till another day, she decided. Sarah couldn't see herself going out much in the near future.

But what if there wasn't another day? What if Scott threw her out and changed the locks? It was the sort of thing her husband might do. He was not a man who took kindly to being crossed, let alone betrayed. As much as she hated to admit it, those photos had made her look as if she were having an affair with Phil.

No, she would have to collect all of her things today whilst she had the chance.

Sarah took the exit that would lead her down to McMahon's Point, her attempts at a more pragmatic mood disappearing with the sight of the tall block of harbourside apartments that she'd called home for the last year. A happy home, she'd thought, despite Scott's many absences. She *did* understand that he'd been facing business difficulties during the last few months, with the mining industry not doing well, metal prices at an all-time low. His frequent business trips still irked her, however. But his returns were always extra joyful, last Friday night even more so after what she'd been through that day. She'd woken last Saturday morning with a delicious smile on her face.

Of course, at the time, she'd still been ignorant of the true reason behind Scott's insatiable sexual appetite. And whilst the memory of some of his demands was slightly shocking, she'd also been secretly thrilled that at last she'd taken a less passive role in their sex life. On top of that, if she was brutally honest, she'd found her husband's highly erotic lovemaking wildly exciting and extremely satisfying, her many orgasms addictively powerful. So she'd dressed and gone in search of Scott the next morning, already turned on by the thought that they would have the whole weekend together.

She hadn't been turned on for long…

Sarah groaned, annoyed with herself for revisiting that painful encounter one more self-destructive time.

'What a bastard,' she muttered angrily as she drove down the ramp that led to the underground car park, stopping at the bottom to swipe her key card through the machine so that the security gate would rise. It was annoyingly slow, but at last she could drive through. Despite telling Cory confidently that Scott would be at work, she was still relieved to see that his car space was empty. She parked her red hatchback into her own allotted spot, locked it up then hurried over to the bank of lifts that would carry her up to the luxury high-rise apartment that Scott had bought a week before their wedding. Clearly, he'd wanted to impress his new bride. And he had.

It wasn't the penthouse. But it was only one floor down from the top and was simply huge, its wide wraparound balconies having views to die for. The plate-glass window in the main living room formed a perfect frame for the Sydney Harbour Bridge, with the Opera House underneath it in the distance. The same view applied to the floor-to-ceiling windows in the master bedroom. At night, it all looked magnificent.

There were two guest bedrooms aside from the master suite, each with their own en-suite bathroom. Add to this two formal receptions rooms, a home theatre, another powder room, a gym and a kitchen that was large enough to satisfy the caterers Sarah employed whenever they had a dinner party. Which up till now was at least once a month. Sarah could cook but cooking several courses for a large number of guests—their dinner table seated twelve—and trying to play hostess at the same time was beyond her.

After letting herself into the apartment Sarah stood in the spacious marble-floored foyer for a long moment, remembering how impressed she'd been when she'd first seen this place. Despite not having been brought up poor—Sarah came from a middle-class upbringing—she'd been overawed by the size of the rooms, the expensive fittings, the elegant imported furniture. She hadn't wanted to change a thing.

Sarah made her way down the carpeted hallway to the master suite. As she entered what had once been her favourite area in the house Sarah kept her eyes averted from the neatly made king-sized bed, trying desperately not to think of how it had looked last Saturday morning with its tangled oil-stained sheets, not to mention the long blue chiffon scarf that had been draped haphazardly over the black lacquered bedhead. But despite her best efforts, Sarah *did* think about it, her mouth drying at the memory of how turned on she'd been by Scott binding her wrists like that; how he'd poured body lotion all over her and proceeded to show her exactly how much he knew about a woman's secret fantasies. When he'd flipped her over and poured more lotion over her entire back, she hadn't protested. Just pleaded for him not to stop.

And he hadn't…

Oh, God.

Must not cry over last Friday night any more, she told herself sternly. *Just get all your things and go!*

Sarah hurried on across the thick cream carpet and into her walk-in wardrobe, where she pulled down the two large cases that they'd taken on honeymoon to Hawaii. She'd been happy then. Very happy. Scott had seemed happy, too.

Maybe that had all been an illusion. Maybe he'd always been a bit bored with her in bed. Sarah imagined most rich men eventually got bored with their trophy wives, which was why they traded them in for newer models a lot, or took mistresses, women who did even more kinky things than what she'd done with Scott last Friday night. Maybe those rumours about Scott and Cleo were right after all.

No—*no*. She refused to believe that. She hadn't really believed it then and she didn't believe it now!

Well, if you didn't believe it, why did you rush into the hotel bathroom and throw up when the investigator said there was not a shred of evidence of Scott and Cleo having an affair?

The truth was, at the back of her mind, where old tapes from the past were stored, she *had* believed it. Of course she had. She was programmed to believe that most husbands were cheaters, and their silly wives forgave them much too often. It haunted Sarah to think what she would have done if the investigator had said the opposite. That yes, Scott was having an affair with Cleo. Would she have confronted him? Would she have left him? Was she actually leaving Scott *now*?

Perversely, the question of her forgiving him would probably never arise. Clearly, her husband believed she'd been unfaithful. More than likely, he would want a divorce. If there was one thing Sarah knew about Scott it was his black-and-white thinking. It was both his strength, and his weakness. Whilst she'd always admired his straight-down-the-line character, plus his total adherence to honesty and integrity, Scott could be slightly one-eyed over things. There was no grey in his thinking. Forgiveness would not come easily to Scott, not if he thought he'd been wronged. And he believed she'd wronged him.

Pushing aside this distressing train of thought, Sarah turned to begin taking some clothes off their hangers when she suddenly caught sight of herself in the full-length mirror that hung on the back wall of the walk-in wardrobe. Dear God, but she looked a fright. Her hair was awful, having not been washed properly in days. The need to recondition her straw-like locks with her own lovely products suddenly became a necessity. It wasn't as though Scott was going to come home unexpectedly and catch her, naked, in the shower. She had plenty of time to be out of here before he left his precious office.

But she still hurried, wanting to be out of the place as soon as possible.

CHAPTER THREE

WHEN SCOTT DROVE into the underground car park and saw Sarah's car parked in its allotted space, the frustration he'd been feeling at not finding her at Cory's house revved up a notch. She hadn't been sick at all, had she? She'd snuck home here whilst she believed he was at work, no doubt to collect her things, plus possibly anything else she fancied. He'd heard of such things happening to other men who'd come home to find their houses stripped clean.

This furious thought stayed with him during his ride up in the lift, his angry mood lessening once he let himself into the apartment and discovered that nothing was missing. The artwork was still on the walls and all the expensive knick-knacks still there.

When he called out to Sarah, however, she didn't answer, leaving him with the sudden far more awful thought that maybe she'd brought her car back—it had been a Christmas present from him—and just left it, then taken a taxi off to Lord knew where. The realisation that Sarah might have done such a thing, that she was leaving him permanently, and that he would never have the opportunity to find out the truth, made him feel sick to the stomach.

It was then that he heard the faint sound of water running somewhere. Recognising the sound, Scott dashed down the hallway to their bedroom, where he noted that the bathroom door was shut. Clearly, Sarah was having a shower. Scott could not deny the relief that flooded him. But there were some other confusing emotions too. Surely he wasn't hoping she'd come home seeking a reconciliation? Surely she didn't expect him to *forgive* her?

Glancing to the left of the bathroom door, he saw that their walk-in wardrobe door was open. Scott marched over to stand in the doorway, his hands curling into fists as he stared down at the two open cases on the floor, his teeth clenching down just as hard. Okay, so she wasn't looking for a reconciliation, then. Good. All Scott wanted—or so he told himself—was an explanation of her actions.

It had niggled him all over the weekend that he'd been neglecting Sarah lately, leaving her alone way too much, not giving her the kind of attention that she'd obviously been secretly craving. Last Friday night had shown him that, at least. She'd been a different woman in his arms that night. Wild. Wanton. Bold. The kind of woman another man would do anything to get, and whom a husband would never be able to forget.

Scott groaned at the possibility that Sarah might not have been thinking of him when he'd been inside her last Friday night. She might have been thinking of the man she'd been with that lunchtime, whom she'd probably been with every time he went away on business.

The sudden silence from the bathroom coincided with his mood turning very dark indeed. Scott threw off his suit jacket and tie, flicked open the top button of his shirt before kicking off his shoes then stretching out on top of the bed. His stomach churned as he waited for his unfaithful wife to emerge, but his mind remained hard, and cold.

Sarah dried herself quickly, wrapping her wet hair in a towel before grabbing the long pink silk robe that she kept on a hook on the back of the bathroom door. Not an overly sexy garment, it was nevertheless pretty and very comfy with three-quarter-length sleeves in the kimono style. No way was she going to leave it behind. Pulling it on over her flushed nakedness, she tied the sash loosely around her waist before tossing the towel aside then drying her hair properly with her hair dryer, which was much more powerful and efficient than Cory's. *With a much better result*, she thought as she ran her fingers through her long straight silky locks before opening the bathroom door.

The unexpected sight of Scott lying on top of the bed brought a gasp of alarm to her lips. Despite his nonchalant pose—his hands were linked behind his head and his ankles were crossed—there was nothing nonchalant in his chilly grey gaze.

'I gather you're not staying, then,' he drawled, his voice as cold as his eyes.

Sarah could not find her tongue, fear drying her mouth and making her heart pound behind her ribs. She'd never been afraid of Scott before but she was at that moment.

'No,' she croaked out at last. 'I...I just came to get my clothes.'

Scott uncrossed his ankles then sat up abruptly.

'There's no need to sound so petrified, Sarah. I would never hurt you. Surely you must know that.'

'You hurt me last Friday night,' she threw at him.

'Now you know that's not true,' he ground out, standing up and towering over her. 'You enjoyed every moment of what we did last Friday night. Please don't add hypocrisy to your adultery.'

Her hand whipped up to slap him but he grabbed it before she could make contact with his face.

'Come now, Sarah,' he said. 'Let's try to act like adults here, shall we?'

For a long moment she thought he was going to pull her against him. The intent was in his glittering grey eyes. Her already racing heartbeat accelerated further. When he released her, she could not decide if she was relieved or disappointed.

A rueful smile twisted his mouth.

'I suggest you go put some more clothes on and we adjourn to somewhere less…dangerous. I find myself unable to focus with you nearly naked like that. All I can think of at this moment is how much I still want you, despite everything.'

Sarah's mouth dropped open at his startling admission. Even more startling was the fact that she wanted him just as much. How perverse was that?

It rattled her, this irrational but powerful urge she had to close the space between them, to reach up and kiss that hard, angry mouth of his.

His eyes narrowed on hers, perhaps glimpsing the crazy jolt of desire in their depths. For suddenly, his hands reached out to grab her shoulders, dragging her against him as his head swooped.

She could have fought him; could have been the

ultimate hypocrite. But she didn't, moaning under his quite brutal kiss, melting against his big strong body, her lips and her hips betraying her own frantic desire.

Insane. All of it. Sarah knew he still thought she'd been unfaithful to him. But right at this moment she didn't care what he thought. All she cared about was the here and now. And the here and now was turning her on to a degree that surpassed even last Friday night. She kissed him back with a quite savage need, telling him without words that she was still his, no matter what he believed.

When he wrenched his mouth away, she groaned in protest, staring up at him with wide glazed eyes.

'God, Sarah,' he ground out, then kissed her again, obliterating every sensible thought with the wildness of his passion. His mouth stayed glued to hers whilst he stripped off her robe, tossing it aside with careless abandon. By then she was trembling violently, but not from cold. A large lock of hair had fallen across her face, and eyes. She stared through the strands up into his lust-filled face. It thrilled her, this knowledge. She was already lost to the mindless world he'd created last Friday night; a world of excitingly erotic pleasure, which didn't seem to possess a conscience, only a craving for constant satisfaction.

His hands slowly scooped her hair back from her face, bundling it into a tight bunch at the nape of her neck as he pulled her head back, his captive hold doing wicked things to her traitorous body. He glared down at her, his face flushed, his breathing ragged.

'Don't go thinking this means I forgive you,' he threw at her.

'I've done nothing for you to forgive,' she managed

to say. But he only laughed, then kissed her again, kissed her and touched her till she was beyond protest, let alone wordy explanations. When he scooped her up and dumped her sideways across the silvery-grey quilt, she just lay there, quivering with need whilst he hurriedly undressed. And then he was on top of her, and inside her, and she was making those animal noises again, holding him tight as she opened her legs wide and wrapped them high around his back. She moved with him, moaning his name and reaching for that moment when her flesh would shatter around his. Her climax came with a rush, making her cry out, wracking her body with wave after wave of pleasure. It was brilliant. Glorious. She gasped with the electric pleasure of it all.

But the moment the tsunami of ecstasy began to wane, common sense blasted back into her brain, bringing with it the crushing reality of what she had just done.

'Oh, God,' she groaned, her tongue giving voice to her acute dismay. How could she have let him do that, believing what he still believed? How could she have enjoyed it, knowing this? At least last Friday night, she hadn't known about those photos, or what Scott had been thinking.

Her face crumpled as she agonised over what he was thinking now. Possibly that she was the worst person that had ever lived.

His face betrayed a momentary confusion before his eyes grew cold once more. He withdrew abruptly, not looking down at her as he stood up and dressed. After that, he picked up her robe, his gaze scornful as he tossed it over her outspread nakedness.

'I'm going into the kitchen to make coffee,' he grated out. 'Join me there when you're decent. We need to talk.'

Sarah squeezed her eyes tightly shut as she gripped the robe with both hands, already regretting everything, the heat of the moment fast becoming a distant memory. What on earth had possessed her? She couldn't make sense of it. It wasn't love that had propelled her into Scott's arms just now. It had been something more basic than that. Something primal. Something that would not be denied. Was it just lust, or a cavewoman instinct that demanded she lay claim to her man in the way women had been doing since time began?

That last explanation made some kind of sense, Sarah conceded as she put her robe back on and made her way reluctantly to the kitchen. But she didn't like either thought. Because both made her vulnerable to Scott. He had to be made to understand that she could not stay with a husband who didn't believe what she was about to tell him. She didn't want his forgiveness. She wanted his trust!

Sarah swallowed at the sight of her bare-chested husband busying himself in the kitchen. Lord, but he was a superbly built man, muscles rippling down his back, his arms, his chest. At the beginning of their relationship, she'd found his size somewhat intimidating, till he showed her just how gentle and tender he could be. After that she'd felt supremely safe in his arms. Not so any more. He no longer inspired that safe, secure feeling in her. Instead, when she looked at him, her whole insides quivered with a fear that was dangerously exciting. *He* was dangerously exciting. She wondered if this was what her poor mother had felt for her serial cheater of a husband. Sarah could see now that desire could make a woman weak. Weaker than love, in a way. It was a horrifying concept and one that she vowed to fight.

Such thinking forced her to ignore the stupid feelings that kept fluttering in her stomach. 'Why aren't you at work?' she asked brusquely as she levered herself up on one of the breakfast bar stools.

He turned and carried two mugs of steaming black coffee over to the counter.

'I couldn't work so I went looking for you,' he said. 'You weren't at Cory's so I came home.'

Sarah refused to feel flattered by his leaving his precious office to search for her. 'You could have called me.'

He made a scoffing sound. 'Don't you think I tried? You had your phone turned off all weekend. Then, today, when I tried again, it was engaged.'

She dropped her eyes to the coffee. 'I was probably talking to Cory.'

'Not Philip Leighton?'

Her head jerked up, her eyes widening.

'Don't play the innocent with me, Sarah. I know who the man in those photos is.'

Any confusion Sarah was suffering from suddenly changed to outrage. 'My God, you had those photographs investigated, didn't you?'

'What on earth did you expect?' Scott slammed back at her. '*You* wouldn't tell me anything. You refused to offer any explanation.'

'I'd have told you everything if you'd shown me those photos when you first arrived home. But you didn't. You had to have your pound of flesh first, didn't you?'

'Perhaps I was distracted by the passion of your greeting,' he said with cold anger in his eyes. 'And the quality of your lies.'

'My *lies*?' Sarah was genuinely thrown. 'What lies?'

'You said you'd gone out at lunchtime last Friday and bought me a special anniversary present,' he elaborated in rock-hard tones. 'I knew for a fact that you were actually in a bar, then up in a hotel room with another man.'

Her cheeks reddened with anger. 'I *did* buy you an anniversary present,' she insisted heatedly. 'In a boutique on my way out of the hotel where I wasn't doing anything to be ashamed of. I can show it to you if you like.'

'It's a little late for that, don't you think? Unless I'm very much mistaken, we're headed for the divorce court. I'm just grateful that we decided to put off having children for a couple of years. Thank God for the pill, is all I can say.'

Sarah's whole world stopped with his mentioning the pill; she couldn't remember the last time she had taken it. Had it been last week, last month? The blood drained from her face at the thought of the possible consequences of her naivety and she groaned.

'What is it?' Scott said as he glared at her. 'What's wrong?'

CHAPTER FOUR

As SARAH FACED the unfaceable, the blood continued to drain from her head, which had been in a total fog since all this started. But it wasn't in a fog now. It was in shock.

She'd fainted a couple of times in her life before. Neither time had been pleasant. But she remembered how she'd felt just before it happened. The clamminess. The sense that everything was tipping out of kilter. This time she recognised the symptoms before disaster struck, slipping off the stool to sit on the tiled floor with her head dropping down between her knees.

'What in hell are you doing?' she heard Scott ask in an alarmed voice. 'Are you ill?' he added, coming round to hunker down next to her. 'Should I call an ambulance?'

'No,' was all she could manage. It was just shock and, yes, a lack of food perhaps. She hadn't had any breakfast. Or lunch for that matter, Cory having gone to work this morning before she got up. He'd fussed over her yesterday, forcing her to eat and drink something. With him gone she'd neglected herself.

'I'll be okay in a minute,' she added weakly at

last. 'Just feeling a bit faint. If you want to help then make me some toast. And put plenty of honey on it.'

'Toast,' he repeated, sounding totally flummoxed. But he stood up and his trouser legs disappeared so Sarah assumed he was doing as asked. Finally, she felt well enough to get up, but her legs were still shaky as she climbed back on the stool and reached for her coffee, grasping the mug with shaky hands. She'd begun to shake inside as well, still not having come to terms with what she'd realised a little while ago. It was said that fate was cruel. But it wasn't fate. It was her own stupid fault.

Sarah smothered a groan, her stomach contracting at the thought that a child might have been conceived after last Friday night. Her stomach contracted with horror at the thought. A baby should be born out of acts of love, not acts of black jealousy. She could also have conceived today, which wasn't much better. But better than last Friday, she supposed. She'd sort of known what she'd been doing just now.

Sarah shook her head in denial of this last thought. She hadn't known what she was doing at all, had she? Not really. She'd been putty in Scott's hands.

Her eyes went to those hands as he spread the toast with butter first. They were large hands. Large and strong, with calluses on their palms from where he'd done hard physical work for many years. He hadn't always been a businessman in a suit.

'Feeling better?' Scott asked as he placed the toast in front of her.

'A little. Thank you.' Avoiding his questioning eyes, she took a few bites of toast, swallowing them down with some coffee.

Thirty seconds passed before he spoke again. 'It's time you told me exactly what happened at that hotel last Friday, Sarah. And I want the truth.'

Sarah placed the mug back down on the white stone counter, took a deep gathering breath then glanced up at his large and uncompromising face.

'The truth,' she repeated, sounding calmer than she felt. For Sarah wasn't at all confident that he would believe her. He might think she was making it all up. Still, if that was the case, then she could suggest he speak to Phil. Phil would back her up.

Half an hour ago, she would have told him to stick his demand for the truth, but things were different now. The possibility that she might be having Scott's baby had changed everything.

Sarah gulped, then started. 'I went there with Phil to meet a private investigator who had some information about you.'

'*Me?*'

'Yes, you. Phil approached me that morning in the staff room and told me he had it on good authority that you were having an affair with your PA, Cleo.'

'*What?* That's ridiculous and you know it!'

Sarah wasn't going to be put off by Scott's bluster. 'Is it? Cleo's an attractive woman. On top of that she's a widow.'

An angry colour slanted across Scott's high cheekbones. 'I am *not* having an affair with Cleo. As for her being a widow, I'll have you know that Cleo is still very much in love with her dead husband. She would never even look at another man, let alone sleep with one.'

'How do you know that?'

He looked totally flummoxed. 'Well...I just know!'

'You know because you talk to her,' Sarah pointed out harshly. 'Which is more than you ever do with me.'

'For pity's sake, we just talk about business, not personal things. We spend a lot of time together.'

'I am well aware of that,' Sarah said drily.

'Look, this is all getting off the point, which is supposed to be you explaining the content of those photos.'

'I'm just getting to that. I was supposed to meet up with this PI in the hotel bar. But he didn't show up. While we were there, waiting for him, Phil got a call saying that he was tied up watching someone from the balcony of his hotel room upstairs and couldn't come down right at that moment, suggesting we come up instead.'

Scott gave her a sceptical look. 'That doesn't make sense, Sarah. Why couldn't he just tell you whatever he had to tell you over the phone?'

'Phil said he didn't like using mobile phones to relay sensitive information, especially when dealing with celebrities.'

Scott made a scoffing sound. 'So I'm a celebrity now, am I, as well as an adulterer?'

Sarah felt her face flushing. 'I know you're not an adulterer, Scott. The man told me there was absolutely no evidence of your having an affair with Cleo, or any other woman; that he'd watched you for weeks and—'

'Watched me for *weeks*? Good God, what is this? Who hired this guy? Oh, I get it. Leighton hired him, didn't he?'

'Well, yes, he did. Look, I know it all seems a bit odd but it wasn't my idea. Phil's a divorce lawyer and was worried about me after he heard the rumours. He asked his usual investigator to look into it without consulting me.'

'Touting for business, was he? Or was it something more personal than that?'

'I don't know what you're talking about.'

'Haven't you wondered yet who might have sent those photos, Sarah? Blind Freddie can see that if what you say is true, then it had to be a set-up. Luring you to the hotel like that. Getting you to go up to a room. Tell me, was the PI actually in the room when you got up there?'

Sarah frowned. 'No…not at first. He left a note saying he had to step out and follow someone for a few minutes. He didn't arrive till some time later.'

'Making it look like you had enough time to have sex with Leighton before you left.'

Sarah's frown deepened. 'But that would mean that…that…'

'That Leighton was the person who set it all up,' he finished for her.

'But why?'

'Why do you think? He's probably in love with you.'

'Oh, that's ridiculous,' she denied heatedly. Yes, he had invited her out to dinner during the week she'd worked under his mentorship. But only the once. She'd quite enjoyed his company but there'd been no chemistry between them. At least on her part. Then she'd met Scott and Phil had become just a friend. Quite a good friend, actually. Sarah often ran into him in the staff room where she occasionally gave vent to her annoyance at how often Scott went away on business. He was always very sympathetic. Still, it was probably her fault that he thought something had gone wrong with their marriage. But she could see nothing in his behaviour to warrant believing he had romantic feelings towards her. He never flirted, or gave her lustful glances. He never stepped out of line. Ever!

'You're quite wrong,' she stated firmly. 'It has to be someone else. Some woman who's probably in love with Phil and followed us because she was jealous.'

'And what? She just happened to know my phone number?'

'It wouldn't be hard for anyone at work to find out your business number, Scott. It would be in the files.'

'That's a stretch, Sarah. Of course, there is an alternative explanation.'

'What?'

'That you actually *are* having an affair with your work buddy.'

Scott's ongoing distrust hit Sarah like a physical blow. She closed her eyes and shook her head.

'It's a well-known fact that an affair can spice up a bored spouse's libido,' he went on ruthlessly. 'And you were a different woman last Friday night. And then again, today. The virgin I met and married would never have acted like that.'

Her eyes flew open, dismay banished in favour of outrage. 'If you honestly think that, then I feel sorry for you,' she snapped.

'Then how do you explain it?'

'You want the truth?'

'That's exactly what I want.'

'When I was told that you were having an affair with Cleo, I didn't want to believe it, but I still went into a total panic. While I was waiting for the PI's report, I began thinking that maybe you'd grown bored with me in bed—that maybe you'd only married me because I *was* a virgin,' she went on before he could agree with her. 'Anyway, I was so relieved when I found out you weren't having an affair that I actually threw up.'

'God, Sarah.'

'Yes. I know. And yet, when you believed that I was having an affair you came home and proceeded to ravage me endlessly, proving that men and women are totally different creatures.'

Scott grimaced as he thought back to his behaviour last Friday. 'I do regret the way I acted afterwards.'

'Really? I haven't seen much regret. You still believe today that I was having an affair and just look at us! Tearing each other's clothes off. It's madness.' Sarah paused as the weight of her words settled in the silence between them. She needed some space away from Scott, time to gather her thoughts and plan her next steps.

'I'm going to leave, Scott, and I suggest you don't try to stop me.'

He straightened, his broad shoulders squaring as he faced her with narrowed eyes. 'Are you planning on leaving me for good?'

'I don't know yet. We'll have to wait and see.'

'What does that mean, exactly?'

'It means I need some time away from you, Scott. Time to think and to work out what I should do.'

'I don't want you to leave,' he growled. 'Look, I'm sorry for what I did. Sorry I jumped to conclusions. Sorry I acted like a bloody idiot. But we've sorted that out now so there's no need for you to leave. We still love each other, don't we?'

'No,' Sarah said, resisting the temptation to accept his apologies and just stay. 'Scott, we don't even *know* each other. I can see that now. We got married way too quickly. All we have between us is lust. And that's not enough for me. I need to have a husband who truly loves me, and trusts me unconditionally.'

'You expect too much.'

'Perhaps. But I refuse to settle for less.' Her mother had settled for less. And look where that had got her? Dead, at forty-five.

'You didn't trust *me* unconditionally,' he pointed out harshly. 'Underneath, you believed I was having an affair with Cleo.'

A guilty colour crept into her cheeks. 'Then I'm as bad as you. Hardly a good recipe for a happy marriage.' Or good parents, she thought bleakly. Of course, there might not be a baby, but Sarah wasn't hopeful.

Still, she might be lucky…

With a heavy heart, she stood up, putting her shoulders back and facing her husband with as much courage as she could muster. 'I'm going to pack now, Scott, then I'll be leaving. And please…don't try to stop me.'

His top lip curled derisively. 'What point would there be in that? You've clearly already made up your mind to go. To abandon your vows. Did they mean so little to you?'

His barb cut her deeply. She'd meant every one of her vows, but how could she stay with Scott if there was no trust between them? She shot visual daggers at him. 'I'll ignore that,' she bit out. 'But if we keep arguing in this way, Scott, I can't see any hope of a reconciliation.'

'And if you keep working in the same law office as that man, then I feel the same.'

That rocked her. 'You can't possibly expect me to quit my job?'

'You will if you ever want me to take you back.'

His comment stopped Sarah in her tracks and she laughed at the sheer arrogance of her husband. 'Take me *back*? Can you hear what you're saying, Scott? It's *me* who has to decide if I'll take *you* back. And right now, I think the answer to that is a definite no.' Despite her heart breaking into little pieces, she lifted her chin and set defiant eyes upon him. 'I'll be at Cory's,' she said, her voice only wobbling a little. 'I'll let you know what I decide in due course.' Sarah hated that she sounded like a lawyer, but it was the only way she could survive at this moment without breaking down.

Scott sank down onto the nearest chair as Sarah left their apartment, but he didn't try to stop her. His words had been reckless and he could have kicked himself for behaving like such a Neanderthal. Did he not know Sarah at all? Of course she wouldn't respond to such arrogant threats!

Scott felt suddenly powerless and bereft. He had wanted his treacherous wife to leave and now she had. So why did he feel that he had just made the biggest mistake of his life?

CHAPTER FIVE

HALF AN HOUR later Scott headed out to see exactly how much Sarah had taken with her. Just about her whole wardrobe, he noted with a sinking heart, only a few of her long evening gowns left behind. He swore as he ran his hands through his hair. This couldn't be happening to him. They'd been happy. He loved her. And she still loved him, no matter what she'd said. It was all a bloody nightmare!

A tortured groan ripped from Scott's lungs as he faced the fact that Sarah had just actually left him for real. It was one thing to talk about a divorce. Quite another to face the reality of it.

God, but the place seemed so empty without her, he thought despairingly as he made his way back through the bedroom. At the foot of the king-sized bed he stopped, his gaze settling on its crumpled quilt, plus the indentation of where her body had lain. It seemed impossible that just over an hour earlier they'd been on that bed together, making love with a passion that had blown his mind.

Sarah had said that they didn't love each other, that it was just lust, but Scott didn't believe that. He'd experienced plenty of lust in his life and what he felt for

Sarah went way beyond that. He'd loved Sarah from the first moment he'd set eyes on her. Loved her and wanted her like a man possessed.

'And damn it all, I'm going to get her back!' he vowed, and marched down the hallway to what he called his thinking room. Not his study. His gym.

Over the past year whenever Scott was presented with a business problem—and there'd been plenty—he'd come in here, climb up on the exercise bike and pedal away. Not too fast. Just a nice steady rhythm whilst he stared blankly out at the view and set his mind to analysing the problem, usually coming up with a plan of action before too long.

Scott wasn't so optimistic of success this time. He'd finally accepted that his actions last Friday night had been beyond the pale. He hadn't been too nice to Sarah just now as well, letting his temper and his male ego get the better of him. She'd every right to be more than furious with him. He'd really messed things up this time.

Scott suspected that the odds of his securing Sarah's forgiveness any time soon were about the same as the odds of his keeping that nickel refinery open. But he had to try something, or go quietly mad. Changing into his gym gear, he climbed up onto the bike and began to pedal. And pedal. And pedal, his normally pragmatic brain firing up his feet as he struggled with his emotions. Despite knowing that he still loved Sarah, he was also totally frustrated with her.

Why couldn't she see that it was Philip Leighton who'd orchestrated this whole nightmare? It was obvious to him. Why wasn't it obvious to her?

Clearly Leighton was a clever devil, plus an ongoing risk to Scott's goal of getting Sarah back. If she continued to work with him he might somehow poison her mind further. Or come up with some other devious scheme to make trouble for their marriage.

Scott groaned in despair at the realisation that he was powerless to persuade Sarah to quit her job. She wasn't the kind of girl who wilted under fire. She was a courtroom lawyer, after all. But Leighton wasn't the only problem—the startling lack of trust in their marriage would have to be addressed too.

Still, it galled Scott to think of Leighton taking advantage of this moment, hanging around his wife every day at work, worming his way into her affections. If Scott had any chance of saving his marriage, he'd need to speak to Leighton—man to man.

Scowling, he glanced up at the clock—twenty past four. Jumping off the bike, he retrieved his phone from his trouser pocket, brought up the right number and pressed call.

'Goldstein & Evans,' the female receptionist answered. 'How may I help you?'

'Good afternoon. My name is McAllister. Scott McAllister. I was hoping to see Mr Leighton this afternoon.'

'Have you seen Mr Leighton before, Mr McAllister? Are you a client of his?' Clearly, she didn't recognise his name. So much for his being described by Leighton's investigator as a celebrity.

'No. We've never met before.'

'I'm afraid Mr Leighton is busy in a meeting for the rest of the afternoon. I could make an appointment for you to see him later in the week.'

Scott smiled a wry smile. He wasn't about to be

put off by that old 'in a meeting' chestnut. 'That won't do, I'm afraid. I need to see Leighton today. It's urgent. I'm sure he'll see me if you let him know who's calling.'

'Might I ask you the reason you wish to see Mr Leighton?'

'No. It's personal.'

'Personal…'

'Yes. Please tell him that I will be there to see him at five-thirty.' And he hung up.

After a quick shower, Scott put on his new black suit, a crisp white shirt and skinny red tie. Since marrying Sarah his wardrobe had been overhauled and updated, Sarah insisting that he had to look the part if he wanted politicians and wealthy business colleagues to take him seriously. Which he did. He also didn't want to feel in any way inferior to the man he was about to meet. He couldn't help but notice how well dressed the lawyer had been in those photos. Very elegant. Scott knew he could never look elegant. He was much too tall, too broad-shouldered, too big. But he could look impressive. And intimidating. And seriously rich. Which was what he was aiming for.

A final check on his appearance in the vanity mirror left him mostly satisfied. Handsome he would never be but he wasn't ugly by a long shot. His facial features, though on the large side, were symmetrical, his nose was straight and his eyes—which were the same pale grey as his father's—were supposedly sexy. His thick brown hair was annoyingly wayward so he kept it cut very short. He quickly ran a comb through it, glad now that he hadn't shaved, the dark stubble his face was sporting giving his macho looks an added edge. Last but not least he slipped on the gold Rolex wristwatch that he rarely wore but which his father had bought when he'd struck gold two decades earlier. Unfortunately, the mine in question had soon petered out, as had happened with most of his father's finds.

Scott scooped in a deep, gathering breath, picked up his wallet and keys, then set out to do battle with a foe that he vowed not to underestimate. For if he did, things could quickly go belly-up. It was a risk to confront Leighton, but it was a bigger risk to sit back and do nothing. Sarah was upset right now, which could make her vulnerable to a man like Leighton.

Leighton's secretary looked up as he strode into her office, her dark brown eyes showing curiosity as they ran over him. Scott wondered if she knew Sarah; or knew that he was Sarah's husband.

'Mr McAllister, I presume,' she said, smiling as she stood up.

'The one and the same,' he agreed, and smiled back at her.

'Mr Leighton said to take you straight into him the moment you arrived.'

Did he now? Scott thought ruefully as he was shown into his enemy's office.

Leighton was even more handsome in the flesh than in his photos. Handsome and smooth and supremely confident. He came forward to greet Scott with a dazzling smile and hand outstretched. Scott's first reaction was to bypass any pleasantries and just go for the jugular, but he suspected that wouldn't be smart. He had to outmanoeuvre this slime bag, not fall into any of his traps. And there would be traps,

Scott was sure of it. So he took the offered hand and resisted the temptation to crush all his elegant fingers to pulp.

'So pleased to finally meet you, Scott,' Leighton said, doing the old politician's trick of covering their handshake with his other hand, aping a false warmth. 'Sarah has told me so much about you.'

'Really? She hasn't mentioned you,' Scott said, his iron control slipping a little as he pulled his hand away.

A mistake, he quickly realised, Leighton's brows lifting as though he was puzzled by his visitor's attitude.

'I see,' he said slowly, giving a good impression of working out why Scott might want an urgent appointment with a divorce lawyer. 'Would I be right in assuming you're seeking my help in a professional capacity?'

You wish, Scott almost snapped, but held his tongue just in time.

'Actually no,' Scott was pleased to announce. 'That's not why I'm here at all.' And he handed him the phone with the first of the many photos already on the screen. 'I've come to ask if you have any explanations for these photos that were sent to me last Friday afternoon.'

Leighton frowned as he scanned through the photos before glancing up at Scott, his expression seemingly shocked. 'Has Sarah seen these?' was his first question.

'Of course.'

'What did she say?'

Scott recounted Sarah's explanation, letting Leighton think he'd shown her the photos last Friday, not the next morning.

'And you believed her?' he said, sounding surprised.

'Of course,' Scott retorted, ignoring the stab of guilt which accompanied the lie. 'Sarah would never lie to me.'

'Of course not,' the oily bastard said with a smirk. 'If that's what Sarah said happened, then that's exactly what happened.'

Scott adopted his best poker face. '*You* sent me those photos,' he said, his quietly controlled voice a credit to him, considering how furious he was inside. But Scott knew it was never a good idea to let an enemy see weakness. And losing one's temper made a man look weak.

Leighton was clearly taken aback at the unexpectedness of Scott's accusation. 'Why would I do something like that?'

'The why is obvious,' he returned smoothly. 'You want my wife for yourself and you're prepared to do anything to have her, even set her up so that it looks like she was having an affair with you.'

The man actually smiled. 'I'd be careful what you say in the presence of a lawyer, if I were you. That could constitute slander.'

Oh, yes, he was a clever bastard. But Scott was ready for him. 'Don't threaten me, Leighton,' he countered coolly. 'Give me forty-eight hours and I'll know all there is to know about you. All your dirty little secrets.'

Suddenly, Leighton didn't look quite so confident, or so handsome. His cheeks puffed out, his close-

set eyes darkening as he blinked incessantly. 'I…
I've done nothing to be ashamed of,' he blustered before suddenly pulling himself together, clearing his
throat and straightening his tie before speaking again.
'You're nothing but a rough-neck bully, McAllister.
Sarah would be better off without you. You think
I haven't worked out what happened when you got
those photos and that telling little text? You didn't
believe Sarah at all. You came storming home and
did something awful to her. That's probably why she
didn't come to work today. Because she's sporting a
black eye. Or worse.'

'I would never hit Sarah,' Scott said with cold fury,
though he was close to hitting *him*. Still, he had been
close to the mark. He *hadn't* believed in Sarah and
Scott already knew that he would have to work very
hard to get her to forgive him. If she ever did, that
was. Meanwhile, this manipulative creep wasn't about
to go away. But he'd tripped himself up just now.

'How did you know about the text that came with
the photos?' Scott asked. 'I deleted it before I came
here.'

Leighton just smiled. 'What text? I know nothing of any text. Now I think this meeting is over,' he
stated with an arrogance that needled Scott no end.
'Unless, of course, you have something else to say.'

Scott smiled, but somehow he restrained himself.
'Stay away from my wife.'

Leighton smirked again. 'That's up to Sarah, don't
you think? Or do you plan on dictating who she can
have as friends in future? That's the usual tactic for
bully-boy husbands.'

'You're a dead man.' The unwise words fell out of

Scott's mouth before he could stop them. Furious at his stupidity, Scott whirled and marched over to the door, flinging it open then striding quickly past the wide-eyed brunette. He didn't have the satisfaction of seeing the fear that filled Leighton's eyes, or the way the coward slumped down in a nearby chair, his legs having gone to jelly.

CHAPTER SIX

'So let me get this straight,' Cory said as he set out the Chinese food on the breakfast bar in the upstairs kitchen. 'Scott was there when you came out of the shower, after which you had fantastic make-up sex, but didn't make up at all, despite you telling him what really happened at the hotel last Friday and his eventually believing you. Did I get that right?'

'It was never make-up sex,' Sarah refuted heatedly. 'It was just sex.'

'Right,' Cory said slowly, then shook his head at her. 'Not like you, sweetie.'

'No,' she choked out, on the verge of tears again. 'I don't know what's got into me. Ever since last Friday night all I can think about is having sex with that bastard.'

Cory's eyebrows arched. 'Really? Wow. Okay, so what's your problem, then? Why are you here instead of at home in bed with Brutus?'

Sarah grimaced. 'You don't understand, Cory. I married Scott because I was in love with him and I thought he was in love with me. Now I'm not sure he ever loved me.'

'Rubbish. He's always been crazy about you.'

'That's not the same as love. If he truly loved me, and believed I truly loved him, then he would have trusted me. And respected me more. I didn't see any evidence of either last Friday.'

'Oh, come now, Sarah, be reasonable. The man was mad with jealousy at the time. You're a lawyer. You know about temporary insanity. Cut the poor guy some slack.'

'So now he's a poor guy instead of Brutus, is he? You men sure do stick together.'

Cory gave her a droll look. 'I'm just trying to make you see his side of the story. Look, let's start eating this food before it gets cold. What do you think of the wine?'

Sarah automatically lifted her glass to her lips before she remembered that she might be pregnant. Wincing, she put the glass back down again.

'What is it?' Cory asked immediately. 'Is it off?' He picked up his glass and took a sip. 'Nope. Tastes great.'

Sarah suppressed a groan. She hadn't wanted to tell Cory about her pregnancy scare but he was too intelligent to fool for long. 'I...I can't have any alcohol,' she told him reluctantly. 'Not till I find out if I'm expecting a baby or not.'

That floored him. Sarah knew exactly how he felt.

'But you're on the pill,' he said, clearly perplexed.

'I've forgotten to take it lately,' she confessed, still shaken by this realisation. She sighed a heavy sigh. 'Like I said, I'm not myself. My brains have been well and truly scrambled.'

Cory pulled a face. 'Am I right in presuming you didn't tell Scott you'd forgotten to take the pill?'

'Are you mad?' Sarah said, then shuddered. 'Of course I didn't tell him. No way.'

'But why, Sarah? The possibility of your having a baby together might help solve all your problems.'

A weary sigh puffed from Sarah's lungs. 'Spoken like a man again. Having a baby doesn't solve a relationship problem, Cory. If anything it complicates things. Women don't have to marry these days just because they're pregnant. They don't have to stay married, either.'

Cory looked taken aback. 'You're thinking of actually divorcing Scott?'

Just the thought of divorcing Scott made Sarah feel nauseous. 'I didn't say that,' she hedged. 'But I need to step back from my marriage for a while and do some clear thinking.' She sure as hell couldn't think clearly when she was around Scott.

'Perhaps that's not such a bad idea,' Cory said thoughtfully. 'Like they say, distance makes the heart grow fonder. Now eat up. You could be eating for two, remember?'

She ate the food in thoughtful silence, not really tasting it, her mind elsewhere.

A baby, she started thinking. A real live baby. She had always wanted to start a family with Scott, but not like this. So why hadn't she dashed out and bought a morning-after pill today? Why had she just come home here and cried her eyes out, like some helpless idiot?

Because it was too late to do anything now. She couldn't remember the last time she had taken a pill, so reckless she'd been! What a mess she had made of her life.

'You're quite welcome to stay here as long as you like,' Cory offered after they'd finished eating and they were clearing up together. 'There's been a delay in starting the renovations so things will be staying the same for a good while yet.'

'Thank you, darling,' she said, and came round to give him a hug. 'You are such a good friend.'

'True,' he said with a smile.

The front doorbell ringing made his smile fade. 'If that's Felix come to beg my forgiveness then he hasn't a hope in hell.'

Sarah laughed. 'You know you always forgive him in the end.'

'That's because I'm a Libra,' he said soulfully as he headed for the stairs. 'Wish I was a Scorpio, like you. Then I would invite him in for a drink, tip some hemlock into his glass from my poison ring and send him on his way.'

Scott heard Sarah's laughter from where he was standing outside Cory's front door. Not totally broken-hearted by their separation then, he thought rather bitterly. Unlike himself. Maybe he'd been right when he wondered if she'd kept her virginity to ensnare herself a rich husband. Maybe she now planned to take him to the cleaners in the divorce court.

And maybe you should stop thinking like some suspicious jealous fool and set about doing what you came here for. Getting the woman you love back!

'Scott!' Cory exclaimed on opening the door. 'It isn't Felix,' he called up the stairs. 'It's Scott.'

No more laughter now. Just silence.

'Come in,' Cory said. 'Sarah and I have just finished eating. No food left I'm afraid but I can offer you some wine…'

'I just came to talk to Sarah,' Scott said stiffly, not sure what to make of the drily amused tone in Cory's voice.

'She's upstairs in the kitchen. I dare say you'll want to be alone. I'll go down the local for a while,' he added, grabbing a jacket from the coat rack on the wall and disappearing out of the front door.

Scott was making his way up the steep steps when Sarah appeared at the top of the staircase. Her arms were crossed and her expression was not happy.

'I thought I told you not to contact me,' she said sharply. 'I said I would contact you when I was ready.'

Anger did become her, he thought, noting her wildly glittering eyes and high colour. She'd looked like that this afternoon when he'd been inside her. There was something about Sarah in a temper that stirred the caveman in him. The temptation to ignore her hostile body language and just sweep her into his arms was acute. He liked the thought of her fighting him, of her lashing out at first. He would welcome her blows. Absorb them. Be aroused by them. Scott felt confident that she would surrender to him in the end. But at what cost afterwards? He'd come to reason with her, not ravage her.

Scott shoved his hands into his trouser pockets, ignoring his erection and adopting a composed demeanour. 'I assumed you might like to know what happened when I dropped in on Leighton just now,' he said in a creditably calm voice.

Sarah sucked in sharply, her arms falling away to

her sides. 'You *didn't*!' she exclaimed, not sure if she was annoyed or thrilled.

'What did you expect, Sarah? That I would not confront the man who's meddling in our marriage?'

'What…what did Phil say?'

The muscles under Scott's granite-like jaw tightened considerably. 'Look, I have no intention of having this conversation standing on a staircase. Either you come down or I'll come up.'

'I'll come down,' Sarah said, then wished she hadn't. Far better that she have Scott sitting safely on the other side of the breakfast bar than next to her on Cory's large squashy lounge. But she could hardly change her mind now. Scott had already whirled and was stomping down the wooden steps.

Sarah followed him into Cory's far too cosy living room, switching on the overhead lights as she did so, despite there being two corner lamps on already. The last thing she needed right now was to be seduced by a romantic ambience. Bad enough that just the sight of Scott in that brilliant black suit had her practically salivating with desire for him. Weird. She'd chosen that particular suit for him because she'd wanted him to look more sophisticated during his business meetings. More…impressive. Looking sexy had not been on her agenda. But he looked more than sexy in it tonight. He looked…dangerous.

When Scott plonked himself down in the middle of the maroon velvet sofa, Sarah chose an adjacent armchair, perching on the end of it without a shred of her usual social grace. Clasping her hands nervously on her jeans-clad thighs, she swallowed, then leant even further forward.

'So what did he say?' she asked, driven by equal measures of anxiety and curiosity.

'He backed up your story,' Scott replied, his eyes not leaving hers.

A rush of relieved air escaped from Sarah's tightly held chest.

'I could have told you he would. Because it's the truth. Did you, um, show him the photos?'

'I did.'

'I'll bet he was shocked.'

'Not nearly shocked enough,' Scott said drily. 'On top of that, he mentioned the text that came with the photos. Yet I'd already deleted that.'

'I...I don't understand...'

Scott's face filled with exasperation. 'What's not to understand, Sarah? It's plain as the nose on your face. Leighton set you up, then organised for those photos to be taken. *He* sent them, along with the text.'

'I still find that hard to believe.' And she did.

'Believe it, because it's true.'

'But *why*?'

'Leighton is an ambitious bastard. He has his eyes on a career in politics and to be successful you need the right kind of wife. And you fit the bill, darling, in every way. You have the looks, the poise and the smarts. You're a girl in a million.'

Sarah ignored the flattery in his words and concentrated on the heart of the matter. 'But to do what you say he's done is just so evil!'

'It worked, though. You left me.'

'It wouldn't have worked if you'd trusted me.'

Scott's sigh was heavy. 'I know, but surely you can

appreciate how bad things looked. Any man would have been worried.'

'Worried. Yes. But that's no excuse for what you did last Friday night. You should have shown me those photos as soon as you got home.'

Scott smothered a groan. 'Do we have to go through this all again? Look, I know I was wrong and I'm sorry. I made a mistake. All you have to do is come home and we can work through this. We still love each other, Sarah. You know we do. Look what happened today.'

How could she forget? She only had to look at him to remember every mind-blowing moment. She could still feel the effects of that orgasm, deep in her body. Sarah struggled with the various emotions bombarding her; not the least was the temptation to surrender all her pride and common sense, and just say yes. *Yes, I'll come home. Yes, we'll go on as if none of this has ever happened.*

But she couldn't. Because that was what her mother had done. Continuously forgiven the unforgivable and taken her husband back. Sarah now suspected she had a clue as to why she'd done that—the pull of sexual desire and physical satisfaction. But she refused to do that with Scott, no matter how exciting a lover he'd become. A marriage could not be founded on lust alone. It needed love to survive.

'I can't do that, Scott,' she said. 'I'm not ready to come back just yet.'

'When will you be ready, then?' he asked softly.

'I'm not sure I'll ever be ready.'

Sarah was taken aback by the look of horror on his face.

'You don't mean that,' he said, clearly shaken. 'You have to give me a second chance.'

Sarah steeled herself to stay strong. 'I don't *have* to do any such thing, Scott. Like I said, I need time away from you just now.'

Scott sighed and ran his hands through his hair. 'Fair enough. How long do you need?'

How long? Maybe after she found out if she was pregnant or not, she could come to a decision. If there was to be a baby, it would be wrong not to make an effort to fix things between them. Maybe the lust that seemed to be all she felt for Scott at this moment could turn back to love…

'Two weeks,' she said. She would know for sure in two weeks.

Scott looked horrified. 'Two weeks? That's one hell of a long time.'

'Not really.'

'And will you be going back to work during that time?'

'Of course. I'll be going back tomorrow.' And going to see Phil too. She suspected Scott was telling the truth and that Phil was behind those photos, but she wanted to speak to him first to get his side of the story.

'How can you work with someone who set you up like that?'

'I don't work with Phil, Scott,' she pointed out archly. 'He just works at the same firm. I don't have to see him if I don't want to.'

'But you do want to, don't you? You'll run off and see him first thing in the morning.'

Sarah stiffened, her back straightening as her chin

lifted. 'I think I have the same right to confront him as you. To give him the opportunity to give me his version of events.'

'God, I have to get out of here before I say or do something I'll seriously regret,' Scott said, jumping to his feet. 'Two weeks you said? Okay, I'll give you two weeks. But after that I'm done with this marriage.'

Scott's statement shocked her to the core. She'd imagined he would always be there for her if she wanted him.

Sarah stood up to face her very frustrated-looking husband. 'Scott, I…I…' She didn't have a clue what to say. She just hated him looking at her the way he was presently looking at her.

'You don't have to say anything, Sarah. I get the picture. I'm to be made to suffer for what I've done. I can understand you wanting to leave me—I've behaved badly, but I've apologised for that. What I don't understand is why you would continue to associate with the bastard who caused all this trouble in the first place. You want my trust, but won't do me the courtesy of having nothing to do with Leighton. I'm beginning to suspect that you never loved me at all— perhaps this is what you always wanted. A divorce after a suitable time span and a gravy-train alimony which will set you up for life.'

'That's not true!' she denied, horrified. Little did he know it but she didn't need his money. She had quite a bit of her own, inherited after her mother died. How else could she have travelled the world for two years after her mother's funeral?

Of course, he didn't know that. She hadn't told

him. It had been her own secret nest egg, her safety net in case her marriage hadn't worked out.

And it hadn't, had it?

'I don't want any of your damned money,' she threw at him.

'What do you want, then?'

'A husband who loves and trusts me! Look, Scott, we are going around in circles arguing like this. I just think we need some time apart. I'll call you after two weeks and we'll talk.'

He swore, then shook his head at her. His laugh smacked of frustration. 'I don't need any time apart. I want you home, in my bed and in my arms.'

Sarah hated the way her body reacted to his impassioned words. It wanted the same thing. But she knew it wasn't the right thing to do. Scott would think she was weak. Which was what she'd been so far where he was concerned. In the past, she'd given in to whatever he wanted to do. She hadn't made a fuss when he'd kept going away on business. She hadn't insisted he take her with him sometimes, like that last time when he'd only been going to a hotel on the Gold Coast. She'd bitterly resented his taking Cleo. Sarah knew she should have said something instead of pretending she didn't mind.

But she refused to play the compliant, accommodating little wife any longer. It was time to make her stand.

'I'm sorry, Scott,' she said staunchly, 'but that won't be happening. I believe I have the right to ask for this small space of time. Please respect my wishes. I'll be in contact after the two weeks are up.'

He stared at her as if he couldn't believe this was

happening to him. But his shocked expression soon changed to a sullen anger and he stormed out of the house, slamming the front door as he did so.

A stunned Sarah staggered over to the sofa and slumped down in the middle of it, all the breath leaving her lungs. She shuddered to think what he'd say if she ever had to tell him she was pregnant, but she'd kept the possibility a secret from him.

Oh, God. A baby was a complication she didn't need right now. She needed to sort her marriage out without feeling pressured to make unwise decisions. She needed Scott to stay well away from her.

The front door opening and closing had Sarah's back stiffening against the sofa. But it wasn't Scott. It was Cory.

'I just saw Scott roaring up the road like some kind of maniac,' her friend said as he sat down next to her. 'I gather, by the look on your face, you didn't sort anything out.'

'Oh, Cory,' Sarah cried unhappily, then burst into tears.

CHAPTER SEVEN

A SET OF red lights forced Scott to abandon his suicidal speed. He still slammed his hands against the steering wheel, angry more with himself than Sarah. He'd lost his temper. That was the long and the short of it. Though, damn it all, she *was* being very difficult. How did she think he felt about having her work in the same place as that slime ball?

Still, he hadn't handled that at all well, had he? Not that negotiation was ever his strong point. He hated having to manipulate people, or promise to deliver things that down deep he knew he couldn't deliver. Which was what being a businessman was all about. He much preferred the simple life of a miner. Mining was cut and dried. You either had a mine worth mining or you didn't.

Scott imagined marriage was pretty much like a mine. You either had one worth keeping, or you didn't. Till this last hiccup, Sarah had been a wonderful wife. He couldn't have asked for better. His accusation that she'd married him for his money did not ring true. A materialistic woman wouldn't have refused his offer of a free credit card and a generous monthly allowance, the way Sarah had. She'd have taken everything he was offering, instead of adopting an independent stance, informing him that she earned a good salary and preferred to pay for her own clothes and things.

The lights turned green and Scott drove on more slowly, his mind turning over as he tried to work out what Sarah wanted from him other than more abject apologies. If he thought flowers and diamonds would work, he'd try them, but he suspected such gestures would cement him as being one of those husbands who thought he could buy his wife's forgiveness and affection. Which left what? Communication, he supposed. Women did like to talk. But how could he talk to her when she'd forbidden him to contact her?

Two weeks. Two long bloody awful weeks. He hadn't been two weeks without Sarah since their wedding night. He hadn't been a *week*. Even when away on business, he would ring her every night and tell her how much he loved her and missed her. Scott ached to call her right now but he knew without even trying her number that she would not answer.

Two weeks. He was going to go stark raving mad!

Sarah cried on and off all night, the next morning seeing her so drained and puffy-eyed that she rang in sick again. Of course, this time she would have to get a doctor's certificate, the firm she worked for being very strict about such things. In a way she was glad that she wouldn't be going into work. She didn't want to face Phil just yet. To discover he was behind the problems in her marriage and to tell him exactly what she thought of him. On top of that, she could ask the doctor when she could reasonably take a pregnancy test.

Cory gave her the number of his local surgery but she wasn't able to get an appointment till late that afternoon. By the time Sarah was ushered in to see the doctor shortly after five, she was feeling both anxious and stressed. Going to the doctor always made her feel that way. But the elderly lady doctor was very nice, taking her blood pressure then listening to Sarah carefully as she explained that her marriage was going through a difficult time, that she was now temporarily separated from her husband but was worried that she might have fallen pregnant.

The doctor frowned at her. 'I hope you don't take this the wrong way, Mrs McAllister, but is the reason for your separation anything to do with domestic or sexual abuse?'

'Good God, no!' Sarah blurted out.

'Sorry. But I had to ask. Over the years I have seen lots of women in my surgery who are victims of such things, and I have to check this isn't the case with you.'

'No—no. The sex between us is fine. I just… We just… Well, it's hard to explain.'

'I understand. Would you like to see a marriage guidance counsellor, perhaps?'

Sarah knew instinctively that Scott wouldn't agree to that.

'Not just yet,' she hedged. 'Not until I find out if I'm pregnant or not. When do you think I will know for certain?'

'Probably not for another week at least. It takes a while for the egg to be implanted in the lining of the womb, which then releases the hormone that the test is looking for. There is a blood test you could take but I see no reason for that. Best to just wait till your next period is due then use one of the home testing kits you can buy over the counter. They're quite reliable. There's no need to come back to see me. I understand you don't actually live in this area. Meanwhile...' She picked up a pad and jotted something down on it before giving it to Sarah. 'I would suggest you take one of these vitamin tablets daily. They have folic acid in them. Also keep off the alcohol. Do you smoke?'

'No.'

'Good. Now, do you need a doctor's certificate for today?'

'Yes, I do. I didn't sleep much last night and I simply couldn't go to work this morning.'

'You do look tired. And I can see you're quite stressed. Your blood pressure is up too. I think, under the circumstances, that you should take the rest of the week off. I won't give you any sleeping tablets but I want you to rest. Watch TV. Read a book or two.'

Sarah doubted she could read at the moment but she liked the idea of resting and watching TV.

'Thank you so much,' she said when the nice doctor wrote out the certificate.

'My pleasure,' the woman said, and smiled at her. 'Look after yourself, dear. And come back, if you ever want to.'

'Ah, you saw Dr Jenkins, did you?' Cory said when Sarah relayed her visit in detail that evening. 'She's a love. Getting a bit long in the tooth but still very with it.'

'I liked her a lot. Now what are we going to eat tonight?'

'Search me. Pizza do? I don't feel like cooking.'

'Neither do I. But I'll cook tomorrow night.'

A phone started to ring, Sarah recognising the tone immediately. She retrieved her phone from her bag and saw that it was Scott. Her breathing quickened, just seeing his name. Her heart wanted to answer him, but her head stepped in and said no. He had to learn to respect her wishes. But it was with some regret—and a smattering of guilt—that she switched off the phone.

'Scott, I presume?' Cory asked.

'Yes.'

'So when are you going to tell him about the baby?'

'When there *is* a baby, Cory. Not before.'

'I didn't realise you could be this tough.'

'Neither did I,' she said with some surprise.

'Poor Scott.'

'There's nothing poor about Scott,' she said ruefully.

'True. Still, I wouldn't wait too long to tell him, if it turns out you *are* pregnant. Scott's not a man who likes to be kept in the dark.'

Sarah blinked as Cory's words sank in and she imagined telling Scott the news about a baby. For all his anger and arrogance, Scott would be a wonderful father. But would he welcome the news of a child conceived during the darkest moments of their marriage, or would it spell the end for good? For a moment, Sarah felt a faint chill run down her spine. Only time would tell.

CHAPTER EIGHT

By Friday that week Scott was tearing his hair out. And so was Cleo.

'You can't go on like this,' she told him as she walked into his office and deposited another mega-sized coffee on his desk. 'All you do is drink coffee when you should be seeing about your cash-flow problems. If you don't do something about it soon, your whole business might go down the tubes.'

'I don't give a hoot about the business,' he growled, and meant it. Which shocked him. But not as much as the apparent disintegration of his marriage. 'All I care about is Sarah.'

'Then ring her, for pity's sake!'

'I've tried. She's switched her phone off.'

'Then go and see her. It's not as though you don't know where she is.'

'If I thought a personal visit would work, I would. But you didn't see her the other night. She'd just slam the door in my face.'

'What on earth did you do to make her so mad at you?' Cleo asked.

Scott sighed. 'Aside from my myriad mistakes where the photos were concerned, I suspect it was my demanding she quit her job which put the tin hat on everything.'

'Oh, dear,' Cleo said, and shook her head. 'Never a good idea to make your wife's decisions for her, especially about her career. Sarah is an intelligent girl, Scott, who can make her own decisions. It sounds like you just come over as a controlling husband. Trust me when I tell you that's not the way to a girl's heart.'

Scott was taken aback by the note of irony in Cleo's voice. 'Sounds like you have some experience with controlling husbands.'

An unhappy flicker flashed through her eyes. A memory of something not at all pleasant. 'My father-in-law was not a nice man to live with,' she said. 'He was very possessive. Very controlling. He made life… difficult…for his family.'

Scott frowned. 'But I thought he died before you even met Martin.'

'He did. But Doreen has told me a lot about him.'

'I see.' Scott knew that Cleo's mother-in-law lived with her nowadays, having moved in after her son's death from cancer three years earlier. From what he gathered they were very fond of one another. Very close.

Thinking of fondness and closeness catapulted an image of Sarah back into his mind. Scott suppressed a groan at the thought that he wouldn't be able to even *talk* to her for another ten days. How on earth would he cope? Already he was drinking too much every evening. And eating loads of junk food. He didn't even feel like exercising any more. As for work…he hadn't been lying when he told Cleo he wasn't interested in work. He wasn't.

The trouble was it wasn't just him depending on McAllister Mines. Thousands of employees were relying on his keeping his company solvent, people he liked and valued. To continue to neglect the business was close to criminal. Some of his other varied investments would probably survive—he'd put quite a bit into real estate over the years—but a couple of the mines, plus the nickel refinery, needed money now, and plenty of it.

'I suppose I can't ignore the business for ever,' Scott said with a sigh. Much as he would like to at the moment. 'So! How are you going with finding me another silent partner? One with more money than sense.'

Cleo's face lit up as it did when she became involved in a research project. 'The best one I've been able to find is Byron Maddox, only son and heir to the Maddox Media Empire. During his twenties, he worked for his father as an executive but they parted company—business-wise—a few years back. Now he has his own company, called the BM Group. It's not on the stock exchange but is reputably doing very well. *Business Review Weekly* listed him as number eleven on Australia's rich list in June last year. Technically he's not a billionaire yet but close to.'

Scott nodded. He'd actually met Byron Maddox at the races one day last year and had liked him. The man definitely had charisma, and loads of smarts. Maybe too many. Still, as the saying went, beggars couldn't be choosers.

'Okay,' he agreed. 'Set up a meeting with him ASAP.'

'Already onto it, boss. Unfortunately, the man himself is in America at the moment. Family business according to his PA. Anyway, he'll be back in Sydney at his head office early next week. She's going to get back to me with a suitable date and time for you two to meet.'

'Excellent. Whatever would I do without you, Cleo?'

'You'd be broke. And I'd be unemployed.'

'Not for long,' he muttered, picked up his coffee and took a deep swallow. He didn't see Cleo's exasperated eyes, or the determined set of her mouth. Neither could he read her mind. Which was just as well.

Sarah had just eaten an omelette—Cory was away in Melbourne on a weekend architectural conference—and was packing up the dishwasher when the doorbell rang.

The sound sent electric currents charging through her veins. It was Scott. She just knew it was Scott.

What to do? Ignore it? Pretend no one was home?

A bit difficult with the TV on downstairs as well as most of the lights.

Whilst she stood there, waffling, the doorbell rang again. This time she turned and made it to the top of the stairs before stopping, hotly aware of her galloping heart and churning stomach.

A voice suddenly shouted through the door. 'It's just me, Sarah. Cleo. Please let me in.'

'Cleo…' A whoosh of air puffed from Sarah's lungs as she hurried down the steps and along to the front door. She didn't even stop to think what her husband's PA could possibly be doing here, she was so glad it wasn't the man himself.

Sweeping the door open, she almost gave the woman a hug. But one look at Cleo's somewhat grim face made her step back in alarm.

'What is it?' she asked straight away. 'Is it Scott? Has he been hurt?'

The look Cleo gave her was not one Sarah was used to seeing on Scott's PA. Whilst Cleo in general was not an overly smiley person, neither was she a grump. Right at that moment, however, she looked very grumpy indeed, her big brown eyes narrowed, her nicely shaped lips pursed with displeasure.

'If you mean has he been hurt in some sort of accident,' Cleo said sharply, 'then no, he hasn't. But he's hurting all right. Hurting so much that he can hardly put two sensible thoughts together. I couldn't stand the prospect of another week of watching the poor man suffer so I decided to come here tonight and try to talk some sense into you.'

The censorious tone of Cleo's words pricked at Sarah's pride, plus her temper. Who did Cleo think she was, coming here like this and criticising her actions? The jealousy that had been simmering away in Sarah for some weeks infuriated her further. But before she could fashion a suitably cutting reply, Cleo's face softened, her next words full of self-reproach.

'I'm sorry. That was uncalled for. I know you love Scott. And I know he must have done or said something awful to make you leave him. But he hasn't been himself since he got those photos. I just…well…I just had to try to do something to make things right between you two. He doesn't have anyone else to speak up for him, you know. No parents or close friends. All he has is you.'

'And you,' Sarah said, her own attitude softening.
'Not really. I'm just his PA.'

Sarah sighed. 'I think you're way more than that,
Cleo. He often speaks of you. He admires you enor-
mously.' Which was true. It sometimes irked Sarah
how much he complimented Cleo.

'Scott's a good man,' Cleo said. 'And a great boss.
He actually cares about the people who work for him,
which is a rare commodity in this day and age. Not
this last week, though. He's lost all interest in the
business.'

This final piece of news amazed Sarah. She could
never have imagined anything interfering with Scott's
work ethic. But it was some comfort to hear that the
problems they were having had affected him to such
an extent. Maybe he did love her after all. Love, however, wore many faces, Sarah knew from experience.
The kind of love she wanted from Scott had to include trust, and respect, not just physical attraction.

'I'm sorry to hear that,' Sarah said. 'But he's
brought all this on himself. Look, I don't know
how much you know about what happened. Though
clearly, Scott confides in you,' she added a little wasp-
ishly. 'Why else would you be here? I mean, you obviously knew where to come to find me.'

'Scott does not *confide* in me,' Cleo denied somewhat sternly. 'But I can't help gleaning things in my
position. Look, do you think I could come in? Not
only is it chilly out here, but there's something I wish
to say to you. In private,' she said quietly, glancing
around at the people who were walking by on the
pavement, one of whom went into the house next
door, throwing them a curious glance as he did so.

Sarah didn't want to be lectured by her husband's PA, but neither did she want to be rude to her. She liked Cleo, on the whole. But she did envy her position in Scott's life, a position that contained more true intimacy than she had. He spent more time with his PA than his wife; took her away on business trips with him; asked her opinion on things. No doubt she'd seen those appalling photos and jumped to the same horrid conclusions. It was obvious that her sympathies were all with Scott.

With some reluctance Sarah led her into the downstairs lounge room, switching off the TV whilst Cleo seated herself on the sofa. It was warmer inside the double-brick building, but Sarah still switched on the electric heater that sat in the old fireplace and looked a bit like a real fire, with faux black coals surrounded by fake flames.

'Would you like some coffee?' Sarah asked with arms crossed. 'Or a glass of wine perhaps?' There was plenty in the fridge, Sarah no longer imbibing. This thought reminded her of the pregnancy testing kit that she'd bought today, despite knowing it was still too soon to get a reliable result, though the salesgirl in the chemist shop told her that this new test could detect a pregnancy earlier than the older ones.

How long, Sarah wondered, before temptation would get the better of her and she'd take the test?

'No, I don't want anything to drink,' Cleo replied brusquely. 'I won't be staying long. I see that you're not happy with my coming here. But I simply *had* to come.'

The intensity in her voice—and in her eyes—had Sarah uncrossing her arms and sinking down on the sofa next to her. Without thinking, she reached out to touch the distressed woman on the hand.

'I'm sorry,' Sarah said softly. 'I'm not normally this rude. What do you want to say to me about Scott? I promise that I'll listen.'

'It's not just about Scott. It's about marriage.'

Sarah blinked. 'What about marriage?'

Cleo shook her head, her dark eyes clouding over. 'It's hard, Sarah. Being married. Very hard, especially when your husband doesn't treat you right...' Her voice drifted off, as did her gaze.

Sarah frowned, wondering if she was talking about her own marriage. Yet according to Scott, Cleo had been a devoted wife. She'd certainly not become a merry widow, that was for sure. But was that because her marriage had been supremely happy, or simply horrid?

Cleo appeared to give herself a mental shake, as though forcing herself out of her bleak thoughts and back to the problem at hand.

'Be thankful,' she said firmly, 'that you have a husband who is alive and well and who loves you more than anything else in the world. He might not be perfect but then are you? Scott knows he jumped to a wrong conclusion about those photos and is truly sorry. So please, give him a second chance, Sarah. He deserves it. Talk to him, at least.'

Sarah grimaced. 'I really don't know what to say to him right now.'

'Well, nothing is being achieved with what you're doing. By the time you're ready to talk to Scott he might not be ready to talk to you. Look, communication is the answer to a good relationship. You must talk to Scott, tell him all your hopes and fears. Make him tell you his. Let down all your defences—and your pride—and tell each other everything. Make him see what you want in life, and in a husband. I'm sure he's up to the challenge, Sarah, because he does truly love you. And I know you truly love him.'

'How do you know that?' Sarah threw at her, both inspired and anguished by her advice. For how could she tell Scott *everything*? Some things were too private, too…shameful, in a way.

Cleo's smile was soft. 'One only has to see you two together to know. It's in the way you look at each other. It's all in your eyes.'

Sarah wasn't so sure about that. She'd learnt last weekend that what she'd seen in Scott's eyes was good old lust, not love. The same with herself. Maybe that was all it had ever been. That, combined with companionship, plus the added bonus of not having to worry about money. Lots of marriages faltered on the matter of money. She wondered what Cleo's husband had done before he got cancer. Whether money had been a problem for them. Not that she would ever ask. But she suspected their marriage might not have been the utopia Scott had always implied it had been.

'Promise me that you will at least call him,' Cleo urged. 'Tonight. Don't wait. You don't have to rush back to him, if that's not what you want. But at least talk to him, Sarah. Please.'

Sarah still didn't really want to talk to Scott. Not yet. But after what Cleo had told her about Scott's distraught state of mind, to not do so would brand her a coward, and very cruel. Hopefully, she was neither.

But she would not be going back to him. Not yet. Not till she knew if there was to be a baby.

And maybe not even then...

'All right,' she said, though her reluctance was obvious.

'Promise me,' Cleo repeated firmly.

'I promise.'

'Tonight?'

'Yes. Tonight.'

Cleo heaved a huge sigh of relief as she stood up. 'Thank you,' she said.

Sarah levered herself up also. 'Are you sure I can't get you anything?'

'No. I've done what I came for. I'll be going now. Oh, but before I go, could you promise me something else?'

'What?' Sarah asked with a hint of impatience.

'Don't tell Scott I came to see you. He wouldn't be at all happy with me.'

'All right, then,' Sarah said, privately agreeing with Cleo's request. It made sense. Scott would not like to think that his PA was meddling in his private life. 'I won't mention your visit.'

When Cleo smiled, Sarah saw how very attractive the woman could be with the right clothes, plus the right hairstyle and make-up. Quite stunning really. Not that she wanted her to be stunning, Sarah conceded as she saw Cleo out. Not with the amount of time she spent with Scott. Far better that she looked her usual bland and rather boring self.

By the time Sarah closed the front door behind Cleo she was frowning, troubled by the realisation that she still felt jealous of the woman, despite it being obvious that there was nothing for her to be jealous about. Her mother had been a very jealous woman, she recalled. Obsessively so. Sarah wondered if the tendency to jealousy was an inherited factor. She didn't want to be jealous. She hated how it twisted a person's mind and made them miserable.

Of course, her mother had had every reason to be jealous, with her husband being a philanderer of the worst kind. Her mother used to excuse her frequent temper tantrums by saying it was because she loved Sarah's father so much. Sarah's frown deepened as she trudged slowly up the steep stairs. Was obsessive jealousy linked with obsessive love? She didn't like that concept. Didn't like it at all.

Sarah straightened her shoulders and lifted her chin, steadfastly ignoring the deep well of insecurity that had plagued her ever since her parents' divorce, not to mention her mother's suicide. The doctor had called her mother's overdose an accident, a combination of prescription pills and alcohol. But Sarah knew differently. Her mother had killed herself, all because her chronically unfaithful husband hadn't loved her. Had *never* loved her. According to her mother he'd only married her because she fell pregnant. Not with Sarah herself, with her older brother, Victor. Then, when her husband had started to seriously stray, her mother had tried to keep him by having another baby. *Her.*

Babies didn't strengthen a bad marriage, Sarah knew. Which reminded her of her own possible pregnancy. Her heart fluttered at the thought that she might be going to become a mother, her hands lifting to press gently on her flat stomach.

'Are you already in there?' she whispered.

Sarah wasn't sure if she was still horrified at the thought, or secretly thrilled to pieces. She wanted to have a family, but only if she had the right man as the father; a man who loved her and trusted her. She'd thought that man would be Scott, and that any children they had would be conceived out of love, not some wild burst of black rage and jealousy.

One thing Sarah *was* sure of. When she rang Scott tonight—as she'd promised Cleo—there would be no mention of a possible pregnancy. Neither was she going to agree to go home to him. Hell, no. Sarah was also determined not to be alone with Scott till she knew for sure that he was the same man she'd first thought he was. Decent and strong and civilised, not the primitive caveman he'd become since getting those photos. She found that man way too intimidating, too dangerous, too perversely sexy. Not that she hadn't always found him sexy. Now, however, Sarah found herself quivering at the thought of having sex with him, her mind filling with erotic images that were primitive and wanton and way too disturbing.

'Oh, God,' she cried softly, and stumbled up the rest of the stairs.

CHAPTER NINE

SCOTT WAS SPRAWLED out on the chesterfield in his study, downing his third whisky, when his phone rang. Sighing—he despised talking on the phone—he extracted it from his trouser pocket, his rather sluggish heartbeat stopping altogether when he saw the identity of his caller. Sarah!

For a brief moment he contemplated not answering—what was good for the goose was good for the gander!—but he couldn't resist finding out what had made her change her mind and contact him before the stated fortnight was up. The thought that she might have finally realised how bloody-minded she was being did not ease his frustration as he lifted the phone to his ear.

'To what do I owe this honour?' he drawled caustically.

Sarah gritted her teeth. She'd known underneath this wasn't a good idea. She herself wasn't ready to talk to Scott, especially when he'd obviously been drinking. But a promise was a promise.

'I thought,' she said with much more politeness than she was feeling, 'that we might talk.'

'Really? So you finally believe me about that bastard, Leighton?'

'I haven't even spoken to Phil,' Sarah admitted.

'Why not?'

'I, um, didn't go to work this week.'

'Why not?' Definite surprise in his voice.

No way was she going to tell him the truth. 'I've had a sinus infection,' she said, choosing a problem she was susceptible to. Though usually not in the colder months. 'I should be ready to go back next Monday. But I doubt I'll be able to put my mind on the job till we sort things out between us. Which is why I think we should have a long talk this weekend.'

'I'm not much good at long talks,' he pointed out.

'True,' she agreed. Scott had always been a man of few words, the strong, silent type who didn't open his mouth except to give directions and make decisions. He wasn't interested in just talking for the sake of talking. Sarah herself wasn't a natural gossip or a chatterbox. Neither was she given to telling her life story at the drop of a hat as some females did. Cory had been the exception, perhaps because he had a highly empathetic nature. Even so, Cory didn't know absolutely *everything*. And Scott...well, he knew next to nothing, really. He was entirely ignorant of all the sordid little details of her ghastly home life.

It came to Sarah that she didn't know all that much about *his* upbringing, either. Which wasn't right. Even before Cleo had said so to her, she'd known that a married couple—especially ones who might be about to become parents—shouldn't have any secrets from each other. They should know each other like the backs of their hands. Sarah was forced to concede that if she'd told Scott the full truth about her father—not to mention her bastard of a brother—then he would have known instinctively that she'd *never* be unfaithful to him.

It was definitely high time to remedy that situation; time to do something constructive to save their marriage. Running away never solved anything. She'd done that after her mother had died and it hadn't achieved a single damned thing. Yes, she'd seen the world, but she hadn't really *seen* it for a long time, grief and depression dogging her footsteps. She probably should have stayed at home and had some counselling first. But then she would have missed her amazing experiences in Asia where she'd kept out of the large cities, staying in lots of small villages and living the simple life. Witnessing first-hand the love those families had for each other had been better than any counselling. What she wouldn't give to be back there now.

Sarah sighed. No point in thinking like that. Their world was not her world. Her world was Sydney and Scott and a marriage that was floundering.

Perhaps this time counselling might be some kind of answer.

'Look, I know you definitely don't like talking for long over the phone,' she said, 'so how about we meet somewhere for lunch tomorrow?' Sarah hoped that meeting with him in a public place would stop her from being distracted by the disturbing desires that being in his presence kept producing.

'Sorry. No can do. I'll be at Randwick races at lunchtime tomorrow. Have to present the trophy for the first race. It's the McAllister Mines Stakes. Why don't you come with me?'

Sarah was seriously tempted. She'd always loved going to the races with Scott, loved the vibrant atmosphere, loved looking at the horses, plus the way he always seemed to back the right horse to win. He was lucky like that. But whilst a racecourse offered her the safety of a public place, she wouldn't have the opportunity to have any kind of deep and meaningful conversation with Scott. He'd be constantly surrounded by officials and other owners and trainers, all trying to talk him into buying a horse, something he'd always vowed never to do, claiming that owning a racehorse was an even riskier investment than owning a mine.

As much as she still wanted to say yes, in the end Sarah decided against it.

'I'd rather not,' she said with some regret. 'How about dinner tomorrow night instead?'

'How about I come over to see you right now?' he counter-suggested.

Sarah sucked in sharply, hating the way her traitorous body leapt at this proposal.

'I don't think so, Scott,' she said stiffly. 'Could we just stick to dinner tomorrow night, please?'

His sigh was heavy. 'All right. Where?'

'It doesn't matter where. You choose. Preferably a place with plenty of room where we won't be squashed in like sardines.'

'I'll get us a table at that seafood restaurant you like down on the quay. I can never remember the name.'

'The Seafood Palace?'

'Yes. That's the one.'

'You'll be lucky to get a table there on a Saturday night.'

'I'll get a table, don't you worry. What time?'

'Eight?' she suggested. By then she'd be starving. *Though for what?* came the corrupting thought. Oh, hell…

'That's miles too late,' Scott said. 'Make it seven.'

Sarah resigned herself to a long and frustrating evening. 'All right. Seven.'

'I'll pick you up at a quarter to.'

Sarah winced. She didn't want to be alone in a car with him; didn't want him driving her home afterwards. But she knew she was being silly. This was about them trying to smooth things out—pouncing on her in the car was not Scott's style. 'Very well. Pick me up, then.'

'Good,' he said. 'It's good to see you letting go of some of that stubbornness, Sarah. See you tomorrow,' he said and then hung up on her.

His rudeness startled her at first, and Sarah sniffed haughtily as she whirled and stalked into the guest bedroom where her eyes lit on the pregnancy testing kit sitting on the bedside table.

'I am *not* stubborn,' she muttered under her breath. 'I am, however, possibly pregnant.'

She picked up the kit and carried it into the bathroom where she opened it and read through the full instructions, tempted beyond bearing to take the test. Common sense kept telling her that it was still too soon for the test to be reliable, and that nothing was to be gained by getting a false negative. Nothing but false comfort. In the end, common sense won, Sarah shoving everything back in the box, unused, and marching out of the bathroom, leaving the damned thing behind.

But the thought of her possible pregnancy haunted her for hours that night. What would Scott say if she *was* pregnant? Would he be pleased, seeing it as the means to mend their marriage? Or would he be suspicious and accuse her of infidelity again?

Of course, suspicion over the identity of the father didn't cut it these days, Sarah conceded, a simple DNA test always putting the matter to rest. But she would hate to see initial scepticism in Scott's eyes. She was right when she said that this ultimate form of distrust would be the kiss of death where their marriage was concerned. But perhaps she was putting the cart before the horse. Maybe there wouldn't be any baby.

But feminine instinct whispered to her that there was. Sarah didn't fall asleep till the early hours of the morning.

CHAPTER TEN

SARAH SIGHED AS she looked at the pile of clothes scattered over the bed. Truly, she was acting like some teenager going on her first date, trying on and discarding practically everything in her wardrobe.

'It's all Cory's fault,' she muttered as she started hanging some of them back up again. They'd had a brief text exchange this morning where she'd confessed she was going to dinner with Scott tonight and he'd replied that it was a good idea and she was to wear something extra sexy.

Stupid advice, given she was trying to resist the temptation to have any further sex with Scott. If she dressed extra sexy it would definitely send out the opposite message to him.

Still, whilst dressing *extra* sexy was out, Sarah found herself wanting to at least look sort of sexy.

The trouble was Sarah didn't dress even sort of sexy. Not the way some women did. She didn't wear low-cut tops or too tight, too short skirts. Her choice of wardrobe was very elegant and feminine, flattering but never provocative, her mother having shown her how to choose colours and clothes that complemented her fair hair and willowy figure. Sarah never dressed in anything too dark or too bright. At work, she combined cream or taupe suits with soft silky blouses in pastels or delicate florals. Her skirts, whilst nicely fitted, were kept to knee length, and she always—always—wore stockings, expensive stockings that had a faint sheen and drew the eye to her shapely calves and slender ankles. She also always chose shoes and a bag in a nude colour, which went with everything. For after-work wear she usually wore dressy dresses, several of which would have done for dinner tonight.

But Sarah wasn't happy with any of them, finally settling on a pair of champagne-coloured crepe trousers that had a matching jacket, which she'd bought two years ago and which occasionally made an appearance during the cooler months. It was the middle of May, and Sydney's Indian summer was definitely on the wane. This evening was sure to be quite cool. Of course, the restaurant would be heated so she needed to wear something nice underneath in case she had to take off her jacket. Sarah had an awful feeling that she might be feeling hot around Scott.

A rather erotic shiver rippled down her spine at this last thought. Oh, Lord!

Finding the right top proved surprisingly difficult. She discarded her usual choices. Wearing a cami was just too bare. In the end, she chose a gold beaded top, which she'd bought on sale and never worn. Admittedly, it was still sleeveless but it had a scooped neckline that wasn't too low.

Sarah finished off the outfit with nude high heels, a gold clutch purse and gold jewellery. Nothing too much. Just a slim chain around her neck, which had belonged to her mother, and some small gold ear studs she'd bought for herself overseas. None of the jewellery Scott had bought for her. Not that there was all that much. He wasn't a gift giver in the main. Though he did present her with some lovely cultured pearls on their wedding day and a diamond pendant with matching earrings on her birthday last November. For Christmas he'd bought her the red car.

By six thirty-five Sarah was dressed and fully made up, but still she dithered. Maybe she shouldn't wear her hair down. Scott *loved* her hair down. It had been down on the day they'd first met. Maybe she should put it up. Tightly up. No, she didn't have the time to do that. She compromised by putting it up at the sides, using two pearl-encrusted combs that were pretty and feminine and which she often wore to work. Not on that fateful day fifteen months ago, however. That day, her hair had been fully out, falling in a sleek creamy curtain over her shoulders and halfway down her back. Since then, she'd had it cut a bit. Now, it stopped just short of her shoulder blades. But it was still her crowning glory. Or so her mother used to say.

Thinking of her mother did Sarah the world of good. Because it reminded her why she had to resist Scott's sex appeal tonight and concentrate on fixing their relationship. Or try to. Which meant having some long discussions over dinner, telling him all the things she'd never told him before, then finding out his own deep dark secrets. He was sure to have some. Everyone did, didn't they?

Just before a quarter to seven, Sarah picked up her purse and started making her way downstairs. The doorbell rang before she reached the bottom step, her heart jolting to a stop before lurching into an agitated rhythm. Scooping in a huge lungful of air, she let it out slowly then forced herself to keep going, lecturing herself all the while.

Play it cool, girl. Cool and calm. Tap into some of that natural poise people keep saying you've got. Don't, for pity's sake, start going ga-ga over the man, no matter how good he looks or how sexy you find him.

The lecture worked well till she opened the door and saw Scott standing there, dressed in the sort of clothes that added to his macho appeal. Dark jeans, an opened-neck white shirt, covered by a smart jacket. It wasn't an outfit she had chosen for him, or that she'd ever seen in his wardrobe. Clearly, he'd been out clothes shopping, wanting to wear something new for her. Maybe it felt like a first date to him as well.

'Looking good, Scott,' she complimented, doing her level best to ignore the fluttering in her stomach.

'Not as good as you,' he returned, his gaze hot and hungry as it roved over her.

Sarah scooped in another gathering breath. 'What? This old thing?' she tossed off nonchalantly.

His smile almost undid her feigned cool. God, but it was a sexy smile. Not all teeth. Just a wry lifting at the corners of his mouth and a knowing light in his glittering grey eyes. 'I haven't seen that top before,' he said. 'Anyway, you look fabulous. But then, you always look fabulous.'

'Wow. Flattery, Scott? That's not like you.'

'I'm a desperate man tonight. Come on. Let's get going.'

'I have to lock up first.'

'Cory not home?' he asked whilst she did so.

Sarah noted an oddly knowing note in the question, the reason for which eluded her. Perhaps he'd noticed that Cory's car wasn't parked in the street. Not many terraced houses in Paddington had off-street parking.

'On a Saturday night?' she hedged. 'You have to be joking. Where's *your* car?' she added as she glanced up and down the street.

'Just round the corner. This is a dreadful street to park in at the weekends.'

'I should have taken a taxi to the restaurant,' she told him as they walked along together.

'That's not what I wanted,' Scott returned, his hands slipping into his pockets. 'You don't get to hold all the cards in this, Sarah. You have to consider my wishes as well if you want us to get back together.'

When she stopped and gaped over at him, Scott laughed. 'You should see the look on your face. Truly, Sarah darling, a lawyer should never forget that there are always two sides to a story. I might have done the wrong thing last Friday night, but you haven't exactly played nice this past week.'

Sarah had always found personal criticism a hard pill to swallow, especially one that rang true. She'd been so busy feeling sorry for herself that she hadn't really stopped to think how those photos had affected Scott. Even when Cleo had come over last night and pointed out how much he was hurting, she hadn't really taken it on board. Scott's comment now hit home, making her feel terrible.

'You're right,' she said. 'I haven't. And I'm sorry.'

'No need to apologise. Look, I can admit when I'm in the wrong and I behaved badly last week. I wish I could turn back the clock. But perhaps you overreacted a little too? If you'd just stayed, we could have eventually sorted everything out. Instead, we've both ended up being miserable and lonely all week.'

Sarah refused to let him whitewash what he'd done. Or put the blame on her. Her father used to do that with her mother, tell her she was overreacting and that it was all her fault if he looked at other women. Which was what he used to claim in the beginning. That he was just *looking*. And her poor silly mother had swallowed that. For a while...

Sarah had no intention of backing down. 'I don't agree with that at all, Scott,' she replied. 'Nothing would have been sorted out if I'd stayed. What happened last weekend showed we have some deep-seated problems in our relationship.'

'Would you care to elaborate on that?'

'I will when we get to the restaurant—did you manage to get us a table at the Seafood Palace?'

'I did. Money talks all languages. It gets men like me the most beautiful wives and the best of tables.'

Sarah stared up at him. 'You still think I married you for your money?' she asked, startled.

Scott just shrugged. 'To be honest, Sarah, I have no idea why you married me.'

'I married you because I loved you,' Sarah answered, feeling quite angry with him for doubting her motives. But it put a different perspective on why he might have believed her unfaithful to him. 'I've always wanted you,' she added, anxious now to convince him. 'Right from the first moment I set eyes on you.'

'That's another thing which bothers me,' he ground out. 'You were a virgin when we met. It doesn't make sense that you lusted after me the way you seemed to but not any other man before me. It's not like you wouldn't have been pursued by the opposite sex before, Sarah. You are one hot-looking babe.'

Sarah winced, then sighed. She should have told Scott the truth about her upbringing from the word go. Then he would understand why she'd been so wary of men for most of her life. She vowed then and there to do what Cleo had suggested last night. Tell Scott everything.

Well...perhaps not *everything*! She wasn't about to mention her pregnancy scare till everything had been sorted out to her satisfaction. Why make more trouble, if there was no need?

'I understand your confusion,' she told him with utmost sincerity. 'But there are reasons why I was still a virgin when I met you, reasons which will take a while to explain. Could we wait till we get to the restaurant? Then I'll answer all your questions. And you can answer some of mine,' she finished up firmly, determined not to lose control of tonight's conversation.

CHAPTER ELEVEN

THE SEAFOOD PALACE was five star plus, from its top-class menu to its setting overlooking Sydney harbour. The dining room was spacious, with the tables not too close together, each one covered in a crisp white linen cloth and set with the best of cutlery and glasses. In the centre was a small crystal candlestick—complete with a not-too-high candle—which the *maître d'* lit with a flourish after he showed them to their set-for-two table. Undoubtedly it was the best and most romantic spot in the house, situated in a semi-circular alcove that had a huge bay window, affording its privileged diners a magnificent view of the water and the nearby Harbour Bridge.

'Andre will be your waiter for tonight,' the suave *maître d'* informed them as he held out the chair for Sarah. 'Enjoy,' he added, flashing Scott a wide smile before leaving them in the hands of the eager-faced young man.

And well he might smile, Scott thought wryly, given the tip he'd promised the man for securing him this table on such short notice. At the time, Scott's only intention for tonight was to impress the pants off Sarah—quite literally. He'd honestly thought he could get her back via the mutual chemistry that still sizzled between them. That was why he'd left the races as soon as he could today and gone clothes shopping, determined to show up looking his best. He'd thought his plan had worked when she'd opened the door and practically drooled. But somehow things had become sidetracked during their walk to the car. Her stating that she should have taken a taxi had annoyed him, and soon he'd been saying things to her that would have been better left unsaid. But the damage was done now, and, if he was brutally honest, he did want answers to the questions he'd posed.

Meanwhile, perhaps it would be a good idea to soften her up with some champagne. Sarah liked good champagne. But when he asked her if she wanted a bottle or just a glass, she disappointed him by declining altogether, saying she was sorry but she wasn't allowed to drink alcohol whilst taking the antibiotics for her sinus.

'Just some sparkling mineral water for me,' she said, smiling up at their waiter.

Talk about the best-laid plans of mice and men, Scott thought frustratedly.

'In that case bring me a beer,' he added, feeling quite put out.

'What kind, sir?'

'Any of the pale ales will do.'

Sarah hated lying to Scott but what else could she do? She had to give him some reason for turning down her favourite drink. It wasn't the right time to tell him that she'd forgotten to take her pill for some time and now she might be pregnant. But only *might*. Tonight was supposed to be about the past, not an unproven future. Sarah picked up the menu and started studying it, suddenly aware that she didn't have much of an appetite. Nerves gathered in her stomach at the thought of telling Scott the unvarnished truth about her totally dysfunctional and somewhat sordid family life.

'You order for me, will you?' she asked him, and put down the menu. 'I always like what you order more than what I order, anyway.'

'True,' he replied with a rueful smile. 'You can be indecisive at times.'

'Not something anyone would ever accuse you of being,' she countered with a dry laugh.

'I usually know what I want,' he told her, his eyes colliding with hers across the table.

And there it was, the same hunger Sarah had glimpsed in those glittering grey depths on the first day they'd met. This time, however, she refused to surrender to its primal pull. She would not let him seduce her tonight. No way! She'd come here to talk to him. Nothing else.

Still, it took a real effort to drag her eyes away from his and pretend to inspect the view.

'It's a very pretty spot here at night, isn't it?' she said, striving for a casual tone.

'Very,' he agreed in an annoyingly smug voice. It came to her that he honestly expected her to come home later tonight. It also came to her that behind her steadfast resolve to resist him lay the wickedest of temptations. *It wouldn't hurt to go to bed with him, would it? At least you might sleep tonight for a change.*

By the time her eyes returned to his, she wasn't

so sure that she would say no to him, underlining his accusation of her being indecisive at times. Perhaps if she started talking about all those things she hated talking about, she would stop being turned on. Nothing guaranteed to make her feel cold inside more than remembering the life she'd led at home.

But before she could launch into her sorry tale, Andre returned with their drinks, Scott grabbing the opportunity to order at the same time, choosing fresh rock oysters for their entrées, grilled barramundi in a lemon and parsley sauce for the main, along with salad side dishes, finishing up with the most decadent-sounding chocolate cheesecake for dessert.

'With ice cream, not cream,' he added.

'You do love your ice cream,' she said after the waiter departed.

Sarah realised she already knew a little more about Scott's upbringing than he did about hers. She knew his mother had died when he was very young and he'd been brought up by his father, who'd been a less than successful prospector. Intelligent, though, having a degree in geology. He'd home-schooled Scott, home being a Kombi-van in which they'd traversed every state in Australia, looking for that pot of gold. His dad had occasionally made a killing, finding a few valuable opals at Lightning Ridge, plus a couple of decent-sized gold nuggets, their proceeds funding the purchase of those parcels of land that had eventually proved to contain true treasure. Whenever money ran seriously low, his father would get work in one of the coal mines and they'd live in a local caravan park, where Scott ran wild and free.

'That was the life,' he'd told her once.

Thinking about that now, she rather agreed. Anything would have been better than her own stressed and distressed existence.

'Time for you to do that explaining, Sarah,' Scott said, breaking the rather tense silence that had enveloped the table. 'We're alone, so no more excuses, please.'

Sarah picked up her mineral water and took a sip before speaking. Her mouth had dried, her throat thickening with her memories. When you'd never really told anyone the total truth about something it was very difficult to know even where to begin.

'My father didn't just have one affair,' she blurted out. 'He was a serial cheater for as long as I can remember.'

Scott didn't seem shocked, though his expression was thoughtful.

'He never bothered to hide his dalliances,' Sarah swept on. 'Sometimes he would go off with some woman for the whole weekend. It used to drive Mum mad. The rows they had were monumental.'

Now Scott was frowning. 'Why didn't she just leave him?'

Sarah laughed. It was not a happy laugh. 'I used to say exactly the same thing. Lots of times. But no,' Sarah added after another sip of mineral water, 'she always took him back. She said it was because she loved him. And maybe she did, in her own masochistic way. She would never have divorced him if he hadn't left her first. For a younger, but very wealthy woman, by the way.'

'I see. What did your father do for a crust?'

'He used to sell quality cars. You know. Ferraris

and Porsches and cars like that. He was a good sales-
man, too. Made an excellent living. We never wanted
for anything, financially, not even after the divorce.
Dad gave Mum the family home and paid for my
education so I can't complain about that.'

'It sounds like your life was better after the divorce,' Scott pointed out.

'Oh, it was, for a while. It was a relief to have Dad
out of the house. But an even bigger relief to never
have to see my bastard brother ever again!'

CHAPTER TWELVE

THE ARRIVAL OF their oysters interrupted Sarah's story at this startling statement, Scott wondering what her brother had done to make her talk about him like that. Something not very nice, he was sure. Her face had twisted with the memory, her eyes filling with distaste.

'What did he do to make you so mad with him?' he asked quietly after the waiter left.

'Victor. His name was Victor. Lord, what *didn't* he do? The creep. He was five years older than me and by the time I turned thirteen he was eighteen. And a total sex addict. Watched porn on his computer all the time. Treated his multiple girlfriends like crap. Cheated on all of them. Like father like son, I guess.'

'He didn't try anything with you, did he?' Scott said, worried now.

'No, but he enjoyed using his power to scare me into thinking he would. He'd threaten me and generally made my life hell every way he could think of. When he started *accidentally* coming into the bathroom we shared when I was in there, I went and bought a bolt so that I could lock it from the inside.'

Scott swore and another deep shudder ran through her.

'That's terrible, Sarah,' Scott said, beginning to understand why she'd stayed a virgin for a long time. 'But not all men are like that,' he added gently.

'I know,' she said, and smiled at him. 'But it took me a long time to trust one again. I just didn't like them. Or trust them. Even when I first went to university, I was still wary. Whenever a male student took an interest in me, I blew them off, quick smart. Then Mum died and I think I must have had some kind of breakdown.' She gave him a guilty look, then. 'Her death wasn't an accidental overdose like I told you. It was suicide.'

When tears pricked at her eyes, Scott decided enough was enough. Any more soul-shattering stories could wait till later, when she was safely in his arms and he could comfort her properly.

'I think, my darling,' he said with a warm smile, 'that you should stop talking about upsetting subjects for now and just concentrate on eating these truly delicious oysters. I am no longer curious over why you were still a virgin when we met. And I can see how your being an unfaithful wife would be the last thing you would ever do. I'm just sorry I ever pushed the issue in the first place. So let's forget about distressing confessions for now… If I'd known what you went through…'

'I want to be honest with you,' Sarah replied as she stabbed one of the oysters with her fork. 'And for you to be honest with me. If our marriage is to survive, we can't keep secrets from each other.' Especially big ones like she'd forgotten the pill and just might be pregnant.

Sarah opened her mouth to confess but the words simply wouldn't come, her panicky mind finding all sorts of excuses not to tell him, the main one being she might not be pregnant at all! Why risk more trouble? Far better to wait till she was sure that Scott really did love and trust her before hitting their fragile marriage with added stress.

And a baby was definitely added stress.

Meanwhile, everything else had to be aired. Like her private financial stash. She hoped it wouldn't make him angry that she'd kept that a secret.

'There's one more thing I must tell you,' she said.

Scott looked alarmed.

'No, nothing too dreadful,' she hurried on. 'It's just that I inherited a substantial amount when Mum died. The house for starters—which I sold—and quite a bit of cash. So I definitely didn't marry you for your money,' she told him with a touch of acerbity, having been cut that he'd even thought for a moment that she might be a gold-digger. 'I have plenty of my own. Though not enough, unfortunately, to bail out that refinery of yours. From what I gathered, that's going to take millions.'

'You're right about that,' Scott said ruefully.

'You're welcome to what I've got,' she offered rather impulsively.

'Thanks, but no thanks. You might need it one day, the way the mining industry is going.'

'You're not really in deep financial trouble, are you, Scott? I mean, I wouldn't have suggested this restaurant if I thought you were going broke.'

'Don't trouble your pretty little head about that. I'm not an idiot. I have plenty of assets and a steady private income from other sources. I have more than enough to pay the bill. And to support a wife. When and if she ever comes home... I nearly went insane this last week. I miss you, Sarah. I want you to come home.'

Sarah sighed. Trust him to use this opportunity to bring that matter up. This was why she hadn't wanted to see him in the first place. That, and the uncontrollable lust he kept evoking in her. She missed him too. Or she missed his body. *That* was what seemed to be uppermost in her mind at the moment. Oh, God, everything was such a mess. 'I...I'll think about it,' she said. 'Now let's just eat our food.'

They ate the oysters in silence, Scott clearly not happy with her decision. Or her lack of it. When the waiter came to clear their plates, he ordered another beer for himself and a second mineral water for her.

'For a girl who wanted to talk,' he said after the waiter departed, 'you've gone quiet all of a sudden.'

If he knew the reason behind her fraught silence, she'd be in big trouble. With great difficulty, she refocused her heated brain on why she'd agreed to this dinner date in the first place. Unfortunately, this meant she had to look across the table at Scott, and into those sexy eyes of his. Her casual shrug was a sham. There was nothing casual going on inside Sarah.

'I guess I've told you everything I wanted to tell you,' she said, doing her best to stay calm. 'I needed you to understand what has made me the way I am. Why I react to things the way I do. If we'd talked more before we married, things might not have gone so wrong last Friday. You would have trusted me more. You would have known that it would have been impossible for me to be an unfaithful wife.'

'Yeah, you're probably right. I rushed you to the altar. But damn it all, Sarah, I don't regret it. I do regret not trusting you and I regret what I did last Friday night. But you have to admit, what we did, it was pretty amazing. You were something that night! I'm crazy about that girl and I want more of her.'

Sarah felt his hunger right through every pore in her body. Felt her own desire too, from the tips of her erect nipples right down to the melting heat between her thighs. Thank God the waiter arrived back with their drinks, breaking the dangerous moment and letting her have a breather.

'Well, I'm not so crazy about that girl, Scott,' she managed to say once they were alone. 'She's way too much of a pushover for my liking. Now could we kindly get back to discussing things that really matter?'

'Like what?'

'Like why *did* you rush me to the altar? Why did you marry me at all?'

CHAPTER THIRTEEN

SCOTT WAS SO taken aback by her questions that he was speechless for a few seconds.

'Well?' Sarah prompted.

He finally found his tongue. 'You know very well why I married you,' he threw back at her. 'I was madly in love with you, woman. Trust me when I say it wasn't just a matter of lust. I know how lust feels and that wasn't what I felt for you.' He'd fallen madly in love with her. Absolutely. But what he'd also felt was fear. Fear that he'd somehow lose this incredibly beautiful, bright creature if he didn't marry her quick smart; that if he didn't put his ring on her finger then one day soon some other better-looking, more charming, more sophisticated man would come along and win her away from him. He couldn't risk that so, yes, he'd rushed her to the altar whilst she was still as bewitched with him as he was with her.

But ultimately, it hadn't worked, had it? That man he'd feared had come along, and even if Sarah hadn't fallen into his arms, *he'd* believed she had. And in doing so, he'd risked the one thing he feared most of all. Losing Sarah.

But you haven't lost her yet, you fool, whispered the voice of reason. *Use your brains, man.*

Scott knew women liked to talk, but it hadn't been a big part of his upbringing. His father only opened his mouth to show him something or impart knowledge. Scott only knew a handful of details about his father's past life, and quite frankly this hadn't bothered him, but it seemed women just had to know everything about everyone. Scott had learned this over time. He'd had girlfriends before Sarah. But confiding didn't come naturally to him and Sarah had seemed to understand this. In the beginning, that was. Clearly, she no longer liked his close-mouthed reticence. It was time to talk about the one subject he hated talking about. The past.

But first he had to answer her question over why he'd rushed her to the altar.

'If you want me to be brutally honest,' he began, 'I married you because I wanted to have you all to myself, twenty-four-seven. I didn't know the reason then for your wariness about the opposite sex, but I could see you weren't the sort of girl who'd live with me, or become my mistress. So marriage seemed the only course of action, and the sooner the better. Like I said, I was crazy about you, Sarah. I'd never felt anything even close before to what I felt for you. To be totally honest with you I wasn't too fond of women for a good while after I found out the ugly truth about my mother.'

'*Your* mother?' Sarah queried, startled.

'Yes. You see, she didn't die when I was a baby. That's just a lie I tell to hide the truth.'

Sarah sat up straighter in her chair, stunned by this highly unexpected revelation.

'She also wasn't married to my father,' Scott went on. 'She was a good-time girl Dad picked up when he struck gold once. Their fling finished once the money ran out and Dad took off again for the outback. He didn't realise at the time that he'd left behind a piece of himself. Anyway, to cut a long story short, a couple of years later, when he was flushed with finding some black opals, he looked her up again. She was living on some kind of hippie commune by then, up near one of the Northern NSW beaches. Imagine his surprise when he came across a little toddler who was the spitting image of him, running around the front yard, stark naked, whilst she was inside totally out of it in a pot-smoking haze.'

'Good Lord! What did he do?'

'Paid her some money and took me away with him.'

'Didn't she fight him for you?' Sarah couldn't imagine any mother letting her child go that easily. She certainly wouldn't have. She'd have created bloody hell!

'No. She told Dad he was welcome to me—that I was an uncontrollable brat and she'd never wanted me anyway.'

'Oh, Scott,' Sarah said sadly, her heart going out to him.

'No need to feel sorry for me,' he said matter-of-factly. 'I don't remember her or miss her. And Dad was a great dad. A little unconventional but he loved me to death and I felt the same way about him. He didn't tell me the truth about my mother till I was a grown man and could take it.'

Sarah blinked back her tears but didn't say a word.

'I did look my mother up a few years ago,' Scott went on, 'more out of curiosity then need. But she'd died a decade or so earlier. Too many drugs, I guess. The funny thing was this old junkie who'd known her said she was never the same after Dad took me away. That all the life went out of her. So maybe she sort of loved me after all.'

'I'm sure she did,' Sarah said soothingly.

Scott wasn't sure of any such thing. Women liked to romanticise situations, he'd found. Still, perhaps it was a nice thought, but not one that he wished to dwell on.

'Enough of this,' he said a bit sharply. 'I've never seen the point of rehashing old hurts. Let's just concentrate on the here and now, which is enjoying each other's company, and our next course.' Which he spotted being brought to the table.

They did enjoy the barramundi. Sort of. Sarah's mood remained a little sad, however, Scott frustrated that she refused to have even one glass of wine with the main course. He knew the directions always said you couldn't drink alcohol with antibiotics, but surely one glass wouldn't hurt. It might relax her; put some joy back into her.

Of course, there was another way to relax her...

'I think we might skip dessert,' he said, glancing across the table at her, his eyes glittering as he made his meaning clear.

CHAPTER FOURTEEN

SARAH TRIED NOT to blush. But it was no use. The image of Scott doing wicked things to her sent heat zooming up from her chest to her neck and into her face. Her throat was parched as her heartbeat quickened.

'Are you trying to turn me on, Scott?'

'Am I succeeding? Be honest now.'

'Yes,' she choked out.

'Let's go, then.'

'I am not going back to our apartment with you, Scott. Not yet.'

'I didn't ask you to. Cory's place will do just as well for tonight.'

Sarah knew she was fighting a losing battle but she refused to relent easily. 'Cory might have brought someone home by now,' she said in a desperate defence.

'Not very likely. He's at a conference in Melbourne.'

Sarah gasped. 'How did you know that?'

'He texted me this afternoon and told me so, something which seemed to slip your mind, Miss Honesty.'

Sarah gritted her teeth. 'I'm going to kill him.'

'I wanted to kiss him.'

'Oh, really?' she said archly. 'I didn't think you cared for him in that way.'

He grinned. 'Neither did I. Maybe it has something to do with my wife neglecting her marital duties this past week.'

Sarah rolled her eyes at the cheek of him. But it was no use. A smile grabbed her mouth and soon she was laughing. 'What chance did I have, with you two conspiring against me?'

'No chance at all. I'll just get the bill and we'll go.'

'I need to visit the powder room first.'

Scott scowled gently. 'Is this another delaying tactic? You won't make a dash for it out of the back window, will you?'

'Maybe I should.' And she meant it. For nothing would be solved by going to bed with Scott. They still had a lot of talking to do, on both sides.

But the compelling nature of her desires would not be denied. Sarah wanted Scott to make love to her tonight, all night. And maybe all tomorrow. She wanted him to take her to that hot, heady place again where logical thinking ceased and the only thing she cared about was her next orgasm, along with all the wild dizzying pleasure in between. That was where she'd been that fateful Friday night. And she wanted to experience that again.

Her legs almost didn't support her when she rose and made her way unsteadily to the powder room. As she washed her hands she didn't dare look at her reflection in the wall mirror, afraid of what she might see. Her mother perhaps, that poor tragic creature whom Sarah physically resembled but who didn't have one ounce of willpower when it came to her husband.

I will not be like that, Sarah vowed as she left the room. *I will not!*

Scott was waiting for her, the bill paid, wasting no time ushering her outside and into the small car park set aside for patrons of the restaurant. The touch of his hand in the small of her back sent little shivers running up and down her spine. They didn't speak during the short drive home, Sarah not even glancing over at him. She didn't want to see smugness in his face, or desire. She had enough to contend with trying to handle her own.

This time, Scott was able to park close to Cory's house, some of the other inhabitants of the street obviously having gone out.

'It's a bit chilly in here,' he said once they entered the hallway.

'Cory hasn't installed heating or air-conditioning yet,' Sarah told him. 'It's to go in with the renovations. But that's been delayed. There's a great little heater in here though,' she said, leading Scott into the downstairs living room.

'And a great big sofa,' he added, turning her in his arms and kissing her before she could do a single thing. Not a slow, tender, loving kiss. A hard, hot, hungry kiss, which echoed the frustration both of them had been feeling all week. She accepted his tongue avidly, sucking on it as she wanted to suck on *him*. When he wrenched his head away she moaned in protest.

'Don't worry,' he growled. 'I feel exactly the same way.'

Sarah extricated herself from his grip to turn on

the heater and take some of the cushions from the sofa
and throw them on top of the thick shag rug that lay
in front of the heater. Because no way was she going
to have sex with Scott on that lounge like a pair of
horny teenagers.

'Good thinking,' he said, tossing aside his jacket
before pulling her into his arms again.

Another savage kiss completely obliterated any lingering doubt Sarah might have had about doing this,
confirming in her mind this was what *she* wanted.
There was no question of being seduced, or in any
way coerced.

'Too many clothes, sweetheart,' he muttered when
his head finally lifted.

'Yes,' she agreed throatily, her hands going to the
buttons on his shirt.

He laughed and just yanked the shirt off over his
head, exposing his magnificent chest to her touch.

And touch him she did, her fingernails scraping
over his skin as they slid through the sexy matt of
curls that covered the middle of his chest. When they
moved over his nipples, he groaned a raw animal
groan. When she did it again, his hands lifted to grip
her wrists.

'Best stop that,' he muttered. 'It's doing dreadful
things to me.'

'Good,' she said, and bent her lips to them instead.

'You've turned into a witch,' he growled. 'But I
love it.'

She lifted her head, determined not to let him think
she was his again, just because she desired him. 'This
isn't love, Scott. This is just lust.'

'That's a matter of opinion, sweetheart. But if you

want total honesty, then right now I don't give a damn what it is. I want you as I've never wanted you before, and if I don't have you in the next twenty seconds, I think I'm going to explode.'

Without further discussion and with little finesse he stripped her of her clothes then spread her out on the rug, ogling her naked body whilst he took off the rest of his own clothes, at which point it was Sarah's turn to do the ogling.

Scott was all man, she thought breathlessly. Big and strong, with a body that was as powerful as it was intimidating. She stared at the size of his erection and wondered how it ever fitted inside her. But it always did. Beautifully. Wondrously. Bringing her pleasure without even having to move.

But when it did…

He lay down and surged into her without preamble, the way he'd done the other day. Everything happened just as quickly as then too, both of them climaxing in no time, shuddering and shaking with the intensity of their rapid releases.

'Geez, Sarah,' Scott groaned as he collapsed across her, his weight making *her* groan in protest. He quickly rolled off her, Sarah gasping with relief.

'Sorry,' he said from where he lay beside her, his breathing still ragged. 'Didn't mean to squash you. When I've got my breath back we'll go have a shower together and I'll show you some more interesting moves.'

'More interesting?' she echoed, trying not to sound as instantly excited as she was.

'That's what you want, isn't it? Or would you prefer we do it the way we used to do it? Under the bed-covers with the lights off.'

Sarah winced. Surely she hadn't been as boring as that, had she?

Not quite, she conceded, but things sure hadn't been as adventurous as this. She'd never said no to Scott when it came to sex, but she'd been a passive partner, possibly because her lack of experience made her feel less confident. She'd always left everything up to Scott. Maybe he thought she was too shy for more adventurous activities. Just thinking of standing up naked in a shower with him and having him wash her all over was doing her head in. Not in a bad way, either.

She looked over at him and he smiled.

'I love it when your eyes go all smoky like that. I know you were angry with me for last Friday night, but the sex was great, wasn't it? *You* were great. A bit naughty. But hot as hell.'

'*You* were the one who was naughty,' she pointed out, desperate to stop her mind from unravelling with desire.

He laughed. 'Oh, sweetheart, you are such an innocent! But that's what makes you so attractive to me. And why I fell in love with you. Because you were different from all the other women I've ever dated, none of whom I ever wanted to marry.'

Sarah levered herself up on one elbow to stare down at him. 'Are you saying you married me because I was a virgin when we met?'

'Partly. But I also wanted to be in a position to protect you.'

'*Protect* me?'

'Sure. A woman of your obvious attractions needs protection from the big bad wolves in this world.'

Sarah had to admit that when she was with Scott, she did feel safe and secure. Till recently...

'Too much talking,' Scott said, and abruptly sat up. 'Come on. Let's go shower.'

CHAPTER FIFTEEN

SARAH SHIVERED AS Scott led her from the warm living room, down the cold hallway and into the rather ancient bathroom that hadn't been updated in years. It was very clean, though, Cory meticulous when it came to housework. There was a small strip heater on the wall, which Scott immediately turned on, followed by the taps in the shower.

'Not exactly built for two, is it?' Scott said drily as they waited for the water to get hot enough.

'At least it d-doesn't have a shower c-curtain,' she stammered, her teeth beginning to chatter.

Scott gave her a droll look whilst he rubbed her goosebumped upper arms with his large hands. 'Just think. We could be at home right now, with ducted air-conditioning and a huge two-headed shower stall.'

'Don't tempt me,' she replied.

'Could I?'

'No.'

'We'll see, Miss Stubborn. We'll see.'

Scott loved the way her lovely blue eyes widened, then glittered with an intoxicating mixture of shock and excitement. This new sexy Sarah bewitched him even more than the shy virgin, because she promised a lifetime of erotic pleasure with her as his wife. He refused to believe that she had any intention of actually leaving him...that she would let one rotten misunderstanding ruin their relationship. Yes, he'd hurt her badly by not trusting her. He could see that now. But surely she would forgive him. She wouldn't have come to dinner tonight at all if she hadn't been having second thoughts about her actions. Neither would she have let him have sex with her if she didn't still love him. Sarah thought it was lust driving her but he knew differently. It was love. It had always been love. He was sure of it, he thought as he followed her under the jets of hot water, resolving to leave no stone unturned in seducing the woman he loved into coming back home with him.

It was a snug fit all right, Sarah conceded once Scott slid the shower screen shut behind them. There was nowhere to escape the streams of water beating down over her head, plastering her hair to her skull and back. There was hardly room to lift her arms to scoop the wet locks back from her face.

'Oh!' she gasped when he turned her round and she felt his erection pressing against her bottom.

'Hand me that soap there,' he ordered roughly.

Her hand trembled as she picked the cake of soap up off the inbuilt soap dish, not sure what he intended to do, not sure now if she was capable of stopping him. Sarah might be a relative innocent when it came to sexual experience but she wasn't ignorant.

She gasped again when he began rubbing the now wet soap over her nipples. Lord, but it felt fantastic!

Her heart started galloping and she had the devil of a time stopping herself from moaning with pleasure. In the end she did.

'You like that?' he rasped in her ear.

'Mmm…' was all she could manage in reply.

'Sorry, sweetheart, but it's time to move on.'

When he slid the soap down over her stomach, Sarah sucked in sharply, fearful that if he rubbed that soap over her more intimate parts she would come straight away. But amazingly she didn't, Scott skilfully avoiding her clitoris and concentrating on the less sensitive areas. But she still became terribly tense, every muscle she owned tightening in anticipation.

'Dear God,' she choked out at one stage.

'Prayer won't help you tonight, sweetheart,' Scott warned her, then abruptly turned her round. 'Now do the same to me,' he ordered as he handed her the soap then leant back against the tiled wall, giving her enough room to follow his command.

Sarah didn't dare disobey him this time. Hell, she didn't *want* to disobey.

She echoed everything he'd done to her, rubbing the soap over his chest, concentrating on his nipples. Though smaller than hers, they were fiercely erect and just as sensitive, by the sounds he started making: low, raw groans that she found deliciously arousing, making her want to hear more. And more.

Her hand dropped away from his chest, drifting down over his rock-hard abs to the tip of his erection. When she brushed the cake of slippery soap over it, he swore, then grabbed her hand, stopping her from going further.

'No?' she enquired mischievously, her eyes as excited as his.

'No,' he growled, switching off the taps and slamming back the shower screen so hard that it rattled.

'But I *wanted* to,' she protested even as he reached for the towels.

'I wanted you to do it too,' he told her, shoving one towel into her hands whilst he kept the other. 'But I have other plans for you right now.'

Sarah trembled, her head spinning with desire.

His smile was so sexy. 'Shall we go?'

The downstairs living room was nicely warm when they returned, Scott wasting no time pulling her down onto the rug with him.

For a big man Scott was a quick mover. Before Sarah could blink he slid down her body and put his mouth where the cake of soap had recently been. She cried out when his lips took a rather ruthless possession of her swollen clitoris, sucking the electrified tip till it was impossible for her to stop herself from coming. This time her cries carried a degree of exasperation. She hadn't wanted to come; hadn't wanted the edge to be taken off her desires.

But strangely, that didn't happen. Yes, for a few moments she experienced a wave of post-orgasmic languor, but Scott put a stop to that when he slid back up her body and started kissing her nipples. That woke her up again. Big time. After tormenting her breasts for a while, he returned to her gasping mouth, inserting his tongue and cupping her cheeks at the same time. It was a long, slow, wet kiss; an intimate and very loving kiss, which Sarah found both incredibly arousing and strangely emotional.

This wasn't just lust, she realised as she clasped Scott close and wallowed in the moment. This was love—honest to goodness, lasting-for-ever love. How could she have ever thought otherwise?

When he finally stopped kissing her, she looked up into his flushed face. 'I do love you, you know,' she said, her stomach going all squishy inside.

'I sure hope so,' he returned, then smiled a wry smile.

'Aren't you going to tell me you love me too?'

'Haven't I already told you that enough already? How many times does a man have to prove himself to you? I love you too.'

Quite a lot, Sarah conceded whilst hugging her happiness, the knowledge that this was love driving her and not just lust bringing a playfulness to their lovemaking that was both fun and exciting.

She could already tell that he liked what she was doing. A lot. Frankly, she'd never seen him so large or so hard.

A choking sound escaped his throat when she bent her head, first to the tip, then to the rest of him, only taking him a few inches before withdrawing then doing it all over again. Gradually, she sucked him in deeper and deeper, but he seemed determined not to surrender, his iron control frustrating her. In the end, Sarah only just managed to take him back into her mouth before he came, shuddering into her as he cried out like a wounded animal, his hands tangling in her hair at the same time.

CHAPTER SIXTEEN

FIFTEEN MINUTES LATER Scott was in pleasurable agony. Perhaps because Sarah had insisted she be on top. The sight of her riding him in a state of such naked abandon did things to him that were almost criminal. Hell, he was going to come if she didn't stop.

His groan carried both agony and ecstasy. 'Hell, Sarah.'

'Sorry. Did I hurt you?'

'You're killing me. Look, just keep still and talk to me for a short while.'

'You don't like to talk, especially during sex.'

'I do right now.'

Sarah sighed an exasperated-sounding sigh. 'But I was having such fun. I've only just learnt how to do this properly and you want me to stop.'

'You'll have lots more opportunity for more practice when you come home with me.'

'*If* I come home with you, don't you mean?' she said archly.

Lord, but she would try the patience of a saint! Maybe he shouldn't bother with her pleasure. Just give in to his own. But damn it all, he didn't have much going for him at the moment except the persuasion of great sex. The trouble was she looked so utterly gorgeous without any clothes on.

Scott loved looking at her. Sarah's body was perfect in every department in Scott's opinion, from her slender shoulders to her tiny waist to the gentle swell of her hips and bottom. And then there were her soft silky thighs and that delicious area in between, which currently had him imprisoned within its hot wet depths.

God. Better not think about that! Otherwise his asking Sarah to stop and talk would not work at all. He was already perilously close to coming.

'Stop wriggling and start talking,' he commanded roughly.

'Truly,' she tut-tutted, lifting her arms to wind her rather dishevelled hair up into a topknot, the action lifting her pretty breasts with their fiercely erect nipples. Her stretching up also lifted her bottom slightly, Scott only just managing not to groan.

'So what do you want me to talk about?' she asked.

'How about telling me how you came to be best friends with Cory?'

'Cory?' she repeated, looking perplexed.

Scott wasn't at all jealous of her close friendship with Cory. He thought it quite sweet. But he *was* curious.

'But I've already told you about Cory. We met at uni and we…well…we had the same interests. Liked the same books and movies.'

Scott could see that she was slightly uncomfortable explaining how their friendship began. 'I get the impression you were more than just friends at one stage,' he said with a burst of intuition.

A guilty colour entered her cheeks.

'Out with it, Sarah,' Scott insisted. 'Honesty, re-member?'

'Okay—okay. The truth is I sort of fancied him to begin with. I mean, he was a hunk and by then I think my hormones were willing to bypass my history. So when he asked me out I said yes. Then, when he asked me back to his flat—he wasn't living here yet—I went.'

'Didn't you know he was gay?'

'Not in the slightest. He acted like he found me as attractive as I found him.'

'So what happened when you got back to his flat?'

'Nothing much. We kissed a few times.'

'You *liked* kissing him?'

'I thought I did. I hadn't experienced *your* kisses then, don't forget. I now know that Cory's kisses were like mineral water to your champagne.'

Scott tried not to preen at her compliment. But his male ego was pleased all the same.

'What happened after that?' he asked.

'We moved into his bedroom and started taking off our clothes.'

'And?'

'He broke down and said he was sorry but he couldn't go through with it. He confessed that he was gay but was afraid his parents would hate him and that his life would be ruined. He told me that he'd thought if any girl in the world could make him straight, it would be me. But it hadn't turned out that way. He said he didn't like kissing me and he knew that he wasn't capable of having sex with me.'

'Right. Awkward. What did you do then?'

'I felt like crying but Cory was doing enough for both of us. So I cuddled him and told him he was being silly and that I would go with him to tell his parents the truth the very next day.'

'And did you?'

'Yes, of course. I don't make idle promises. Anyway, they were fine with it. Said they'd already suspected. The upshot was I stayed the day with his family—Cory had two younger sisters—and we all just clicked. We've been good friends ever since.'

'I see,' Scott said. 'So what happened to your hormones after that?' he went on, his curiosity fully whetted by then. 'They sound like they were definitely on the move at last. Not dead and buried any longer.'

'True. But I still wasn't prepared to just jump into bed with anyone. He had to be someone who was physically attractive and whom I could trust with my body. I did look around, believe me, but no one did it for me. Till you came along…'

Scott's heart turned over. Something else stirred as well. Not that his erection had ever really gone to sleep. It had just been distracted for a while. 'I still can't imagine why you found me so attractive. A big, ugly brute like me.'

Sarah's smile was a very Mona Lisa smile. 'You're not at all ugly and you know it. But if you want me to be brutally honest, no pun intended, then I don't know why, either. You were nothing like the fantasy first lover I'd pictured in my head. You were too big and too old and way too intimidating. All I know is that I wanted you from the first moment I set eyes on you.'

'Well, you have me,' he returned thickly. *Till death*

do us part, Scott hoped. 'No more talk now. I have myself under sufficient control to continue, so go ahead and have your wicked way with me...if you so desire.'

'I do so desire, my Lord and master,' she said with a sexy smile, and began riding him again.

Scott clenched his teeth hard in his jaw, determined to outlast her this time.

It was still dark when he woke, his back aching a little from falling asleep on such a hard floor. The rug wasn't thick enough to cushion a man of his size and weight, especially with Sarah sprawled on top of him. The days of his sleeping rough in the outback had long gone. He was used to creature comforts now; used to sleeping in big soft beds in air-conditioned rooms. Sarah too, he imagined. She might have felt wretched during her growing up years but she obviously hadn't wanted for much—materially speaking. Her admitting to having such a substantial amount of money of her own had come as a surprise, but a pleasant one. Clearly, his own financial successes hadn't influenced her feelings for him. She'd said she loved him at first sight and he believed her. A week ago he hadn't been at all sure.

Tonight had certainly shown him how much he loved her. The way he'd felt when she was making love to him had been almost beyond love. Life without her would be impossible. But he felt a little more confident that all would be well. Eventually. Though he suspected Sarah wasn't about to relent about her two weeks' break. Still, he could bear that, now that he had hope.

In the meantime he had to get them both into a proper bed. Not the one downstairs. That was Cory's. Sarah would have been sleeping this past week in the guest room upstairs. Somehow he managed to carry her up the narrow and rather steep staircase without waking her, though she did stir slightly, nuzzling into his neck and muttering something in her dreams. The state of the guest bedroom startled him. First, the bed was covered with clothes. On top of that, the room was on the chilly side. Finally, he succeeded in getting her into the bed, after which he quickly piled the clothes onto a corner chair before diving in after her. She immediately snuggled into him, her body deliciously warm. Scott might have woken her if he hadn't been knackered himself. They'd outdone themselves tonight, making love several times before exhaustion had taken over.

CHAPTER SEVENTEEN

SARAH WAS BROUGHT back slowly to consciousness by Scott shaking her and saying her name.

'Sarah, wake up,' he growled when she kept her eyes dreamily shut, loving the warmth of the thick quilt that enveloped her. 'I need to talk to you, damn you.'

His swearing at her did the trick, her eyes snapping open to see Scott standing beside the bed, glaring down at her. He was naked, except for a towel slung low round his hips, his dripping body and wet hair indicating that he'd just climbed out of a shower. He was also holding the pregnancy testing kit she'd carelessly left on the bathroom vanity.

Oh, dear God...

Sarah swallowed. 'Yes?' she squeaked.

'What's this?' he growled, waggling the box at her.

Sarah's stomach swirled with nausea at the thought he might jump to all the wrong conclusions. Again.

'It's a pregnancy testing kit,' she said, trying her best to sound perfectly innocent and not worried sick.

'No kidding,' came his droll reply. 'I can read, you know. Since we both know it hardly belongs to Cory, then I can only presume you bought it. What I want to know is why? Did you forget to take the pill one night, is that it?' he added, scowling.

'Well, yes and no,' she replied, sitting up slowly whilst holding the bedclothes up over her bare breasts. 'I mean, I didn't just forget one night. I actually haven't taken the pill for some time now.'

His frown darkened. 'And why was that?' he demanded to know.

Sarah knew there was nothing for it but the truth.

'Complacency, security, recklessness. I don't know why. It wasn't until last Saturday that I realised how mistaken I was. But by then taking my pill was the last thing on my mind. I didn't even remember it till you mentioned it last Monday. If you recall, I nearly fainted on the spot. You've no idea how shocked I was at being so stupid. On top of that, I wasn't exactly thrilled at the idea of conceiving a baby through acts of jealousy and revenge. Or even from that lust-crazed quickie we'd just had a few minutes earlier. Though that was preferable, I suppose,' she added bitterly. 'After that, there didn't seem be any point to going back on the pill till my period arrived.'

'Which it obviously hasn't,' Scott said as he shook the box in his hands.

'No,' she agreed wretchedly.

'So, *are* you pregnant?' he asked her. 'Have you taken this test?'

'No. It's too early to tell. I just bought that test on an impulse. The doctor said that I should wait at least another week to be sure.'

'I presume this is the same doctor who prescribed you the antibiotics for your phantom sinus infection,' he said rather caustically.

Guilt had Sarah colouring hotly. 'I had to say something to explain why I couldn't drink at dinner. I knew you knew how much I loved champagne.'

'No kidding. How inventive of you. By then you should have told me the truth, Sarah,' he bit out, his eyes like shiny steel. 'I can almost understand why you didn't tell me straight away after you realised you might have fallen pregnant. You were still mad at me. But I cannot forgive you for keeping it a secret last night. All that talk of honesty and trust over dinner was just so much crap, wasn't it? I'm beginning to think that you were right when you said there was nothing left between us but lust. At least on your part.'

Sarah winced at the coldness in his voice. 'Try to understand my point of view,' she pleaded. 'I didn't tell you about my possibly being pregnant because I didn't want you using it as a weapon to get me to come back before I was ready.'

Sarah knew, the moment the words were out of her mouth, that they were a mistake.

His eyes narrowed even further, his top lip curling up with disgust. 'And wouldn't that have been just criminal!' he threw at her, his voice savage with sarcasm. 'What a terrible thing to do, to ask your wife to come back because she might be having your baby. Totally deplorable! Well, you don't have to worry about that any more, sweetheart. Because I don't think I want you back. Maybe if it turns out you really are pregnant I'll think about it. But just right now I can't even stand to look at you. I'm out of here!' And so saying he threw the testing kit on the bed before storming out of the room.

Stunned by how quickly everything had rocketed

out of control, Sarah stayed where she was, listening to Scott stomping down the stairs, her heart racing, her head spinning with panic-driven thoughts.

I can't let him leave the way I did last Saturday morning. I have to make him see that I do really love him and that I was wrong to lie to him. And that I'm sorry. So terribly, terribly sorry. I should have told him about forgetting the pill and the possibility of a baby straight away.

Silent tears were streaming down her face by the time she bolted out of the bed to run down the stairs after him.

'Go away, Sarah,' he snapped without looking at her, concentrating instead on pulling on his clothes.

'No!' she choked out. 'I will not go away, not till you hear me out.'

Finally, he turned to face her, his shirt in his hands, his cheekbones spotted red with fury. 'There is nothing you have to say that I want to hear.'

'Scott, please…' She glanced down at herself, then lifted her hands to wipe away the tears. 'Sorry.'

The word come out in a ragged sob. Her shoulders started to shake as she peered up at him through flooded eyes. 'Please don't go, Scott. I love you. I've always loved you. I wish I'd told you about the pill business but I was afraid.'

'Of what?'

'Of ending up an emotional mess like my mother. Of never knowing if you really loved me, or you were just staying with me because I was having your baby.'

His face softened then. 'God, Sarah, how could you possibly think that? A baby would be nice, but it wouldn't make me love you more. Or want you more. It's you I married, Sarah. *You.*'

He dropped the shirt and gathered her tenderly into his arms, warming her trembling body with his own.

'I think it's time I took you home,' he murmured as he stroked her hair down her back. 'What do you say, Sarah?'

'Yes, please,' she blubbered against his bare chest.

'Everything will be all right now,' he said as he stroked her. 'Trust me.'

CHAPTER EIGHTEEN

SCOTT WAS GLAD they had two cars to accommodate all of Sarah's things. Lord, but he had no idea how she'd crammed everything into that small car of hers, despite it being a hatchback. It was full to the brim yet his car still had clothes draped all over his back seat and boxes of shoes piled high on the passenger seat. Thank goodness he'd been able to find a parking spot close to Cory's house last night, otherwise packing would have been a slow process.

'Ready to go now?' he asked Sarah as she stood next to her car, frowning as though she'd forgotten something.

'Just have to get one last thing,' she said without looking at him.

'Okay. I'll wait here for you.'

Her reappearance with the dreaded pregnancy kit in her hands reminded Scott how close he'd come to wrecking any chance of a reconciliation after he'd found that damned thing in the bathroom. Just the sight of it still raised his blood pressure a notch, but he clenched his mouth tightly shut, making no comment as she put it in her own car. But it took a real effort to control himself. By the time they climbed in behind their respective wheels and drove off, Scott was relieved to be in a separate car to Sarah for the drive home. That way he wouldn't say anything inflammatory to her the way he had earlier.

It also gave him the opportunity to think about things.

It wasn't like him to lose his temper like that. He was usually way more pragmatic, priding himself on his ability to stay calm under pressure. His father had been a laid-back fellow, rarely raising his voice and never being violent in any way, except when pushed to the limit. Though he confessed he *had* hit the roof when he'd discovered the existence of a secret son—a very neglected secret son. Still, that was understandable. No one liked seeing children—especially their own—being mistreated.

Scott had always believed he was a chip off the old block. Ugly outbursts of anger were simply not his style, though, damn it all, he'd been sorely tested ever since those wretched photos had arrived. He'd certainly been tested that day in Leighton's office. And tested too by Sarah's own highly emotional and sometimes contrary behaviour. He'd really seen red this morning once he'd realised she'd lied to him the previous night over dinner, especially when she'd gone on and on about trust and honesty.

Still, in hindsight, he could see why she hadn't told him about her possible pregnancy. And, yes, he could understand that during the distress of last weekend's events all thought of the pill and falling pregnant had gone right out of her head. But once she'd remembered she should have told him. No question about that. And she shouldn't have made up all that rubbish about having a sinus infection and not being able to drink because she was on antibiotics.

A wry laugh escaped his lips at the sheer inventiveness of her lie. She'd make a fabulous trial lawyer one day, no doubt about that. And a good mother too, no doubt, if and when the time came. Sarah would want to do everything right. Scott figured he'd make a pretty good father, too. He'd had a very good example. Frankly, now that he thought about it more calmly, Scott wasn't unhappy about Sarah having forgotten her pill. A baby would be good for them both. They'd always planned to have a baby. One day. When Sarah's career was more established and when she was ready for it.

Maybe that was the reason behind Sarah's panic. Because she wasn't ready for parenthood. Or more likely, she believed *he* wasn't. An understandable belief, given he'd been spending so much time away on business. Scott could see now that he'd been neglecting her. Neglecting her *and* his marriage. He'd started taking her for granted. No wonder she'd thought he was having an affair. And no wonder he'd believed *she* was. He could see now why she'd bolted, why she was worried about their future relationship.

Scott sighed. Maybe he should tell her that. Admit his failings and at least talk to her a lot more, reassuring her that things would change in future. And he would keep telling her he wouldn't mind a bit if she was already pregnant, as long as she didn't. The only difficulty was how to bring such a topic up in the conversation without it seeming forced, or false.

Scott felt lucky when an opportunity for such a conversation came up as he was helping Sarah unpack

her car. Perversely, it was the pregnancy testing kit—
which Sarah had thrown onto the floor in front of the
passenger seat—which did the trick. Picking it up, he
started to read the instructions on the back of the box.

'It says here,' he remarked, doing his best to sound
casual, 'that this is a very sensitive test and can pick
up a pregnancy quite early.'

Sarah sighed as she took the box out of his hands.
'Yes, I've already read all that. The girl in the chemist shop said it was the best. But the doctor said it can
still give a false negative if you take the test before
your next period is due.'

'But it might not,' he countered. 'And let's face it,
you don't know when your next period is due. You've
totally stuffed up your hormones. Maybe you should
just take the test and see.'

Anxiety was instantly etched on Sarah's lovely
face. 'I don't want to do that, Scott. I keep thinking
about the horrible argument we had last week. What
if I fell pregnant that Friday night? What if this baby
was conceived in anger and revenge? I wouldn't like
that so I'd rather not know yet, thank you very much.'

'I can understand your feelings on that subject,
Sarah,' Scott said in reassuring tones, 'but maybe
it's time for you to rethink what happened that night.
Look, we'd both had scares that day over our love for
each other and we both wanted to lay claim to each
other the way men and women have been doing since
time began. With sex. If you recall, you were as provocative as I was demanding.'

Sarah frowned, her expression thoughtful, his
carefully reasoned words obviously striking a chord
with her intelligent brain.

'Well, yes,' she said slowly. 'Yes, I do see that that's what *I* was doing, anyway. I was seriously rocked by the thought that you were having an affair with Cleo.'

'How do you think I felt when I looked at those photos?' he pointed out, deliberately keeping his voice calm.

She pulled a face. 'Mmm. Yes. They were pretty damning. Cory told me you were just acting like any man would have, but I wouldn't listen to him.'

'You should have, Sarah. Cory's a smart man. But back to our rethinking the events that Friday night. You can't deny that it was great sex. The best we'd had so far. Though last night was pretty darned good too.'

Scott loved it when she blushed. His virgin bride was still deliciously enchanting.

'Trust me,' he went on, 'when I say that along with my feelings of jealousy and anger that night, I never stopped loving you. Never! If we made a baby that night then it will definitely be a baby born of love.'

'Oh,' she said, and promptly burst into tears. Which was not quite the reaction Scott had in mind.

Suppressing a groan, he gathered her into his arms and held her close. She wept for a while but not for too long, gathering herself reasonably quickly, he thought, then reaching up to kiss him on the cheek.

Such a simple kiss but it moved him, touching his soul more than any of the passionate kisses she'd given him last night. Because it was full of forgiveness. And love. A pure, sweet, loving love. Nothing to do with lust.

'Thank you for that,' she said as she smiled softly up at him. 'And I love you too. Very much. And I'm not so worried any more about being pregnant. What you said just now… It…it made all the difference.'

'I hope so, Sarah,' he returned, not entirely convinced that she felt truly happy about falling pregnant that night. Which was fair enough. It hadn't exactly been a night of romance. His lovemaking had been raw and, yes, vengeful. There was no denying it. But the passion and love behind his jealousy had been real. God, yes. 'I still feel I haven't said enough how sorry I am for not trusting you.'

'Stop now,' she replied quickly, and laid a gentle hand on the cheek she'd just kissed. 'They say love is never having to say you're sorry.'

He laughed. 'Now that's a load of old rubbish. I should have crawled on my hands and knees to beg your forgiveness. I know I crossed the line that night and my feeble attempt to whitewash my behaviour is totally unacceptable.'

'True. But we have to move past all that now, Scott. I'm ready to. Honest.'

'Honest?' he echoed, and smiled a wry smile.

'Absolutely,' she said. 'Aside from your heartfelt apology just now, I had some time to get my head together on the drive over here. I feel much better about our marriage and I've come to a decision.'

Scott swallowed. 'And what decision is that?'

'As soon as we get the last of these things upstairs, I'm going to go take that test.'

CHAPTER NINETEEN

SARAH REGRETTED HER decision the moment she made it. But it was too late to back out now. With fumbling fingers she opened the box and extracted the white plastic stick. For a long moment she just stared at it, as if it was a fearful thing. Which it was. A powerful, fearful thing that had the power to make her feel... *what*, exactly? Happy? Unhappy? Confused? Impatient? Or all of those things. Did she want the test to be negative, or positive? She wasn't sure any more. Wasn't sure of anything except that Scott loved her.

So she clung to that reassurance and rather numbly did what the instructions said to do. But as she waited for the hormones to give her a result a truly weird sensation came over Sarah; a light-headedness that left her dizzy and dazed and just a little disoriented. She had to sit down on the toilet again—quickly—leaning forward till enough time had passed for her to reach for the stick.

Her face drained of more blood as she stared at it.

Scott could not believe how tense he was, waiting for Sarah to come out of the bathroom. He paced the bedroom like an expectant father in a maternity ward. When she finally emerged, her face was pale but she wasn't crying or anything. She just looked… shocked.

'Well?' he prompted when she didn't say anything.

'Yes,' she choked out, nodding rather blankly. 'It was pink. Very pink.'

'Wow!' Scott exclaimed, beaming over at her. 'Wow!'

'I'm going to have a baby,' she said in stunned tones. 'A real baby.'

'So it seems, sweetheart,' he said, then strode over and scooped her up in his arms, whirling her round and laughing as he hadn't done in ages. It took him a little while to realise Sarah wasn't laughing.

He planted her back down on her feet and looked at her with suddenly worried eyes. 'You are happy about the baby, aren't you?' he asked anxiously. 'You're not still upset over…you know…' His voice trailed off, his heart squeezing tight at the thought she might still hate the idea of having conceived a baby that Friday night.

She blinked up at him a couple of times, then slowly, wonderfully, she smiled. 'No, I'm not upset about that any more. I wasn't lying when I said your lovely words made all the difference. It's just that I didn't think I would feel quite this…overwhelmed. It's one thing to imagine you might be pregnant, but when you know you definitely are, it's an entirely different feeling. Most girls fantasise about becoming mothers but the reality of it is a little daunting. I…I hope I'll make a good mother.'

'You'll make a terrific one.'

'I would like to think so. Still…it's a big thing, having a baby, isn't it? It changes your life.'

'Only for the better,' he reassured her gently. 'We'll become a family, Sarah. Our own family, to fashion the way we want it to be. Neither of us have families. Now it's you and me and little whatsit.'

'Whatsit?' Sarah threw him a pretend scowl. 'Our baby is not a *whatsit*. It's a boy or girl. Or both.'

'It can't be both,' Scott snorted.

'Unless it's twins,' she exclaimed in a startled tone.

'Good Lord! But that would be awesome. Or maybe you're just a very fertile little minx. Either way it's still good news, isn't it?'

'What? Oh, yes…yes. I suppose so.'

'You seem a bit stunned by the idea.'

'I am. I really am.' Her hand lifted to wipe her pale forehead. 'I've gone a bit dizzy, all of a sudden.'

'Could be because you haven't had any breakfast. And neither have I. I'll get you a glass of juice. Then let's drop everything and walk up to Dino's and have a celebratory eat-up.' Dino's was a trendy little café not far from their building, which served breakfast all day every day as well as the most delicious pancakes. They often had breakfast there on the weekends. Lunch too. With the sun out and the day promising some pre-winter warmth they could sit at one of the outdoor tables in the back courtyard. They weren't that popular because of the noise that came from nearby Luna Park, but neither of them minded the sounds of happiness.

'I'd like that,' Sarah said, then shook her head. 'Twins!' she exclaimed as he took her elbow and steered her out into the kitchen.

'Could be,' he told her. 'My father was a twin.'
'You never told me that.'
'Didn't I?'
'No.'
He shrugged. 'I'll tell you over brunch.'

CHAPTER TWENTY

'WELL?' SARAH PROMPTED as soon as they'd ordered their food and sat down at one of their favourite outdoor tables.

'Well, what?' he replied.

'You were going to tell me about your father being a twin.'

'Oh, yes, so I was,' he said with a cheeky smile. 'They weren't identical twins. Similar in looks, but nothing like each other in nature, Dad said. His name was Roger and he was a right rebel. A risk taker. He died when he was eighteen. Got killed falling off a motorcycle.'

'That's sad. But I don't know about their being all that different in nature. Your dad didn't exactly follow the conventional path in life, did he?'

'Well, no, but he wasn't a risk taker.'

'Really? Then why did he buy old mines and plots of land which everyone said were useless?'

He frowned at her, then laughed. 'I never told you that, madam, so where did you get that little nugget of information from?'

Sarah grinned. 'Remember the day we met?'

'I'm hardly likely to forget it,' he said in droll

tones. 'It was very difficult to sit in that boardroom, conducting business with a hard-on the size of Centrepoint Tower.'

'Hush up,' a blushing Sarah said as she looked hurriedly over at the nearest table, which was occupied by a couple and their two small children. 'There are children here.'

'Sorry. Okay, out with it.'

'Well, I was bored to tears that day and had nothing better to do than look you up on the Internet. Not that it was all that informative. You really are not very communicative with the media, are you? I couldn't even find a decent photo—just one with a hard hat on where you looked like a union leader. A rather weather-beaten one. Trust me when I tell you I wasn't impressed. I didn't fancy you at all till I saw you in the flesh. Not sure why I did then, either. You were a long way from being my fantasy man.'

'That's sweet of you to say so.'

'I did tell you that I was going to be honest from now on.'

Scott laughed. 'In a selective manner, that is.'

'I promise I will tell only little white lies in future.'

'That's a comfort. So what did you fancy about me, once you saw me in the flesh?'

'Just about everything, I guess. But most of all I liked the way you looked at me. It made me feel very…sexy.'

'Yet you held out on me till our third date.'

'I didn't want you to think I was easy.'

'Sweetheart, have you forgotten you were a virgin?'

'No. But you didn't know that at the time.'

'You'd be right there. I was quite blown away once I found out.'

'You *were* rather surprised.'

'True. I'd never come across one before.'

'Not even when you were younger?'

'Nah. I was into older women at that stage.'

'And now?'

'Now I'm just into you.' His smile was wonderful and warm, with just a hint of wicked promise. Sarah suspected that as soon as they got back home she wouldn't be putting all her things away till much later. Scott would be whisking her off to bed. She recognised that glint in his eye only too well.

Their food arrived, hers a simple serving of poached eggs and fried mushrooms on toast whilst Scott was presented with a huge pile of pancakes with a side dish of vanilla ice cream. Sarah knew that all conversation would cease till Scott had eaten. Already his whole concentration was on pouring the maple syrup onto the first pancake, his steely grey eyes lighting up as his taste buds salivated.

Sarah didn't mind his obsessed state, using the quiet to enjoy her own food, taking her time and washing each delicious mouthful down with some freshly squeezed orange juice. Scott was still eating when she finished, so Sarah put down her cutlery, leant back in her seat and admired her surroundings. It was lovely and warm where they were sitting, the sounds of laughter and rides from Luna Park adding to her happiness.

And she *was* happy. Happier than she'd been in her whole life. If anyone had told her she would have felt this happy a little over a week ago, she would not have believed them.

And it wasn't just because of the baby. Or babies, if it turned out she was having twins. Her happiness came from the new depth of understanding that she'd forged with Scott. She felt confident now that their marriage would go the distance. And that was very important to her, especially now that she was having a baby. She personally didn't want to ever suffer the wretchedness of divorce. She certainly didn't want her children to have to endure the distress and loneliness of their parents' separating.

There was only one thing that still bothered her a bit, but which she didn't want to address at this stage. Why risk spoiling things today? But sooner or later she would have to tell Scott that she wanted the father of her children to be a more stay-at-home dad, not going away on business trips all the time with his PA. Weirdly, as though reading her mind, Scott himself brought the subject up over coffee.

'I've been thinking,' he said, 'that in future, I'm going to cut down on going away on business.'

'I'd really like that,' Sarah said. 'It did annoy me how often you were going away. And how you always took Cleo and never asked me,' she added, trying not to sound jealous, but not entirely succeeding.

Scott frowned at her. 'I didn't think you'd be able to drop everything at your work and come with me.'

'I suppose I can't. Not always. But I would have liked you to ask occasionally.'

'Point taken. Look, I'm in the process of finding myself a business partner. I *was* looking for more of a silent money-bags-type partner but instead I'll look for someone who wants to be more hands-on. That way he can take some of the load off me when it comes to going away. How does that sound?'

'It sounds good,' she said.

'We'll also have to buy a proper family home. Can't raise a family in an apartment. We'll need a yard. One big enough for a dog. Got to have a dog. I always had a dog when I was growing up. A kid needs a dog.'

'I always wanted a dog, but Mum refused to get one. Said they dropped hair all over the place.'

'We'll find one that doesn't drop hair.'

'Gosh, this is all so exciting. Can we go look at some family homes this afternoon?'

'Nope. Once you finish your coffee we're going home. And then we're going to bed.'

CHAPTER TWENTY-ONE

'WHERE ARE YOU GOING?' Scott asked when Sarah suddenly threw back the bedclothes and climbed out of bed.

They'd made love on and off all afternoon, Scott being extra gentle, Sarah laughing at his worry over *disturbing the babes*. Nothing too athletic or too deep was the order of the day.

'But they wouldn't be the size of two peas yet,' she told him at one stage when she'd wanted to be on top. 'And there might only be one pea.'

Scott didn't say anything at the time but he felt absolutely certain that she'd conceived twins, the same way he'd been certain that that diamond mine he'd bought a year ago would prove not to be the worked-out dud everyone else imagined. And he'd been right. Already it was showing a decent profit. Scott believed he was right about Sarah having twins as well. Which thrilled him no end.

Strange, really. Having children had never been a huge urge for Scott. Neither had marriage, for that matter. But everything had changed once he met Sarah.

An image formed in his mind of how it would

be, standing by Sarah's side as she pushed two tiny babies into the world. His heart swelled with love at the thought. Love and pride.

It amazed him how excited he felt about becoming a father, now that it was actually happening to him for real. Scott aimed to give his own children the same things his father had given him. Plenty of time spent with them, a degree of discipline, lots of love and, yes, definitely a dog.

Not that he planned on spoiling his children. That didn't work. He'd seen the results of rich parents spoiling their children and it wasn't pretty.

So no spoiling, except in matters of time and love. Sarah was right about his cutting down on those business trips, though. Hopefully, Cleo would be able to find him that hands-on business partner before long.

The bathroom door opened and Sarah emerged, quickly diving back under the covers where she cuddled up to him. This time they just talked, trying to work out what suburbs they would buy a house in.

'I do like the northern beaches,' he said, 'but the traffic is always awful. It would take us for ever to get to work.'

'True. But it is nice on the north side, especially the beachside suburbs. Why don't we look for a suburb which has a good ferry service?' Sarah suggested. 'Manly Beach maybe. Then we wouldn't even have to drive to work. We could catch the ferry together and hold hands.'

Bringing up the subject of work put a slight dent in Scott's contentment. The thought of Sarah continuing to work in the same firm as that snake Leighton did not sit well with him. But he just knew she wouldn't like his asking her to quit again. So he didn't. Not right at that moment. But he suspected it wouldn't be long before he said something. He wasn't the kind of man who would let his wife continue being in the company of a man like that.

'I suppose we should get up,' Sarah said with a resigned sigh. 'I need to hang up my clothes properly. We just dumped them on the floor of the walk-in wardrobe, remember?'

Scott remembered. 'I'll help you,' he said, 'then we should eat again. I don't know about you but I'm starving.'

'You're always starving,' she said smilingly. 'But you're right. I am a bit hungry.'

'That's because you're eating for three.'

Sarah punched him in the ribs. 'Will you stop saying that? We don't know it's twins.'

'No. We don't. It might be triplets.'

He laughed at the look of horror that crossed her face.

'Don't even *think* such a thing,' she chastised. 'Now, no more of that nonsense. Time to get up and get to work.'

Scott winced. That *work* word again. Hell on earth, but just the thought of Sarah being anywhere near that bastard brought out his caveman side. Still, it wasn't the right moment to bring the subject up. She seemed so happy.

He should have known that he wouldn't be able to keep his big mouth shut for long.

CHAPTER TWENTY-TWO

'How on earth did you get all this stuff in your one little car?' Scott asked her as he helped her put away her clothes properly.

'Fury, I suppose,' Sarah said with a shrug. 'I just jammed it all in.'

'You really were very angry with me.'

Sarah's mind flew back to that Saturday morning when he'd shown her those photos. It seemed a lifetime ago now. 'You have no idea,' she confessed. 'I could cheerfully have killed you.'

'I deserved killing.'

'Indeed. But perhaps I should have stayed and had it out with you instead of flouncing off the way I did.' Sarah was finally forced to face that she'd always run away from distressing situations rather than confronting them. Hopefully, she wasn't going to be like that any more.

'I think the blame rests wholly and solely on me, my darling,' he said. 'I was totally in the wrong.'

'But with mitigating circumstances,' she said.

Scott smiled. 'Spoken like a lawyer. By the way, did you let Cory know the good news?'

'No,' she said, clearly astonished with herself. 'I forgot.'

'Better let him know, don't you think?'

'He can wait till later this evening. It's only just after five. He's probably still in the conference, learning how to build some more icons like the Opera House.'

'True. Okay, I'll go see what I can rustle up for an early dinner whilst you finish up here,' he suggested.

'Sounds like a good plan.'

Sarah was humming happily as she put her shoes away in her walk-in wardrobe when she suddenly came across the anniversary present that she'd bought Scott and never given him. She'd originally hidden it at the back of one of the shelves, planning to give it to him on the morning of their anniversary. Now, she picked up the small plastic bag in which lay the even smaller box, her heart filling as she went in search of Scott. She found him perched up on a kitchen stool, searching his phone for something.

'All finished?' he asked without glancing up.

'Just about,' she replied, clutching the plastic bag with suddenly nervous hands. What if he didn't like what she'd bought?

'So what would you like me to order in to eat?' he asked her, finally looking up. 'There's nothing much in the fridge or the cupboards to cook with. I've been living the life of a lazy bachelor whilst you were away, not going to the supermarket and existing on take-away. Thank God for the cleaning service, that's all I can say, or you'd be coming home to a tip. I was lost without you, my darling. Totally, utterly lost. So what's it to be? Thai, Chinese, Indian?'

Sarah's stomach turned over at the thought of anything spicy. 'Could we just have toast and pumpkin soup?' she requested. 'I know that's there. And you can follow up with some of your favourite chocolate ice cream. We always have heaps of that in the freezer.'

'Done!' he said, smiling. 'So what's that you have there?'

'It…it's the anniversary present I bought you. It's not wrapped up, I'm afraid,' she added, and walked over to sit down on the stool next to him.

She handed him the plastic bag and watched, her heart thudding, as he drew out the small black leather box. His eyebrows arched. 'Jewellery, Sarah?'

Sarah knew Scott wasn't a ring-wearer. Had refused to have a wedding ring. But the moment she'd seen this particular ring in the shop window, she'd felt compelled to buy it. Perhaps because it represented the stability and security she'd always experienced with Scott but which had been seriously rocked that day.

'Yes,' she said, her voice firmer than her emotions. 'I hope you like it.'

Scott determined to like it, no matter what it was. But when he flipped open the lid of the box and saw what lay inside, *liking* was not even close to his emotion.

It was a man's ring. A gold ring, with an intricately woven design on top that looked like an eight on its side. Scott knew what the sign meant. It was the mathematical symbol of infinity. His father had taught him maths as a kid, drawing all the symbols and signs in the sandy outback soil with a stick. This one had intrigued Scott at the time, his father explaining that the continuous loop meant it never ended.

'But that doesn't make sense, Dad,' he'd said. 'Nothing goes on and on for ever.'

'Numbers do,' came his father's logical reply. 'And space.'

And true love, Scott thought, a lump in his throat.

'I love it,' he said as he slipped it on the bare third finger of his left hand, surprised that it fitted. Smiling, he leant over to kiss her on the cheek. 'It's perfect. Like you.'

'I'm not at all perfect,' Sarah replied, smiling back at him. 'But I do love you. I will love you till the end of time. That's what this ring represents to me. Our everlasting love.'

When Scott's face fell Sarah almost panicked. Had she been over the top with her declaration? Didn't he love her the way she loved him?

'God, Sarah,' he said, turning the ring round and round on his finger. 'Now I feel awful. I didn't buy you anything at all. I forgot. I'm so sorry.'

'It doesn't matter,' she said. 'Presents don't matter. Not really.'

'I think they do. Getting this lovely present showed me that. I'll buy you something tomorrow, my darling. Something special. And we'll go somewhere extra special tomorrow night for dinner.'

'It'll be Monday night,' she pointed out. 'Most of the good restaurants are closed on a Monday night.'

'Yes, you're right,' he mused. 'Tomorrow's Monday…'

His eyes carried worry as he looked deep into hers.

'You won't reconsider not working for that mob any more? I can't stand the thought of you being anywhere near that Leighton bastard.'

Sarah stiffened. She understood completely that Scott didn't want her working in the same building as Phil. And to tell the truth, she had her doubts about staying at Goldstein & Evans as well, now that she was pregnant. They were a rather gung-ho legal firm who expected their employees to give one hundred and ten per cent. And whilst Sarah was a dedicated lawyer who enjoyed her work, her priorities had changed with her pregnancy. But it was a matter of principle that she go to work the following morning. A matter of her husband trusting her, not of her just doing what he ordered her to do like some old-fashioned chauvinist.

'I'm sorry, Scott,' she told him soothingly. 'I understand your feelings entirely. But I will be going to work tomorrow morning. I can't just up and quit. It would make it very hard for me to get another job. People would think I was flighty and unreliable. But you're right. I will start looking around for another position, okay?'

'Okay,' he said with decided reluctance in his voice.

'Trust me,' she said.

'I do trust you,' he countered. 'I just don't trust Leighton.'

CHAPTER TWENTY-THREE

DESPITE SARAH ARRIVING at work a good fifteen minutes before the official start time of eight-thirty the next morning, the place was already abuzz, with most of the offices filled with busy, busy people. For the first time since her early days of working at Goldstein & Evans, Sarah experienced a totally negative reaction towards the atmosphere. She didn't find it heady the way she once had. Just hectic.

Several people asked her how she was feeling after her week off, but none of the queries seemed sincere, no one actually stopping to speak to her for more than a few seconds as she walked past. It also bothered her that she couldn't just dump her handbag and head off to the staff room to use the coffee machine the way she usually did. Fear of running into Phil there had forced her to buy herself a takeaway coffee downstairs instead.

Sarah slumped down at her desk, annoyed with that fear, annoyed with herself for not realising sooner that Phil did fancy her. If she had, she wouldn't have used his shoulder to cry on whenever Scott went away on business. But she had. Stupidly. She hadn't encouraged his interest, but she hadn't discouraged him, either.

Not that that gave him any excuse to do what he'd done. Had he honestly thought she'd run to him, if and when her marriage broke up? She'd never fancied him. Never! Now she actively hated him, the way she hated her slime bag father and brother. Sarah regretted that she'd never confronted either of them and told them what she thought of them. Instead, they'd got away with the reprehensible way they'd both behaved. She should have at least torn verbal strips off them. Not that it would have dented their consciences one iota. It would have been water off a duck's back. But at least it would have given her some satisfaction. And made her feel slightly better.

Phil shouldn't get away with what he'd done, either.

Gripping her large takeaway coffee with both hands, Sarah stood up and walked slowly out into the main corridor, turning right and heading towards the family law section, sipping as she went. Adrenaline had her heart racing, all her inner muscles tightening as she drew closer to Phil's office.

His very attractive secretary was at her desk, looking rather smug as usual.

'Is Phil in, Janice?' Sarah asked politely enough.

'He's busy,' she replied sharply as she looked Sarah up and down.

'I need to speak to him,' Sarah went on. 'Could you please let him know that I'm here?'

Just then the door to Phil's office opened and the man himself walked out, his eyes also running over Sarah, though not with the same hostile regard as his secretary. 'I thought I heard your voice,' he said with an oily smile. 'Did you want to see me?'

Sarah had no intention of confronting him in front

of Janice, so she smiled back at him, hiding the way her skin crawled at his almost lascivious appraisal. Sarah knew she looked good. She always looked good when she came to work. Today's outfit was a pale pink Chanel suit, matched with a cream silk blouse that had a ruffle framing the pearl-buttoned front, a style that flattered her willowy figure and her fair colouring. Her hair was up in a neat roll and her make-up was perfect, her perfume subtle yet sexy. Elegant pearl drops fell from her neat lobes.

Sarah didn't object to men giving her admiring looks but she hated being ogled. Her stomach tightened with rage, but still she smiled.

'Yes, I do want to see you, Phil,' she said sweetly. 'I'm in need of some legal advice.'

His eyes lit up with pleasure, not compassion. 'Of course, dear girl. Anything for you. Do come in.' He waved her into his office. 'Hold all calls, will you, Janice?'

The back of Sarah's neck prickled as she walked into the office and Phil closed the door behind her.

'Why don't we sit over here?' he said, directing her to a long grey leather sofa that rested against a far wall. His office was one of the largest, his status very high in the firm.

She didn't object, despite her skin crawling some more. He sat unnecessarily close to her, his expression full of feigned concern. He might have picked up one of her hands if they hadn't both been cupped tightly around her coffee.

'You don't have to tell me what the problem is,' he started straight away. 'You've left your husband, haven't you?'

'I…yes…I did.' Not a lie. She had. For a while.

'I'm not surprised. You may or may not know this but your husband came to see me last week and made all sorts of vile accusations about some photos someone sent him. Photos of you and me at the Regency hotel that Friday lunchtime.'

'He did tell me about his visit to you,' Sarah admitted stiffly.

'Did he tell you that he threatened to kill me if I came near you ever again?'

'No, he didn't,' Sarah confessed, slightly shocked at Scott's threat.

'You're well out of that marriage, Sarah. Look, I know that you didn't come to work all last week and it worried the life out of me, thinking what that bully of a husband might have done to you. The thought of his abusing you in some way gave me nightmares.'

'Scott would *never* hit me,' she defended hotly, thinking that if Phil was so worried about her then why hadn't he tried to call her?

She understood full well why he hadn't. First, he didn't really care about her. And second, Scott had scared the living daylights out of him.

'I wouldn't be too sure of that,' he sneered. 'McAllister comes from a rough and tough background. He has violence written all over him. You could do so much better, my dear,' he said, then actually dared to place his hand on her knee. 'You deserve a man who would appreciate you as his wife, someone who would give you the kind of life to complement your beauty and your brains.'

'And are you imagining that that man would be you, Phil?' she asked him, struggling to keep the dislike out of her voice. She hadn't set out to trap him into incriminating himself, but couldn't resist the temptation.

That disgusting hand on her knee actually moved in what he no doubt thought was a seductive circle.

'You must know how I feel about you, Sarah,' he murmured, his eyes locking with hers. 'I've admired you ever since you came to work here. You are the kind of woman any man would want. When you married McAllister I couldn't believe it. The man has no class, or culture. He's nothing but a thug in a suit. But at least now you've seen the error of your ways and you've finally come to me. *Finally*,' he repeated, that horrible hand daring to inch up onto her thigh.

Sarah could not bear another second of his vile touch, slapping his hand away and jumping to her feet at the same time. 'My God, you don't honestly think I would leave Scott for you, do you?' she threw at him, only just stopping herself from throwing the coffee at him as well. 'Even if your rotten plan had worked and Scott and I broke up permanently, I would never turn to you.'

He seemed totally thrown by her outburst, his massive ego clearly unable to take in exactly what she was saying.

'But you said you left him,' he blurted out. 'You came to me and said you wanted a divorce.'

'I did leave Scott,' she countered furiously. 'But we're back together again now, stronger than ever. Your appalling plan didn't work in the end. And I *never* asked for a divorce. I said I wanted some legal advice. So tell me, Phil, what would you advise a girl in my position to do? You do realise that Mr Goldstein is not too partial to claims of sexual harassment against his employees.'

Sarah saw the instant fear in his eyes and knew Scott had his character pegged right. The man was a total sleaze and an out-and-out coward.

'You have no proof of anything,' he said shakily as he stood up. 'It's your word against mine.'

'Is it just? Well, maybe my word might have more sway with the boss than yours.'

'If you go to Goldstein, you'll be making a big mistake,' he spat at her. 'My father is an important man, a senator and a very close friend of his. You won't win.'

'Oh, lovely. And there I was, thinking you must be mad about me to do what you did.'

'I'm not that mad about any woman,' he snarled, his handsome face twisted into an ugly mask. 'Lord knows what I was thinking,' he went on nastily, shrugging his shoulders and straightening his tie as he looked down his finely chiselled nose at her. 'You might be beautiful, sweetheart, but you obviously don't have any taste. Fancy taking up with that big lug when you could have had me. The mind boggles.'

Her mind certainly did. God, the arrogance of the man! And the sheer vanity.

'Scott is more of a man than you'll ever be,' she stated firmly. 'What's laughable is that I used to like you. I thought you were my friend, someone I could turn to for advice. I couldn't believe it at first when Scott said you'd set me up so that I would look like a cheater. But I soon saw that he was right. Though he was wrong about your motive. You never really wanted me, did you? You just wanted to cause trouble.

To make me miserable. It was all because I'd bruised your male ego.'

His laugh was scoffing. 'Well, it certainly wasn't because I couldn't live without you. But I was sick to death of your complaining about hubby going away all the time, so I decided to give you something to really complain about. Which reminds me. Your husband could be having an affair with his PA, for all I know. I didn't have him investigated at all. That was just an excuse to get you to go to the hotel with me. My main aim was for your stupid husband to think *you* were having an affair. I figured if in the fallout I managed to get a bit of that delicious arse of yours then I'd count that as a bonus.'

Sarah managed somehow not to reel back. 'Scott was right,' she said coldly. 'You are disgusting.'

Fear zoomed back into his eyes. 'You can't prove anything.'

'Maybe not, but mud sticks, Phil.'

'It sure does. What if I say you did sleep with me that day? That you told me you loved me and you were going to leave your husband for me, but I told you I didn't love you back—that everything you're now saying is just the revenge of a woman scorned.'

Sarah shook her head. Scott had been so right. Leighton was a slimy bastard who wasn't to be trusted. For a moment she felt rattled, but then she reminded herself that she'd faced slimier men in court.

'I'd say you'd be wasting your breath,' she returned coolly. 'Because I'm out of here as of now. You're not worth the hassle of a law suit. Or anything else. Time will take care of you. I just wanted the opportunity to see you face-to-face and tell you what I think of you before I resigned.'

'You're resigning?' he asked, his mouth dropping open.

'I sure am. And I won't be back.'

'But what reason will you give for resigning?'

Her smile was a little wicked. Let the creep worry.

'Oh, I'll think of something,' she said airily, and with that she whirled and marched over to the door, flinging it open to find Janice standing right next to the door, obviously listening to what had gone on. The girl's face was flushed and she seemed quite upset. Sarah, however, had never felt better. There was something very cathartic about having some revenge, no matter how small, on the man who'd almost ruined her marriage.

'I'd stop sleeping with him if I were you,' Sarah called over her shoulder as she strode off, tossing the half-drunk coffee in a nearby bin on the way. 'The man's a total sleazebag and a big-time loser.'

CHAPTER TWENTY-FOUR

SARAH'S SMILE WAS wide as she walked the three blocks to Scott's office. God, but it felt so good to be out of there, and not just because she'd escaped Phil's toxic presence. Sarah hadn't appreciated till this moment that she hadn't been overly enjoying her job for some time. She'd liked some of her clients and cases, but not the constant pressure of having to win. Goldstein & Evans had a 'win at all costs' policy, which could be wearing after a while. They also expected you to work long hours, without getting paid overtime. Which had been fine by her to begin with. But it wasn't the sort of workplace she envisaged enduring once she had a baby.

Whilst Sarah didn't want to abandon her career entirely for motherhood, neither did she want to be one of those mothers who gave over all the caring of her children to nannies and day-care centres. That wasn't the kind of family life she craved. If she expected Scott to stay home more, then the same should apply to her. Sarah believed in equality in a marriage.

Sarah didn't ring Scott to tell him she was coming, keeping the news of her resignation as a surprise. He was going to be so pleased, she thought as she rode the lift up to his floor. Her smile was still in place as she pushed open the door that had McAllister Mines written on it in silver lettering.

'Hi, Leanne,' she said happily to the forty-some-thing receptionist. 'The boss in?'

'Sure is.'

'Great. Looking good, Leanne. New hairdresser?' Leanne was sporting a chin-length honey-brown bob with blonde highlights, which was more youthful than her previous style.

'Yes. *Yours*. Thanks for the tip.'

'My pleasure.'

Sarah made her way down the corridor to Cleo's door. When knocking elicited no answer, she popped her head inside, only to find the office empty. The door into Scott's office was open, however, and what Sarah saw in there had the ready smile fading from her face. For there was Cleo, standing in front of Scott's desk, wrapped in Scott's arms. One of his hands rested in the small of her back, the other was stroking her thick dark hair with what looked like ten-derness. He was murmuring something soft and reas-suring, and Cleo... Cleo sounded as if she was crying.

Instantly, the most horrible thoughts rushed through Sarah's head.

They are *having an affair.*

It's been going on for ages.

Scott has just told her about the baby and Cleo is devastated.

Sarah's first reaction was to turn and run. Maybe she could hide in the powder room for a while and come back later. Pretend she hadn't seen a thing.

A few days ago, she might have. But not today.

Today was the beginning of the first day of her new marriage, one which embraced honesty and total trust, not with wild bursts of jealousy.

Taking a deep gathering breath, Sarah calmed her mind, letting common sense push aside those other hasty and quite irrational thoughts.

Of course they are not having an affair.

Scott loves you and Cleo isn't that kind of woman.

You have to trust him the way you want him to trust you.

There is some other explanation for what you're seeing.

Swallowing, Sarah came forward to stand in the doorway to Scott's office, discreetly clearing her throat so that they knew someone was there.

Scott glanced up over Cleo's shaking shoulder, startled to see Sarah standing in the doorway. She'd said she was going to drop by at lunchtime so that they could go shopping together, but it was hardly that yet. He froze inside, aware that what she was seeing would not look good. No wife would be happy to find her husband with his arms wrapped around his weeping PA. Sarah wouldn't be a typical woman if she didn't jump to the wrong conclusion.

But if she did, then everything they'd achieved over the weekend would be ruined.

A fierce dismay was enveloping Scott when something wonderful happened. Sarah smiled at him, lifting her eyebrows in a way that betrayed irony rather than jealousy. She'd trusted him. Dear God, but it was an incredible feeling, bringing a lightness to his suddenly heavy soul that seemed almost miraculous.

He smiled back, lifting his shoulders in a light shrug, suggesting that he was the innocent victim of circumstance here, not some dastardly bounder.

Relief claimed Sarah when he smiled back at her, not a smidgeon of guilt in his face. Thank God she'd trusted him and not fallen into that self-destructive trap of jealousy and false assumptions.

'Hi there, darling,' he said ruefully. 'Cleo's having a bad day.'

'Oh, God, Sarah!' the woman herself cried, wrenching away from Scott's arms as if she'd been struck by lightning. 'It's not… You mustn't think… Oh, God…'

'I don't think anything,' Sarah immediately reassured her. 'Honestly.' Coming closer, she reached over to the box of tissues that Scott kept on his desk, pulled out a great wad and handed it to the still-sobbing woman.

'It's the anniversary of Martin's death,' Scott explained as Cleo mopped up her face. 'But she forgot. Till just a minute or two ago.'

'I see,' Sarah said gently.

'I've never forgotten before,' Cleo wailed, sniffling into the tissues, confusion in her voice. 'I always put flowers on his grave on the anniversary of his death,' Cleo choked out. 'I usually take his mother with me.'

'No reason why you can't still do that,' Scott said. 'Go ring Doreen now, and take the rest of the day off.'

Cleo immediately brightened. 'Are you sure?'

'Positive,' Scott said firmly.

'You are so good to me. Your husband is a wonderful man, Sarah. And a wonderful boss.'

Sarah just smiled, still slightly rattled by her initial reaction to seeing Cleo in Scott's arms. For a terrible moment there she'd let distrust raise its ugly head once more. Still, at least she hadn't let it take root. But it had been a close call.

'He certainly is,' she agreed, and linked arms with Scott.

'Off you go,' Scott told Cleo.

'Yes—yes. Right. I'm off. See you tomorrow, then, Scott. I'll just tidy up my desk and shut down my computer.'

Sarah was glad when Cleo closed the door on her way out.

'So, *madame*,' Scott said as he turned her to face him, at the same time flicking her a questioning glance. 'Are you early for lunch or did I lose track of time again?'

'I am early,' she told him smugly. 'I'm also unemployed. I resigned this morning. And I refused to work out my notice.'

Scott's eyebrows almost hit the ceiling with surprise. Sarah noted, however, that behind the surprise lay a heap of satisfaction.

'What happened? No, don't tell me, Leighton hit on you and you lost your cool.'

'Not at all,' Sarah said, having resolved during the walk over to his building not to tell Scott about her confrontation with Phil. No way did she want him charging over there and threatening to kill Phil again. So she sidestepped that part and went straight to the reasons she'd given the big boss for her rather abrupt resignation.

'From the moment I sat down at my desk this

morning,' she began, 'I knew that Goldstein & Evans wasn't the sort of place I wanted to work in either during my pregnancy, or after I have our baby. Not because of he-who-shall-not-be-named, but because it just doesn't have a parent-friendly atmosphere. Being a mother has to be my priority from now on, Scott. Being a crusading lawyer will just have to play second fiddle till our children are well on the way to growing up. Not that I intend to give up my career, mind. I might apply for a job at Legal Aid, part-time. They do very good work and it's not as though I need to earn a six-figure salary. Or do I?' she asked with a sudden jab of worry. 'You're not on the verge of bankruptcy, are you?'

Scott laughed. 'Not just yet. God, but you've no idea how happy you've just made me. But what reason did you give for resigning? And how on earth did you get away with not working out your notice?'

Sarah grinned. 'I confess that I told a few little white lies. Though there was some truth in what I said.' And there was. 'I explained that I was pregnant, though I did let Mr Goldstein think I was a little further along than I actually am. I admitted that I didn't have a sinus infection the previous week but had been suffering from shocking morning sickness. I just hadn't wanted anyone to know I was pregnant just yet. I also said my doctor had advised me to give up work for a while but I'd stubbornly refused. He accepted my resignation straight away and I came here to see you.'

'You are a seriously naughty girl,' he said, laughter in his eyes. 'But a seriously brilliant one as well.'

'True. Would you like to kiss me now?'

* * *

Scott would have liked to do more than kiss her. But Scott knew that Cleo was probably still in the outer office, tidying up and collecting her things. So he settled for just a kiss, after which he suggested they go have coffee then do some shopping.

'So what are we shopping for?' Sarah asked.

'Your anniversary present. I was going to return your idea and buy you a lovely eternity ring. And I probably will still do that. But now that you've quit your job I've decided on an added gift.'

'Oh? What?'

'A second honeymoon,' he announced.

Scott loved the joy that filled Sarah's face.

'I know how much you like Asia,' he went on, 'so I was thinking of a stay at one of the luxury beach resorts in Thailand. What about Phuket? I saw an ad for this fabulous resort there during the long week you were away, when I had to resort to watching television into the wee small hours. We could leave ASAP. What do you think?'

'Oh, I'd love it. But what about your business? Aren't things a bit sticky at the moment?'

Scott shrugged. 'Things are going to be sticky in the mining business for a long time. Our relationship is far more important than work, Sarah. We deserve some time together after what we've been through.'

'But what about this new business partner you're supposed to be getting? What about your cash-flow problems?'

'That's not so acute now that my diamond mine is producing. I have enough ready cash to keep everything afloat for at least a month or so. As for acquiring a new business partner… Cleo can handle that whilst I'm away. She knows the business inside out. She'll enjoy being the boss for a while. Besides, it's not as though we're going to be gone for all that long. Two weeks, max.'

Sarah blinked up at him. 'Heavens, I don't know what to say.'

'Just yes will do.'

Sarah shrugged. 'Okay. Yes.'

'There's a travel agency on the ground floor. We'll pop in there and see what can be arranged, post haste. But first…' He strode over, opened his office door and put his head out. 'Good, she's gone. Now…'

He returned to sweep Sarah into his arms and kiss her as he'd been aching to do. Both of them were breathing heavily by the time his head lifted.

'No,' she said when she saw that glint in his eye.

'Why not? We're married.'

Sarah had to laugh. 'What about the travel agency?'

'It's not going anywhere. Besides, this won't take long.'

'I'm not fond of quickies,' she told him even as her heartbeat accelerated.

'You could have fooled me.'

It was a glowing Sarah who sat next to Scott in the travel agency, saying yes to absolutely everything he suggested. Her arm was hooked through his and she simply couldn't stop smiling. Life was just so good. Not only did Scott love her to death but she was having his baby. Or babies. Going on a second honeymoon together would be the icing on their cake of happiness. It didn't really matter where they went. She would still enjoy it.

'So what do you say, darling?' he asked her for the umpteenth time.

She couldn't for the life of her remember what his question was about. Still, she trusted him to choose well. After all, she'd already trusted him with her life.

'Absolutely yes,' she said. 'It all sounds wonderful.'

'Are you quite sure you can be packed by tomorrow?' Scott asked her after they'd left the travel agency.

'*Tomorrow!*' Sarah exclaimed, gasping and grinding to a halt.

Scott grinned. 'I knew you weren't listening properly. But you said yes so it's a done deal. We fly out for Bangkok at four tomorrow afternoon. Think you can be ready in time?'

Sarah sucked in sharply. 'I guess I'll have to be. Oh, Lord, I have no idea what clothes to pack.'

'Not too much. We're going on a second honeymoon, remember? Clothes will not be a priority.'

'Spoken like a man. I will still need something for every possible occasion.'

Scott rolled his eyes. 'There are shops over there, you know. We can always buy whatever you might forget. Along with that eternity ring I was going to buy you today, but which we now don't have time for.'

'We certainly don't,' she said. 'I have to get home and start packing. And I'll have to go to the hairdresser in the morning. Oh, Lord!'

'They do have hairdressers over there as well,' he pointed out with a wry smile.

'True,' she agreed, all anxiety leaving her as she lifted sparkling eyes to the man she loved. 'Gosh. Tomorrow! Oh, I can hardly wait.'

Scott pulled her close. 'Neither can I, my darling. Neither can I.'

* * * * *

If you enjoyed
THE MAGNATE'S TEMPESTUOUS MARRIAGE
why not explore these other fabulous
Miranda Lee stories?

THE ITALIAN'S RUTHLESS SEDUCTION
THE BILLIONAIRE'S RUTHLESS AFFAIR
THE PLAYBOY'S RUTHLESS PURSUIT
TAKEN OVER BY THE BILLIONAIRE
A MAN WITHOUT MERCY

Available now!

AUTHOR NOTE

I WOULD NORMALLY write an epilogue to this story, but this is Book One of a series and I do not want to pre-empt anything that happens in Book Two, which will be Cleo's story.

I will not, however, leave you in suspense over the baby issue. Sarah is having twins. Not identical. A boy and a girl.

MILLS & BOON®

MODERN™

POWER, PASSION AND IRRESISTIBLE TEMPTATION

0517/19

MILLS & BOON®

EXCLUSIVE EXTRACT

Ruthless Prince Adam Katsaros offers Belle a deal –
he'll release her father if she becomes his mistress!
Adam's gaze awakens a heated desire in Belle.
Her innocent beauty might redeem his royal
reputation – but can she tame the beast inside…

Read on for a sneak preview of
THE PRINCE'S CAPTIVE VIRGIN

"You really are kind of a beast," Belle said, standing up.
Adam caught her wrist, stopped her from leaving.

"And what bothers you most about that? The fact that
you would like to reform me, that you would like for your
time here to mean something and you are beginning to see
that it won't? Or is it the fact that you don't want to reform
me at all, and that you rather like me this way. Or at least,
your body likes me this way."

"Bodies make stupid decisions all the time. My father
wanted my mother, and she was a terrible, unloving person
who didn't even want her own daughter. So, forgive me if
I find this argument rather uncompelling. It doesn't make
you a good person, just because I enjoy kissing you. And
it doesn't make this something worth exploring."

She broke free of him and began to walk away, striding
down the hall, back toward her room. He pushed away
from the table, letting his chair fall to the floor, not caring
enough to right it as he followed after Belle.

He caught up to her, pivoting so that he was in front of
her. She took a step backward, then to the side, butting up
against the wall. Then, he caged her between his arms,

staring down at her. Her blue eyes were glittering, her breasts rising and falling rapidly with each breath.

"This is the only thing worth exploring. Not what could be, but what you have. The fire that burns between you and another person. For all you know, in the days since you've been here the entire world has fallen away. And if we were all that was left… Would you not regret missing out on the chance to see how hot we could burn?"

She shook her head. "But the world hasn't fallen away," she said, her trembling lips pale now, a complete contrast to the rich color they had been only moments ago. "It's still there. And whatever happens in here will have consequences out there. I will help you, Adam, but I'm not going to give you my body. I'm not going to destroy that life that I have out there to play games with you in here. You're a stranger to me, and you're going to remain a stranger to me. I can pretend. I can give you whatever you need when it comes to making a statement for your country. But beyond that? I can't."

Then, she turned and walked away, and this time, he let her go.

Don't miss
THE PRINCE'S CAPTIVE VIRGIN
by Maisey Yates

The first part in her
ONCE UPON A SEDUCTION trilogy

Available June 2017
www.millsandboon.co.uk

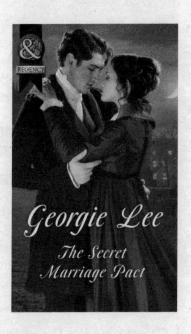